Fallen Angels: The Amulet of Osiris

_By_

Marcus Malcolm

To Paullet, with all my love.

Acknowledgment

It was the love, intrigue, and fascination with the field of cosmology that sparked my quest to truly embark on this joyful, time-consuming quest to write a story that was long in the making.

I wish to extend my appreciation to the great thinkers and scientists in their different fields of studies who made it possible for others who are not their peers to acquire information and disseminate it.

In the process of intensive researching and writing this book, I received invaluable assistance from several people. As such, I want to take time to acknowledge some who gave me valuable advice.

Firstly, I would like to thank my sister, Marcia Malcolm, who gave her time to help me identify some of the mistakes. Secondly, thanks to those people who shall remain nameless although they were quizzed endlessly about certain topics, and they also provided pertinent and insightful information. Finally, thanks to all who made an input in this manuscript, and I sincerely hope that you all enjoy the story as it unfolds.

***

Where should I start? To tell the tale of human beings or angels who have walked amongst us and the help they have provided in guiding us, mere mortals, is truly phenomenal. This is the tale of one such being who walked amongst us humans.

As I am sitting here on my balcony in my Manhattan apartment overlooking the other huge skyscrapers and bright light of the city, gazing at the night sky, and reflecting on my life and my journey to where I am now, it seems so surreal. But here I am, the embodiment of flesh and blood and the perseverance of my ancestors and the Mighty God above heaven and earth to guide my path.

My very human existence would not be possible if it were not for one such character that I met when I was a young, freckled-faced, innocent, impressionable, starry-eyed teenager on my father's farm nearly ten long years ago in Lancaster County, Pennsylvania. There, I met a wandering stranger at my gate looking for work. The stranger was welcomed on my father's farm and changed my whole life and what was expected of me in my traditional female role. To say the stranger changed my whole life is not an understatement. I am celebrating life, drinking, and savoring the taste of champagne, which was considered taboo in the community where I grew up.

I fell madly in love with this suave stranger, and I would have gladly and willingly dedicated my whole life to him, but he was a gentleman and never took advantage of me, and for that, I became more eternally grateful and remained in love with him over the years. Why I fell madly in love with this stranger was because he was different from the boys or men in my small community or, for that matter, the wider world.

Growing up in my small ultra-conservative community, I would spend countless hours with him, chatting, questioning him, and becoming more curious while learning from him and absorbing all the information. We interacted so much that I realized that I was starting to think like him and dare to dream of a greater role for me in the wider world. I became curious about the world and resistant to the various institutions that seemed to dominate our lives. The stranger encouraged me to develop my mind, to think widely, to let no one have unfettered access to my mind or to let nothing, person or institution, restrict my thought process. Where I was brought up, in a patriarchal society, the mindset was that females must know their roles and be restricted in every way possible, and that type of thought process still exists today in this modern twenty-first century.

The stranger has opened my eyes to the world in this fight between the force of good and evil. We wish that somehow goodness comes forth from things or people who are impeccable, but good sometimes comes from the force that is not unblemished in this life. The stranger has shown me the bad, the good, the complexities, and the beauty within people's nature. He has shown me the awesome, inspiring attributes of hope and reaching beyond our humanity to connect to a greater force within the universe.

Not only has the stranger changed my life, but he has allowed me to see and witness things that no mortal being has seen in my small village of Lancaster County. Growing up in the village, I was quite agnostic, but being close to my friend, the wandering stranger, reaffirmed my faith in a greater power above and to fall madly and deeply in love with this beautiful, gorgeous, unique blue planet we call Earth.

To tell the story like many other stories, I must start at the beginning.

About the Author

Contents

Chapter 1

It was an extremely hot and humid day in the Valley of the Kings in the land of Egypt, where a massive excavation project was being undertaken by about thirty-four men. The Valley of the Kings was where a lot of the pharaohs and the upper echelons of Egyptian society were buried in the past. The heat from the sun was quite intense, burning into the skin of the men, and there was little relief as they wiped the sweat from their faces with their small hand towels and the back of their hands.

Because of the oppressive heat, the work was slow, tedious, and tiresome as the thirty-two Arabic men dug the sandy soil quite carefully and methodically, not wanting to create too much disturbance in the area. The other two men, who seemed as if they were the project supervisors, were of German ancestry and issuing orders to the rest, who were mostly Egyptian, African, and Lebanese men with thick, guttural Arabic accents. The two Germans were extremely tall, dressed in khaki attire, black shiny boots, and hats covering their heads. The men had a small white paper with a map drawn on it to the location of what they were digging and searching for, regardless of the fact that they were unable to find the elusive object.

As the men continued digging, the two Germans were pacing, talking to themselves, and seemed extremely worried above the excavation site. The men were worried because they were behind time in finding what they came to Egypt to acquire for their benefactor. It was more than two months, and it seemed they were nowhere close to finding the priceless artifact they were digging for; however, they were diligent under the hot sun.

The men who were excavating the site were told that they were not searching for any Egyptian pharaoh tombs, gold, or silver but a specific small iron object shaped like an egg containing an amulet. The workers were further encouraged that whatever artifacts they dug apart from the amulet were theirs to keep or to dispose of in whichever way they chose and on their own time.

As the men dug, four of them entered a catacomb, and one of the men touched a small indentation on the tomb wall. Suddenly, the sandy soil gave way, and the men fell around thirty feet below in a chamber. Four Egyptians fell, and they landed on some pointed spears made of iron. The spears were extremely narrow at the pointed end, covering the entire floor; they gored the men's entire bodies, and they were killed instantly as their rich red blood flowed inside the damp, musky chamber. The chamber floor was covered with cobwebs and pristine brown sands, which gave the room a musky smell. Dust and sand covered everything in sight, and it made everything inside look eerie.

Two of the Egyptian men saw what was happening and started calling the other workers to the plight of their four coworkers. The two Germans heard the commotion and came down and entered the catacomb where the other workers were gathered with consternation etched on their faces. The two Germans quickly issued orders for two ladders to be tethered and extended down the chamber, where the four men fell to their deaths. The ladders were extended, and the German supervisors ordered ten of the men to climb down the ladder to retrieve the bodies.

The ten men started descending the ladder rungs and looked terrified of what they might encounter in the lower chamber of the tomb. They reached the bottom one by one, and the two Germans came down quite hurriedly, excitedly, but unconcerned for their coworkers' dead bodies. There was nothing but death surrounding them… Whatever half-hearted attempt the Germans had made to rescue the fallen fell short.

The two Germans suddenly started talking excitedly in another language, which the workers of Arabic ancestry could not comprehend in any form. The two Germans were quite excited because they realized they had inadvertently found the entrance of the burial tomb which they had been searching for the past two months. The men all looked around the burial tomb and saw a narrow entrance to a concealed chamber. The two Germans entered the concealed chamber, followed by the ten workers who came down to tend to their dead coworkers. The men were all walking further into the concealed chamber, and so were out of sight of the other workers above the excavation site.

As the twelve men walked in single file into the chamber, they were greeted by something unexpected.

In a blinding flash, iron spears from all directions came at them. The spears gutted the ten men's bodies but passed through the Germans. As the blood oozed from the men's bodies, the sight of the iron spears passing through the two Germans' bodies was the last frightful thing the ten men saw as they died with the realization that the two Germans who were working with them for the past two months were not human.

The two Germans walked further into the chamber as iron spears continued to shoot from all directions. In the right-hand corner of the chamber, a small rectangular rock structure about three feet in height and about a foot in width covered with an old rotting Egyptian cloth was the only remnant of the space. One of the Germans went over to the rock structure and blew away the cloth. He used his hand to hit the top of the rock structure, and it fell apart, revealing sand and something wrapped up in rotting papyrus paper. He hurriedly and eagerly took up the papyrus paper to see what it had been concealing. As he peeled it away, an egg-shaped object made of iron or bronze came into view. The men opened the object to reveal a glittering gold amulet, which came fully into view.

The two Germans were elated – the fruit of their labor would soon be in their hands. They quickly took out a small, rectangular, black graphite box and inserted the amulet. The two men exited the chamber and climbed on the ladder to the upper surface where the rest of the workers were. They told the workers to go below in the chamber because there was plenty of gold and other precious stones. One German had the amulet in the graphite box, took it out, lifted it above his head, and showed the workers. The workers, with greed in their eyes, started descending the ladder in a mad rush to retrieve the treasures.

As the man held the amulet above his head, it started glittering in the sunlight. Suddenly, the sky became dark and cloudy, and lightning and thunder were streaking across the area. A large number of white vicious-looking apparitions started emerging into view.

The German who held the amulet above his head felt as if electricity was coursing throughout his body. The other German saw what was happening and came to the realization that he could not control the amulet, so he inserted the amulet into the black graphite box. As if on cue, the lightning and thunder ceased, and the black clouds disappeared along with the vicious-looking apparitions.

The two Germans stared at each other, and the one named Heinz said, "Seems as if the rumors were right that only our kind can control the power of the amulet."

They then went to their Toyota Prado Jeep, took two grenades out of the car, pulled the pin, and threw them in the chamber where the workers were searching for treasures. The two grenades created a huge explosion, and the whole site caved in, burying the workers. The Germans went into the sports utility car and drove away in the direction of Cairo, the capital of Egypt.

Above a small knoll, an Egyptian man named Mohammed Fayol lay on the ground with a huge binocular tied around his neck, watching the excavation site. The man had on a white Galabeya, which is a loose fitting ankle length robe, and a fez, which is a hat worn on the head. The man was not a devout Muslim, but he just found that type of attire was more suitable in the unforgivable blistering heat.

The man thought that the two Germans had seen him because he saw them looking up at him many times. When one of the Germans took the amulet and held it above his head, the glare from it caused a small pain in the man's stomach because the stark reality dawned on him that they had found the Amulet of Osiris, the Egyptian God of the dead. The Amulet of Osiris had lain buried for centuries upon centuries, and now it was to be unleashed in the twenty-first century in the modern world. The man was in a real state of panic because he knew he could not confront the two Germans unless he wished for an early death.

As the German's Toyota Prado Jeep sped away, the man jumped in his car and, from a safe distance, started following their car. The man knew that by even following the Germans, his life was in danger. The man was aware of the fact, but he could not stand back and not do anything. The man always thought that if a life was worth saving, then some risk must be taken to preserve that life, irrespective of the danger. As he drove and followed the two Germans, the man tried to formulate a plan to retrieve the amulet. The man was aware of what his inaction meant in not trying to retrieve the amulet, what it would mean for this world. The man thought that he would do all he could do to retrieve the jewel so as to prevent these men from having control of the spirit of the dead.

***

On a cold morning in New York, a Caucasian man named Malakai, in an apartment in Manhattan, received a call from The Curator at the Cairo Museum in Egypt. The man had just woken and was half naked, only wearing blue Old Navy shorts and a silver amulet around his neck. He was extremely tall and not too muscular. As his cell phone rang, he jumped out of bed to answer the phone.

"Hello," he said.

"Is this Malakai? It is me, Fayol, from the Cairo Museum in Egypt."

"Yes, it is me, my friend. We have not spoken in a long time," said Malakai.

"Malakai, oh my God! They found it! They found it in the Valley of the Kings!" said Fayol, who was quite distraught and speaking in an erratic manner.

"Found what?" asked Malakai.

"They found the Amulet of Osiris in the Valley of the Kings, and two men are now leaving for the Cairo airport to take a flight to New York, where they will deliver it to The Alliance Organization. I tried, but I was unable to stop them from acquiring the amulet. I have a picture of the two men. I will send it to your cell phone in the next two minutes. One of the men is tall and muscular. He is the bodyguard, and the other is short, fat, and has an extremely nervous disposition. They are on an Air Cairo flight, which will be landing in the next ten hours," said Fayol.

Malakai paused and asked, "What do you want me to do with the Amulet?"

Fayol then said, "I need you to retrieve the Amulet and destroy it before the Alliance Organization can get their hands on it."

"Do you know where the two men will be staying in New York?" asked Malakai.

"They will be staying at some apartment in Brooklyn; I got the address from a customs official at the Cairo Airport. I will send the address when I send the picture. Your best bet is to be at the airport and follow them clandestinely to their destination because their address could be wronged," said Fayol.

"By the way, the cell phone you are using, is it a disposable phone?" asked Malakai.

"Yes, it is a disposable phone. I stole it from a store merchant the other day. I will burn it when I am finished speaking to you," said Fayol.

"Good, because you know I cannot afford for anything to be traced back to me," said Malakai.

"Malakai, I also need to tell you that if you retrieve the amulet from the men, you can only open the box for a few seconds. If you do open the box for more than a few seconds, it will bring hell on earth. You have got to stop them and prevent them from delivering the amulet to the Alliance Organization. The fate of the world is in your hands, my friend, because if they get to deliver the amulet, there will be chaos in this world and the next. I am sorry to drop this on you, but it is in your hands now. Take care, my friend," said Fayol.

After Fayol finished talking to Malakai, he immediately went outside the yard where a small fire was burning. He took out the disposable cell phone and threw it in the fire. He did not want anything to be traced to him or to Malakai.

Fayol stared into the fire, watching the phone burn, and began to reminisce about the first time he met Malakai. The memories came back to him as fresh as if it were not twenty-five years ago. He had just lost his wife and two children to a terrorist bomb attack at a café in Cairo. The café was mostly frequented by Christians in Cairo, hence the reason for the bomb in a predominantly Muslim country. He went into the café with his wife and children, and just as they were seated, he realized that he had left his wallet in the car glove compartment. He got up and rushed to his car to retrieve the wallet, and as he was going back to the café, a bomb went off, killing his wife and two children and all the patrons in the café.

After the death of his family, Fayol lost all hope in humanity and engaged in the apostasy of his faith. He lost faith and, in his mind, he could not fathom why a God who is about love and protection of the innocent would allow his wife and children to die needlessly without the chance to live. He was so distraught that one day, he drove many miles into the desert near the pyramid of Giza. He looked around to ensure that there was no one nearby and took out a revolver to commit suicide. As he put the revolver to his head to squeeze the trigger, a figure emerged from nowhere, held his hand, and said, "No matter what the circumstance is, Sir, life is really a gift from The Creator of the Universe. Do not throw away the most precious gift He offers you. You are capable of handling whatever travail you are undergoing, even though you may not realize it now. It is within you to deal with it."

Fayol was totally flabbergasted by the stranger's presence and asked, "Pardon me, stranger, how come you appear from nowhere to stop me from committing suicide?"

"It is not your time today nor tomorrow to die. Your life is worth saving. Do you know how precious it is? Contemplate what you were going to do and tell me if you think your problem would be over?" asked the stranger.

"I was trying to exorcise the pain that I go through night and day," said Fayol.

"Trust me, my friend, I would know if you take your own life now, it would be the beginning of endless pain in the next life," said the stranger.

"What is your name, my good man?" asked Fayol.

"I am Malakai. Permit me to ask, why do you want to commit suicide?"

Fayol explained what had happened to him with regard to his wife and children and the constant pain and guilt of not being able to save them that terrible day. Malakai told Fayol that things happen in the world that people have no control over, and he must accept and forgive himself even though sometimes there will be no understanding of the matter.

Fayol was so glad to unburden himself to Malakai that he invited Malakai to his home in Cairo. Malakai did not mind and ended up staying at Fayol's house for a month before he left for the States. They kept in touch with each other by using disposable phones. Occasionally, Malakai would send United States dollars to Fayol through a remittance service by an intermediary.

After hanging up the phone, Malakai started to ponder the situation. The news from Fayol was like a thunderbolt to his plan, and he knew the consequence of inaction and the urgency of the situation. He looked across the room and started staring at the beautiful Caucasian woman named Georgina in his bed. She started stirring from under the white sheet as the early morning light descended into the room.

"Good morning, darling," said the beautiful woman.

"Hey, my sweet, you are finally awake," said Malakai.

Georgina kicked the sheet with her right foot and jumped out of bed to go to the bathroom. She had on matching black lacy thong underwear and a bra that seemed to accentuate her curves. She was an extremely tall, beautiful woman with long, beautiful, flowing blonde hair that reached to her shoulder. She had long, gorgeous legs and two beautiful rounded breasts.

Around five minutes later, the beautiful female emerged from the bathroom, undressed, and jumped back into the bed, pulling the white sheet and blanket over her body. "Darling, come back to bed; remember, we do not have much time with each other," said Georgina.

"Georgina, I will be there shortly. Let me go and brush my teeth," said Malakai.

Within a few minutes, Malakai came out of the bathroom, and Georgina proceeded to turn on the radio to a popular rhythm and blues station in New York, Power 105.1. The disc jockey started playing old Rhythm and Blues' sung by one of Georgina's most cherished Rhythm and Blues artists, Mr. Teddy Pendergrass. "Just because you're mine." Georgina and Malakai loved music. Both had an eclectic taste in all genres of music.

Georgina was covered with a blanket in the bed, and as Malakai approached the edge of the bed, he dragged the sheet off her beautiful body. He loved to look at her. He loved her body, her ass, her breasts, and her long beautiful, svelte legs. There was nothing on this woman's body he did not love, and he appreciated every curve, every fiber that made up her whole being.

Malakai was still standing on the side of the bed. He proceeded to pull Georgina closer to him, and as he pulled her, he gave her a gentle smack on her bottom. Malakai, standing at the side of the bed with Georgina's back facing him, took both his hands to pull her body at the hips in a more upright position and started kissing her neck. Malakai slowly slid his hands upward until his hand settled on her breasts, wherein he proceeded to feel and squeeze them as it gave him an exhilarated feeling. Malakai released the hold he had on Georgina's body, quickly got undressed, and jumped into the bed. Georgina's back was turned as Malakai entered the bed, and he quickly snuggled up to her soft body. As he entered the bed, Georgina used the remote and turned up the music, and they started making love with the slow, soulful rhythm and blues music, an accompaniment to their lovemaking.

Malakai liked the feel of her rather firm buttocks on his thighs. Malakai resumed kissing the back of her neck, then slowly continued tracing his tongue on her back. After a few more minutes of kissing Georgina's back, he spun her around and began to kiss her lips. He loved to kiss her, to taste her lips. Georgina then gently took her hand and directed his mouth to her neck. She enjoyed the feel of his wet tongue on her neck as it gently caressed and gave her an exhilarating feeling.

After a few minutes of kissing Georgina's neck, Malakai moved his tongue eagerly to her breast as his hand wandered all over her body, gently touching and caressing every inch of it. Within a couple of minutes, Georgina's body started to be in a state of spasm as she screamed with ecstasy as she climaxed.

Malakai then proceeded to enter her and thrust and thrust until he had his orgasm. They hugged each other in the bed while the music kept on playing on the radio station. The rhythm and blues song of Teddy Pendergrass echoed in their small Manhattan bedroom. It had a special significance to both, but more so to Georgina. As she continued listening to the rhythm and blues lyrics of the songs, a tear came to her eyes, and she took her right hand and wiped it away.

Chapter 2

Around two hours after their sexual escapade, Malakai woke up and told Georgina that he had some business to take care of in Brooklyn. He told her that because they were going on a long journey the next day, she should stay and get as much rest as possible, and he would be back later in the night. Malakai went to the bathroom, where he quickly took a shower and got dressed by putting on his blue jeans, black polo shirt, and long black leather trench coat with his dark Ray Ban sunshades. He kissed Georgina goodbye and left the apartment with a small bag.

After Malakai left the apartment, he walked two blocks and then headed for the train station. He got on the number four train then came off at Wall Street wherein he took a number two train which was going to Brooklyn. The number two train stopped at Church Street, and Malakai exited the train station.

Malakai started walking briskly up the steps of the subway to the street level. He did not like being underground because he liked the smell of fresh air. As he emerged from the subway, he took a deep breath and started observing the streets. Church Street was busy as always, with lots of traffic and people of all ethnicities going about their business. He went into the McDonald's and ordered some chicken Mac- nuggets, fries, and a soda. Malakai consumed the meal and then left the restaurant.

On leaving the restaurant, Malakai began to observe the cars that were parked along the street. He needed a car to take him to John F. Kennedy International Airport. He was looking for a car that was not too conspicuous and one that did not have an alarm. Suddenly, he noticed a black Toyota Camry with the windscreen all fogged up, indicating it was parked for a long time. He quickly reached into his left pocket and took out a master key. Malakai then walked to the door with his key in hand, observing first if there was any alarm on the car. He did not notice any and proceeded to insert the master key into the car door. The car door opened quite easily, and he jumped inside, started the car with the master key, and drove away in the direction of the airport.

On reaching the John F. Kennedy International Airport, Malakai took out his phone to check if the Air Cairo flight from Egypt was on time. The flight was indeed on time and landed at JFK. Malakai parked the car at a location wherein he could observe who was coming out of the airport. He then picked up his phone again to look at the picture of the two men. With the picture cemented in his brain, his only option now was to wait for the two men to emerge from the airport.

Within thirty minutes Malakai saw two men who fitted the description of the picture he had on his phone coming through the door of the airport. One of the men was tall, gruff-looking, and had an olive complexion. The other man was much shorter, with an obvious paunch, and had a very pensive look on his face to the point of being very worried about something. The shorter man who had an inhaler inserted in his nostril was breathing quite heavily as if he were gasping for his last breath.

Malakai instantly realized that the taller man wearing a brown jacket over his suit was the bodyguard, and any action that he had to take, the bodyguard had to be dealt with first. The shorter man had a bearded face and was wearing a black business suit covered by a black jacket. The two men then went into a line that was securing yellow cab taxi service. They waited in line for five minutes then they were ushered into a yellow cab taxi.

Malakai started his car and waited for the two cars to move ahead of him before he drove off, following the yellow cab with the two men. Malakai did not want the two men to suspect that they were being followed. So he kept his distance. The yellow cab taxi drove on Linden Boulevard, then turned on Kings Highway, then after around ten minutes, turned into an apartment complex known as Clarendon Garden.

Malakai noticed that the complex was one of those old complexes that were built around the fifties or the sixties that did not have any gate. He did not turn into the complex; instead, he drove onto the service road and parked the Toyota Camry, where he could see the two men alighting from the yellow cab.

Malakai quickly opened the small bag that he had with him and took out a black wig, which he put on his head. The wig made Malakai look like a decrepit old man. He also took out a cologne bottle from the bag and sprayed it on his body. The scent of the cologne was to mask his scent from the men. Before he exited the car, he pushed his hand into his coat pocket, took out an instrument, and pressed the button that was on it, and suddenly, an elongated-looking fiery steel sword emerged from the instrument, which he promptly wrapped with two pieces of newspaper. The elegant steel blade under the newspaper was further secured with two elastic bands.

Malakai got out of the car and started walking like an old man with the support of the steel blade disguised as a walking cane towards the entrance of the building. The two men who came out of the taxi were just ahead of him but did not notice him as he hobbled along the walkway. As the two men reached the entrance door, the shorter one took out a key to unlock the door. Malakai started to walk a little faster now because he did not want to lose sight of the men when they reached their apartment.

Malakai pushed his hand into his coat pocket, took out his master key, and unlocked the entrance door. He could still see the two men as they walked up the stairs to the second floor. He hurriedly looked around to see if there were any other individuals around, but he could not see anyone coming out of their apartment.

Malakai quickly climbed the stairs and, with keys in hand, went to the door adjoining the men's apartment. Just as the shorter man opened the door to their apartment, Malakai spun around and kicked the taller man in his chest. The force of the kick pushed the taller man through the door entrance and, in the process, knocked over the shorter man. Malakai quickly shut the door. Just as the taller man was getting up off the shorter man, Malakai grabbed the sword and, with one fell motion, brought it down on the taller man's neck. The taller combatant's neck was completely severed, and blood started spewing all over the apartment. Malakai turned his attention to the shorter man, who was still lying on the floor in full panic mode.

"Please don't kill me, please," said the man.

Malaki raised the sword and put it at the man's neck and asked, "Do you know why I am here?"

"No," said the man.

"Where is the package you are going to deliver to the Alliance Organization tomorrow?" asked Malakai.

"Package, what package are you asking about? I do not have any package." said the man.

Malakai pressed the sword closer to the man's neck and said, "Since you are not able to give me the package, I may as well chop your fucking head off as I did with your companion."

In a quivering voice, the man said, "Okay, it is in that black bag, but please do not kill me."

Malakai said to the man, with the sword still pointed at his neck, "Get up slowly off the floor and take the package out of the bag."

The man got up off the floor, slowly opened the bag, took out a small black box, and placed it on the table inside the room.

"Open the box," said Malakai.

The man took off the cover of the box to reveal an object covered in a white piece of cloth, and through it, he could see the object was made of pure gold. The man proceeded to remove the white cloth to reveal a thick, round object covered in pure gold. Malakai realized it was the Amulet of Osiris.

"Close it!" said Malakai.

The man, almost shaking, said, "If you take the contents of the box, you know they will be coming after you in the night and in the day, and you will have nowhere to run or hide."

"I doubt they will be able to find me," said Malakai.

With one swift motion, Malakai decapitated the man, and blood started spewing all over the apartment. Malakai was not worried about the blood or the bodies because they were not human beings. Malakai knew no human eyes would be able to see them after five minutes because their bodies would turn to dust. Although they lived and blended quite well among the human population, they were, for all practical purposes, indiscernible to the average man or woman. They possessed vast powers, and the only way to terminate their life force was to separate their brain from their spinal cord. Some human beings were aware of them long ago and called them the spirit of a long-lasting realm that walked among humans, amassing power, and now ruled the earth, becoming the ultimate power on earth.

Malakai quickly wiped the blood that was on the sword on the shorter man's shirt and pressed the button that was on the sword for it to retreat into the sheath. He quickly picked up the box and put it in his coat pocket. Malakai then made a quick glance around the apartment to ensure he did not miss anything. He went to the door, opened it slightly, and looked to see if there was anyone outside. He did not see anyone, and he closed the apartment door and departed.

He went into the car and drove back onto Church Street, where he parked the car and entered the train station. Malakai went on a train and arrived in Manhattan after midnight.

Around an hour after Malakai had left the apartment in Brooklyn, a man in one of the most prestigious office buildings in Manhattan was calling the house phone in the Clarendon Garden apartment. There was no response. The person calling the house phone ensured that the phone rang for a minute. After the person hung up the phone, he called another number in Brooklyn. "Hello," said the man answering.

"Hello, am I speaking to Roberto?" asked the man in the Manhattan office building.

"Yes, this is Roberto. How can I help you?"

"You are speaking to Vallencourt, sector chief of the Alliance Organization. I need you to go by an apartment complex named Clarendon Garden. It is around five minutes from your apartment. Two men are supposed to be taking a valuable item to the Alliance Organization tomorrow, but I am calling the apartment number, and there is no one answering the house phone. The apartment number is B4, call me and tell me what you observe. Is that clear?"

"Yes, I am leaving now to go by the Clarendon Garden apartment. I will call you on my cell phone as soon as I am inside," said Roberto.

"Good," said Vallencourt.

After hanging up the phone, Roberto took the time to compose himself with the realization that something was afoot. The man's voice on the phone was commanding and terrifying at the same time. He was glad to be getting a call from Vallencourt because he was just a low-level street soldier and Vallencourt was the sector chief for the Alliance Organization. He did not imagine that he would ever be getting a call from somebody of that stature. Roberto was excited that he could be of use to Vallencourt, and he hoped that he would be able to fraternize with him one day.

Roberto quickly picked up his cell phone and his dark glasses, jumped into his car and drove over to Clarendon Garden. When Roberto arrived at the entrance of the building, there was an entrance door that was locked, and he waited outside until he saw an old African-American lady coming outside. And as she came out, he held the door and went inside the building. He looked at the door number downstairs that he was searching for but did not see it, and he hurriedly climbed the stairs. As he reached the top of the stairs, he saw the number on the door.

Roberto went to the door and turned the lock, and the door lock opened, and he went inside the apartment. It was a small two-bedroom apartment with a single bathroom and sparsely decorated with a few pieces of furniture. He looked around the apartment and did not see anyone apart from a small blue hand luggage which was opened on the table. Roberto took out the cell phone he had in his pocket and called Vallencourt. "Sir, I am in the apartment, and there is no one here, only one small blue opened hand luggage on a table," said Roberto.

"How did you gain access to the building and enter the men's apartment?" asked Vallencourt.

"I waited for someone to come outside the building and then went inside, and then I went to the room number of the apartment, and the door was unlocked," said Roberto.

"Look into the small bag on the table and tell me if there is a small black box in it?" asked Vallencourt.

Roberto went over to the table and investigated the small bag but could not see any small black box. He did not do anything wrong, but speaking to Vallencourt, he felt nervous and fearful.

"Sir, there is no black box in the bag, only a few items of clothing," he said.

When Vallencourt heard the response from Roberto, all the blood seemed to drain from his face to make him whiter. He was aware of the ramifications of such failure, especially as he was put in charge by the top boss to acquire the Amulet of Osiris. Failure was not an option because he knew there would be consequences if he was unable to deliver the amulet to the Alliance Organization. "Do not leave the apartment. I will be sending two of my most trusted agents there in the next ten minutes to see what they can find," said Vallencourt.

After hanging up the phone, Roberto was feeling a little tired, so he decided to take a seat on one of the beds. As he sat on the bed contemplating and waiting for the two men to arrive, Roberto thought he wanted to be more involved in this caper.

Around seven minutes, the room felt a little warm, and suddenly, two men dressed impeccably in black suits and wearing dark glasses emerged out of thin air into the room. One of the men was a tall, straight-faced African American, and the other was a tall Caucasian with long blonde hair.

"You are Roberto?" asked the tall African American.

"Yes sir," said Roberto rather nervously.

"Did you touch anything apart from the hand luggage?" asked the tall Caucasian man.

"No," said Roberto.

The tall African American man went to the table and started searching inside the hand luggage. He did not find what he was searching for, and he moved away from the table and removed the glass that was on his face; simultaneously, the Caucasian man followed to reveal eyes that were fiery red. The two men went about looking on the wall and the floor of the apartment for around five minutes, then suddenly re-inserted the glasses on their faces.

The African American then pushed his hand into his trouser pocket, took out an iPhone, and called Vallencourt. "Sir, they were both killed. There is blood all over the place, on the floor and the wall. I cannot pick up any clue who may have terminated their lives. All I can tell is that there was a brief struggle, and they were beheaded quite quickly because of the blood spat pattern. Plus, I can categorically state that the box with the amulet is not here. Also, I think how they were professionally eliminated, it had to be one of our kind."

"Fuck! Fuck! Come here! I need to gather my thoughts. Tell Roberto to see if he can pick up anything on the streets," said Vallencourt.

***

When Malakai opened his Manhattan apartment door, Georgina was fast asleep in the bed. He went into the bathroom quietly and quickly got undressed and took a shower. As the water from the shower was beating on his head Malakai was pondering on the day's event and wondering if he should inform Georgina. He decided against informing her about his adventure. Malakai came out of the shower, grabbed one of the white towels that was in the bathroom, and wrapped it around his body. As he came into the room, Georgina was wide awake. "How was your day?" she asked.

"Ok," responded Malakai. He then asked, "Georgina, did you set the alarm to wake up early in the morning?"

"I did, now come to the bed," said Georgina.

Malakai promptly went to bed. As Malakai cuddled up to Georgina with his naked body, Georgina turned to him and said, "Malakai, I do love you; you are mine, and I am yours."

Malakai responded and said, "I do love you too, babe. I am always yours."

Malakai then grabbed Georgina's body tightly, had her forcefully sit on top of him, and started kissing her, enjoying the softness of her lips. Malakai knew that it would be the last night like this. They wouldn't be seeing each other like this again because of tomorrow's long journey. He released Georgina's body from his tight embrace, and she straddled his legs as she directed Malakai's penis inside her vagina. She thrust on his penis until they both climaxed and went to sleep, exhausted from their lovemaking.

At exactly four-thirty the alarm went off, and both Malakai and Georgina got up out of the bed quite groggily, and Georgina went into the bathroom first, then Malakai followed to take a quick shower. After both were finished dressing, Georgina made the bed, and both grabbed their coats and left the apartment with Malakai carrying a small brown knapsack.

Malakai and Georgina then went into the subway station, where they took a train to Grand Central Train Station. When they arrived at Grand Central Train Station, they purchased two tickets to upstate New York.

Around three hours after they had left Grand Central Train Station, the train arrived at Upstate New York. Malakai and Georgina came off the train to a small town named Keene in Essex County. In the town, Malakai secured the services of a taxi to take them to Mount Marcy. Mount Marcy is the tallest mountain in New York State, with a height of five thousand three hundred and forty-three feet. The mountain was surrounded by lush, green vegetation, which got a lot of rainfall coming from the mountain.

As the taxi arrived at Mount Marcy, Malakai paid the taxi driver, and he drove off. Malakai and Georgina started to walk briskly up the mountain. Mount Marcy's terrain is not difficult to traverse, but it could be very tiresome if whoever was walking the trails was not prepared for the arduous trek up the mountain. There were four primary walking trails to reach the top of Mount Marcy, with the Southern Trail being the most difficult and isolated and posing the most danger to a climber's health. The top of Mount Marcy offered spectacular views, especially in the summer months of the surrounding areas. At the top of Mount Marcy, the wind speed tended to pick up because of the higher elevation.

Malakai and Georgina decided to take the Southern Walking Trail. As they began the ascent into the mountain, a gentle mountain breeze blew across their faces. Malakai felt at peace in the mountains and could afford to be even a little playful and carefree as he started feeling up Georgina's bottom. He grabbed Georgina's arms to bring her closer to him and said, "I will be waiting eagerly for you in our Manhattan apartment when you return."

"I will return to you as quickly as possible; I am going to miss you. I cannot afford to lose you; remember, I am yours, and you are mine," said Georgina. She then took both her hands, grabbed hold of his head, and started kissing him tenderly, savoring the taste of his lips. It was a long goodbye kiss, filled with passion and intensity, well aware that it would be their last day on earth.

After they had finished kissing and embracing each other, Malakai and Georgina resumed their trek up the mountain. They occasionally stopped for brief moments to view the terrain and take in the amazing sights of the mountain range.

***

Around six hours after they started the ascent into the mountain, they finally reached the peak. Malakai looked at Georgina to see how she was doing and coping with the climb up the mountain. He was aware of the fact that she was much weaker, and he blamed himself for having her stay this long on mother earth. Georgina was a little winded but composed and prepared for the long journey.

At the highest peak of the mountain, there are two huge boulders, one concealing the entrance to a cavern inside. Only a few living beings were aware of this hidden entrance. Malakai approached the slightly smaller boulder and as he was about to push the boulder to gain access to the cavern, he noticed some disturbance around the area. A few small rocks generally give way when the boulder has been moved in a hurried manner. Malakai thought that someone had recently used the entrance. His thoughts switched immediately to danger. He quietly ushered Georgina into the cavern and told her to be quiet and be careful just as he was pushing the boulder back in place sealing the entrance.

Malakai and Georgina were walking stealthily through the cavern. He did not know what to expect, and he did not want to be caught by surprise. Around ten feet away, Malakai saw a shadowy figure emerging from around a boulder. Malakai, and Georgina stopped, then continued walking towards the person.

"The Great Malakai and his tall Bitch," said the person emerging from the shadow. The shadowy figure who came into the light was a tall, muscular-looking man with a mean disposition dressed in all black. He was carrying a rather long, heavy-looking sword. The sword was meant to intimidate whomever he crossed paths with, especially in a fight. "I am Daemon, and I am here to make sure no one leaves the planet before I have searched them thoroughly." Daemon started staring intently at Georgina and asked, "Do you understand?"

"I know who you are," said Malakai.

"Then you know not to fuck with me. I will start with your Bitch first," said Daemon.

"Permit me to ask, what are you searching for?" asked Malakai.

"I am searching for an amulet in a black box. Do you or your Bitch have it?" asked Daemon.

"No, and we are not going to let you search us, not now or tomorrow. Do you get that, Daemon?" asked Malakai.

"That's going to be a problem. I was instructed by The Alliance Organization if I cannot search both of you, I must take your fucking heads, plus I will rather enjoy searching your woman!" said Daemon. He was enjoying himself and had a smirk on his face that was quite lascivious when looking at Georgina. In addition, he was full of confidence in himself because he did not see any weapon on either Malakai or his woman.

Georgina was quite apoplectic. She did not like being disrespected and especially being called a bitch. She quickly moved a couple of yards away and said, "Malakai make sure you chop off his fucking head."

Daemon lifted his sword off the ground with both hands in a backward motion in the air and, with one motion, directed the weapon towards Malakai's head. Malakai easily sidestepped the blade as gracefully as a matador with a charging bull and, in one motion, pushed his hand into his coat pocket to take out the Onoro sword. Malakai quickly pushed the button, and the elongated flaming steel started protruding instantly, like clockwork.

The sight of the flaming blade protruding almost froze Daemon. He had heard stories of the flaming blade, but he thought it was just a myth. Malakai smiled, quite aware of the effect that the flaming Onoro sword had on his fighting enemies. In the whole universe, there were only two Onoro swords ever made; one was with Malakai, and the other one was with his adopted father on an island. The Onoro swords were made of the finest steel technology not known to humans from a galaxy so far away that Malakai had never known but was told to him by his adopted father. From when Malakai was a boy, he was taught the art of sword fighting by his adopted father until he was a young man. Malakai's adopted father instilled patience in him when he was practicing sword fighting by slapping his hand each time he rushed into attack needlessly like a wild animal.

As Malakai and Daemon fought, Malakai realized that all the bravado was gone from Daemon. Malakai realized that Daemon's attacks were quite lumbering like a man who lost all his self-assurance.

Chapter 3

A high school female geography teacher with her class of fifteen students was on the highest mountain range in upstate New York, Mount Marcy, exploring the topography. Below the mountain was a verdant forest with wide varieties of vegetation. The teacher, whose name was Rose Winter, was a very skilled climber. Rose was a beautiful Caucasian woman, around five feet nine inches with a thick eyeglass that concealed the beauty of her face. She had long, beautiful, full black hair that extended to her ample breasts. She was dressed in a pair of tight-fitting blue jeans, a brown jacket, and hiking boots.

Rose told the students to wait on her while she descended into a cavern. As she was out of sight from her students, she held onto a rock to catch her breath. Suddenly, the rock gave way, and she fell, hitting her head. Lucky for her, she fell on some bushes that were growing inside the cavern. She was quite grateful for the bushes because they helped to cushion her fall inside the cavern. She felt a sharp pain coursing through her body, but the pain was most acute in her head.

She felt quite dizzy and was struggling to regain her composure. Her glasses were broken in pieces, so she just took the broken frame off her face. The pain was subsiding, and as she was clearing her face, she noticed that her eyesight was almost perfect. She did not need the glasses. She could not fathom why her eyesight was so much clearer, but in her present circumstances, she could not afford to dwell on that now, being in an isolated cavern.

As her eyesight became sharper, she saw three figures arguing with each other, and suddenly, she noticed two individuals with swords drawn lunging at each other in the cavern. She let out a small scream, and the three individuals noticed her, but the two individuals who were fighting kept on attacking each other until the individual who was not involved in the fighting approached her in a curt manner. Rose noticed that the person approaching her was a female. She was dressed in blue jeans and boots and a black trench coat. Rose thought to herself how odd that someone would be in the cavern. She pushed the thought out of her mind as the stranger approached her, wondering if she was in any danger.

As the strange female approached her, Rose could not help but admire her beauty and her regal look, although her complexion seemed quite pale. As she was walking towards her, she seemed to be almost gliding than walking in the isolated cavern. As the stranger approached her, Rose noticed that she made a gesture with her right hand, and suddenly, she seemed to be almost in a trance. "What are you doing here?" asked the strange female.

Rose was taken aback by the strange female curt question and said, "I am here with my students exploring the topography of the mountain when I saw this cavern and decided to explore it before bringing in my students."

"What happened to your glasses?" asked the strange female.

In her confused state, Rose started talking extremely fast because she was dazed and confused. "I fell from the opening of the cave and hit my head, broke my glasses, and now I am here talking to you."

The strange female then said to Rose in a very commanding voice, "You are here on our film set, and you need to leave now because a storm is coming this way."

Rose's eyes then diverted to the two men who were fighting and thrusting their swords at each other's heads. Rose could not help noticing the sword of the shorter man. It seemed like it was on fire. Suddenly, the shorter combatant kicked the other man in his stomach, and the force of the kick pushed the other individual back behind a large boulder and out of Rose's sight.

Around two minutes later, the shorter fighter emerged from behind the boulder and approached Rose and the strange female. As the male fighter approached Rose, the female said, "This young lady was viewing our film set."

The male was a little puzzled but said, "Did you tell her she has to leave the area because a storm is approaching?" The male then said, "Where are my manners? I am Malakai, and this lovely lady is Georgina." He reached for Rose's hand to shake it when Rose realized how warm his hands were as she shook them, and she noticed he was looking intently at her body. Rose also realized that Malakai was extremely tall. He also had on a tall black trench coat and was devilishly handsome. Unlike Georgina, who was quite pale, he was quite dark. The male then asked, "What is your name?"

Rose responded, "I am Rose, and I was just exploring the cave to ensure that there is no danger before my students, who are outside, climb down." Rose then explained how she had fallen and hit her head and broken her eyeglasses but then added strangely that she could see better without her glasses.

The two strangers looked at each other, then Malakai turned to Rose and said "You need to leave now. We are going to leave any moment now because a storm will be here in the next five to six hours. We will be exiting at a different point from here."

Georgina thought that Rose was quite beautiful, and she could sense with what they called a woman's intuition that Malakai was attracted to her but pushed the thought out of her mind because where they were going, they would be unlikely to see her again, and she knew Malakai had an undying love for her and would never disrespect her by propositioning another woman in her presence. On the other hand, she thought that Rose was quite lucky to be alive because when she had seen them in the cave, her first thought was to kill Rose, but it would cause too many complications because her students were outside the cave.

As Malakai and Georgina were walking further into the cave, Malakai said, "Let me go and tell Rose not to tell anyone what she has seen inside the cave."

"All right, but please hurry back," said Georgina.

"Will do," said Malakai.

Malakai hurriedly left to catch Rose before she exited the cavern.

As Rose was about to climb out of the cavern, Malaki came rushing towards her, gasping for air, and said, "I need to speak to you for a few minutes."

"Certainly," said Rose.

"I am hoping that it is not too much to ask of you not to tell anyone what you have seen inside the cavern," said Malakai.

"I am going to tell everyone in the world," said Rose with a cheeky grin on her face.

"Guess what," said Malakai. "No one will believe you."

Rose looked at his face, and he had a devilish smile revealing a beautiful set of white teeth. Rose thought to herself how odd that she had just met this stranger, and she did not feel fearful, considering that they were inside a cavern. "You know, you are a devil!" said Rose.

Malakai responded, "You may be right about that, but seriously, I would appreciate it if you do not tell anyone what you have seen inside the cave."

"Okay, I will do that for you. My lips are sealed," said Rose as she took her right hand and placed them over her lips. She somehow felt safe with this man she had just met, and she did not know a god damned thing about him or what he was about, and she was conscious that she was even flirting with him slightly because of his devilishly handsome face

Malakai then started looking intently at her face. He suddenly had this epiphany and knew it would be risky, but it seemed now the only way to extricate himself from his present predicament. Malakai was mindful that the Alliance Organization would be searching everywhere for the amulet, and because of Georgina's weakened state, she would not be of much help in a fight.

"Why are you looking at me like that?" asked Rose.

"I am looking at you, wondering if I can trust you?" replied Malakai.

"I told you that I won't reveal what I have seen here today," said Rose.

"It's not about what you have seen inside the cavern, but something else that is on my mind. I know trust must be earned, but frankly, I do not have the luxury of time. I want to give you something to hold securely for me until I return to collect it," Malakai then looked intently at Rose and asked, "is that okay with you?"

Rose was a little puzzled and responded, "Before I respond to your question, I want to know what you are giving me to hold securely for you, and for that matter, what do you do in terms of occupation?"

Malakai smiled and said, "Firstly, I am going to give you a small box containing an amulet. I want you to please secure the content of the box until I return to collect it. Secondly, about my occupation, I produce documentaries for television, and I am also an amateur archaeologist."

"Now that you have answered my questions, I will secure the content of the box until you return to collect it," said Rose.

"By the way, are you married, and do you have any children?" asked Malakai.

"No, no, and I also live alone," said Rose.

Malakai then took the knapsack off his back, opened it, took out the small black box, and gave it to Rose.

"Please take care of this box and keep it securely for me. Please promise me!" said Malakai in a stern voice.

The sternness of Malakai's voice caught Rose completely by surprise. "I said I would keep it securely for you, I promise you!" said Rose, elevating her voice.

"My apologies for raising my voice, but you must know how important this box is to me. I am depending on you to keep it safe for me. Please do not show anyone!" said Malakai.

"Okay, apology accepted. I will secure the box for you," said Rose.

Malakai then reached for Rose's hand, grabbed it firmly, kissed it, and said, "Thank you so much."

Rose was a little surprised by his tenderness in kissing her hand, but her immediate thought was to get off the mountain with her students before the impending storm. Rose gave Malakai her cell phone number, her home phone number, and her home and school address.

"I hope you are satisfied now that I have given you every detail about where to find me in New York. Anyway, I must bid you adieu and get to my students," said Rose.

After saying goodbye to each other, Malakai walked briskly to catch up with Georgina. He was aware of Georgina's temper and jealousy of other beautiful women and he dared not want that jealousy to flare up today of all days, when they were leaving mother earth.

As Malakai was out of sight and around the corner, Rose ran to where she saw the two men fighting behind the large boulder. She did not know what to expect, but she was damned sure not going to leave the mountain and not satisfy her curiosity. If there was a dead man behind the boulder, she wanted to know and to inform the authorities. As she reached the boulder, she did not see a body or any blood splattering. She looked around intently but could not see a body; satisfied, she hurriedly left the cavern to rejoin her students.

Rejoining her students, Rose told them that a storm was coming their way, so they would have to leave the mountain. She was glad that she came up Mount Marcy using the primary trail because, apart from it being the most popular for hikers; it was also the least challenging of all the four trails up the mountain. Rose and her students quickly descended from the mountain, and within five to six hours, they were at the bottom. They jumped into the bus that took them to Mount Marcy and headed back to Brooklyn.

Malakai and Georgina stayed on the highest peak of Mount Marcy until the wind started to become fiercer because of the impending storm. Malakai took off the knapsack that was on his back, and he and Georgina started taking off their clothes. He put the clothes into the knapsack, and when they were all finished, Malakai went and hid the knapsack under some rocks.

When the storm finally arrived with all its ferocity, Malakai and Georgina jumped off the cliff, and suddenly transformed their bodies to a fiery flame. With the aid of the raging wind, both Malakai and Georgina were propelled into the earth's atmosphere, being transformed into fiery flames.

Both Malakai and Georgina landed on a Chondrite Meteorite, which was quite stony and common in the Earth's atmosphere. There were around twenty to twenty-four million Chondrite Meteorites at any given time in Earth's atmosphere, but the vast majority tended to burn up into dust and settle on the earth.

Familiar of the fact that they could not stay on the Chondrite Meteorite because it would burn into dust, Malakai and Georgina still transformed into a white fiery flame and hurled themselves into space onto a small asteroid. The asteroid's surface was black, quite rocky, and cold, and both were insouciant to the coldness. The asteroid was orbiting around the sun as all asteroids do and taking them to their destination. Malakai was extremely glad that they landed on the asteroid because all the consternation that he had about Georgina's weakness could now be alleviated for the journey to her home world.

Malakai and Georgina transformed into the white fiery flicking flame on the small asteroid. They did not want any prying human eyes to see them, especially with the closeness of The International Space Station and the prevalence of human exploration of space.

As Malakai and Georgina were travelling farther and farther through space at breakneck speed on the cold and rocky asteroid, a voice appeared out of nowhere and said, "Do not move and stay in your present form to allow me to scan you."

As Malakai and Georgina looked up, they saw a figure emerging out of the shadow of the blackness of space coming into view. It was as if they were staring at the statute of The Colossus of Rhodes, one of the seven wonders of the ancient world. The figure was huge and not exactly seventy cubits like The Colossus of Rhodes, but was extremely tall, dressed in a black cape and skintight shorts displaying muscles from head to toe. On his back was a shiny, elongated sword around fifteen feet in length. Malakai heard of this individual before but had never encountered or seen him before the present moment. His name was Ornias Junior, and he was aligned with the Alliance organization. Although his name was quite notorious, he hated his name, so whenever one is addressing him, you have to address him as "My Lord."

Malakai felt the penetrative gaze of Ornias Junior scanning them, but he could do nothing at the present moment. He was so glad that he had given the amulet to Rose for safekeeping because he would have resented fighting an enemy not knowing their weakness or strength. Malakai gazed at the imposing figure and asked, "My Lord, have you finished scanning us as yet?"

"Yes, go on your way," said Ornias in a deep, booming voice.

"Permit me to ask, My Lord, what were you searching for?" asked Georgina.

"None of your business, and go on your way before I change my mind!" said Ornias Junior.

With Ornias' imprimatur, both Malakai and Georgina went on their way to their destination. Malakai knew the fact he would soon have to separate from Georgina because they were going to separate destinations. Georgina did not belong to The Milky Way Galaxy but to The Andromeda Galaxy. Her journey to Andromeda Galaxy would take so much longer, and although Malakai was going into deep space, Georgina's destination was another galaxy.

Georgina was looking quite pensive and started staring into the only star in our solar system. Looking into the sun gave her some sort of solace, knowing it was time for Malakai to leave for his destination. She was going to miss him without a doubt, but it was the path that had been chosen for them before they were even born.

"Darling, it's time for me to leave," said Malakai.

"I know, and I hate that you have to," said Georgina.

Malakai reached over, grabbed her, kissed her, and said, "Goodbye darling, I will be eagerly awaiting your return on Earth."

With one final kiss, Malakai hurled himself off the asteroid; still transformed into a white fiery flame to a larger asteroid. The larger asteroid was much colder but had a smoother rock surface. Malakai had no intention of staying on the asteroid because he was going into deep space, into the center of the Solar System. He kept leaping from asteroid to asteroid, ensuring he was travelling in a straight line until he was in deep space.

Malakai could feel the intense pressure and coldness on his body. He was using most of his energy to withstand the coldness and intense pressure. He accepted that this was where he had to come to continue surviving. In his younger days, he was not able to relate or accept that this was where he had to come just to continue existing, but as time went on and he grew older, he grew to accept it. His elders taught him that he was no different from some sea birds like penguins or sea turtles, that no matter where in the world they were, when it was time to procreate, they would have to return to where they were born, but in his case to regenerate and restore his body to its full potential.

Malakai's destination was at the center of the galaxy, to a supermassive black hole known as Sagittarius A*. This supermassive black hole greatly impacted the whole Milky Way Galaxy by limiting the formation of stars and could sometimes emit light brighter than the sun. Supermassive black holes form when two or more massive stars collide, and they have mass five to ten times that of the sun. Supermassive black holes take in matter, but they also can spit it out, especially when they gobble up too much matter quickly in their surrounding orbit.

Malakai dived off the final asteroid and into the gravitational field of the huge black hole, and it was as if he were travelling at lightning speed. As Malakai entered into the event horizon of the supermassive black hole, he stared into space, gazing at the uniqueness that was planet Earth, and started to think about the complexities of the wider universe. Scientists defined the universe as space and time with the interaction of matter and light. However, the universe is so much more than that and so much more complex.

Human beings can only comprehend and appreciate the concept that God is outside of space, time, light, and matter because, before the creation of the universe, God existed. God is everlasting. He created the universe and can transcend space and time. It is rather patently obvious that the universe is the living embodiment of God, displaying his power, greatness, and grandeur. A planet or a galaxy is not everlasting because they can be destroyed over time, which often occurs; however, even if a hundred galaxies were destroyed, that does not mean that the universe can be destroyed because the universe remains indestructible because the sustenance of it lies within the power of the creator, who is God.

Life is only unique to one planet in the whole universe, and if life is only unique to planet Earth, then planet Earth is unique like life itself. Malakai appreciated the beauty of deep space, seeing stars and even galaxies formation, but his true love was the blue planet Earth. Malakai loved Earth's flora and fauna, the fishes, the oceans, lakes, rivers, the clean smell of fresh air, food, the love of a woman, sex, music, sports, poetry, reading a good book, friendship, laughter, colors, and its diversity of people. All these things were unique to one planet in the whole universe, and that was planet Earth.

Malakai thought planet Earth was totally unique and amazing and was specially created by God for mankind to be his home planet. Because of the uniqueness that is planet earth, which is the home of mankind, mankind must care for it, like a well-manicured garden.

Mankind must utilize Earth's resources by taking care of the soil, partaking in the consumption of the fruits of the trees, and partaking in the consumption of fish in the oceans. Animals on land should not be used for sport because they are unique in their own ways, but only where necessary to satisfy man's consumption of protein in their diet.

As Malakai plunged further into the supermassive black hole, it was as if he were in a suspended animation. His brain was no longer conscious because of the unbearable heat and the massive amount of energy going in and out of his body. It was as if his body was reconstructed each time he entered the black hole.

Theoreticians always postulated that time and space in a black hole no longer existed, but Malakai would not know because his brain was no longer conscious, and all he was waiting for was for the black hole to spit him out when the process of reconstruction of his whole being was completed to be back on Earth.

Chapter 4

Vallencourt was in his posh Manhattan office seething with rage, and when he was this angry, he tended to sweat profusely like a racehorse at a derby. Vallencourt was a tall, muscular man with broad shoulders and impeccably dressed in the finest Italian suits. He knew for fact that failure to deliver the amulet meant that he would not be occupying his stylish Manhattan office in the near future. His very existence on this planet meant that he would have to find the amulet wherever it was and by any means necessary, and he did not have the slightest clue who could have acquired the amulet without leaving the slightest trace.

Vallencourt decided to retrace the steps of the two men from Cairo. He called a contact in Cairo that was responsible for the excavation and acquisition of the amulet. Vallencourt told the man at the other end of the line that the amulet had disappeared, and the two men who were to deliver it were dead. He told the man he was just trying to retrace the journey of the two men from Egypt to America and if there was anyone watching or observing their movement.

The man at the other end of the phone call in Egypt paused and then told Vallencourt that there was a man named Fayol, who is the curator of the Cairo Museum who was clandestinely watching them doing the excavation. The man told Vallencourt that he did not think Fayol had anything to do with the death of the men or the disappearance of the amulet but regarded Fayol as a harmless pest and a nuisance. Vallencourt told the man that he would send two of his agents to Egypt on an Air Cairo flight to interrogate the man and that he would have to pick the men up at the Cairo Airport the next day.

After hanging up the phone, Vallencourt called his two trusted agents and told them that he was sending them to Cairo to interrogate someone who may know or may not know something about the disappearance of the amulet. Vallencourt further told the agents that they should use whatever means necessary to get the information.

As the two agents walked out of Vallencourt's office, his secretary called him and told him that Mrs. Sonia James from the Internal Revenue Service was there to see him about a pressing government matter. Vallencourt told his secretary to send Mrs. James to his office. Vallencourt's office door opened, and a beautiful African American woman around five feet six inches walked in, dressed in a black professional business suit with an attaché case in her right hand. Vallencourt was angry, seated behind his desk, and did not want to be bothered by any visitor, but he got out of his chair, shook Mrs. James' hand, and told her to have a seat. Vallencourt then asked Mrs. James, "What can I do for you or the government today?"

Mrs. James cleared her throat and said, "I am here on behalf of the Internal Revenue Service, and we noticed that this organization does business all over the world, yet we can find no discernable way to confirm that your organization is contributing to the tax base of our country." Mrs. James suddenly noticed that Vallencourt's disposition was changing in front of her eyes. His mood was getting angrier and darker. Still, she asked, "Can you say why this organization is not paying its fair tax?"

A visibly upset Vallencourt did not even want to entertain the lady in front of him, much less listen to her question, so he interjected. "Our organization does not have anything to do with your government, and where we operate around the world is our business."

Mrs. James looked at Vallencourt and knew he was trying to intimidate her, maybe because she was a woman, but she was not going to back down from getting answers to her questions. She considered herself a professional woman working on behalf of the tax authorities and she fervently believed that as long as a business made money, they should pay their fair share of the tax stipulated by the United States Congress. Mrs. James then said, "As long as your organization is a commercial enterprise and operates within the boundary of the United States of America, it is our business."

"You need to leave and stop wasting my time because I honestly do not think you know who you are speaking to about mundane tax issues. Our organization operates wherever we want in the world, and we do not concern ourselves with your trivial tax issues," said Vallencourt.

Mrs. James' demeanor remained calm and poised, and she retorted, "Since you are not amenable, I will have to bring the wrath of our government on this organization to make you more tax compliant. As soon as I arrive back at work, I will make my findings in a report and pass it on to my superior."

Vallencourt, quite exasperated, asked, "Are you threatening me within my own organization?"

Mrs. James got up out of her chair and was on her way out of the office when she turned around nonchalantly and said, "Take it as you will; I am just stating a fact. Goodbye, Mr. Vallencourt. Have a good day!"

Mrs. James exited Vallencourt's office, and he was more infuriated than before the lady had entered his office. The curt and dismissive manner in which Mrs. James spoke to him was way too much for him to take from someone of that ilk - whom he believed was way below him, as he regarded her as an insect that needed to be crushed like a cockroach.

Vallencourt's eyes became quite red, and he became invisible. And he raced out of his office into the elevator, trying to catch Mrs.

James. The elevator descended to the ground floor, and as it opened, Vallencourt was just in time to see Mrs. James exiting the building.

Vallencourt followed her still in an invisible form to her red Honda CRV. Mrs. James opened her car and put her attaché case on the backseat. She put on her seatbelt and drove away from the area with Vallencourt seated in the front seat without her knowledge. Mrs. James continued to drive until the road traffic was not too congested, and she started increasing the speed. Suddenly Mrs. James heard the unmistakable voice of Vallencourt that said, "Say goodbye. This is your last day on this earth, Mrs. James."

Mrs. James started shrieking in terror as Vallencourt took the steering and yanked it from her, and directed the car into the oncoming traffic coming from the opposite direction. The car crashed into an oncoming Mack truck with a container attached to it. The Mack truck crushed the Honda CRV, killing Mrs. James. Vallencourt was still in an invisible form as he looked at the crashed site with the Honda CRV mangled and Mrs. James' lifeless body bleeding. Callously, he remarked, "I do not think that report will be written now."

The accident caused huge traffic to pile up as Vallencourt walked away and the oncoming sound of an emergency car speeding towards the crashed site became audible in the background.

When Rose arrived at her apartment in the night, she was so fatigued, although glad to be home. She locked the apartment door, put her bag on the table and went straight for the refrigerator to get something to drink to quench her thirst.

The apartment was a small two-bedroom, consisting of one bathroom and a living room, which she converted to part dining room. The apartment was beautifully decorated and fully carpeted, except for the kitchen. She loved her apartment; it was her sanctuary from the hustle and bustle of everyday life. She turned on the television in her bedroom and then went into the bathroom, where she undressed and took a long hot shower. When she came out of the shower, she lotioned her body and put on her night clothes before telephoning her friend, Angela Stanton. They chatted for a few minutes then Rose went straight to her bed.

Rose woke up Saturday afternoon feeling much more energetic because she had had a long, restful night's sleep. She was feeling hungry, and she went into the bathroom, brushed her teeth then went into the kitchen to prepare scrambled eggs and toast.

After she finished eating, Rose took her bag that was on the dining table and started to unpack. She took out the black box that Malakai gave her for safekeeping. Rose opened the box only to discover a glittering round object looking like a bracelet. She took it out, examining it thoroughly, and realized it was made of pure gold. Rose thought the amulet was valuable, but she had made a promise to the man she met on the mountain to secure it. She stretched across the table and grabbed a small basket filled with red apples. The basket was filled with a combination of real and artificial red apples. She picked up one of the artificial apples, unzipped it and placed the bracelet in it. Rose then took the empty box and placed it in a compartment in the breakfront.

When seated around the dining table, Rose's mind drifted to the incident on Mount Marcy with Malakai. She was rather intrigued by his presence on the mountain. She detected that he was also intrigued with her and seemed to be attracted to her in the way he kissed her hand. Rose suddenly snapped out of her fanciful thinking and started wondering why she had not asked Malakai about the relationship he had with the woman, Georgina. She could sense a level of hostility with Georgina, and most of all, it suddenly jolted her that Georgina had told her they were filming a movie, but she had not seen any camera...

She told herself that maybe the camera was placed where the men were fighting and carefully hidden in the cavern. She started pondering what had happened to the other man and if Malakai had really killed him, why she was unable to see the body or any blood at the spot where they were fighting like wild animals. Rose told herself all those unanswered questions would have to be postponed until she met Malakai at some other time.

***

As the Air Cairo plane landed in Egypt, the two men quickly disembarked and made their way outside, where a white Ford Explorer was waiting for them. "I am Lucan," said the driver.

"I am Thornbird," said the Caucasian agent. "The other agent is Rochester," pointing to the tall African-American man. "We want to leave Egypt as quickly as possible as soon as the interrogation is completed."

"That will not be a problem. However, it is now nine o'clock, and Mr. Mohammed Fayol closes the museum at ten o'clock and reaches home at eleven. Your best bet is to interrogate him at his home, where he lives alone," said Lucan.

"Okay, that sounds like a good idea to interrogate him at his home. So what do we do now for the next two hours?" asked Rochester.

"Let me take you to a café in Cairo where they have the finest belly dancers," said Lucan.

"Great idea, I would love to see a little of Cairo's nightlife," said Thornbird.

The men entered the car and drove in the night to an upscale gated neighborhood. It stopped at an establishment painted in garish red color. A security guard armed with a high-powered rifle dangling across his back approached the car and opened the door. "Welcome to our establishment, where we have the finest belly-dancing girls."

"Thank you!" said Rochester as he got out.

As the men entered the establishment, they were ushered to a table that seated three. The ambiance of the place was quite impressive with the moonlight reflecting through the glass windows providing ambient lighting. The place was packed with fascinated male onlookers who were eagerly anticipating the night's performance. The men ordered their drinks, and just as they were paying the waitresses, the music came on, and a lone belly dancer approached the stage.

The floodlight was now on the belly dancer gyrating and swaying her hips. The belly dancer was scantily clad with her huge bust slightly covered, her midriff exposed, and her hips covered with a long skirt and a split at both ends. The midriff of the belly dancer displayed beautifully toned stomach muscles that seemed to enhance her sensuality.

This girl made belly dancing quite sensual and exciting, and she was quite skillful at her craft. The young belly dancer appeared to be in her twenties and she was quite beautiful, and the men in the audience were quite enthralled and started clapping in appreciation of her performance.

At around quarter to eleven, the men left the belly dancing establishment. They drove into a middle-class community. Lucan slowed the speed of the car and pointed out Fayol's house to the two men. Afterward, Lucan took out his smartphone, showed them a picture of Fayol, and told the two men that he would be waiting for them at the entrance of the complex on the other side of the road. While the car was still driving, the two men in the backseat of the Ford Explorer simply disappeared from the car.

Rochester and Thornbird appeared from thin air into Fayol's dining room, where he was sitting around his dining table, having his dinner and playing Arabic music. Fayol jumped out of his chair and instantly picked up the knife he was eating with and slipped into his pocket.

"Mr. Fayol, please sit in your chair. We are here to ask you a few questions, and depending on your answers, we are going to see if you live or die," said Rochester in a way-too-friendly manner.

"What? What questions do you want answered?" asked Fayol in a rather nervous voice as he sat back into the chair. Fayol came to the instant realization that Malakai must have acquired the amulet.

"What do you know about the Amulet of Osiris?" asked Thornbird.

"Not much. I know it was excavated a few weeks ago in The Valley of The Kings," said Fayol in a more confident voice.

"Did you contact anyone in the States about the amulet?" asked Rochester.

"Of course not. Why would I contact anyone in America? I do not know anyone in America to contact about the amulet. My only concern was about precious Egyptian antiques being taken out of the country. These ancient artifacts belong to the people of Egypt," said Fayol.

Fayol's response was not to Thornbird's suitability, so he turned around and increased the volume of the Arabic music that was playing in the background. He went to the kitchen and lit the gas stove with a match, and turned the knob to the maximum to increase the flame. Thornbird then went into the dining room, grabbed Fayol from around the table and led him into the kitchen.

"I am done playing with you, Mr. Fayol. I need some honest answers. Tell me, who has the amulet?" asked Thornbird.

Thornbird, with one motion, instantly grabbed Fayol by the front of his shirt and hoisted him to an iron towel rack in the kitchen.

He then grabbed a couple of the towels that were in the kitchen and lit them on the stove. Thornbird then placed the lit towels under Fayol's feet, which were a foot away from the fire. Fayol started to swing his feet and scream, as the flame was reaching up to Fayol's feet. The pain was almost unbearable, and Fayol was struggling to free himself from the iron towel rack to which he was attached.

"Now tell us who has the amulet?" asked Rochester.

Fayol did not respond to the question, and the two men looked at each other quite quizzically. Fayol realized that the two men were going to kill him, and he was damned sure not going to betray Malakai. Fayol started to mutter something that the men could hardly understand in his native Arabic language. "My God, my Savior, forgive me of my many sins. I render my soul to you and your son Yeshua," said Fayol.

Fayol believed that a man was what he said he was and the name he wanted to be called, and not what anyone chose to call him, especially a deity. Fayol did not use the name Jesus but the Jewish name, Yeshua. Fayol's belief was further strengthened when Malakai told him that was the true and accepted Jewish name.

"So you are not going to tell us what has happened to the amulet?" asked Thornbird.

Fayol ignored the two men, aware that they intended to kill him regardless of whether he answered their questions. As the fire started to burn his feet, Fayol tried his utmost best to block the excruciating pain. His mind drifted to a more peaceful and happier place as he saw the apparition of his wife and children beckoning to a more peaceful place.

The fire started to burn Fayol's groin area; the pain was so excruciating that he came out of the trance-like state he was in, and he started to scream and kick his feet. With Fayol kicking and screaming, the shirt that he was wearing that held him to the curved towel rack tore, and he fell to the kitchen floor. Fayol quickly inserted his hand into his pants pocket, took out the knife, and hurled himself at Thornbird's chest, and the force of Fayol's weight knocked him over on the kitchen floor.

Fayol quickly jumped on Thornbird's body and started slashing his neck with the knife. As the blood from Thornbird's neck started to spew on the floor, Fayol kept slashing and slashing. Fayol was trying to decapitate Thornbird's neck because he remembered Malakai told him only by removing the head can you terminate his life force. The knife, however, was used for eating and not for cutting. Therefore, Fayol was not able to sever Thornbird's head. As Fayol continued to slash Thornbird's throat, Rochester saw what was happening to his companion and quickly placed a kick to Fayol's ribcage, and he knocked Fayol off Thornbird.

The pain in Fayol's ribcage was so acute that it seemed all of Fayol's ribs had broken. Fayol started gasping for air as his lungs started to collapse. Blood started pouring out of Fayol's mouth, and he started to drift into an unconscious state.

"So you wanted to terminate my life on this planet where I do not belong," said Thornbird.

Thornbird was so enraged with Fayol trying to decapitate him that he hurriedly got up off the floor, and as his skin started to heal immediately, he kicked Fayol in his head. The force of the kick knocked Fayol's head straight into the cement wall. Fayol started bleeding profusely from his mouth and head and was gasping for oxygen. "You will never find the Amulet of Osiris, you alien beast!" said Fayol. With one last gasp for breath, Fayol succumbed to his injuries.

The men were left more puzzled than before because they knew Fayol was the answer to where the amulet was, but now, he was dead. They started searching the apartment for any clue to the whereabouts of the amulet, but it was a futile effort.

Just as they were getting ready to leave the house, Rochester went into the kitchen and turned on all the knobs on the gas stove. He took one of the towels that was burning on the floor and used it to light the curtain in the kitchen, and then he took the lit towel and carried it into the bedrooms and lit the curtains. Within minutes, the whole house was engulfed in flames, and the two men immediately disappeared into thin air.

***

As Lucan was in the white Ford Explorer waiting and smoking a cigarette, Rochester and Thornbird appeared. "What took you so long?" asked Lucan.

"Mister Fayol did not want to convey any information to us, so we had to use deleterious means to try to get the information. We still did not get much information. Did he have any friend who was helping him spy on you during the excavation process?" asked Rochester.

"No, he was alone. Fayol tends to keep to himself after the death of his wife and children," said Lucan.

"Guess that is the end of our business in Cairo. We have a few hours before the early flight to America. Can you take us back to the belly dancing establishment before we bid adieu to Egypt?" asked Rochester.

"It would be my pleasure before I take you to the airport," said Lucan.

Chapter 5

It was Sunday morning. Rose got out of bed, prepared her breakfast, and after consuming it, she took a shower, dressed then left for church. It was a rather lovely Sunday morning as she entered the church, looking quite radiant in a blue dress and matching heels with her skin glowing, looking as cool as a cucumber. She greeted her pastor, exchanging pleasantries with other members of the congregation and the usual lustful look by some of the men in the church.

Rose was neither a devout Christian nor a regular attendee of the church, but whenever she was in the mood, she would go and offer praise to God. She sometimes struggled with her religious beliefs and even sometimes regarded herself as agnostic. Her loss of faith sometimes occurred whenever she observed grinding, abject poverty, wars that killed the helpless and the innocent, racial and religious bigotry and forest fires that destroyed the environment and killed countless animals. She comforted herself by acknowledging that there must be a God in the creation of the universe and the complexities of life because for something to exist there must be a creator.

As she took her seat on the church bench, the pastor started preaching about faith, love, and referencing 1 Cor.13: 4-8, admonishing the members to be kind and loving to each other and the wider community. It was a lofty and passionate sermon by the preacher, followed by a hymn titled "Blessed Assurance, Jesus Is Mine" before they closed in prayer.

After the service had ended, the pastor of the church descended from the pulpit and started thanking the members for coming to the Sunday service. The pastor was a rather tall, handsome, muscular looking African American man named Reverend Watkiss and extremely devoted to his Christian faith. He was dressed impeccably in his white shirt covered by a navy blue jacket and black pants. As Reverend Watkiss approached Rose, he held out his rather large hand to shake Rose's hand. "Glad that you could make it this beautiful morning for the service, Miss Winter. I was going to call your cell phone when I did not see you for the last two weeks in church. Please, come back next week," he said.

"I have been really busy, but today it seemed such a lovely morning not to come and worship the Lord," said Rose.

"Anyway, thank you for coming. Be good, and may the Lord continue to protect and shine his light upon you," said Reverend Watkiss.

"Thank you, and the same to you, Reverend," said Rose.

After bidding goodbye to the pastor, Rose went to a restaurant where she ordered some food to take home. On reaching home, Rose ate and watched television. She was single, and she was quite insouciant about dating and relationships. She is a woman who treasured her independence, and frankly, she did not meet any man to whom she was attracted and wanted to take the ultimate plunge into a relationship. Rose felt that life was too transient, and relationships can be too complicated sometimes, and she wanted a simple, non-complicated one if she ever found a compatible partner.

Rose went to bed around ten o'clock on Sunday night after preparing her school lesson for her Monday classes. She had a rather lovely day attending church service in the morning and greeting her pastor. As she lay sleeping, her subconscious mind started drifting and dreaming about Malakai. The image of him kissing her hand and the gentleness of his lips touching and caressing her skin heightened the sensation. As she continued in her dream state, Malakai's mouth departed from her hands upwards to her lips; the sensation was too intense, and she woke up and opened her eyes.

Rose was sweating slightly, and she reached over her night table and took a small hand towel to wipe the sweat from her forehead. Fully conscious, Rose started staring at the white ceiling, wondering why this man whom she had just met briefly was on her mind, and now she was even dreaming about him, not even knowing if she would ever see him again in her life.

On Monday morning, Rose entered her classroom feeling quite rested and energetic and looking forward to meeting her students. As Rose entered her classroom, an African American student named Anton got up from around his desk and rushed to assist Rose with her bags and books. Anton was one of the students who had accompanied Rose up Mount Marcy and also Rose's favorite student. He was dressed in black jeans and a woolen pull over. "Good morning, Miss Winter. I hope you had a restful weekend," said Anton.

"Good morning to you, too. I did have a restful weekend. Take your seat, and let us commence the class," said Rose.

As Rose started the lecture, she felt at ease because she was quite proficient in the pedagogy of her beloved subject. Geography came naturally to her because she loved the outdoors and was always curious about rock formations, mountains, the different continents, and how human activities impact the natural environment.

Rochester and Thornbird had just disembarked the Air Cairo flight at the John F. Kennedy International Airport and were rushing back to Manhattan to report to their boss, Vallencourt. As the men entered the elevator, they saw a female rushing to catch the elevator. Rochester held the elevator door and a beautiful blonde female entered, wearing blue jeans in high heels and a gorgeous sexy white blouse barely covering her ample bosom, and slung over her shoulder was a brown Louis Vuitton bag. Her name was Wildflower,

Vallencourt's beloved daughter. She was not only beautiful but quite stunning and mesmerizing. "Thanks for holding the elevator door, gentlemen. Are you going to see my dad?" asked Wildflower.

"Yes, we are," said Rochester.

As the elevator door closed and ascended to the twentieth floor, the three occupants came out and entered a large grey room with a receptionist. The receptionist directed the three individuals to Vallencourt's office. Rochester opened the door to reveal a spacious office with exquisite office furniture overlooking the Manhattan skyline. When Vallencourt saw his daughter, he got up from around his office desk and gave her a tight embrace and a kiss on her jaw. "My darling, when did you come back from Europe?" asked Vallencourt.

"Last night, I flew from Heathrow Airport to JFK, and I said first thing in the morning I will come to look for you," said Wildflower.

"It is truly good to see you, my beloved daughter," said Vallencourt.

"Gentlemen have a seat. I am glad that you are here to help us with a situation of utmost importance. We had located The Amulet of Osiris in Egypt, and it was being transported to us last week by two couriers, but when they reached New York, the amulet disappeared, and the two couriers were terminated. I sent these two agents, who you know, to Egypt to see what they could find out, and they are just returning. Gentlemen, go ahead and tell us what you found out about the disappearance of the amulet," said Vallencourt.

The men relay to Vallencourt their interrogation of Fayol and what he told them before he died. In the end, the men were still puzzled about who could have the amulet in their possession and what they were going to do with it. Vallencourt relayed to the group the urgency of finding the amulet to deliver to his boss. He further asked them to add some more agents to the mission and see what they could find out by going to churches and even bars and restaurants while keeping their ears on the streets.

As the weeks and months went by, the agents toiled on the streets, bars, restaurants, churches and even in some civic organizations in the five boroughs of New York, interrogating any likely suspects about the missing amulet, but it was a tiresome, futile effort.

One day, the phone rang in Vallencourt's Manhattan office, and it was the indelibly deep menacing voice of his boss.

"My Master, what can your servant do for you?" asked Vallencourt.

The caller on the phone told Vallencourt it was nearly a year since the disappearance of the amulet, and he had better retrieve it before the end of the summer. As Vallencourt's boss hung up the phone, Vallencourt was feeling more petrified; he was sweating more profusely and feeling terrified, and his stomach was tightening and churning the content in it, allowing flatulence to make musical symphony in his expensive Italian designer pants.

Vallencourt rushed to the bathroom to relieve himself of the food in his stomach and the liquid in his system. He knew that not delivering the amulet meant an end to his existence on this earth.

***

It was more than a year that Rose took her class on the field trip up to Mount Marcy and she was feeling quite tired from work. The summer was fast approaching, and Rose was looking forward to it, to get some extra rest and to catch up on some books she wanted to read in her leisure. She had just gotten her passport and was hoping to do some travelling to Mexico or anywhere that was tropical. She had never travelled outside of the United States of America and decided that this summer was going to be the summer she would go on a vacation. She had always wanted to travel overseas for a long time, but money was always *tight* on a teacher's salary, and there were always other contingencies that had to be taken care of immediately, such as her rent and utilities.

***

Friday evening, Rose was on her way home when she stopped at a restaurant to pick up some food to take home. As she was taking out her purse from her handbag to pay the cashier, a small book fell from her handbag. Rose was quite oblivious that her diary had fallen from her handbag, and as she was collecting her food, she heard a deep voice, "Excuse me miss, I think this fell from your handbag," said a man speaking with a Spanish accent.

"Oh my goodness, thank you! That is my diary," said Rose.

As Rose extended her hand to shake the man's hand, she noticed that he was dressed in blue jeans, a white t-shirt, and sneakers. He was not very tall, just a couple more inches taller than her, with thick black hair on his head.

"You are welcome, miss. I am Roberto Sanchez. Your name is?"

"I am Rose, nice to meet you. Glad to know that there is a decent man in Brooklyn," said Rose.

"I do not know about that. I am only doing my civic duty. When a beautiful lady drops her diary, you pick it up for her," said Roberto, laughing.

"I see you are quite jovial. Anyway, it is a nice quality to have, a good mark of a gentleman. Keep it up!" said Rose.

"So tell me, I do not see a ring on your finger. Is there someone special in your life, I mean a boyfriend?" asked Roberto.

"Do you not think it is kind of personal and invasive for you to be asking me that type of question, considering the fact that we just met, and I do not know you?" asked Rose.

"I agree that we just met, and you do not know me, but you heard the expression strike while the iron is hot, and you are one hot mamacita!" said Roberto.

Rose was not sure why she laughed heartily, but maybe it was the compliment, the Spanish word he used, or how Roberto said it.

Roberto was quite taken by Rose's beauty, and he was instantly attracted to her in a feverish kind of way. He wanted her, and he was damned sure as hell not going to allow this moment to pass without asking her out. "So, can I get your phone number?" asked Roberto.

"No, you may not. I am not going to give my number to a stranger!" said Rose.

"Since you are so enamored with my little gesture of being a gentleman, why don't you let me take you to dinner tomorrow night?" asked Roberto.

"Why do you want to take me to dinner?" asked Rose.

"It is quite obvious you are a beautiful woman, and I want to get to know you better," said Roberto.

"I see," said Rose.

"So, are you going to have dinner with me tomorrow night?" asked Roberto.

Rose took a minute to ponder Roberto's date invitation and finally gave in to the request to have dinner the following evening at an agreed restaurant. She told him that she would meet him at the restaurant at seven PM sharp because she did not want to give him much detail about herself. Roberto happily agreed, and Rose went home with her take-home prepared meal.

When Rose arrived home, she turned on the television and watched CNN to catch up on the latest news while she ate her take-home meal. She was glad it was Friday because she would be able to get some extra rest for her weary body. After watching television for three more hours, she went to take a shower and then went to bed.

On Saturday, Rose woke up around ten o'clock and prepared her breakfast of bacon, toasted bread, and scrambled eggs with orange juice. After consuming her breakfast Rose started to ponder why she accepted Roberto's invitation for dinner. She was not at all attracted to Roberto because she liked men who were tall and lanky, but she liked his sense of humor. She did not mind going out on a Saturday night and staying out late because she would have Sunday to rest and recuperate her weary body.

At around five in the evening, Rose got off her sofa, took a shower and started dressing for her date. She wore a short, sexy blue dress that clung to her body from her closet with black high heels and a small purse in which she put some cash, her cell phone, and her credit cards. When Rose finished dressing, she called a cab to drop her off at the restaurant.

When Rose arrived at the restaurant at approximately five minutes to seven, she looked around to see if Roberto was in the restaurant, but she did not see him, and she was a little peeved at his tardiness. The restaurant had a waiting area with a wide brown leather sofa. Rose took a seat on the sofa and told herself she would wait another ten minutes for Roberto. Rose gazed into the restaurant and noticed that there were not many people in there, but the restaurant was nicely decorated with white tablecloths and shiny utensils with nice soft lighting all over the restaurant.

As Rose waited, she wondered if Roberto was not coming and if it was all a prank. At around fifteen minutes after seven, Rose got up and was about to exit the restaurant when she saw Roberto rushing into the restaurant. "I am sorry, my dear, I was having some mechanical issues with my car. Please forgive me for my tardiness," said Roberto.

Rose was fuming at Roberto's lateness and angry that she had to wait so long for him to arrive at the restaurant. "It's an inauspicious start to a first date. Your tardiness tells me that I am inconsequential because you could call the restaurant or call a cab. Therefore, I am leaving," said Rose.

Roberto was not late. He was sitting outside in his car and saw when Rose entered the restaurant. He wanted to see how long Rose would wait because, in his mind, the longer she waited, the more he thought Rose would be desperate for male companionship. He was absolutely blown away when he saw Rose enter the restaurant and how beautiful and desirable she looked in her dress.

"Please do not go. I will try to make it up to you somehow. Don't you see - Rose and Roberto - those names go together very well, like sugar and spice," said Roberto.

Rose was still angry, but she smiled when Roberto said their names were similar to sugar and spice. Rose then decided to stay to see how the night would unfold for their dinner date. Roberto and Rose were ushered by a waiter to a table adjacent to a glass window where both of them could see the night sky and the traffic on the roadways.

"You look absolutely sexy!" said Roberto.

"I really do not want to hear that now, not after I have been waiting for so long," said Rose.

"Pretty please, with a cherry on top. Can you forgive me?" asked Roberto. "You know what; let me call the waiter to bring a bottle of wine to cool you down."

Roberto motioned his hand to a waiter, and he came and took their orders. Roberto ordered a medium rare steak served with white rice and vegetables, while Rose ordered shrimp baked in a butter sauce, served with white rice and vegetables.

"Roberto, now that I am less angry and drinking this lovely wine, tell me about yourself," said Rose.

"There is not much to tell. I work as an accountant because I enjoy working with numbers. Numbers do not lie, unlike people. I am also a passionate sports fan who would like to be an athlete but does not possess the physical attributes, but alas, my time has passed. What is your story? Why don't you have a man? I am assuming you do not have a man. Do you have a man?" asked Roberto.

"Well, for your information, if I did have a man, I certainly would not be having dinner with you or with anyone else. I work long hours as a lecturer and frankly do not have the time to go on dates," said Rose.

Roberto really did not care about what Rose was saying or her questions. He was telling his own lies about being an accountant. Roberto was sexually excited by Rose, and he was awestruck by Rose's beauty. He wanted to take her to bed tonight after they finished consuming their meals. Each time he looked at Rose's face, especially her eyes and lips, he was filled with ravenous desire for her, and he wanted to possess her completely and gratify his sexual appetite. "So, I am going to order some chocolate cake for dessert. Then we leave here and go to my place for a drink and spend a little time together," said Roberto.

"Why would I want to go to your place? I do not know you, plus I do not trust you. All you have been doing all night is leering at me, so hell no, I am not going to your place, not now or never," said Rose.

"Bitch, how you going to play me like that?" asked Roberto.

"Who are you calling a bitch? You are the bitch. Because you invited me to dinner, I must go to your house with you. You piece of filth, I am an independent woman, and I will pay for my own dinner," said Rose.

Rose's cell phone started ringing in her purse, and she took it out and answered. It was Anton, and she told him that she would call him back in the next five minutes.

"Oh bitch, you will be paying for both dinners," said Roberto.

As Roberto was walking away from the table, Rose took up her cell phone and turned on the camera. "Roberto, Roberto," Rose called his name. As Roberto turned around, Rose used her cell phone and took a picture of him walking out of the restaurant.

Roberto was furious about how the entire date with Rose unfolded, as he was hoping that the date would culminate with her in his bed making passionate love. He thought he would just wait and follow her home and rape her to teach her a lesson. As he was sitting in his car watching the entrance when Rose would make her exit, it quickly dawned on him that she had taken his picture, and he did not know if she had sent it to the police or to her friends.

Growing increasingly furious, he realized he wouldn't be able to carry out his malicious plan. Swearing that if he ever saw her again, he would restrain his twisted desires, Roberto drove away from the restaurant, his tires screeching and smoke billowing.

Inside the restaurant, Rose was apoplectic. She was presented with a bill for over three hundred dollars, which she promptly paid on her credit card. She was angry at herself for even taking the date in the first place and cursed herself for not following her instinct to leave when he arrived that late for a first date. She swore off dating any man for now because every time she made the plunge into the dating world, it always ended in disaster.

Although Rose was angry, she was also grateful in the sense that she did not make the mistake of allowing Roberto in her life. She was glad that she did not give him any detail of her life, like where she lived and worked or her phone number. It was, in a sense, quite cathartic for Rose because, as a woman, she was aware of her value as a human being not to take substandard treatment from any man, and certainly not a man who wanted to take her to his place on a first date.

As the waiter returned with her credit card, Rose picked up her cell phone and returned Anton's call. Anton was calling about some school assignment from his car, which was due on Monday and wanted an extension until Wednesday. Rose gave him the okay and asked him to pick her up at the restaurant.

Within ten minutes, Anton arrived at the restaurant with his girlfriend in the front seat of his car. Rose entered the backseat, and Anton quickly drove Rose home and bid her goodbye. When Rose reached into her apartment, she undressed and went straight into the shower. As the water was coming down on her body it was as if it was washing the awful date experience away.

Chapter 6

On Sunday morning, as Reverend Watkiss was on the pulpit in his church preaching to his congregation, a blonde woman with a broad white hat and elegant red dress with matching high heels walked into the church. As the blonde lady walked in, everyone in the church turned around to stare at her alluring figure, including Reverend Watkiss, who stopped preaching momentarily to catch his breath. The blonde lady was not only mystifying and beautiful but quite mesmerizing, alluring, and she was walking like she was on a fashion catwalk. She sat down in one of the aisle seats with most of the men's eyes transfixed on her.

As the blonde lady sat in her seat, she glanced around the church and noticed that it was quite a beautiful church artistically decorated with religious symbols of the cross. She also noticed that the church had a mixed congregation of African American, Caucasian, and Hispanics.

When the sermon ended, Reverend Watkiss came down off the pulpit to greet his parishioners and wished them well for the coming week. As he was moving from aisle to aisle, the blonde lady sat in her seat until Reverend Watkiss came to her seat. "Welcome to our humble little church. We are extremely glad you could join us to worship on this auspicious day. Your name is?" asked Reverend Watkiss.

As Reverend Watkiss was extending his hand to shake the blonde lady's hand, she grabbed his hand and shook it and said, "I am Sheryl Wildflower and I need to speak with you privately now."

"You will have to give me a few minutes to wish my congregation goodbye," said Reverend Watkiss.

"Ok, I will wait for a few more minutes," said Wildflower.

As Reverend Watkiss was moving down from aisle to aisle greeting his congregation, he was just mumbling mundane platitudinous stuff because he was petrified of this female visitor. He was aware of who Wildflower was and the power she wielded over human lives. He was wondering in his mind what she could possibly want from him, and even though he was petrified, he was intrigued by her presence in his small church. Fifteen minutes after the church was empty, Reverend Watkiss turned and said to Wildflower, "Please follow me to my office."

Reverend Watkiss' office was extremely small, with a mahogany color desk, and a desktop computer and three chairs. Reverend Watkiss extended his hand and said, "Please have a seat and tell me why you are here."

"I prefer to stand. I am here seeking your assistance. Have you heard of the Amulet of Osiris?" asked Wildflower.

"No, and what does that have to do with me?" asked Reverend Watkiss.

"It disappeared many months ago in Brooklyn, and I want your help in acquiring it. You will be well compensated if you help me to acquire it. I promise you anything your heart desires," said Wildflower.

"I do not see how I can help you because I do not know of any Amulet of Osiris, nor do I have it to give you," said Reverend Watkiss.

"Look, I do not wish to engage in semantics with you. I know you have certain abilities to see in the past and into the future, just like you are aware of who I am. I am asking you to use your abilities to see what you can find or what you can see in the past," said Wildflower.

"My gift does not work like that. I do have to have a personal experience or interaction with that thing or person to see the past or the future in an episodic way and even sometimes I cannot see anything," said Reverend Watkiss.

"I cannot give you anything to go off because I do not have anything. All I am asking you to do is see what you can find, and I will be back next week Sunday for any information you can provide," said Wildflower.

After concluding her business, Wildflower left Reverend Watkiss' office. As she was outside the church door, Reverend Watkiss glanced outside his office window to see Wildflower enter a brand new dark blue Mercedes Benz as she drove away from the church premises. Reverend Watkiss was extremely worried; he was aware that he was dealing with powers that he preached against and warned his members to shun them at any cost if they wanted any connection with God.

Reverend Watkiss tried his utmost best to keep his clairvoyant ability a secret. There are just a handful of people alive who knew of his psychic ability. He knew that when he went into his psychic trance to see into the past or the future, he was treading in a world of the supernatural, that was of the spiritual and demonic realm, and they could see him and report to their master in the realm of the living. He lied to Wildflower about not hearing about the Amulet of Osiris. He knew that Osiris was the God of the Dead in ancient Egypt, and he ruled the spirit of the dead by the power of the amulet. Reverend Watkiss pondered what the lady who entered his office wanted with the Amulet of Osiris.

***

As the supermassive black hole Sagittarius A* belched out some of its light content into space, Malakai was hurled into space as a big white blob of light. He was thrown into deep space from the black hole. He quickly jumped on an asteroid that was orbiting the sun. He felt energized and wished he was on earth. As Malakai continued to speed through space on the asteroid, he gazed at the sun and contemplated its effect on life on Earth. Malakai accepted the realization that all life will come to an end in the next couple of billion years because the sun is at a mature stage in its life cycle, and at some stage, its life cycle will end. Sadly enough, our second closest stars, Proxima Centauri and Alpha Centauri, are not closed by that they could merge to prolong the sun's life as happened with some stars in certain galaxies.

While Malakai appreciates the sun because it sustains life on Earth, it can also be deadly when a planet does not have a magnetic field that surrounds the planet, which is called a magnetosphere that deflects solar radiation and could destroy the planet's atmosphere. Earth is a habitable planet because of its magnetosphere.

Malakai hurled himself off the asteroid that he was on to a larger one. He kept leaping from asteroid to asteroid because he wanted to arrive on Earth as quickly as possible. Malakai was waiting to see a small comet that was heading into the direction of Earth's atmosphere before he could leap off the last asteroid. Within five minutes, he saw a small comet, which he hurled himself on, still transformed into a fiery blob of light resembling a cartoonish ghost. The comet rock entered into Earth's atmosphere, and it started breaking apart. Malakai did not want to land anywhere on Earth, so he skillfully manipulated the small comet to land on the top of Mount Marcy. By this time, the comet was completely breaking apart, turning to dust as it became part of the landscape.

As he landed on the top of Mount Marcy, he was transformed into his human form but was now fully naked. His body was much darker because he was at the zenith of his power and would not be returning to deep space for now to reconstruct his body. Malakai quickly climbed from the extreme top of Mount Marcy to the secret boulder entrance. He pushed the boulder and entered the cavern where his clothing remained hidden, and quickly put on his clothes and exited the cavern.

As he started to descend the mountain, there was a cool breeze blowing as if welcoming him home. As it was summer, he started seeing people coming up the mountain. He was glad to be home, appreciative of the trees and grasses, the view that the mountain offers, and inhaling the fresh mountain air through his nostrils.

Around three hours after taking the Southern Trails, Malakai arrived at the bottom of the mountain. He took one of the taxis that were carrying visitors to climb the mountain. The taxi dropped him off in the town of Keen, and from there, he bought a ticket to get on the train to New York City.

***

The next Sunday morning, Reverend Watkiss was quite apprehensive as he stared at his congregation. He had prepared for his Sunday morning sermon, but his mind was elsewhere, and he was hoping that, by some miracle, the dark force of this world would not enter his church. As Reverend Watkiss started preaching, Wildflower walked into the church and took her seat. She was attired in a light blue dress that accentuated all her curves on her body. Reverend Watkiss continued to preach, not wanting to highlight his nervousness, and when he was finished preaching, he came off the pulpit to greet his congregation. As he reached the bench where Wildflower was sitting, he extended his hand to shake her hand, which she shook. "Do you have any answer for me?" asked Wildflower.

"I tried, but I am not getting anywhere. Without personal contact, it is extremely difficult to go back in time," said Reverend Watkiss.

"Then try harder because I am depending on you, and I do not take refusal kindly from any man," said Wildflower.

89

Visible upset from Reverend Watkiss's lack of help, Wildflower stormed out of the church and as she was going down the church steps, her shoe heels slid, and she started to fall and was caught by a woman. Wildflower composed herself and said, "Thank you for preventing me from falling. I am grateful for your help. By the way I am Cheryl Wildflower. Your name is?" asked Wildflower.

"I am Rose, and I am glad that I could be of help to you."

"You are quite beautiful," said Wildflower.

"So are you," said Rose.

"Do you have a car?" asked Wildflower.

"No, I was just going to call a cab," said Rose.

"I will give you a ride in my car," said Wildflower.

As the two women went into the car and drove away from the church premises Reverend Watkiss came on the church steps. His whole body became a nervous wreck when he saw Rose enter the car with Wildflower. He went back into the church to his office and sat in his office chair, deep in his thoughts.

Wildflower and Rose were chatting, laughing and enjoying each other company when Rose told her to stop the car to pick up something to eat at a restaurant. Wildflower then suggested to Rose that it would be a better idea if they both went into the restaurant and had a meal. Wildflower parked her car, and both women went into the restaurant.

Both women were ushered to a table by a female receptionist at the restaurant. As it was a Sunday, the restaurant was packed with patrons consuming their meals. Wildflower ordered a bottle of wine, and while they both were drinking, a waiter came and took their orders. Wildflower ordered cheesy pork chops with spicy apples served with garlic mashed potatoes, while Rose ordered barbecue chicken served with spicy smoked sweet potato salad.

The woman consumed their meals while they chatted and laughed, and Rose was enjoying her meal and felt more at ease in the company of Wildflower because she thought at least she was not trying to take her home to sleep with her like most men would want to do and take out their twisted sexual desire. When they were both finished consuming their meals, they both ordered fruit cake for dessert, and Wildflower paid the bill.

After two more hours, the women left the restaurant for Rose's home. Fifteen minutes later, they arrived at the apartment, and Wildflower asked Rose if she could come up for a few minutes. Rose thought it was a little odd but told her she could come up to her apartment.

Rose opened her apartment door and they both entered the apartment. "You have a lovely, cozy apartment, and I like the decor," said Wildflower.

"Thank you, and have a seat on the sofa," said Rose.

"So you live alone and do not have a man?" asked Wildflower.

"I told you that already. Can I get you a glass of wine?" asked Rose.

"Oh yes, by all means, bring the bottle and come sit with me on the sofa," said Wildflower.

Unbeknownst to Rose, wildflower is bisexual and is deeply attracted to her appearance, body, and her personality. She was called Wildflower because she loved both men and women. She did not stay in one camp, but she loved to dabble in both camps. She was blown away by Rose's beauty. She wanted Rose the moment she met her when she stopped her from falling on the church step. She hoped that the wine Rose was bringing her had enough alcohol to intoxicate her and dull her senses. As Rose sat down and they started drinking the wine, Wildflower moved closer to Rose and looked deeply into her eyes. She grabbed Rose's head and started to kiss her sensuously full lips. For a brief moment, Rose reciprocated Wildflower's kiss before she pushed her off. "Wait a damn minute, I am not a lesbian. I like men," said Rose.

"You were reciprocating to my kiss. Are you sure you are not a lesbian?" asked Wildflower.

"Yes, I am sure I am not a lesbian," said Rose indignantly.

"How are you sure when you have never tried it? I do love men also, and I do enjoy a big stiff dick once in a while, but women are my passion. I do love the softness of a woman's body," said Wildflower.

Wildflower was indignant; a woman of her stature and beauty was never denied anything in her life. She generally takes what she desires until she is sated. She was so full of passion for Rose and wanted to devour Rose's taut, young, supple body. She was thinking about what action to take against Rose for her rejection of her advances when suddenly Rose's cell phone rang. She took the phone out of her handbag and went into the kitchen to answer the phone. "Hello," said Rose.

"Hello, Rose, it is Reverend Watkiss. Are you with her, Wildflower?"

"Yes, what is this about?" asked Rose.

"Can you go into a room that I can speak to you privately?" asked Reverend Watkiss.

"You can go ahead and speak. I am in the kitchen, and she is in the living room," said Rose.

Rose did not know what Reverend Watkiss was going to say, but his voice sounded so fearful, as if she was in danger. "Please listen to me carefully. I will explain another time. Please do not reveal anything to her, ask her to leave, and do not come back. It is a matter of your own safety. Please trust me on this, and do not tell her who you were speaking to on the phone," said Reverend Watkiss.

Rose hung up the phone and went back into the living room, quite confused about Reverend Watkiss's warning about Wildflower.

"Do you mind me asking who you were talking to on the phone?" asked Wildflower.

"I do mind. It was one of my church sisters who saw me enter your car, and I told her you were over my house and you are leaving now because I am getting tired and need to get some sleep" said Rose.

"I guess it is goodbye then. Am I going to see you again?" asked Wildflower.

"I guess not because you are into girls, and I am not. Therefore, it is best we say our goodbye now," said Rose.

As Wildflower walked out of Rose's apartment and closed the door, Rose breathed a sigh of relief because she thought it could have gone so much more awkward, spurning Wildflower's sexual advances. She was thankful to God for these small mercies.

Rose went and sat on her sofa, pouring over the day's event in her mind. She thought every time she went out with both a man and a woman, they only desired her body. She thought jokingly that it must display or written on her forehead to come and "fuck me because I am desperate." She thought that she would take a total break from dating anyone for now because it always seemed to end in disaster. She was also puzzled by Reverend Watkiss's behavior because his voice sounded so fearful of Wildflower and for what purpose or reason.

Chapter 7

Malakai arrived at his Manhattan apartment at around seven o'clock in the evening. He was extremely glad to be home, but he hated when Georgina was not home. He went straight into the bathroom to shower then afterward went straight to the bedroom to get some sleep.

Malakai got up the following morning and went straight into the shower. After Malakai came out of the bathroom, he packed a travelling bag with some clothes and took some cash out of a safe he had in his apartment. He left the apartment and went straight to a parking garage where he generally parked his car. He went to the parking garage office, gave them his ticket and paid the fees.

The car was brought around the front by a worker whom he tipped with a hundred dollars. Malakai opened the car, which was a black Lincoln Navigator and put his bag on the back seat. He drove to a gas station, where he filled the gas. Malakai began driving and leaving out of Manhattan he started thinking about Rose and the gamble he took by giving her the amulet. He hoped that she kept the amulet safe and did not tell anyone about it. He knew there would be repercussions within the Alliance Organization if the amulet was not delivered, and they would kill anyone who had it.

As the car picked up speed on the open road, Malakai wanted to arrive at Rose's school before she departed for the day. He wanted to surprise her and see how she would react to his presence at the school. As he entered Brooklyn, he saw a man selling some roses on the side of the road. Malakai stopped and purchased a bundle of roses. Malakai knew Brooklyn quite well, and he arrived at the school in the afternoon and parked at the entrance, where he could see who entered and exited the premises.

As he waited, Malakai finally saw her coming out of the school entrance door with her handbag over her right shoulder and another bag in her left hand. She was dressed in a black pantsuit and looked quite elegant in the afternoon sun. Malakai watched Rose walking until Rose was almost near the sport utility car, and he said, "A Rose by any other name would smell as sweet. Hello, Miss Rose Winter."

The expression on Rose's face was one of total surprise and disbelief, and as she got over the unexpected visit by Malakai, she said, "Damn, you sure surprise me, Mr. Malaki, and quoting from Shakespeare, Romeo and Juliet."

"I see that you still remember my name," said Malakai.

"You have not forgotten mine also," said Rose.

"Do you drive?" asked Malakai.

"No, I am taking the bus," said Rose.

"Come with me. I will give you a lift home," said Malakai.

"I do not know you enough to take a drive with you. I do not know if you want to take me away," said Rose.

"Not yet. Do you still have my stuff, Rose?" asked Malakai.

"Yes, I do," said Rose.

"Please come into the car and let me take you home and get my stuff. I promise you I am a real pussy cat. I mean, you no harm. By the way, here are some roses I bought for you," said Malakai.

"Thanks for the roses. I guess I will come with you in your car so you can take me home," said Rose.

"Great, let's go then," said Malakai.

As the car drove away from the school, Rose was glad to see him, and she thought how uncanny, on the last day of the school summer holiday break, this man appeared when she thought she would not see him again in her life. She pointed him in the direction where she lived, and around fifteen minutes later, they arrived at Rose's apartment. "Stay here, and let me go and grab your stuff," said Rose.

"I do not mind coming into your apartment, plus I told you I am a pussy cat. You do not want me to see your boyfriend?" asked Malakai.

"Okay, come with me and help me with this bag. I told you already that there is no boyfriend and I live alone," said Rose.

"Okay, I got you, mademoiselle," said Malakai.

Rose thought he sounded funny when he used the term mademoiselle because she was unmarried, but she was not speaking French. Rose opened her apartment door, and they both entered. "Welcome to my humble abode," said Rose.

"So this is your humble abode. I like it, quite clean and fresh and welcoming" said Malakai.

"Have a seat," said Rose.

Rose then went over to the cabinet and took out the box. Rose wanted to see his behavior when he realized that there was nothing in the box. "Here is the box that you gave me," said Rose.

Malakai took the black box and hurriedly opened it, only to discover that it was empty. He started to panic and started to sweat. "Rose, where is the content in the box?" asked Malakai.

Rose started to laugh as she realized Malakai was overly concerned about the content of the box. "I see that whatever is in that box is unbelievably valuable to you, Mr. Malakai. Anyway, I have had my fill of laughter. The content of the box is on the table in that apple basket," said Rose.

Malakai went to the table and looked inside the red apple basket and did not see anything. "It is not there," said Malakai.

"Look very closely," said Rose.

Malakai looked more intently and still did not see anything. "Rose, please come and look. There is nothing here on the table," said Malakai.

Malakai was getting a little bit exasperated because losing the content of the box would be devastating to his plan.

Rose was in the kitchen drinking some water and came to the table, "Oh my God, it is gone," said Rose.

Malakai was in full panic mode when he noticed Rose starting to laugh heartily and clapping her hands. Rose started rummaging through the basket, then picked up the artificial apple, unzipped it, took out the amulet and inserted it in the black graphite box that was in Malakai's outstretched hand.

"You nearly gave me a heart attack. I see you were laughing at me, panicking. I will get you back for this little joke of yours," said Malakai.

"I could not help myself. I wanted you to see how you were going to react in a stressful situation," said Rose.

"Anyway, from the bottom of my heart, thank you for keeping it safe for me. I certainly owe you," said Malakai.

"You are welcome, Sir. Plus, I did not tell anyone about it," said Rose.

"Thank you again. I am in your debt. By the way, what are you going to do now?" asked Malakai.

"I am going to look about my dinner," said Rose.

"Great then, let me take you out to show my appreciation. Plus, I am starving; I am hungry as a horse. I promise to keep you safe," said Malakai.

"I do not know. How do I know I can trust you?" asked Rose.

"Several months ago, I did not know if I could trust you, but I was in a jam, and you came through for me. Therefore, I am indebted to you. I am asking you the same now. Trust me a little, and come have dinner with me," said Malakai.

"Since you put it that way, I will certainly come with you and have dinner. Watch the television while I get ready," said Rose.

Rose went into the bathroom and took a quick shower, then went into her room and hurriedly put on her clothes. As she was dressing, she thought how odd things could be because a man was in her house, not trying to seduce her but wanting to take her out to dinner. She grabbed her purse off the bed, opened the bedroom door, stepped outside in the living room and said, "I am ready to go now to have dinner."

Malakai spun around from the sofa and got up, staring at Rose for a few seconds. Rose was wearing a deep blue mermaid scoop neck floor-length satin evening dress. Malakai was stunned at how beautiful Rose looked, and he was mightily attracted to her and he said, "You look absolutely stunning and smell extremely nice. Let us go then before you change your mind."

"Thank you for the compliment," said Rose.

Rose closed her apartment door, and they both walked toward Malakai's car. Malakai opened the passenger door for Rose, and she entered the car and told him thanks. As Malakai walked around the driver's side to open the door, Rose stretched across and opened the door and Malakai told her thanks for opening the door. Malakai smiled and thought these little simple gestures tell who a person is and how caring and concerned they are to other people.

"Where are we going for dinner?" asked Rose.

"We are going to have dinner at the River Café on Water Street, near the Brooklyn Bridge. Have you been there before?" asked Malakai.

"No, but I heard it is quite fancy with a strict dress code," said Rose.

"I do not know what is fancy, but I have my jacket and tie in the back of the car. I am going to ask you to assist with the tie when we arrive at the venue," said Malakai.

"Okay, I will assist you with your tie," said Rose.

Rose was feeling great and even liked being out with Malakai. She could sense that he liked her, especially how he kept making furtive glances at her when she was looking in the other direction. She did not mind him stealing a glimpse at her because she was doing the same, and she wondered what was going through his mind and what his expectation for the night was when he took her home.

Malakai and Rose arrived at the River Café and entered the parking area. Malakai got out of the car, opened the back door, took out his jacket and asked Rose for her assistance with the tie. As Rose was assisting with the tie and facing Malakai, she looked at him intently, staring directly into his eyes for a couple of seconds. Malakai wanted to kiss her, but he thought it was a bad idea. Rose finished with tying the tie, and Malakai put on his jacket and they went to the restaurant where they were promptly seated by a waiter.

Malakai and Rose were seated at a table for two that offered a magnificent view of the waterfront and spectacular views of Manhattan. The setting and the atmosphere were quite pleasing to Rose, and she looked at Malakai and asked, "Are we on a date?"

"Thought you knew that already because I had to use surreptitious means to get you out of your apartment," said Malakai.

"Jokes on you because I am glad that you took me," said Rose.

"I told you already, but I am telling you again: you look absolutely beautiful," said Malakai.

"Oh, thank you. Are you trying to flirt with me, Mr. Malakai?" asked Rose.

"Do I have to flirt with you to tell you that you look beautiful?" asked Malakai.

A waiter came, and Malakai ordered a bottle of vintage wine.

"What shall we toast to for tonight?" asked Rose.

"To our nascent friendship and life, hoping that they may prosper and not be transient, so eat, drink and be merry because no man knows what tomorrow brings," said Malakai.

"I will definitely drink to that," said Rose.

Both Rose and Malakai had, for their main course, poached Nova Scotia lobster with cavatelli pasta. As they were eating there was a live piano playing in the background to liven up the ambiance of the place. They chatted and laughed with each other, and both enjoyed each other company while they ate the sumptuous food. When they were finished with the main course, they had chocolate cake for dessert. Malakai paid the bill, and they left around ten o'clock.

Rose enjoyed the night out with Malakai and liked talking with him as they chatted about various subjects. Rose thought Malakai was a good conversationalist in that he listened to her attentively, unlike most men. Her mind started to race, wondering if he was going to kiss her when he dropped her off at her apartment. When they arrived at Rose's apartment, Malakai parked the car and walked Rose to her apartment door. He reached out and held her hand, and for some reason, Rose did not mind the gesture. Afterward, she took her key out of her purse and pretended to fumble it. Malakai took it and opened the door for her, and she entered the apartment. "You can come into the apartment for a few minutes," said Rose.

"Best not for me to come in and ruin our growing friendship. I had a great time at dinner, and I enjoyed your company immensely. I would love to see you tomorrow for a date. Let us go to a soccer match tomorrow and watch the New York City Football Club play the Los Angeles Galaxy at Yankee Stadium," said Malakai.

Rose agreed to the date the following day, and they said goodbye as she watched Malakai walk away from her apartment. Malakai drove back to the motel, and Rose went into her bathroom, had a shower and went to her bed, thinking of the man she first met on Mount Marcy.

The next day, Rose was getting ready for her date to a soccer match with Malakai. Rose was dressed in ripped blue jeans and a white modern off the shoulder blouse and sneakers. Rose's face was covered in a dark glass that gave her an enigmatic look on her face. Malakai pressed her apartment door buzzer and told her he would be outside waiting on her near his car.

Rose came out of her apartment to see Malakai waiting patiently for her beside his car. Malakai was dressed in blue jeans, a red untucked shirt and sneakers. Malakai opened the car, and Rose went in with her brown handbag. They drove to Yankee Stadium, where there was a huge crowd of people of all ethnicities entering the famous arena. As they were seated Rose started looking around at the crowd and said, "Soccer is certainly growing in America because when I was a child, we only played it in high schools and at the collegiate level."

Malakai pondered Rose's remark and said, "The sport has certainly grown because of the immigration of people from South and Central America, the Caribbean and Europe. Therefore, immigration can be a good thing because it creates an economic base for a country where none had existed before."

The soccer match started on the field, and there was fierce competition between the two teams to score and win the game. Malakai was shouting and cheering every move of the New York City Football team when Rose asked him, "Why do you like soccer so much?"

"I like it because of the competitive nature of the game, and as they say, it is the thrill of victory and the agony of defeat. Sport, in general, is a lot like life. Sometimes, you are down, and you have to use every ounce of energy to put yourself on top again. To overcome and win makes life worthwhile living. I recognize sport is an escape from the mundane and grinding of everyday life. Sport not only provides an escape but brings excitement to everyday life," said Malakai.

At the half-time interval, the match score was nil for each team. Malakai took the time to order snacks. The match resumed after the ten-minute break, and the Los Angeles Galaxy scored first, to the disappointment of the crowd. New York City then evened the score after twenty minutes, and then, in the dying seconds before the match ended, the Los Angeles Galaxy scored a fabulous goal. It was a huge disappointment for the crowd, including Malakai, who felt deflated. The game, though, was quite exciting, and most people went away feeling happy about the soccer spectacle.

Rose and Malakai left Yankee Stadium and went to a nice Chinese restaurant to have dinner. The ambiance of the restaurant was quite warm as they sat and chatted and ate their food. They left the restaurant, and Malakai took Rose home. Malakai walked Rose to her apartment and said, "I would love to take you out on another date next Saturday to the zoo and get something to eat on the road."

"That would be great; I have nothing planned for next Saturday. You can pick me up around ten o'clock," said Rose.

"Goodnight, and see you next Saturday," said Malakai.

"Goodnight to you too, Mr. Malakai," said Rose.

Rose closed her apartment door and went into her bedroom to undress and take a quick shower. She came out of the shower and then went to bed. She could not sleep; her mind was solely concentrated on Malakai. She was so intrigued by him and wanted to know more about him and his intentions, and she thought how strange a man not to try to get into her pants during the first few dates. She knew he was interested in her, in the way he looked intently and longing at her, and especially the way he complimented her on her beauty.

After Malakai left Rose's apartment, he went to a small motel where he was staying. It was not one of those expensive motels; it just had the basic amenities of a small bed and a television set in the room. He did not mind because he did not want to draw any unnecessary attention. He took a shower and then went to bed.

As the week progressed, Malakai and Rose called each other, talked incessantly and actually longed to see each other on their next date. On Saturday, Malakai woke up excited and looking forward to seeing Rose. He went into the bathroom and got a quick shower. He then put on his jeans, t-shirt and sneakers as he was going to take Rose on a date to the zoo. He left the motel and drove to Rose's apartment. He buzzed the intercom system, and Rose let him in the apartment. "Good morning, beautiful. Are you ready to go?" asked Malakai.

"Good morning to you, too, and yes, I am ready to go," said Rose.

They both left the apartment, with Malakai clandestinely staring at Rose in her tight blue jeans as she walked ahead of him to the car. Malakai followed the same procedure of opening the passenger door, and Rose did likewise as Malakai entered the car.

Malakai told Rose that they were going to the Prospect Park Zoo off Flatbush Avenue. As they drove and maneuvered through the traffic, Rose told him about her job, the joy of teaching, especially when her students got the idea of what she was trying to communicate to them to make the world a better place, and also her frustration with her low-paying salary. Malakai, in turn, told her life is about give and take, in other words, about tradeoffs that the enjoyment that she received from teaching is going to be offset by the frustration with her salary.

After about an hour and a half of driving, they arrived at the Prospect Park Zoo off Flatbush Avenue. The Prospect Park Zoo is quite small, consisting of about twelve acres. The zoo has over six hundred animals of different species. There are animals such as monkeys, goats, birds of all varieties, sheep, cows' geese, ducks, and a wide variety of other animals. The Prospect Park Zoo is dedicated to wildlife conservation and is involved in the restoration of endangered species.

As Rose and Malakai walked the Discovery Trail viewing the various animals, Rose stopped and held Malakai's hands and started examining them quite intently, as if it was the first time she was holding a man's hand.

"Woman, why are you examining my hands?" asked Malakai.

Rose laughed. Maybe it was the way he called her woman, or maybe it was the way it sounded coming from his mouth. "I want to know why you took me to the zoo?" asked Rose.

"I want to spend more time with you firstly, and secondly, I love animals because you do not find them anywhere else in the whole universe. My blood boils, knowing that some of these beautiful, harmless creatures are going extinct due to mankind's selfish actions," said Malakai

"What other stuff gets you angry, and what do you love?" asked Rose.

"Great questions, but I would have to say exploitation of people makes me angry. What do I love? I would say beauty, the beauty of nature, the beauty of a woman, and the wholesome beauty of a person's character. Let me ask you the same question," said Malakai.

"What do I hate? I would have to say pretentious people, and what do I love? The feeling of being in love and falling in love is a great feeling," said Rose. Rose laughed and asked, "That is the only thing I could come up with. Does it sound rather trite?"

"No, it does not. It just tells me you are a very emotional woman," said Malakai.

"Okay, you tell me, what type of woman do you like?" asked Rose.

"I like a beautiful woman but one with wit which epitomizes intelligence, fun and lots of humor," said Malakai.

Rose was thinking that she was feeling more comfortable and relaxed around this man. She liked his intelligence and enjoyed his conversational style of speaking. Malakai put his right hand around her waist as they walked the trail, and for some reason, she was not that concerned about his flirtatious act. She somehow felt safe with him with his arm around her, plus the fragrance of his cologne smelled so good, as it enveloped her nostrils.

As Malakai and Rose continued on the trail, viewing more animals, they stopped and sat on an outdoor bench that was under a tree. Malakai got up off the bench and started to stretch forth his hand outward, and suddenly, a few birds that were not in any enclosure flew to him and rested on his outstretched hands, chirping and singing in an excited fashion. Rose and a few of the visitors that were closed by were amazed to see the sight of birds behaving that way towards a human being. Rose was mesmerized and smitten and more curious about Malakai.

Malakai and Rose spent another hour and a half walking and touring the outside trails and the different animal exhibits that were showcased by the zoo. They left The Prospect Park Zoo around one in the afternoon when Rose was feeling hungry. Malakai then drove on Flatbush Avenue to the Kings Plaza Shopping Center, where they had Chinese food in the mall. After they finished eating, Malakai told Rose he was taking her shopping in the mall. Rose told Malakai that she only needed handbags. They went into Michael Kors' store, where she selected three bags, and he paid for them in cash. They left the mall, and Malakai drove Rose home.

When they arrived at Rose's apartment Malakai assisted Rose with the Michael Kors bags to her apartment. Malakai then gave Rose the black box with the amulet to reinsert it into the apple basket on the table because he thought it would be much safer in Rose's apartment. Malakai then decided he would depart Rose's apartment and said, "Rose, I am leaving now."

"Thought you were going to spend a little time with me at the apartment before you leave," said Rose.

"I was figuring, maybe you need some privacy," said Malakai.

"Listen to me, and listen well. I love having you around here, if for no other reason, I feel safe with you," said Rose.

"Good to know that I am welcome in your apartment. I can honestly say you are always safe around me, and whatever little power

I have, I will always protect you. That is a promise, my beautiful woman," said Malakai.

"That I wanted to hear more than anything," said Rose.

Malakai was standing near the wall in the living room, and he reached out his hand and gently pulled Rose's hand toward his body. Malakai looked directly into Rose's eyes for a few seconds, and it seemed as if it was an eternity and their souls seemed to melt in each other eyes, and then he kissed her tasting her beautiful lips.

It was a long, deep kiss filled with longing and a ravenous burning desire for her as they seemed to be lost in each other tight embraced in each other arms. He kissed her neck, then traced his tongue upward to her chin, and then he kissed her nostril. Malakai then moved his tongue to Rose's lips and he kissed them. As she opened her mouth, he explored with his tongue slowly, kissing her softly as if there was no tomorrow. Suddenly, Rose's body started to convulse and started to fall backward, and Malakai reached out and grabbed her preventing her from falling to the floor. Rose was a little dazed and confused as Malakai led her to the sofa. Malakai was concerned that something was wrong with Rose, and he was to blame for the convulsion of her body. "What is wrong with you?" asked Malakai.

Rose was fully composed and started laughing. She looked at Malakai, smiling and cuddled up to Malakai on the sofa. She took Malakai's hand and told him to hold her in his arms. As Rose's head lay buried in Malakai's chest, she felt at peace.

"Rose, are you going to tell me what happened to you just now?" asked Malakai.

"I can't tell you because it is embarrassing, and you are going to laugh at me," said Rose.

"Please tell me. I promise I won't laugh," said Malakai.

"Okay, I was having an orgasm, and it was so intense when you were kissing me," said Rose.

Malakai started laughing and kissing Rose's head. "I am sorry. I told you I was not going to laugh, but I could not help it. Seriously, you have nothing to be embarrassed about; it is natural reaction to your body receiving pleasure."

"I am glad you are here with me in my apartment," said Rose.

"There is no place I would rather be than be with you in your cozy apartment," said Malakai.

Rose was extremely happy that Malakai was there, embracing and having her in his arms. Having him there was even better than the many nights she had dreamt of him since she met him on Mount Marcy in upstate New York. She felt good in this man's arms, as it was supposed to be, and she felt elated about this new man in her life. She did not know much about this man she was cuddling up with, but all she knew was that she liked and wanted him, and she hoped that he wanted her the same way.

As they lay on the sofa, she suddenly could tell that he wanted her because she could feel his rather large throbbing erection on her ass as they cuddled on the sofa.

Rose and Malakai stayed cuddled on the sofa until it was time for Malakai to leave the apartment. Rose did not want him to leave but she accepted at some point he had to go home. Malakai, quite smitten with Rose, hardly wanting to leave, said, "Guess it is my time to leave. I will see you tomorrow."

"Take me to a ballet recital tomorrow night," said Rose.

"Ok, I will," said Malakai.

Rose told Malakai what time to pick her up for the ballet recital. They kissed goodnight, and Malakai departed from her apartment. As he was driving to the motel all he was thinking was about Rose. He accepted the fact that he was getting attached to her emotionally, and he wanted to be part of her life. He thought if she knew who he really was, would she still want to be part of his life?

Malakai parked his car in the parking area of the motel and walked to his room. As he was in the process of taking out his key from his pocket, he looked downward and noticed the entrance door floor mat was wet with a shoeprint. He took out the Onoro sword from his pants pocket and pressed the button, and the shiny, elongated steel blade came out like clockwork.

He quietly opened the door, closed it back quietly and gazed inside the room. Malakai froze for a second when he saw a Spanish looking man with his back turned away from the entrance door searching his bag. Malakai's clothing was scattered on the motel floor and some on the bed. Malakai realized that the man was of his kind. He looked inside the bathroom to see if there was anyone with him to set a trap, but he did not see anyone else in the room. With the blade outstretched, Malakai approached the man quietly and pointed the blade at the man's neck. The coldness of the blade froze the man, and the inescapable terror plastered on his face as he turned around to face Malakai. "Sit up on the bed. Who are you, and what are you doing here?" asked Malakai.

"I am Pablo Alcantrez," said the man rather nervously.

"Let me repeat the question again. What are you doing here and searching my clothing for?" asked Malakai.

Malakai pressed the sword deeper into the man's neck to indicate that he was serious and would harm him if he was not honest with his responses.

"I saw your Lincoln Navigator here on Friday, and I want to check you out. I paid the man who rented you the room twenty dollars to tell me which room you were occupying. I just thought that a man driving a Lincoln Navigator should be able to afford a higher-class motel than this seedy one. It, therefore, seems to me like he is hiding and does not want to be found or be seen," said Pablo.

"Why were you searching my bag?" asked Malakai.

"I am searching for an amulet for the Alliance Organization," said Pablo.

"Who do you report to in the Alliance Organization?" asked Malakai.

"I report to Roberto Sanchez. He is the one that hires a bunch of street soldiers to acquire the amulet," said Pablo.

"Did you come alone?" asked Malakai.

"I came alone. I took the bus and came over here to see who you were and if you were hiding something." Pablo looked quite disconsolate and asked, "Are you going to terminate my life?"

"Did you call Roberto Sanchez and tell him you were coming over to the motel?" asked Malakai.

"No, I was not sure what or whom I would find. Can I go now?" asked Pablo.

"I do not see why not," said Malakai.

Pablo was very relieved when Malakai told him he could leave the apartment. He started to mutter in Spanish, "Gracias, gracias." As he was about to open the door, Malakai swung the sword, and Pablo's head came right off, and blood started spewing over the apartment. He did not want Pablo to see his death coming. He thought he owed him that for all the precious information.

Malakai knew that he was not going to allow him to leave the room because once Pablo was out that door, he would be a walking dead man. He thought The Alliance Organization was getting desperate when they were hiring a number of street soldiers to acquire the amulet. He knew he had to leave the motel tonight because, in a day or two, the other street soldiers would be searching for Pablo.

Malakai was aware that he was battling an organization with no qualms about terminating not only his life but also that of one hundred others like him. The Alliance Organization ruled the world, wielding ultimate power on Earth. They could change presidents, prime ministers, and kings at the flip of a coin.

Malakai knew that he did not have much time, and he quickly gathered up his clothing that was strewn on the floor into his bag. He made sure that there was nothing in the room that could tie or identify him to the death of the man. He scrutinized the room and bathroom one last time to ensure that there was nothing remaining of his before he closed the door. It was quite late, after midnight, when he opened his car and put his bag in and drove away from the seedy motel to Manhattan.

Chapter 8

As Malakai left the apartment, Rose locked the door and went straight into the bathroom to take a shower. She came out of the shower and phoned her hairdresser friend, Angela Stanton and told her that she would be coming in the following day to wash and style her hair. Rose hung up the phone after they spoke for a few more minutes.

She went to bed around midnight but was unable to sleep as her mind kept going over the day's events and being in Malakai's arms. She missed him, and her body yearned for him even though she tried to suppress her feelings. She concluded that she was falling in love with Malakai, and she felt exhilarated and giddy like a young schoolgirl. She finally drifted off to sleep with one of the extra pillows on the bed between her legs.

Rose woke around eight o'clock the following morning, glad that school was on summer break and she had the time for herself to do whatever she wanted in the coming days. She prepared her breakfast, showered then called a cab to take her to the hair salon.

The hair salon was owned by Rose's friend Angela Stanton, an African American. She and Rose were the same age, but Angela was an astute businesswoman. She is extremely pretty and tends to look quite flashy and gorgeous, especially to her clientele. She is all about panache, and her business, her looks, her hair, and her clothing reflected that to her clientele. Her Motto was "live for the moment."

As Rose entered the business establishment, Angela was dressed in tight-fitting blue jeans that showed off her alluring, beautiful body. Angela had on a chic black blazer that she left unbuttons to reveal a white blouse. Angela, seeing Rose enter the salon, called one of her assistants to finish the client's hair. She greeted Rose with a hug and air kisses to each side of her jaws. Angela then escorted Rose away from the other clients in the shop to an isolated area. "I thought you were coming into the shop from last week to do your hair. Wait, your skin is glowing, and you seem ecstatic. What is happening to you?" asked Angela.

"I met this great guy, and we have been spending time together nonstop," said Rose.

"He must have a great dick because you are glowing and excited as hell. I want to tell him thanks myself. Tell him I will sing hail to that dick myself," said Angela.

"We have not gone there as yet," said Rose.

"You have not had sex as yet, and you are looking this hot and excited," said Angela.

Rose, smiling like a Cheshire cat, said, "My guy treats me like a lady and does not put any pressure on me for sex."

"Wait, do you still remember how to do it?" asked Angela. Angela had this inauthentic expression on her face and said, "It is quite a number of years since you were involved with a man."

Rose laughed and said, "It is like riding a bicycle; you never forget. Plus, once you go on, you hold on until the deed is done. In addition, I still do have a few tricks up my sleeve."

"When are you going to introduce me to him?" asked Angela.

"Soon, as I am totally confident that he is the one. I will gladly introduce him to you," said Rose.

"Please, Lord, make it happen soon so I can see who is lifting my gorgeous friend's legs," said Angela.

"You are disgusting. We are going out tonight, so come and look about my hair," said Rose.

Angela took Rose to one of her assistants to wash her hair then she went under the dryer. After the drying procedure was completed, Angela took Rose to one of her stations and styled her hair. After around an hour, Angela completed styling Rose's hair and took her to another assistant to do her makeup. After the makeup was completed,

Angela came by and said, "Now you look extra fabulous. Make sure he takes you somewhere that is worth your time."

"He will. I am leaving now. Thank you for looking at my hair and makeup," said Rose.

They embraced and bid each other goodbye, and Rose left her friend's salon all excited as she went home to get ready for her night out with Malakai.

***

Malakai got up in the morning and took the Lincoln Navigator to the parking garage. He did not want to take any chance for The Alliance Organization to be searching for the car, and they picked up the car on any closed circuit camera that they had all around the city of Brooklyn. He had the receipt for Georgina's Mercedes Benz car, so he gave the receipt to the cashier and paid the fee. He drove to the gas station and filled it up, then drove back to his Manhattan apartment.

As Malakai exited the Mercedes Benz, he suddenly started to think about Georgina and wondered if she had reached her home galaxy as yet. Malakai was so preoccupied with Rose that he had almost forgotten about Georgina. He thought that with Georgina's temper if she ever found out about Rose, she would boil him in hot oil and "Bobbitt off his dick."

As for Rose, she would have no compunction about disposing of her, who she would think would be beneath her ilk. Rose would be like an insect to her, to be crushed, especially if she found out that her man was involved with her or worse for Rose if she ever found her man was invested emotionally in this mortal woman. Malakai quickly pushed the thought out of his mind, comforted in the idea that Rose lived in Brooklyn and their apartment was in Manhattan.

Malakai packed his bag with new clothes and took out a brand new Burberry black suit that he was going to wear to accompany Rose to the ballet. He opened the safe that was packed with cash and took out fifty thousand dollars. He closed the safe, picked up his bag and suit and exited his Manhattan apartment. He put his bag and suit into the car and drove away from Manhattan. Malakai felt good on the open road and was looking forward to seeing Rose. He turned on the car radio, and the radio was playing beautiful rhythms and blues songs. Malakai started to sing along to the music that was playing on the car radio as the car sped toward Brooklyn.

Malakai arrived at Rose's apartment at around four in the afternoon. He rang the buzzer at the entrance of the building for Rose to let him inside. Rose was at the door waiting on him as he came through the apartment door. Malakai grabbed her, kissed her and said, "I have missed you, and I cannot stop thinking about you, woman."

"Me, too, you have occupied my every waking hour of the day. Are you still taking me to the ballet recital?" asked Rose.

"Certainly, it is not my thing, but I will certainly accompany you," said Malakai.

"Stay with me. I do not want to be without you," said Rose.

"It was my intention, but I wanted to hear it from you first. Plus, it is your apartment. The invitation has to come from you," said Malakai.

"Go for your things at the motel," said Rose.

"They are in the car outside. By the way, I was having some problem with the Lincoln Navigator, so I changed it for a Mercedes Benz," said Malakai.

Malakai went outside for his bag and suit, and Rose was contemplating if she was doing the right thing by inviting Malakai to stay in her apartment. She was in love with him, and she could not help it. She wanted him nearby every waking minute of the day. She was hungry for his touch and for his kiss, and she liked how he was attentive to her needs. As Malakai came back into the apartment with his things Rose told Malakai to put his bag in the other room.

Malakai got dressed in his brand new black Burberry suit and waited on Rose, who was in her room getting dressed. Around an hour, Rose came out of her room wearing a navy blue evening gown that reached to her feet with a small black handbag.

"You look absolutely fabulous. Gosh, you are beautiful, and I am an extremely lucky man to have you on my arm tonight," said Malakai.

"Thank you, you are good for my self-esteem. You look very handsome and dapper, Kai," said Rose.

"I love your perfume; you certainly smell nice. I love a woman who smells nice. By the way, where are we going?" asked Malakai.

"We are going to the Alvin Ailey Dance Theater to see a performance at New York City Center. Let us go," said Rose.

"Your wish is my command, my queen," said Malakai.

Malakai and Rose left the apartment with Rose feeling so confident and fearless being with Malakai on his arm. They drove and chatted enjoying each other company until they arrived at New York City at The Alvin Ailey Dance Theater. The Alvin Ailey Dance Theater is a modern dance company comprised of a mixed-raced group of dancers.

Inside the theater, there were people of all ethnicities, similar to the dancers that were on the stage. The men were dressed smartly in their jacket suits, and the women were dressed as if they were competing in a fashion show. The dancers were extremely talented and skillful as they soared in the air and propelled their bodies through countless dance routines, dancing to modern and classical music.

Rose was enjoying the performances of the dancers and their various intricate dance routines. It was Malakai's first time watching a ballet performance, which he enjoyed immensely. He looked at Rose and how beautiful and happy she looked, and he whispered to her, telling her thanks for taking him for the experience of watching a ballet performance for the first time in his existence on earth. After the show ended, there was around a five-minute standing ovation by the audience.

Malakai and Rose then left and had a romantic dinner at an upstairs restaurant overlooking the city. They both had chicken for dinner and a bottle of wine. As they both finished eating and drinking the wine, Malakai held her hand and said, "Rose, I do not know why our lives intersected on Mount Marcy, and frankly, I do not care. I am glad that they did, and I am thankful to God for giving me this opportunity, this moment in time, to tell you I am falling in love with you."

"Oh wow, I do not know what to say more than to tell you from the moment we met on the mountain. I have not stopped thinking about you even though I thought I would never see you again. Then, when we met again, I was so blown away by your charm, your intelligence, and, most of all, your gentleness towards me. I am in love with you longer than you can imagine," said Rose.

Malakai leaned over the table, held Rose's hands to his face and kissed them, and then he kissed Rose's lips softly and gently in the restaurant.

Malakai paid the bill, and they both left the restaurant. As they were driving home, Rose was ecstatic to hear Malakai declare his love for her because she was madly in love with him, and she loved the feeling of being in love and the rapturous joy she felt for this man.

They arrived at Rose's apartment around some minutes to eleven. Malakai went into the room where his bag was and undressed then went into the bathroom to take a shower. He came out of the shower, put on shorts and a t-shirt and went into the living room to watch television. Rose undressed in her room and then went into the bathroom to take a shower. She came out of the shower and went into her room where she lotions her body and put on her lingerie.

Around thirty minutes of watching the television, Malakai started feeling drowsy and was nodding away when he heard Rose calling him, covered in her bathroom robe and high heels. She told Malakai to follow her to her bedroom. Fully revived from his drowsiness, Malakai eagerly followed Rose into the bedroom. Rose told Malakai to go to the bed. Malakai obliged her request, stretched across to the bedside table and turned on the radio.

With Malakai on the bed, Rose proceeded to disrobe, revealing black lacy lingerie panty with a matching bra and a garter belt. She spun around as if modeling for Malakai and asked, "Do you approve, sir?"

"Oh yes, I certainly do approve. You are one beautiful, sexy woman, and I am glad and grateful that we are together," said Malakai.

"Should I take them off and come into the bed?" asked Rose, laughing.

"If you took the time to look so beautiful, let me take the time to savor the moment, feast my eyes, and appreciate everything about you," said Malakai.

As Rose continued to model for Malakai, she was glad that he liked her modeling for him. She loved the idea that she was the center of his attention and attraction, and she was turned on by that. She relished the power it gave her. "Most men would want to rip off my lingerie," said Rose.

"I am not most men," said Malakai.

"That is a damned certainty," said Rose.

"I enjoy looking at you, with or without clothing, and I certainly enjoy looking at you in your lingerie. I am a man who enjoys a woman in fine lingerie. That is just me. Anyway, come here. Let me take off each piece with my mouth," said Malakai.

Rose jumped into the bed and straight into Malakai's arms. She could not fathom from all the depth of her mind why she was so turned on and had this unquenchable desire for this man. Was it modeling for him that turned her on, creating that feverish sexual desire? As she jumped on the bed, the radio, which was tuned to a rhythm and blues station, started playing a beautiful soulful song by Otis Redding, *I have been loving you too long.*

Rose roughly forces her tongue into Malakai's mouth, kissing him with reckless abandonment. She hurriedly tried to take off Malakai's t-shirt, but it was not coming off, so she lifted the shirt over his stomach and started kissing his body all over. Malakai then removed his t-shirt while Rose practically dragged off his shorts.

Malakai started to undress Rose, examining and kissing every inch of her body. He turned Rose around, kissing her and tracing his tongue all along the crease of her back. Rose's body felt electrified by the feel of Malakai's wet tongue on her back. Her body felt like it was climbing unsurmountable heights under Malakai's probing tongue.

As the sensation became too intense, she turned around, and Malakai started to suck her ample breast. Rose was so aroused that she went and straddled Malakai's legs and took her right hand, and inserted Malakai's penis inside her moist inviting vagina. Rose began to grind her pelvis on Malakai's penis, and soon after, she started to scream with ecstasy as she climaxed, holding Malakai firmly around his chest.

Rose got up off Malakai's legs and lay flat on the bed. Malakai went and lay on top of her and inserted his penis inside of her vagina. Malakai began to thrust and thrust inside of Rose, and suddenly, Rose clenched her pelvic muscle. Malakai's erect penis remained inside of Rose, but he was unable to thrust inside of her vagina. The sensation was quite unexpected and new, though quite exhilarating for Malakai, who had never experienced something like that ever in his life.

Rose, with a broad smile on her face, looked at Malakai's reaction as he suddenly ejaculated inside of her; her vagina milked every drop of semen from his penis. Malakai came off Rose and said, "Wow that was something totally unexpected and felt so good."

They both went to bed afterward, embracing each other, with Rose sleeping on Malakai's chest. In the morning, they woke up, went separately to the bathroom and came back into bed, where they continued to have sex. Malakai asked and begged Rose to use the same sex technique of clenching her pelvis muscle. They continued to have sex until they were each exhausted and their energy spent, and they went back to sleep with Rose's naked body on top of Malakai.

***

Malakai got up, went to the bathroom, took a quick shower and left the apartment. He went to the supermarket, picked up a few groceries, and then went to the fish market to buy five pounds of red snapper fish. On the way to the apartment, Malakai stopped at the nearest McDonald's and picked up breakfast consisting of two cups of coffee, two fruit and yogurt parfait, and two bacon, egg, and cheese bagels.

When Malakai opened the apartment door, Rose was just coming out of the bathroom. He took the groceries that he bought at the supermarket and put them in the refrigerator and some in the kitchen cupboard. Malakai called Rose and said, "Come and have breakfast."

"You know you are God-sent. I had a great time last night," said Rose.

"I aim to please my queen. By the way, I went to the fish market, and I am going to cook for you this evening," said Malakai.

"I am so looking forward to you cooking. I love a man who can cook," said Rose.

"You, and most women, love a man who can cook," said Malakai.

"Do not worry. I am going to show you how appreciative I am of you later," said Rose, laughing.

Rose was so happy and glad that she was with someone with whom she could express her true self, and most of all, she was with someone who she was madly in love with and passionate about, and he was her man. As she was consuming her breakfast, she thought, *Malakai was so thoughtful going to the market to get breakfast.*

After they finished consuming their breakfast, they went into the living room and lay on the sofa watching television with Rose's head buried in Malakai's chest. A news item came on CNN about a terrorist bombing in Egypt, killing over three hundred people and injuring countless number of people. Rose said, "I cannot for the life of me understand why someone would want to kill so many innocent people."

"They forget why we are here and why we exist as human beings," said Malakai.

"We exist as human beings to praise God. That is what I think in general," said Rose.

"You are not entirely right if I can say so. If I asked you to show me God, you would not be able. Therefore, the reason why we exist as human beings is to help each other and to lift each other up. As a species, we are dependent and interdependent on each other for our existence; therefore, when we help and lift up each other, we praise God with our actions," said Malakai.

"You are saying not to praise God?" asked Rose.

"No, no, all I am saying is our relationships and actions with each other are equally important, as each of us relationship with God. Why? Human beings are flesh and blood; therefore, they exist in a material sense, while God is a spiritual being and does not exist on the same plane of existence like human beings. Let me ask you, what do you think was the greatest story in the bible that is most relevant today?" asked Malakai.

"I do not know. Christ dying on the cross for our sins or the parting of the Red Sea. Am I right?" asked Rose.

"That is your homework," said Malakai.

Rose took up one of the sofa cushions, hit Malakai, and said, "I am not in school."

"My darling, life is school. You learn, grow and adapt, or you die if you cannot adapt to changing circumstances. Take, for example, the dinosaurs; they were not able to adapt to changing circumstances, so they died, given the opportunity to your ancestor," said Malakai.

Malakai and Rose continued to watch television, sharing their life stories, playing, laughing, and enjoying each other company.

At one point, Rose thought, *does it get better than this?*

Chapter 9

In his posh Manhattan office, Vallencourt knew time was running out to deliver the amulet to the Alliance Organization. He had thousands of street soldiers, each one reporting to an agent, and yet they all came up with *zilch*. He thought, *who could be that good and clever not to leave the slightest clue?* He wondered if it was the sworn enemy of the organization, but he thought they would not terminate every life force indiscriminately, leaving no clue.

Vallencourt stepped out of his office and entered the conference room, where he called a meeting to discuss where they were in finding the amulet. Around the table in the conference room were Thornbird, Rochester, and a number of other senior agents. He called the meeting to order and discussed each agent's progress. Vallencourt told the agents that since they were not able to come up with anything, he was going to put someone in charge to replace Thornbird and Rochester as the lead agent. Vallencourt pressed the intercom in the conference room and told his secretary to send the gentleman to the meeting.

The conference room door opened, and a wiry-looking man entered, wearing reading glasses and dressed in a black jacket suit. The man's disposition was quite unassuming, and he looked like an accountant.

Vallencourt said, "Ladies and gentlemen, this is Mr. Wallenstein. He will be in charge of the investigation. Thornbird and Rochester will catch you up on the investigation. Please render any assistance you can give him. The meeting is adjourned."

Vallencourt walked from the conference room back to his office, hoping that Wallenstein could come up with something or some clue that could lead him to the recovery of the amulet. He recognized that he was placing his fate in Wallenstein, but Wallenstein was from the same Sagittarius galaxy, his home world. He knew that Wallenstein possessed a sharp brain capable of spotting minute anomalies of any investigation.

Around three o'clock in the afternoon, Malakai went into the kitchen to prepare fish for dinner. He took two of the red snapper out of the refrigerator and cleaned them with up limes to get rid of the odor. With the fish totally cleaned and dried, he put them in a bowl and applied some seasoning. He cleaned and cut up some onions, small tomatoes, scallions, thyme, carrots, okra, and red pepper. He then stuffed all the vegetables into the fish in the cooking bowl and covered it. This was to ensure that the seasoning was marinated in the fish properly.

After finishing preparing the fish, Malakai took out some red peas from the cupboard, washed them and put them in a small pot to boil on the stove. After boiling the red peas for fifteen minutes, he poured coconut milk into the pot. He applied scallions and thyme, green ginger, pepper, and garlic to the red peas' pot. Malakai allowed the red peas pot to boil for five minutes, then he washed the Uncle Ben's Rice and poured it into the pot with cooking butter. While the rice was boiling, he started cooking the fish on a low flame. When the rice, peas, and fish were finished cooking, he cut two plantains, diced them and fry them in a frying pan with butter.

Malakai set the table and carried the food to the table. He called Rose to the table for dinner as he was opening a bottle of white wine. Malakai said, "I have prepared steamed fish, rice, peas, and fried plantains. Hoping you enjoy the meal, my queen."

"Gosh, the food smells extremely nice. I want to propose a toast to my man," said Rose.

"Go ahead!" said Malakai, excited.

"I want to make a toast to the future. May you always be there with me as my man and… *friend?* I want to tell you also how happy you make me, and I am eternally grateful to have you in my life." said Rose.

"I am also happy that you are in my life, and I do love you," said Malakai.

Malakai and Rose clinked their glasses and sipped. Rose then reached over and kissed Malakai on his lips. They ate and chatted and enjoyed the food. After they finished eating, they stayed around the table, drinking wine, chatting, and just enjoying each other company. Rose thought that this was the type of relationship she had always dreamt of and wanted; an uncomplicated one. But she never thought she would get one where the man *actually cooked* her meals.

They finally got up, and Rose decided she would remove the plates from the table and wash the dishes. After Rose finished looking at the dishes, she told Malakai that she wanted to go for a walk and that Malakai must accompany her to the park.

Rose went into her room and put on her tights while Malakai put on his shorts and sneakers. They closed the apartment door and started walking to the park. Malakai started walking behind Rose, admiring her beautiful body.

As they entered the park, Malakai could not see any other individuals. The park was poorly lit, but he could not see any other individual, so he was not that worried about their safety. Rose was jogging around one hundred yards ahead of him when Malakai took his eyes off her and looked behind him when he thought he heard a sound. There was no one there.

He started jogging to catch up to Rose, who was out of his line of sight. Malakai ran around one hundred and fifty yards when he saw three men, one African-American and two Caucasians, dressed in jeans and t-shirts.

A blend of fear and fury overtook him.

One of the Caucasian men had a knife to Rose's throat. Malakai was furious. He tried to rein in his temper. He was never good with that sort of restraint. "Mister, if you do not remove the knife from her throat and release her now, I will definitely kill you."

"Fuck him up and beat the crap out of him!" said the man holding the knife.

Malakai could see the terrified look on Rose's face, and he knew he had to end this confrontation with the men quickly before any harm befell her. Suddenly, the African American pulled a gun from his waist and pointed it at Malakai's head.

"Listen, my man, we are going to fuck the shit out of your bitch, and we are going to let you watch how a real man fucks your woman."

"Not going to happen, my man. You have ten seconds to remove the gun from my head. I will kill all three of you before I allow anyone of you to even lay a hand on her," said Malakai.

The African American man removed the gun from Malakai's head, carried his hand upward, and came down with force, using the gun as a club directed at Malakai's head. Malakai easily sidestepped the incoming blow, and in one motion, grabbed the gun from the man's hand. Instead of threatening the men with his newfound weapon, he tucked it in his waist instead.

The sight of the gun in Malakai's waist instilled confidence in the men. The Caucasian man who was standing beside the African American rushed toward Malakai and threw a fist at him. Malakai avoided the attack, grabbed the man's hand and pushed it behind his back, pushing it upwards and breaking his hand. The Caucasian man started to scream as excruciating pain shot up his arm.

The African American man saw his comrade screaming in pain and rushed towards Malakai. Malakai saw him coming and kicked his foot, and the African American man fell. Malakai jumped on his back, grabbed the man's hand, and pushed it upward the same way. The man screamed with agonizing pain.

Malakai got up from the African American man's back and confronted the man who was holding the knife at Rose's throat. Malakai could see the fear in the man's eyes but knew he had to be careful. Malakai looked intently at the man and said, "My friend, if you drop the knife, I will let you leave unharmed."

"No fucking way am I going to drop the knife," he said.

"If you do not release her in the next minute, I am going to take the gun out of my waist and kill you," said Malakai.

"Okay, I will release her, if you promise not to shoot me," said the man.

"I *promise*, I will not shoot you, but you must drop the knife," said Malakai.

The man dropped the knife, pushed Rose towards Malakai, and started to run past them. Malakai, in one motion, caught Rose in his arms and stretched out his foot to stop him. The man toppled over, falling to the ground.

Malakai quickly released Rose and jumped on the man on the ground. Malakai ensured that the man felt his full weight when he jumped on top of him, and the force of Malakai's weight knocked the wind out of him. Malakai grabbed the man's arms and broke his two hands. All three men screamed at the agonizing pain they were experiencing. Malakai looked at the men in excruciating pain and said, "Apologize to the lady now."

"We are sorry for holding the knife to your throat," said one of the men.

"If I ever see you again in the park, your life belongs to me. All three of you go now before I change my mind!"

Two of the men got up, and Malakai assisted the one who'd had the knife. As the three men struggled to walk out of the park, Rose ran into Malakai's arms and embraced him tightly. Malakai stroked her back and said, "It's over now, and you are safe. I would not allow them to hurt you."

"Thank you for being here, protecting me," said Rose.

"I will always protect you, my love. Let us continue to walk," said Malakai.

Malakai picked up the knife, and they walked for another thirty minutes before they left the park. Malakai did not want Rose to leave the park immediately. He wanted her to face the fact that even when things go bad, you keep going and not go home and cower.

As they walked home to her apartment, he was glad that Rose was still in high spirits. Malakai thought his trick worked by keeping Rose in the park for thirty minutes. She seemed to forget the encounter with the three men.

As they continued walking, Malakai took the gun and knife and threw them into the sea, which was near the park. After they finished walking, they left the park and entered the apartment. Rose went into the kitchen to get some water. She drank the water and then went into the bathroom to get a shower. After Rose came out of the bathroom, Malakai went and got his shower.

When Malakai entered Rose's bedroom, she was totally naked on the bed. He looked at her appreciatively and said, "This is a picture of you I will always treasure in my heart."

"Thank you. I have been eagerly waiting for you. Take off your shorts and come into the bed," said Rose.

Malakai did as he was instructed and entered the bed. As he lay on the pillows, Rose kissed him passionately, and then she started kissing his neck, tracing and meandering her tongue all over his body. Malakai enjoyed the different sensation of Rose's tongue slowly teasing and caressing his body, with her looking directly into his eyes as if reaching and looking for his soul.

When the sensation was too intense, Malakai held Rose's head, looked directly at her and whispered, "I am yours."

Maybe it was hearing those words, or enjoying tracing her tongue slowly over this man's body or having Malakai's fingers softly touching her erogenous zones, but suddenly, she was having an intense orgasm.

After Rose's orgasm ended, Malakai came off the bed and went to the side of the bed. He called Rose to come to the edge of the bed, where she opened her legs, and he entered her with her legs on his broad shoulder. After a few minutes, Malakai asked Rose to turn around, which she complied, and he entered Rose from behind and resumed his thrusting and cupping her ample breast. Malakai love the feel of Rose's shapely buttocks on his thighs. After a few more minutes of thrusting, Malakai came. Exhausted, he dropped on the bed, embracing Rose.

***

Around two o'clock in the early morning, Malakai, in his repose state, thought he saw a shadow over him, and he opened his eyes to see Rose staring directly at him with anger on her face. He was a little frightened but composed himself and asked, "What's the matter?"

"Who are you? Who the fuck am I sleeping with?" Asked Rose.

"Where is this coming from?" asked Malakai.

"Yesterday, when you were fighting with those three men when one of them had a knife to my throat, you seemed to take great pleasure in inflicting pain and breaking their hands," said Rose.

"I was fucking terrified of what they might do to you. Rose, what did you want me to do, run away and let them have their way with you?" asked Malakai.

"Whose bed would you come into when you run away, leaving me with those pigs?" asked Rose.

"So what is the matter?" asked Malakai.

"I can't have a man in my bed that inflicts pain on other people like that and seems to enjoy it. I just cannot have you in my bed. It goes against everything I stand for and believe in. It is best for you to leave," said Rose.

"Rose, the world is not made up of fairy tales, goodness and righteousness as you imagine. To make the world a better place, you have to fight each day for it, and someone will have to do the dirty work, and that is where I come in to do the dirty work. If I leave, I am not coming back," said Malakai.

"Please, leave," said Rose.

Malakai went into the next room and gathered his things and also the amulet. Before he closed the apartment door, he told Rose goodbye. Malakai put his things into the car and drove to Manhattan to his apartment.

As Malakai closed the apartment door, Rose started crying because she was madly in love with this man and now, he was gone out of her life. She was torn because she could not reconcile his cruelty towards the men even though it was to save her life. She cried until her eyes were swollen with her tears and the audible beat of her heart constantly pounding in her chest, reminding her of the love and passion she felt for this man and all that was lost. She eventually started to sleep after exhaustion from crying in the early morning.

Rose woke up around two o'clock in the afternoon realizing that Malakai was no longer in her bed. She started crying, reminiscing about their time together, laughing, talking constantly, and making love like there was no tomorrow. Her cell phone rang. She looked at it, hoping it would be Malakai, but it was her friend Angela. She did not answer it.

As the week went by, Rose was in her house alone, not wanting anyone over her apartment. She was not eating well and lost weight. She missed Malakai, and the thought of dating anyone else made her become even more despondent. She thought in a lifetime, you only love two or three persons with that wild abandon passion that allows you to walk on water, float through the air, and talk endlessly, even though you may not be the loquacious type. She did not want to settle because she thought settling led to divorce and short-lived relationships, especially when the other person may not genuinely love the other person. She wanted that love and life she had with Malakai, although it only lasted a brief period. She felt within her soul that she genuinely loved Malakai, but she thought she had lost him when she told him to leave her apartment.

***

Malakai went home to his empty Manhattan apartment, totally distraught, and he could not fathom why Rose was acting that way. He accepted Rose was a little idealistic because she lived a sheltered life, oblivious to the harshness and grittiness of real life. He even accepted that maybe he did go overboard by breaking the men's hands, but they had to be taught a lesson.

He could not allow the men to go free without them paying a penalty for their barbarous actions. If he allowed the men to go free, and they went and committed a reprehensible act against an innocent person, how would he feel knowing he could have prevented it?

Malakai reasoned that the law of men cannot address every situation, and if he could distill punitive justice to those who deserved it, he did not have a problem. Malakai was hurting, and as he stared at the ceiling, he missed Rose. He missed her warmth, missed her smile, missed her touch, and most of all he missed having her in his arms.

As the days went by, he tried to put Rose out of his mind, but it was a losing battle.

One Wednesday, he was walking on the street of Manhattan, and the rain was pouring down. He was not going anywhere in particular; he was just walking in the pouring rain, just feeling heartbroken, and as he passed by a storefront, he thought he saw an image of Rose in the falling raindrops.

There was no solace, and as he walked back to his apartment, the pain in his heart seemed as if it would envelop him in melancholy. He arrived back at his apartment, took a large towel, dried off his body, and changed his clothes. After that, he sat at the table, took a note pad and started writing a letter to Rose.

***

Early Monday morning Rose's cell phone rang. It was her friend Angela Stanton. She picked up the phone and answered it. Angela told Rose she was outside her apartment. She must have buzzed her in and opened her apartment door. Angela came inside the apartment, enquiring why Rose was not answering her phone and returning her calls all week.

Rose told Angela what happened between her and Malakai. Rose said, "From the day I told him to leave, I cannot stop crying. I cry every night before I go to bed. I love and miss him."

"Do you still think he loves you?" asked Angela.

"He was hurt when I told him to leave, but I think he still loves me," said Rose.

"Listen to me, Rose, I think you are wrong. You have to eradicate those liberal tendencies, thinking those men were poor and privileged and could be redeemed. Those men deserved whatever they got. Just suppose those men were to harm you. I am glad you were with someone who was able to beat the crap out of them," said Angela.

"Looking at it from your perspective, maybe you are right. What was bothering or galling me is the wanton cruelty and the way he beat the hell out of them," said Rose.

"I am always right, so try to get in touch with him and make it up back. Please come by the shop to get a facial and look about your hair before you see him because you literally look like crap," said Angela.

"Thanks for coming over. I feel so much better," said Rose.

A few minutes later, Angela left the apartment. Rose went into the kitchen and made her breakfast. After she finished her breakfast, she went downstairs to collect her mail from her letterbox; she came back with a handful. As she sat around the table, she noticed one of the letters was from Malakai.

She hurriedly ripped it open and noticed the bold, handwritten letter. The letter stated:

"How do I say I miss you without saying so? How do I say I miss hearing your voice without saying so? How do I say I miss seeing you without saying so? How do I say I miss my friend most of all? Well, for all it's worth, I am saying so. I miss you. I miss seeing your curves. I miss the smell of you. I miss the taste of you. Woman, I miss the essence of you."

As Rose read the handwritten letter, she started to cry. The simplicity and veracity of the words etched and tugged at her heart. She yearned to see Malakai as her heart pounded in her chest cavity, as if telling her brain to surrender to the love of this man. As Rose was putting the letter away on the table, she noticed something else was written on the next side, which stated:

"PS. I am coming by Monday evening around seven o'clock to see you." Signed *M*.

Rose practically jumped out of the chair. She was so excited. She rushed into the bathroom to take a quick shower then she made a mad dash to see Angela to do a facial and to look about her hair.

Malakai arrived at Rose's apartment complex at around quarter to seven. He sat in his car quite apprehensive, not sure if Rose wanted to even see him again, and he thought if she behaved this way of him beating the crap out of some degenerate men, how would she react if she found out the truth about his very existence?

Malakai decided he would have to protect his secret to the utmost of who he is on this earth.

He got out of the car and pressed the buzzer to Rose's apartment. She buzzed him in and opened the door to her apartment. As Rose opened the door, Malakai entered.

She started to cry and said, "I am sorry, and I have missed you like crazy. From the day you left, I have been crying and, I was so unhappy with myself."

Malakai reached out and embraced her and said, "Hush, no more tears. I am here now, and I am not going anywhere."

Malakai picked Rose up and carried her to the sofa. As he put her on the sofa to lie down, Rose said, "Lay with me on the sofa."

Malakai removed his shoes and lay on the sofa. While he was on the sofa, Rose unbuttoned the untucked blue shirt Malakai was wearing and buried her face in his chest. The warmth of Malakai's skin surprised her, but she wanted to feel close to him, and be his woman, and he her man. As Rose lay on his chest she could feel his heart beat pounding in a rhythmical fashion as if offering solace from the outside world.

They lay on the sofa, not speaking, just embracing each other, treasuring the silence and grateful for the time to rekindle their nascent romance.

Around an hour later, Malakai carried Rose into her bedroom. He slowly undressed her and made love to her, after which they went to sleep. Around midnight, they got up and made love. They woke in the morning, and they made love. It was as if they were trying to recapture time lost. Around midday, they were still in bed, and Malakai said, "Woman, I am hungry. You have milked and drained all my semen."

"There was no semen ejaculating inside me the last time. It was just air," said Rose.

"You are certainly right about that because I am drained. Let us order some Chinese Food. I need some wanton soup inside me and some chicken," said Malakai.

"That is a good idea. I will go and call the restaurant," said Rose.

As Rose put on her clothes to go and call the restaurant, Malakai was just thankful to be in her life. He thought he had lost her for good, but somehow, faith decreed that they should be together again, and he was rather gratified for a second chance. The food arrived shortly from the restaurant, and they ate, consuming every morsel of the meal.

When they finished eating, Malakai took a notepad and started writing while Rose was watching the television. Rose looked at Malakai asked, "Kai, what are you writing?"

"I will tell you or show you when I am finished," said Malakai.

Rose continued watching the television but did not really concentrate on what was being shown on the television. She was wondering what Malakai was writing on the notepad, and she became a little panicky and terrified, wondering if he was ending their relationship and going home.

She tried her utmost best to compose herself but to no avail. Her mind was racing and going into overdrive, trying to decipher what Malakai was writing on the notepad. After around fifteen minutes, Malakai said, "Rose, I wrote a poem for you. Please tell me if you like it?"

Woman I see you cry, woman I see your tears.

Woman I see your laughter, woman I see your smile.

Woman I see your mouth that brings me enviable pleasure and pain.

Woman I see those lips, I kiss many a nights and days.

Woman I see that languid look overlooking my stare.

As I gazed upon your curvaceous ample bosom wondering what might have been.

Woman I have an unquenchable yearning for you.

But will time bring about a cessation of my ravenous hunger and desire for you?

They say time will tell, but how will it know if it is never spoken?

Woman, as a man, I need to find love, but I need to find myself too.

Lost in the complications of this life, I am reaching my outstretched hand and body to you.

Are you reaching, or are you reciprocating?

Woman my love knows no bounds, no mountains or hills I would not ascend for you.

Woman I love you, but is that love enough?

—I See You, Malakai

After Malakai finished reading the poem, Rose took the notepad that Malakai was writing on, and she read the poem, trying to understand it and to compose herself about the meaning of the poem.

She was relieved that her thoughts hadn't materialized. She loved the poem, accepting how Malakai revealed his true feelings to her, and she looked at him and said, "I am blushing, I have never had a man write a poem for me. I honestly love it, but why did you decide to write a poem for me?" asked Rose.

"I wrote it for you to express my love for you. I love poetry, and I love to express my feelings to the woman I am in love with," said Malakai.

Rose went over to Malakai and looked intently into his eyes, kissed him passionately and said, "I am your woman always, and I do love you, too."

Malakai slapped Rose on her ass and asked, "Rose, do you have a passport?"

"Yes, I do have a passport?" said Rose.

"By the way, I am taking you to your bank to lodge some money in your account if you do not mind. It is not over ten thousand dollars, so you will not have to provide any explanation," said Malakai.

"Why do you want to do that?" asked Rose.

"I may want to take you somewhere, and I want to ensure that you have an adequate amount of money, and I am going to use your credit card to book the tickets," said Malakai.

"Where are you taking me?" asked Rose.

"It is top secret. It's a place where you can feel the vibrancy and excitement in the atmosphere," said Malakai.

Rose was getting curious and could not contain her excitement. She looked lovingly at Malakai and asked, "Please, tell me where you are taking me?"

"I said it is a secret. Where do you lodge your money?" asked Malakai.

"I lodge my money at Chase Bank," said Rose.

"After we have finished eating, let's go to the bank," said Malakai.

Malakai and Rose left the apartment and went straight to the bank. Malakai gave her nine thousand to lodge in her account while he waited in the car. After finishing the lodgment, Rose came back into the car, and Malakai drove her home.

Chapter 10

Rochester was in his office seething with rage. He had worked extremely hard to get to where he is at in the Alliance Organization. Without notice he was replaced in a second, and the ignominy of it all he had to report to the man who had taken his position. His spirit was crushed, and he did not know what to do, and he was angry. He poured himself a glass of vodka and drank it in one gulp. The vodka calmed him a little, but he was still angry about the situation.

Rochester called Roberto to see if he found anything of significance with regard to finding the amulet. Roberto told Rochester he had not come up with anything, but one of his best street soldiers named, Pablo Alcantrez, was missing, and he could not locate his whereabouts in the city.

Rochester questioned Roberto when was the last time they spoke, and if Pablo told him where he was going. Roberto told him they spoke last week, and he told him he was going to check on some guy at a particular motel in Brooklyn. Rochester told Roberto he was coming to Brooklyn to check on the motel lead and he must pick him up by the train station at Church Street within one hour and a half.

Rochester rushed out of his Manhattan office to the train station, where he bought a twenty-dollar metro card to gain access to the train. Within five minutes a train came, and he went on it. He did not know if he would find anything in Brooklyn, but he was hoping he would be able to find even some small clue to the whereabouts of the amulet. He wanted Wallenstein gone so he was desirous of solving this case. As the train arrived at Wall Street, he came off and entered a number two train that was going by Brooklyn.

Within ten minutes, the train arrived at Church Street, and Rochester came off and walked out of the subway. Roberto was waiting for him as he came out of the subway. Roberto ushered him into his car, and they drove to the motel. Rochester looked at Roberto and asked, "Do you have a picture of Pablo so we can show it to the people at the motel?"

"I certainly do. I have a picture of him in an envelope in the glove compartment. Open the glove compartment and take it out," said Roberto.

Rochester opened the glove compartment and took out the envelope with the picture of Pablo. He looked at the picture and said, "He is an overweight motherfucker, but the picture will do."

As Roberto arrived at the motel, he parked, and he and Rochester got out with the envelope in his hand. They walked to the front desk area, where they saw a Caucasian man at the desk. Rochester approached the man and said, "Good day, Sir, I am Detective William, and this is my partner, Detective Castile."

"I am Kevin. What can I do for you, officer?"

"We are searching for this man. I heard he was here last week making some enquires," said Rochester.

Rochester pushed the picture to Kevin, and he looked at it and said, "Sorry, I do not remember anyone of that type staying at the motel."

"Please look at the picture again to see if you remember anything. I did not say he was staying at the motel," said Rochester.

Kevin looked at the photograph again and said, "Oh, I remembered him. He came here making some enquiries about one of our guests."

"Do you know what he was enquiring about?" asked Roberto.

"No, but I know he was interested in this tall, lanky white guy that drove a Lincoln Navigator ," said Kevin.

"Did you, by any chance, remember the license number of the car?" asked Roberto.

"No," said Kevin.

"Can you look into the computer and tell me his name?" asked Rochester.

Kevin went on the computer and pulled the file, and said, "He registered as Ted Knowles of Baltimore."

"Can you show me the room where he was staying?" asked Rochester.

"Sure, let me take the master key to open the door," said Kevin.

Kevin collected the master key, and the men followed him to the room. The room looked clean to Kevin and Roberto, but Rochester could see the blood splatter near the entrance door. Rochester went in looking for some other clue, but he could find none. Rochester was elated because, after many months of searching, this was the first break in the case. Rochester continued looking for clues.

He asked, "Kevin, was there anything distinguishable about Ted?"

"No, he was quite unassuming and kept to himself, and he did not stay at the motel in the day, only in the night," said Kevin.

After thanking Kevin for the information he provided, Rochester and Roberto left the motel. Rochester told Roberto that the man registered at the motel as Ted terminated Pablo's life force. Rochester surmised that Pablo had stumbled or discovered who had the amulet and was killed because of that knowledge. Rochester decided he was not going to Manhattan as of yet because he figured the amulet and the man who terminated Pablo's life force was in Brooklyn.

He knew the name Ted Knowles of a Baltimore address was a made-up name. Rochester thought he would try to solve the case and reclaim the amulet without the involvement of the Manhattan office and, more specifically, without the involvement of the man who took his position. He thought first he would have to rent a room in a motel to stay for the next couple of days and also pick up a few items at the store, pharmacy and supermarket.

***

Rose and Malakai were in the apartment watching television in the night when Rose said, "Malakai, I am experiencing severe menstrual cramps, and I need you to go and get me an over-the-counter drug named Midol at the pharmacy."

Malakai hurriedly left the apartment and drove downtown to a mall where a pharmacy was located because he wanted to contact an old friend of his who knew Fayol. He parked his car in the mall and walked to the pharmacy. On reaching the pharmacy, Malakai discovered it was closed because it was after ten o'clock. He asked a lady that was walking by where he could find the nearest pharmacy and she told him he could go across the next street. Malakai decided that he would just walk across the road to the next pharmacy.

Malakai quickly traversed the street and entered the pharmacy. He looked around and noticed that there were just a few people in the pharmacy. He asked one of the workers where he could find the Midol drug, and the worker directed him to the cashier. Malakai went up to the cashier and asked him for the Midol. He paid for three packs pushes them in his pants pocket, and as he was opening the door to exit the pharmacy, he heard someone say, "Fuck me, you are the asshole we have been looking for these many months."

Malakai quickly closed the door and ran in the opposite direction of where he entered the pharmacy. As he ran, he looked behind him and he could see two people chasing him. One of the men who was pursuing him was quite a distance away from the other. Malakai ran into an alley only to discover it was a dead end. He turned around, knowing he had to face and fight his pursuers. Malakai knew Rochester, but he was unfamiliar with the Spanish-looking man. As Rochester caught up to Malakai, he said, "Malakai, I need the amulet that you have taken from those two men."

"I do not know what you are talking about, Rochester," said Malakai.

Malakai knew Rochester quite well, and he encountered him twice when he was quite young and travelling all over the country.

"So why were you running?" asked Rochester.

"I am afraid of you," said Malakai.

"Listen, Malakai, I am not joking. If I have to take your fucking head to get the amulet, I will. You know you cannot defeat me because I am stronger, older, plus I am from the Andromeda Galaxy, and you know the rules; the farther you are born from the Milky Way Galaxy the stronger you are," said Rochester.

Rochester pulled out his sword, and Malakai pushed his hand into his waist and pulled out the flaming Onoro sword. Rochester thrust his sword at Malakai, which he blocked like a consummate swordsman. They continued thrusting their swords at each other, but neither man was making any progress with their carefully crafted attack in the alley. The fighting continued, and Roberto caught up to the men practically out of breath. Roberto started to retreat as he saw the tall, white, lanky stranger's sword cut at Rochester's head, and the force of the blow cut the stone bricks of the adjacent building quite effortlessly and came back to block Rochester's sword.

Roberto started to run into another alley because he was fearful that if the stranger defeated Rochester, he would be coming after him next, and he was not a fighter. As the fighting continued,

Rochester kicked Malakai's feet, and he fell flat on his backside, but he was still facing Rochester with his sword still in his hand. As Malakai was getting to his feet, Rochester, wanting to end the fighting, unwittingly rushed and chopped at Malakai's head.

Malakai blocked Rochester's sword and kicked at Rochester's feet. Rochester retreated in that one split moment and Malakai used the sword as a lever and pressed on the sword to somersault over Rochester. As Rochester moved forward and thrust his sword at Malakai, his neck was unwittingly exposed, and as Malakai was landing on his feet, he swung the sword at Rochester's neck and chopped it off. Rochester's decapitated head started to spew blood all over the alley. Malakai stared at Rochester's headless body for around five minutes, and suddenly, the body started slowly turning into dust. Malakai was thankful to God for giving him the strength to defeat Rochester.

As the wind blew away Rochester's body, Malakai said, "I guess rules are meant to be broken because I am from The Milky Way Galaxy, and I defeated someone from The Andromeda Galaxy with my trusty Onoro sword."

Malakai looked up the road to see if he could see the other man, but he was unable to, and he quickly crossed the street to the mall, where his car was parked and drove away into the night. He thought that the Alliance Organization was getting too close, and he would have to get out of town for a few weeks until things cool down.

When Malakai arrived at the apartment, Rose was on the sofa, covered with a blanket. He went into the kitchen to get a glass of water and gave Rose the packet of Midol. Rose asked Malakai to make some tea for her cramps. After she drank the tea, he went and lay with her, gently massaging her back as she lay on his chest on the sofa, watching television.

After watching television for more than an hour, Malakai turned off the television, and they went to sleep in Rose's bedroom. Rose started sleeping, but Malakai was unable to because he was worried about his and Rose's safety.

Malakai knew he could not share any of his life's details with Rose, and he knew that the Alliance Organization would be everywhere in Brooklyn shortly to find out who killed their companion. He was glad he had the foresight to park the car in the mall, so hopefully, the man who was with Rochester and ran away would not be able to see him when he went over the mall. Malakai eventually started to sleep and woke around seven o'clock in the morning.

While Rose was getting a bath, Malakai prepared breakfast of scrambled eggs, bacon, toast, and orange juice. After Rose came out of the bathroom, they sat around the table and had their breakfast. When they finished eating, Malakai asked Rose for her credit card to book the tickets through a travel agency. Rose gave him the credit card, and he booked the tickets. As Malakai was booking the tickets, Rose asked, "Which overseas destination are we going to?"

"We are going to the land of reggae music, the island of the famous Blue Mountain Coffee, blue sea, white sands and authentic Jamaican foods. Yes, mon, we are going to Jamaica," said Malakai.

Malakai got up off the sofa and started to dance and sing, "We are going to Jamaica, the island of reggae music. That is where I am taking my woman."

Rose laughed uncontrollably, seeing Malakai singing and dancing In her apartment. Rose was quite excited and said, "I am so looking forward to the trip, and I can't wait to be there. Malakai, please come here."

Malakai went to Rose on the sofa, and she pulled him closer to her, kissed him and said, "I love you, and I am glad you are my man, and in my life, and I am very appreciative that you are taking me to Jamaica."

"I love you too, but there is no one I would rather take to Jamaica than you. By the way, we leave next Friday, and I need to give you some money to get some stuff for three people," said Malakai.

"Who are these people, and who are they to you?" asked Rose.

"I grew up on the island in my early years with the help of a man name Rodigan. He took me in when my mother and father were killed and raised me, and he taught me right from wrong. Rodigan is married to a lovely lady named Grace, and they have an eight-year-old son named Michael. They are the closest thing to a family I have. He called me Uncle Malakai, and I will have to buy him the latest PlayStation games," said Malakai.

"Sorry about your parents. I did not know, but you did not tell me anything about them," said Rose.

"It is okay, it has been a long time, and I have gotten over it," said Malakai.

He knew he was insincere in telling Rose he had gotten over his parents' deaths because as long as he breathed air on this planet, he would never forget or forgive those monsters who killed his parents. He was lucky that Rodigan was a friend of his dad's who fled with him to Jamaica to find sanctuary.

***

Roberto ran down another street as far away as he could because he was terrified and also a coward. He had never heard or seen a sword cut anything in its path like that, and he was quite fearful that he did not want to encounter the tall, lanky stranger. Roberto remained in the spot where he was for a full hour before he started to look at where the men were fighting in the alley. Roberto was scared but told himself that a man who runs lives to fight another day.

Roberto gazed up the alley but did not see any of the men, so he cautiously walked to where they were fighting, where he saw Rochester's sword lying on the road surface. Roberto realized that Rochester's life force was terminated in the alley. He took out his cell phone and called Vallencourt and explained to him what had happened.

Vallencourt told him to wait because he would be there in the next two hours.

Roberto waited for what seemed an eternity until Vallencourt and his top lieutenants of the Alliance Organization arrived in three black-tinted Cadillac Escalade sport utility cars. Roberto told them that he and Rochester were in the pharmacy buying something when Rochester recognized the man who stole the amulet and chased him down the alley.

Wallenstein asked Roberto how his life was spared, and Roberto told them he ran down another alley because he was afraid when he saw the flaming sword cutting through the rocks and steel. Wallenstein told them it was the Onoro sword made in a galaxy far away to specifically kill their kind and it was only two in existence, and both were stolen when they were to be delivered to the Alliance Organization.

Wallenstein suggested to the men that they must go into the pharmacy to see who the man was on their closed-circuit camera system. Vallencourt was feeling ecstatic because, for the first time in many months, he was getting somewhere to recover the amulet and maybe apprehend the man who caused so many months of anguish in his life.

The men entered the pharmacy dressed in their black jackets and ties and the few customers who were in the store were surprised to see the men who they assumed to be people with authority. Wallenstein went to the cashier and asked for the manager, who she pointed to an African American woman. Wallenstein explained to the lady that they were from the Federal Bureau of Investigation, and they were chasing an extremely dangerous criminal who came into the pharmacy earlier and they would like to see the tape of what he bought and his appearance. The manager explained to the men that the camera system for the pharmacy had been broken for the last three weeks and that if they wished, she could show it to them so that they would not question her veracity.

As Vallencourt heard the woman telling them that the camera system was not working, all the blood seemed to drain from his face, and he became ashen white. He was furious, and it was so apparent on his face. Every time he seemed to get close to some major clue to the whereabouts of the amulet, he was met with a major setback. He did not know where else to turn, and he knew he was running out of time. He asked for suggestions from his men, but they could not come up with any, he therefore decided to go back to Manhattan.

***

The next day, Rose was feeling much better, and Malakai took her to the mall to shop for her trip to Jamaica. She bought quite a number of bathsuits and evening dresses while Malakai bought t-shirts, shorts, bathing trunks, sneakers for himself, and Rodigan and four pairs for Michael. Malakai asked Rose to pick out four high-end name-brand dresses and high heels shoes for Grace. They went to Best Buy to buy the latest PlayStation for Michael and some unlocked cell phones. On their way home, Malakai gave Rose some more money to lodge into her account. They also stopped by a restaurant and picked up food to take home.

Rose was quite excited, and as she entered the apartment with some of the stuff they bought at the mall, she started to pack the suitcases. Malakai told her to keep his stuff with Rodigan and reminded her to pack in the basic stuff, like toothpaste, dental floss, deodorant, and cologne.

In the evening, Rose told Malakai that she wanted to go by the park to jog to ensure that she fitted in her bathsuit perfectly for her trip to Jamaica. Malakai looked at her and said, "Darling, you look perfect, and you will look lovely in that bathsuit." Rose did not seem convinced by the argument that Malakai was making, and Malakai asked, "Are you sure we have to go to the park?"

"Yes, we have to go. I like having you by my side; you make me feel so confident when I am with you. You are my little angel. Do you believe in angels?" asked Rose.

"Yes, I am one" said Malakai.

"Where are your wings?" asked Rose.

"Angels do not have wings; they are spiritual creatures. Plus, how would I fly with my third leg that you cannot get enough of?" said Malakai.

Rose took one of the cushions on the sofa and used it to hit Malakai over his head and said, "You know, you are full of crap."

Malakai and Rose left the apartment and went over to the park. Malakai was glad he told Rose. However, he knew she would never believe him, but at the least, he felt absolved, and he would have a genuine excuse if she did find out at some point in the future. They exercised for one hour before they returned to the apartment.

Thursday night, Malakai and Rose were in bed before they departed on the trip to Jamaica. Malakai told Rose that he would take her with the suitcase to the airport a little early, allowing him time to take the car back to Manhattan. He told her to board the plane, and he would see her on board. Rose agreed, and they continued chatting until they went to sleep, aware that it was their last night before their vacation to Jamaica.

***

Early Friday morning, Malakai and Rose got up and prepared to depart to John F. Kennedy Airport. As Malakai was taking down the suitcase to put in the car, Rose gave Malakai one of the apartment keys and told him it was his now for being her man. They left the apartment, and Malakai drove her to the airport.

When they arrived at The John F. Kennedy Airport, Malakai stopped the car at the Caribbean Airlines departure area. They were flying to Jamaica by Caribbean Airline, which is a regional airline for the Caribbean. Caribbean Airlines flies to the different islands in the

Caribbean, such as Trinidad and Tobago, Barbados, St. Lucia, Antigua and many other islands.

Malakai got out of the car, purchased a cart, and put the suitcase in it. He kissed Rose and reminded her not to wait on him but to check in on the flight. As Malakai walked away, Rose took her cell phone from her handbag and called Angela Stanton. "I am at JFK. I was supposed to call you from yesterday to tell you I am on my way to Jamaica on vacation."

"Bitch, and you are just calling and telling me now? Are you going alone or with your man?" asked Angela.

"My man is taking me to Jamaica. I am so looking forward to being in Jamaica. I am so excited," said Rose.

"I can hear the excitement in your voice. Take care of that man. He seems like a nice person. I thought you said you were going to introduce me to him shortly," said Angela.

"When I come back from Jamaica, I will call you, and you can come and pick us up at the airport, and you will meet him then," said Rose.

"That sounds like a great idea. Enjoy yourself to the fullest and give that man's dick a rest, now and again," said Angela.

"Goodbye," said Rose.

Rose hung up the phone, and as she pushed the cart ahead of her to the Caribbean Airlines checking counter, she was greeted by a friendly, impeccably dressed female customer agent. The customer agent asked Rose for her customer number, and Rose gave her and she promptly checked her in the system. Rose then went and entered the customs area where her passport and ticket were checked again, and after she cleared the customs area, she went and took a seat near the Caribbean Airline gate.

Malakai drove as fast as possible to reach Manhattan, slowing down only when it was absolutely necessary in the high-traffic areas. Malakai arrived in Manhattan within an hour and went straight to the parking garage. He stopped a taxi going by from the parking garage to take him to the subway, where he got on the train to take him to Brooklyn.

Malakai came off the train in Brooklyn and got a taxi to take him to the airport. He was back at the airport within a short space of time and went straight to one of the Caribbean Airlines counters, where he was promptly checked in. He then went into the customs and looked for the gate where Caribbean Airlines was located inside the terminal.

Malakai arrived at the Caribbean Airlines gate just as they were boarding passengers. Malakai boarded the plane and went into the first-class section, where he saw Rose. He quickly sat beside Rose, who had a quite concerned look on her face and said, "I was so concerned you were not going to make the flight."

Malakai kissed Rose and looked around the cabin and noticed that the business class section was not too full and said, "Hush darling, I am here now. I would not want you to go to Jamaica without me."

The flight took off shortly, and Rose and Malakai were on their way to Jamaica. It was a clear, sunny day for the three-and-a-half-hour flight to Jamaica. The flight was extremely comfortable, devoid of any turbulence in the cabin. The airline flight attendants were very friendly, and they served alcohol and meals with a friendly smile.

Malakai slept most of the flight while Rose was quite elated. She kept looking outside the plane window at the clouds and sea. Soon, the plane landed at The Sangster International Airport in Montego Bay, and the passengers disembarked and were greeted by local dancers in their costumes welcoming the visitors to the island. Malakai and Rose went through customs to have their passports examined and stamped and be welcomed to Jamaica.

Rose and Malakai picked up their suitcases, and they were escorted to a tour bus. The driver was a very friendly, black, round-faced man who welcomed them as they entered the tour bus. The driver waited for twenty minutes more until all the passengers that he was supposed to pick up were on the bus. He then drove off to the hotel where Rose and Malakai were staying on the island.

Chapter 11

The air-conditioned tourist bus departed the Donald Sangster International Airport and Rose kept looking around as if she wanted to take in all the panoramic view of the city of Montego Bay. She was clearly quite enchanted as the bus travelled through the picturesque city of Montego Bay and through the idyllic town of Lucea in the adjoining parish of Hanover. The bus travelled another hour before they arrived at their destination at Hedonism Resort in Negril in the parish of Westmoreland.

They disembarked from the bus at the Hedonism Resort in Negril, where they were greeted and welcomed and offered drinks of rum punch. There was a bevy of activities near the front desk as a four-man mento band was playing sweet melodious music as guests of all ethnicities gathered, drinking, eating, and going about their business. The quests were quickly checked into their rooms, with the bellman assisting with the luggage.

Rose and Malakai's room was an ocean view nicely decorated with a king-sized bed, flat screen television, refrigerator, ceiling mirror, and a fully glass-enclosed bathroom. There is also a private verandah Jacuzzi. Rose liked the room and jumped on the bed, asking Malakai to come and join her which he promptly complied, and she quickly rolled on top of Malakai. As they lay on the bed, Malakai said,

"True unmitigated love is the recognition by our spirit that there is someone out there, and when we reach out with all our flaws and idiosyncrasies, love us unconditionally. At least that is my definition of true love."

"You know what? I like being in love. Love is that feeling that I get like I am floating in the air; I can walk on water, especially when I am with you. It is simply the greatest unadulterated high," said Rose.

"I am going to try my hardest to let you walk on water and float in the air," said Malakai.

"I am under no illusion that a relationship takes work and effort, but I am going to try my hardest to be your woman," said Rose.

"That is all I am asking for, to be my woman," said Malakai.

They looked at each other lovingly and lustfully and kissed with animalistic passion. Rose turned around Malakai and slapped him on his ass, and said, "We have all weeks for that, let's unpack and go and explore the property before we go to the orientation."

Malakai and Rose quickly unpacked, changed their clothes wearing shorts, and then exited the room to explore the property. As they walked the property, they noticed that clothing was optional for the guests. They saw several beach bars and restaurants, and with the property being an all-inclusive resort, all drinks and meals were included in the price. They saw several pools, clothing-optional hot tubs, tennis, basketball, and volleyball courts, a gym, and a nude beach.

They went by the beach bar, and Rose ordered a fruit punch while Malakai ordered a strawberry daiquiri. They left the bar and began to walk on the beach. The Negril Beach is world famous for its seven miles of beautiful white sand and glorious blue water. It was quite crowded with people from all ethnicities, vacationing from America, Canada, Europe, South America and Japan. Rose, holding Malakai's hand, said, "I can't wait for tomorrow to go and experience the beach. The water is so clean, warm and beautiful."

After walking on the beach for a few more minutes they went back on the resort property to the orientation. At the orientation, the entertainment coordinators told the guests about the property, entertainment activities, and what to expect and provided suggestions on how to make their vacations more fun and enjoyable for the coming days.

With the orientation completed, Malakai and Rose left and continued to tour the property. They stopped at the gift shop examining a few craft items, and artfully designed t-shirts. Rose bought four of the t-shirts, telling Malakai she wanted to give two to her friend Angela. They left the gift shop and went back to their room to get ready for dinner.

Malakai turned on the television as they arrived in the room and started watching CNN. Rose undressed and went into the fully glass-enclosed bathroom to take her shower. After a few minutes, she came inside the room naked with the white bathroom towel over her shoulder. Malakai stared at his crotch and at Rose and said, "My dick said to tell you that you are practically killing us and to tell you to stop titillating us because we are practically bursting out."

"Tell your horny dick that you must go and get ready for dinner because I am hungry. I swear, sometimes I am walking, and I can feel it inside me."

Malakai got up off the bed and went into the bathroom to take his shower. He came out of the bathroom and quickly got dressed. At around eight o'clock, they left the room for dinner, with Rose wearing a short, flowery evening dress and Malakai wearing a green polo shirt and black shorts.

They went to the Terrace Room dining restaurant, which was offering buffet-style dining of local dishes. The restaurant offered a romantic, intimate dining experience. Rose chose a table which was decorated with white table linen with the utensils and glass nicely arranged, with beautiful, shaped napkins. As it was buffet-style dining, they had to pick up their plates to get their food. They both had the lobster served with baked potatoes, a vegetable platter and a glass of wine. Malakai picks up chocolate cake with cookies for dessert.

After Malika and Rose finish eating, a band starts playing music. After the band completed their set, the main event for the night a local singer took to the stage. The local singer performed a wide variety of songs, with the crowd being very appreciative clapping and dancing along with the performance.

With the performance completed, Malika and Rose got up and started to walk the property, holding hands. They eventually stopped walking and went into the grotto pool area and entered the disco room. They stayed in the disco room, drinking and dancing to reggae and hip-hop music until after one in the morning.

When they arrived back in their room, Rose undressed, went into the bathroom, and invited Malakai inside the bath. She took the shower gel in her hands and applied it to his body slowly and gently, almost in a rhythmical fashion. Malakai did the same to her, enjoying the varied sensation of Rose's touch and appreciating the closeness and softness of Rose's body.

They kissed passionately as Rose turned on the faucet and as the water beat down on their bodies as if trying to extinguish the burning lust, they felt for each other without success. Malakai could not withstand the passion and desire he felt anymore, and he quickly spun Rose around and inserted his penis inside her from behind. She braced her hands on the shower wall while he thrust inside her as the gentle water flowed over their bodies. When Malakai orgasmed, they completed their shower, dried off and entered the bed in the nude.

Rose went into the bed and dragged the sheet over her body, and as Malakai entered the bed, she lifted the sheet, revealing her nakedness in the dimly lit hotel room. Malakai dragged the sheet over both of them, embraced Rose in the bed and started kissing her body. He kissed her passionately, tracing his tongue down to her neck and all over her body. Malakai explored, squeezed, and teased her body with his tongue until she yelled, "Kai, oh my god. Kai, I love you."

Rose's orgasm was quite intense as she looked lovingly at Malakai. Malakai put Rose on his legs, straddling him and inserting his penis. With Rose facing him, he took her breast in his mouth, sucking and squeezing them, enjoying the different sensation. After a while, Malakai changed position to a missionary one. He soon switched position again because missionary was not one of his favorites, and he turned Rose around and reinserted his penis inside her from behind; he enjoyed the feel of Rose's posterior on his pelvic area immensely. As he began to thrust, Rose started to have another orgasm. He continued to thrust as he felt Rose's body shake, and he thrust deeper inside her as he climaxed. They were exhausted from their lovemaking and went to sleep embracing each other.

Malakai and Rose got up around eight-thirty in the morning, dressed and left the room to get their breakfast. Breakfast was served buffet style consisting of local cuisine. After eating their breakfast, which Rose thoroughly enjoyed, they went back to the room. Rose was eager to swim in Negril blue beach water.

Before they left the room for the beach, Malakai insisted that Rose put on an adequate amount of sunscreen all over her body. Malakai helped with applying the sunscreen all over her body, and when he was finished, she reciprocated the favor. They went down to the beach bar and collected their beach towels.

Malakai picked one large white beach chair to lay the towels while he and Rose went into the seawater. Rose took her t-shirt off to reveal a yellow one-piece bathsuit. Malakai could see the men looking at her with approving glances. He looked at Rose admiringly also and said "Woman, you look absolutely gorgeous."

"Thank you, I want to look good for my man," said Rose.

They went into the water with Rose, surprised at how warm the seawater felt on her body. They swam, touched, and frolicked with each other in the clear blue seawater. Rose was extremely happy and enjoying swimming in the clear blue water and asked, "Why do you love the crystal clear blue sea water so much?"

"The simple fact is that there is nothing like this nowhere apart from Earth, and we must fight and protect it," said Malakai.

"I agree we need to protect the oceans and the whole environment because our life and some people's livelihood is dependent on it," said Rose.

Malakai nodded in agreement and told Rose he was going to the beach bar to get two pineapple juices because he was feeling rather thirsty. Malakai came out of the seawater, went to the beach bar and ordered two pineapple juices.

As the bartender gave him the drinks and he was about to carry them to Rose in the seawater, he saw her coming in the lovely yellow one-piece bath suit. He waited at the bar, watching Rose walking towards him just as the bartender turned on the music system and the sweet, infectious, melodious sound of reggae music started playing. The reggae song was "No Goodbye." The song was one of Malakai's favorites, sung by the famed reggae artist named Berris Hammond an icon in the reggae music industry. Malakai started humming along to the sweet, infectious, syncopated beat of the reggae song as Rose walked toward him as if she were on a fashion catwalk. He gazed at her, walking towards him appreciatively like a man fully head over heels for his woman. As Rose arrived at the bar, Malakai asked, "Why did you leave the water?"

"I am too hot and thirsty, and one pineapple juice will not satisfy my thirst," said Rose.

Rose sat at the bar with Malakai, drinking pineapple juice and virgin strawberry daiquiri. She put on her t-shirt, and she and Malakai walked the beach. They came back to the hotel property and had jerk chicken with rice and peas for lunch. They both enjoyed their meal immensely, with both going back for seconds and Malakai adding extra hot sauce to the jerk chicken.

After they finished their lunch, they walked a little and then went back to their room, which was cleaned by the housemaid. Rose went straight into the shower, followed by Malakai. After they were both finished showering, Malakai jumped into the bed beside Rose, embracing her, and both went to sleep fatigued from the day's activities.

They woke at six o'clock in the evening from their slumber and went by the beach bar to get a drink. Rose suggested to Malakai that she wanted to walk to develop an appetite before dinner. Malakai agreed, and they went walking on the property holding hands. As they walked and enjoyed the scenery of the flowers and the birds singing in the trees, Rose was extremely relaxed and happy as a lark. Malakai said, "The scenery is so beautiful, surrounded by beautiful trees and flowers of all varieties and singing birds."

"I agree that the scenery is extremely beautiful," said Rose.

"What is your idea of heaven?" asked Malakai.

"The bible said the street is paved with gold," said Rose. She turned smilingly towards Malakai and asked, "What is your idea of heaven?"

"This beautiful scenery, the sea full of life, animals, plants, music, nature in general, food, sports, and having you beside me. I will take all these things over a street paved with gold," said Malakai.

"Do you think heaven is in the sky?" asked Rose.

"If you are talking where God and his son live, maybe, but man's heaven is right here, beautiful planet Earth. Have you heard the expression from the bible the meek shall inherit the earth? Well, all the bible is saying is that the destitute and the righteous will inherit the earth at some point when God returns to judge all of us," said Malakai.

"So you are saying man's heaven is here on planet earth. To be honest with you, I do worry sometimes about the afterlife, like what happens to your soul in the afterlife?" asked Rose.

"Why worry about the afterlife, which is the unknown? Your duty is to confront what is in front of you that is of material significance. To develop good relationships with your fellowman and be mindful of nature that you have a responsibility to care for the planet Earth because there is nothing like this anywhere in the whole universe," said Malakai.

Malakai did not want to reveal too much to Rose because he did not want her to be too suspicious. He tried to switch the answer about the afterlife because it would spark too many questions. "Let's go and eat now. I am hungry now," said Rose.

They went and had their dinner at one of the restaurants on the resort and watched the local cabaret show. After the cabaret show was finished, they went dancing and drinking at the disco and returned to their room after two in the morning.

Malakai and Rose woke up at nine o'clock in the morning and hurried down to have breakfast because breakfast closed at ten o'clock. Later in the day, they went sailing, indulged in some water skiing and went on the glass–bottom boat ride. As the days went by, Malakai and Rose played tennis, beach volleyball, indulged in windsurfing for the first time, and after swimming, they took time to do a little kayaking. They also went off the property to visit Ricks Café, drank Red Stripe Beer and watched people diving off the cliff and took pictures of the beautiful sunset. They went to a local eatery named Cosmos to sample local cuisine, such as curried lobster, which they thought tasted extremely delicious.

The last night of their two-week vacation at the hotel, Rose was bemoaning that she did not want to leave the resort. The next morning, they settled their bill, and checked out of the hotel and went on the bus that was taking them to the airport. As the bus was transporting them back to the airport, Rose's eyes were glued to the bus window taking all the panoramic view of the towns.

Arriving at The Donald Sangster International Airport, Rose and Malakai came off the bus with their suitcases. Rose stayed with the suitcases while Malakai went and picked up a Toyota Camry motor car, which he had rented online from the Avis Car Rental Company, which is located at the airport. Within ten minutes, he picked up Rose with the suitcases and drove into the town of Montego Bay, showing her the area and stopping at Pier One Restaurant, where they had a drink, taking in the view and taking pictures of the bay.

They left Pier One Restaurant soon after and went to the world-famous Pork Pit restaurant, where they consumed jerk pork and jerk chicken with festival and Red Stripe Beer. They left Pork Pit, and Malakai told Rose as he was driving that they were going to Riu Ocho Rios Resort. He told her he was considering going by Rodigan and Grace before they checked in the hotel.

When they entered the parish of Trelawny Malakai, stopped by the world-famous Luminous Lagoon and explained to her at night, when the water is disturbed, the whole area glows because of special microorganisms in the water called dinoflagellates.

They continued on their journey on the north coast and entered the parish of St. Ann, where the famous Dunn's River Falls is located and where the Riu Ocho Rios Resort is also located. Malakai drove off the main road and turned onto an arterial road.

As they continued on the narrow road, they saw a car speeding ahead of them. Suddenly, it plummeted off the road into a precipice. Malakai accelerated his car to the spot where the car plummeted into the precipice. Malakai and Rose came out of their car, and Malakai quickly descended into the precipice which was around ten feet. The car overturned, and the wheels were still spinning in the wide precipice. Malakai saw that the car was a Toyota Corolla, and it was crushed, with the windscreen smashed and smoke coming from the inside. He bent down on the ground and saw three people: a man, a woman, and a young boy. Malakai asked, "Are any of you hurt?"

"My foot is broken, and my wife's hand is either broken or sprained. The boy is okay," said the man.

Suddenly, a fire started to envelop the car, and Malakai said, "I will help you out of the car and take you all to the hospital. Please do not panic."

Malakai assisted the boy out of the car first and then the woman. The man was a little harder to pull out of the car because he was the driver, and the car steering was blocking his foot. Malakai somehow managed to tilt the steering, thereby freeing the man's leg. The boy and the woman were able to walk out of the precipice, but Malakai had to assist the man by putting the man's arms around his shoulder and slowly walking out of the precipice. As they reached the top of the road, the car was totally engulfed in flames.

Malakai assisted the man into the Toyota Camry, laying his face downward on the backseat. The woman squeezed into the backseat by sitting in a bent position. The boy sat beside Rose in the front. Malakai turned the car around and drove them to the St. Ann's Bay Hospital. As they drove away from the accident, there was a loud explosion of the burning car. The man was experiencing severe pain, but he was trying his best to fight the pain. They arrived at the St. Ann's Bay Hospital within fifteen minutes at the emergency section. They were assisted out of the car by the hospital emergency staff.

Malakai and Rose stayed in the Emergency area waiting section for about an hour when they were called in by a tall, slim nurse. The nurse ushered them into the male section of the hospital where the man they had taken there was lying on a bed, and the boy was standing at the bedside. The man's foot was covered with plaster, and as he saw Rose and Malakai coming, he stretched his hand and expressed his gratitude for taking him, his wife and his son to the hospital. He said his name was John Reynolds, his son's name was Roy, and his wife's name was Patricia. He told them that he used the car as a taxi, and he was rushing to take his family home so he would be able to go on the road to pick up passengers.

Malakai told the man they were glad they were able to assist in taking them to the hospital. Malakai asked John if he could give Roy something from the car, and he responded in the affirmative. Malakai left Rose in the hospital, rushed to the car, took out one of the sneakers and placed it in a black plastic bag. He took the bag with the sneaker and gave Roy who was very appreciative of the gift. Malakai then took out five hundred out of his pocket and gave John. He went to check on Patricia and gave her five hundred United States dollars. John and Patricia told him thanks, and after they chatted a little more Malakai and Rose left the hospital with Rose staring and smiling at Malakai.

As they were driving back into Ocho Rios, Malakai and Rose decided they were going straight to the hotel to check in and visit Rodigan another day. Rose, smiling, said, "I understand now, my homework. Let me tell you this: I am very appreciative of you, and if we don't make it in our relationship, it was a great learning experience, and I will always love you and treasure the time we had together."

"Rose, what are you talking about?" asked Malakai.

"You asked me the other day what the greatest story in the bible is relevant today. I just witnessed it; you are talking about the story of the Good Samaritan," said Rose.

"I love your intelligence, and you are one hundred percent correct, grasshopper," said Malakai.

"One of the reasons I love communicating with you is during the process of interaction, a little of you rubs off on me. Similarly, a little of me rubs off on you," said Rose.

"We are all on a journey that is called life, to learn as we go along and to learn from each other. We exist to help, lend a hand, and lift up each other. That is why we are here. For example, the dress you are wearing, and the slippers you are wearing were all made by different people, therefore, we are dependent on each other for our survival, and we cannot survive by ourselves. Plus, when we do good for each other, angels sing our name in heaven," said Malakai.

Rose, laughing, said, "Amen to that, my brother."

A few more minutes later, Malakai and Rose entered the Riu Ocho Rios Resort property, where Malakai took out the luggage and parked the car. They went to the front desk, where they were checked in on the fifth floor and given an ocean-view room. The hotel is all-inclusive; therefore, all meals and drinks are included in the price. The room was spacious with all the amenities of an air conditioner, king-sized bed, refrigerator stocked with liquor, and satellite television. They unpacked their suitcase and took a shower, dressed and went downstairs to have dinner.

Dinner was buffet style with food of every variety and smelling quite sumptuous in the cool evening air. They ate slowly enjoying the dining experiences and each other company. The food tasted extremely good, and the services were top-class. After an hour and a half, they left the dining area and went to explore the property. The resort had six restaurants, six bars, a tennis court, and two pools, and it is one of those newly built Spanish hotels in Jamaica, consisting of over five hundred rooms.

They went by the beach area and walked barefoot, carrying their shoes in their hands. Rose hugged Malakai and said, "I just love the clean smell of the Caribbean Sea and that salty ocean smell and the feel of sea sand beneath my bare foot massaging it."

"Me too. I do not want to be in a world where these simple things cannot be appreciated and not treasured. Believe it or not, even in Jamaica, where tourism is the main source of foreign exchange, sometimes the poor local resident, around ten decades ago, usually removed the sand and utilized it for their home construction. This practice was ended with better education and awareness that the country's tourism is dependent on the sand and sea," said Malakai.

"Education and awareness is always a good thing. One of the things that I am very appreciative of you is your love of nature and respect for the environment, and that makes me love you even more," said Rose.

Malakai looked at Rose lovingly, wanting to tell her who he really was, but he was scared, not knowing how Rose would respond. He loved her too much, and the incident with the men in the park just cemented his position not to tell her even more because he did not want to cause any more commotion within their relationship. One of the reasons he had wanted to take her to Jamaica was that he'd thought that a romantic getaway like Jamaica might do the trick.

He accepted and knew he could trust her, but telling her such a momentous thing might just shatter their relationship, and somehow, he did not want to take that gamble. He thought that he was going to have some fun with Rose and see how she was going to react to his provocation. He looked at her and said, "You are only saying that you love me because I am capable of taking you on vacation to a place like Jamaica."

Rose looked at Malakai with disgust, could hardly believe what he was hearing from this man who she loved unconditionally, doubting her love, "Malakai, fuck you, I am capable of coming to Jamaica all on my own. Maybe I would not be able to stay at all those grand resorts, but I would be able to stay at the cheaper resort, so fuck you again and get lost." said Rose.

"You know you have a potty mouth," said Malakai.

"I am glad you realize that I have a potty mouth, not only to use it to have you pleasured," said Rose.

Malakai started laughing and slapped Rose on her ass, and said, "I was joking. I was just messing with you."

"Kai, do not touch me nor slap my ass," said Rose.

Malakai rushed ahead of Rose, blocked her way and said, "Seriously, let me apologize to you. I just wanted to see how you would react when I said you do not love me. I know you love me with all my heart, and I love you too with all my heart. Plus, the way you screamed my name when we were making love. Darling, it can only be love," said Malakai.

Rose, smiling, pushed Malakai out of the way and said, "You know what I hate about myself? I cannot stay mad with you for too long."

Rose accepted Malakai's apology, and they kissed and made up.

They left the beach area and went to take in the cabaret performance for the night. The cabaret singer was extremely good, with his repertoire of songs from reggae, hip hop, and rhythm and blues. The cabaret singer's stage performance was also quite immaculate and memorable, as the guests clapped at the end of each of his performances. After the cabaret singer's performance was finished, Rose decided she was feeling tired and wanted to retire for the night.

Malakai opened their room door and rushed into the bathroom to get his shower. Rose went in afterward with a cryptic smile on her face. When Rose came out of the shower, she had a white towel wrapped around her body. Malakai was in the bed in his shorts. Rose went into one of the suitcases, took out two sturdy ties and told Malakai that they were going to have bondage sex tonight.

Rose went over to Malakai and tied his hand to the bed headpost. She dragged off his shorts and then removed the towel that was around her body, leaving her completely naked in the room. She went over Malakai, moved his rock-hard erection out of the way and straddled Malakai, sitting almost on his stomach area. She bent and lowered her chest in Malakai's face. He started kissing her large, gorgeous breast like a hungry, ravenous beast. She removed her breast from his rather greedy mouth and started kissing him passionately as she saw how excited it was making Malakai. Rose suddenly pressed

Malakai's head backward, stopped kissing him and came off him and told him goodnight.

Malakai was totally flummoxed as he stared at Rose's nakedness, and she was not even trying to cover her body to allow his rock-hard erection to go flaccid on the bed. Malakai smiled and asked, "Rose, why are you treating me this way?"

"I said goodnight, Mr. Malakai. Do not disturb someone when they are trying to get some sleep," said Rose.

"Call the police or the FBI because this is inhumane treatment," said Malakai.

Rose laughed and said, "You really want me to call the police with your dick erect and pointing towards the ceiling? I do not think so. My darling, I just wanted to see how you reacted when I played the same game you played on me today by the beach. Tell me truthfully, do you like the feeling or this form of treatment? I do not think so. Therefore, what you do not like, you do not apply to other people and especially to me. I am your woman, and never doubt that I love you again," said Rose.

Malakai smiled and said, "I have learnt my lesson. Now, please do something about my erection because I think I may have blue balls."

Rose went over to Malakai and started kissing him and teasing him with her tongue. She kissed him slowly, deliberately, all over his body until he started begging her to insert his penis into her vagina. She refused his request and watched the visceral reaction it was having on him, and she was enjoying herself with that feminine power she wielded over Malakai. Malakai was begging and pleading, and it was quite an intoxicating feeling. She was getting more turned on as the minutes ticked by slowly in the hotel room.

Rose started to kiss and tease his body when she suddenly orgasm. She savored her orgasmic moment and then went and straddled Malakai, but instead of facing him front way, she turned her back towards him, allowing Malakai to see more of the sex act. She was in control of his penile penetration, and she wanted to have one more orgasm. She thrust on his penis slowly and rhythmically because she did not want to excite him too much for him to have premature ejaculation. As she continued to thrust on his penis, she could feel Malakai's penis getting more engorged and excited. She climaxed just as he ejaculated inside her body. Rose untied Malakai, and they went to sleep embracing each other.

***

The next morning, they got up at nine o'clock and went downstairs for breakfast. Breakfast was buffet-styled on the terrace. Both of them had ackee and salt fish for breakfast, served with boiled white yams, boiled bananas, fried ripe plantains, and toast. As they were eating, Rose took up a piece of the ackee and threw it in a rectangular area where two small green lizards were among some plants.

The two small lizards greedily gobbled up the small pieces of ackee, and three more small lizards came off the plants to join in the consumption of the food. Malakai threw some more of the ackee, and the lizards gobbled up more of the food. Malakai said, "That's the immigration problem we have in America in a nutshell."

"What do you mean?" asked Rose.

"You were born in the United States of America, the most prosperous country in the history of the world. Due to the fact that America is the most prosperous country, some people will want to come there by any means necessary to have a piece of the American dream or to have a higher standard of living. That is people in general; they will always want to better their lives. Bear in mind America is no different than many countries such as Egypt, Greece, Italy, Spain, and England that was extremely prosperous at one time in their history, and people came from all over the globe to live there. All I am saying is that human beings are beneficiaries of planet Earth and not its owner. Therefore, if we are beneficiaries, we need to welcome the weary war-torn travelers," said Malakai.

"Are you saying a country should not have a border?" asked Rose.

"No, I am not saying any such thing. Borders or a wall can be good if it is to protect the citizens of a country. What I am saying is when you see a demagogue talking about immigration, it is always a recipe for disaster. The history of America is one where, when the Irish, Scottish, Italian, and Jews came, there was always some demagogue not wanting to welcome them and almost certainly saying these various groups would not assimilate. These demagogues forgot that America is a melting pot, and if it were not, the country would not be so successful. Samuel Johnson said patriotism is the last refuge of scoundrel, meaning that demagogues always wrapped themselves in the flag of a country and forgot their basic humanity to other people," said Malakai.

"People are always fearful of other people, especially when they do not look like them. We are so tribalized in our outlook that, as you said, as people, we forget our own basic humanity to another individual. We treat each other with total disdain and become unconcern about other people's lives," said Rose.

They finished eating breakfast, then they went swimming on the beach and lounged on a beach chair in the shade. They chatted, drank, and swam until it was lunchtime. At midday, they left the beach and washed off the saltwater using an outside shower. They then went to have lunch. Lunch was all local cuisine giving the visitors a taste of the island food. Malakai and Rose enjoyed the local cuisine and went for additional servings.

Chapter 12

After lunch, Malakai decided he was going to take Rose into the town to do a little sightseeing. They went and changed their attire then left the room and drove off the property. Malakai drove into the town of Ocho Rios, showing her the Reynolds Pier where cruise ships docked. He then drove through the street, driving slowly, showing her the huge hotels along the strips.

Malakai also took Rose to the craft market where she bought a few items. He stopped at a Texaco gas station and filled up the car with gas. He showed her the food market where the local people of the town bought and sold their agriculture produce. When they left the market, they drove and stopped at the duty free shops. Rose was looking at a very exquisite, expensive necklace. Malakai looked at her and asked, "Do you want it?"

"Yes, but I think it is too expensive," said Rose.

"Do not worry your lovely self about that. Let me purchase it for you. Are you my girl or not?" asked Malakai.

"No, I am not your girl, I am your woman, and will always be," said Rose.

Malakai motioned his hand over to the salesman to get the manager. The manager, an ebullient, stocky Indian man with wide-brimmed glasses, came over and Malakai explained that he wanted to purchase the necklace, but he wanted a discount.

The manager gave Malakai the discount and he paid for the necklace in cash. Rose was beaming and told Malakai *thanks* for purchasing the necklace. Malakai told her to take it out of the box and wear it. Rose did as he requested, and as they departed, Rose kept feeling the necklace with her hand as they left the duty free shop. They drove back to the hotel with Rose leaning on Malakai's arms as if not wanting to be out of his presence.

They went straight to their room to get ready for dinner. While they were in the room, Malakai called Rodigan and told him they were staying at the hotel and he will come by on Sunday with Rose. Rose wore a short blue colored dress and the necklace to dinner. After the dinner, there was a cultural performance displaying a slice of the Jamaican culture, involving African dancing, and limbo performances with some of the guests taking part. After the cultural performance ended, Malakai and Rose went dancing until after one o'clock when they retired to their bed.

The next morning, after Rose and Malakai had breakfast, they took their camera and drove off the property to visit the world famous waterfall in Jamaica known as *Dunn's River Fall*. It was a popular destination for tourists visiting the island and for locals wanting to climb the waterfall. The waterfall is about one hundred and eighty foot in height with several small tributaries emptying their water into the beach below. Dunn's River Fall water is supplied by spring water rich in calcium carbonate. The fall is surrounded by lush green vegetation that provides shades from the blistering heat of the sun. Visitors climbing the fall are generally led by a guide who encourages climbers to hold hands, forming a human chain, allowing the climb to be safer and less stressful for first time climbers.

The Dunn's River Fall is located about five minutes from the hotel where Malakai and Rose were staying on the North coast of the island. Malakai parked the car in the carpark and paid the entrance fee to enter the fall. As they entered the park they went to a shop where they rented shoes for the climb. They went by the beach area and bought drinks, chatted with one another until they were ready to climb. Another thirty minutes later, they started climbing the fall by themselves. Since Malakai knew the fall like the back of his hand, so he did not need any guide to take them up the top. They stopped at certain points to take pictures as the cool water came rushing from the hilltop. They stopped at a small cavern-like spot where the water rushed over them, concealing them and they started kissing and fondling each other's bodies. They continued on their way, stopping at various points taking pictures until they finally reached the top of the fall.

Rose decided she wanted to climb the fall again because she enjoyed the cool water running over her body, but Malakai told her they needed to get something to eat before they attempted it. They went and bought lunch of chicken and chips and pineapple juices. After finishing their lunch, they took another hour before they started climbing the fall. Rose felt more confident and was not holding on to Malakai. They stopped at certain point on the way up to the top of the fall taking more pictures until they reached the top of the fall. They returned the rented shoes and drove out of the fall carpark.

Malakai drove – not to their hotel, but near the town of Ocho Rios and stopped off at Island Village. They parked and walked up some board steps and entered. Island Village was a shopping area where there is a wide range of shops of all varieties. There was generally entertainment provided, sometimes of a cultural nature. Malakai loved visiting Island Village because of the beach and the view it offered visitors.

As Malakai showed Rose the place, they walked by Jimmy Buffet Margaritaville full of patrons he took her inside the stores. Rose did not see anything she liked so they kept on walking until they arrived at the beach area where Rose decided she wanted to experience the beach.

They went into the water, and it was warm and inviting, and there were not many people there, so it was even better for Rose to swim freely and enjoy the beach. They had a great time swimming and sitting on the beautiful white sands, until they decided it was time to leave the beach.

As they were walking, Rose saw an ice cream shop known as Devon House Ice Cream. Malakai told her it was great tasting ice cream because they only used local fruits to make it. Malakai went and bought one sugar cone ice cream for her to eat, and Malakai told her he was lactose intolerant, so he did not want any. Rose started eating her sugar cone ice cream and told Malakai it tasted *so* good that he must taste it. Rose looked at Malakai and said, "Please have some, because it really tastes great."

"I do not need any. I told you I am lactose intolerant," said Malakai.

"Have some, it really does taste great," said Rose.

Not really satisfied that Malakai was not having any of the ice cream, Rose took the ice cream cone and pushed it straight into Malakai's mouth. Malakai started eating the ice cream and they bought two more.

They left Island Village and drove back to their hotel room to get ready for dinner. They had their shower, dressed, and went downstairs to have dinner and watched the entertainment provided by the resort. After the dinner, entertainment was finished and Rose and

Malakai decided to retire to their room because they were feeling a little tired.

As they were in bed, Rose started kissing Malakai and asked, "Why does my libido seem so much more enhanced when I am in Jamaica?"

Malakai quite facetiously said, "It is the man you are with. Seriously, you are at a place where you are totally relaxing and enjoying yourself and life, so naturally, your body is going to crave a big dick," said Malakai.

"Okay, Mr. Big Dick man! Take off your shorts and let's have sex," said Rose.

As Malakai took off his shorts and spun Rose around to insert his penis inside her she heard a loud sound and asked, "What is that sound?"

"I am farting all because you insisted that I must eat the damned blasted ice cream!" said Malakai.

Rose turned around and had a good laugh at Malakai's expense. She could not help herself and said, "That was quite funny, the moment you were going to insert your penis, you started to fart."

Malakai had stopped farthing and said, "That erection is not going down by itself, so please turn around and let's have sex."

Rose complied and they started having sex and afterward they went to bed.

They got up Sunday morning and went for breakfast. Malakai reminded Rose that they were going by Rodigan in the hills for the day. Around noon, Malakai put the suitcase with the things they had brought for Rodigan in the car. Rose was elegantly dressed in a short blue dress with matching high heels, and the necklace that Malakai bought adorned her neck.

They drove off the resort property with Malakai looking forward to seeing Rodigan, Michael, and Grace because they were the nearest and dearest thing to a family he had in the world. As they drove by and looked where the car accident had taken place a couple days ago, they did not see the car. Malakai thought more or less it was taken up by a wrecker and taken to a nearby garage.

Malakai looked at Rose approvingly and said, "These people that I am taking you to meet are the closest thing to a family I have in this world. Rodigan is the reason why I am alive today. He can be rather uncouth, but he does not mean any harm. He can be very charming at the same time. Grace is a mother, so she is very protective of her family, and that includes me."

"I understand and I will charm them with my *winning* personality." said Rose.

"That is not a problem! Plus, Rodigan will charm off the panties you are wearing!" said Malakai.

Rose quite facetiously said, "I am not wearing any, so there will not be any to charm off from my body."

Malakai quickly slammed the car brake, and the car made a sudden stop, and said, "Woman I am taking you to see my family and you are not wearing any drawers?"

"I am just joking. I am wearing my G-string," said Rose.

"I know you are joking because I saw when you were putting on the matching G-string panty and bra this morning. I told you I love a woman with wit. Thank you for not disappointing me," said Malakai.

"I should have realized that you were joking because I saw you looking at me. Sorry, let me correct that statement. I saw you *lusting* after me when I was putting them on!" said Rose.

"I was looking at you for sure and even lusting for my woman. Remember, I told you I am a man who appreciates gorgeous lingerie on a beautiful woman," said Malakai.

As Malakai resumed driving, Rose unbuckled her seatbelt and cozied up under Malakai's arms. He extended his left arm over her, embracing her and enjoying the moment. Malakai drove for another fifteen minutes when they finally arrived at a beautiful big house on a hill with a fabulous view of the sea. Malakai stopped at the house gate and opened it, drove inside, and closed the gate.

As they drove inside, the yard there were fruit trees such as mango, breadfruit, orange, banana, ackee, and naseberry throughout the property. Malakai drove closer to the house and honked the car horn, and three people came from inside the house.

Grace was a tall, beautiful black woman and elegantly dressed that displayed an aura of charm and confidence, while Rodigan was a tall, fai-skinned muscular man with long elegantly styled dreadlocks. The young boy was eight years old and devilishly handsome.

Malakai and Rose got out the car and the young boy ran towards them and hurled himself at Malakai. Malakai caught the boy in midair as they embraced each other, and Malakai kissed him on the cheeks and said, "I bought you the newest Play Station and an iPhone. *Hey*, Michael, you are growing so big and tall."

"Thanks for the Play Station Uncle Malakai! I am so glad to see you!"

Malakai walked toward the man and they embraced each other for around a minute. Malakai pulled away from the man embraced and embraced the lady standing beside the man. The woman and

Malakai kissed each other on the cheeks and finally they released each other from their embrace.

Malakai said, "Everybody, this is Rose. She is my woman and the love of my life. Rose this is Rodigan, Michael, and Grace."

Rodigan, Michael, and Grace each took turns embracing Rose and welcoming her to their home. Malakai took the suitcase out of the car and gave it to Rodigan. They all went into the house where Rodigan showed Rose around the house, which was extremely well furnished with local and Italian furniture.

As Rose and Rodigan came back into the living room," Then, "Malakai, my boy, you have certainly chosen wisely, Rose is indeed a beautiful and intelligent woman. Rose you are the first woman he has brought to Jamaica, so you should know how special you are to him, and by extension, to all of us."

"I did not know that I am the first girl that he has brought here."

"I hope you are all hungry because I have cooked up a feast. Let me go into the kitchen," said Grace.

"We had breakfast at the hotel and that was it. We have not eaten since, so we are pretty hungry." said Rose.

Grace went into the kitchen while Rose sat in the living room with Michael watching television. Malakai and Rodigan excused themselves and went into another part of the house to chat. Malakai took the box out of his pocket and showed Rodigan the Amulet of Osiris and told him how he came by it and how the Alliance Organization was searching for it. Rodigan told Malakai that Egyptians believed that Osiris was god of the dead and the amulet gave Osiris or the wearer the power to command the spirit of the dead. Rodigan further explained that the Alliance Organization wanted the amulet to disrupt God plans for human when they die. Rodigan implored Malakai that he could not allow the Alliance Organization to get hold of the amulet and he would have to take it to one of the many volcanoes of Venus to be destroyed whenever he was going back to space.

Rodigan also questioned Malakai if Rose knew who he was and about the Alliance Organization. Malakai told him Rose was ignorant about everything and he wanted to keep it that way.

Grace knocked on the door for the men to come for dinner. They all left the room and went in the dining room where Michael and Rose were seated and waiting around the table. The table was adorned with fine cutleries, glasses that sparkled upon a white tablecloth. The meal consisted of brown stew fish, and grilled lobster. After they consumed the meal, they had pineapple upside down cake and black forest cake for dessert. Rose enjoyed her meal and said, "Grace, the meal was fabulous, I enjoyed it. Thanks for having me here."

"You are always welcome at our table, my dear. Any friend of Malakai is always welcome here," said Grace.

Grace got up and cleared the table of the dishes and said, "Rose, lets go outside to talk."

The two women left the dining room where the two men were chatting and drinking and went to converse on the verandah. They sat on soft comfortable chair facing each other, as if they were sizing the other up.

Grace looked intently at Rose and said, "Malakai is like a son to me. I have cooked and cleaned for him until he decided to leave for the United States of America. I have loved him as my own child. I see that he loves you; there is no question about that. My question to you is: do you love him the same way?"

"Yes, I do love him unconditionally, not because he can take me on expensive vacations. I love him because of the man he is: caring and considerate. I hope that one day he will wait for me as I walk down the aisle as his wife," said Rose.

"I know for a fact that he would love to marry you one of these days but let me caution you: do not rush Malakai. Let him take his time to come to that decision," said Grace.

"Oh, I would never pressure him to make that type of decision," said Rose.

"As women, we are not ignoring all of society's norms. If Malakai wants to marry you, let him buy a big ass expensive ring and put it on your finger and have the wedding ceremony here, at my place! I would be able to arrange everything, including the wedding cake. It is your damned day, have a big or a small intimate wedding with your friends and family, if you so desire." said Grace.

"It would be a small intimate wedding. You see, my parents died in a car crash coming back from church. The other driver was drunk... It's been seven years –"

"I understand," Grace interrupted, not wanting Rose to relive the whole thing. "Sorry to hear about your parents' accident," she said.

"I have accepted it and moved on with my life," said Rose.

"That's the spirit. As human beings, we have to accept that death is a part of life," said Grace, her tone sympathetic.

"Yes. I agree. And, as for the intimate wedding… it's how my parents would have wanted it. Oh!" Rose interjected. "By the way, thanks for those lovely designer dresses because I know Malakai would not know anything about women's fashion!"

Grace smiled, appreciating the change in tone. "You're welcome. Anything to make your day special. Let us go back inside the house to the men.

The women left the verandah and rejoined the men who were in the living room chatting about politics. The women entered the conversation engaging in friendly banter with the men until Grace excused herself and went on the verandah and called Malakai.

Grace explained to Malakai what Rose had said. He grabbed Grace and kissed her on the cheeks and told her *thanks* for talking on his behalf to Rose. Malakai and Grace went back into the living room rejoining Rose and Rodigan. They chatted until around nine o'clock in the night when Malakai decided it was time to depart for their hotel.

They kissed and embraced each other and bid farewell, and Malakai promised he would not stay away that long.

As they drove away from the beautiful house, Malakai was a little bit nostalgic and said, "I really missed this place. I have had a lot of good memories."

"We will be back if you decide to take me. I see why you love and care for them. They seem like decent, lovely people and I like them myself!" said Rose.

"They are good people and the closest thing to a family I have. They are the only people I trust completely – apart from you, of course – in this world," said Malakai.

As they continued to drive back to their hotel, Rose asked, "What was it like growing up in Jamaica as a child?"

Malakai thought for a moment and replied, "It was actually a lot of fun and as a child I was involved in lots of shenanigans especially when I was in primary school at around age six. I remembered once the Ministry of Health sent some opticians to our school to test the students who were having eye problems. Three of my friends, including me, went into the line to see the optician because we wanted to be ditch math class. When it was our turn to see the optician, a tall Jamaican nurse enquired of us what was wrong with our eyes. My friend Lloyd said I have elephantiasis, my second friend said I have polio, my third friend said I have syphilis. As children we did not have a clue what these diseases or sicknesses were. We did not realizing it was not part of the eye. The tall Jamaican nurse held them by their hands and turned towards me and asked what is wrong with your eyes. On seeing the nurse detain my friends, I looked directly in her eyes and said nothing is wronged with my eyes.

The nurse marched all four of us straight back to math class with our tail between our legs."

Rose laughed heartily at the story as they entered on the main road. They soon drove inside the hotel and went upstairs to their room. Malakai and Rose decided they would just spend the night in the room and make the most of tomorrow. They took a shower and went to bed.

***

Malakai and Rose woke quite early the next morning and put on their swimsuits. They left the room and went straight to the beach. They hoped to make the best of the last day at the resort and on the island.

There were not many people at the beach in the early morning. They entered the water, which was kind of lukewarm, but as they started playing and splashing the water at each other, the water became warmer on their bodies. They swam quite a while, enjoying the beautiful clear blue sea water, and each other's company. After a couple hours in the water, they decided to go and have breakfast. They dried off their bodies with a towel and put on their white t-shirts and went to have breakfast.

After breakfast, they went back to the beach and entered the water and swam some more. During the day, they also took part in the beach games, and dancing competition.

Malakai and Rose rented jet skis for one hour and they rode the waves and went as far as they could go in the water with just enough fuel to take them back to the resort. They came back from riding the jet skis and went windsurfing. After the windsurfing ended, they came back on the resort and went in the outdoor Jacuzzi and had lunch afterward.

Having eaten lunch, they went for a walk, then they lay on a lounge chair with Malakai embracing Rose as she lay on his chest.

Later in the evening, Rose went by the spa to get a thirty-minute massage and also went by the hair salon to get her hair looked after for her trip back to the States. Malakai went by the beach bar to have a drink while he waited for Rose. Malakai had many drinks until Rose finally came out of the hair salon to get him and they went upstairs to their room to get ready for dinner. They had their shower, dressed, and came downstairs to have dinner. After dinner they watched the local cabaret show and when it was finished, they went dancing at the night club. They left the night club at around twelve-thirty and went to their room where they made passionate love with each other then went to sleep.

They got up out of bed at seven o'clock in the morning, brushed their teeth, and went downstairs to have breakfast. They quickly consumed their delicious local cuisine breakfast and rushed back to their room to get a shower and checked out of their room.

They left their room at around eight fifteen and went to the front desk to check out of the hotel. Malakai paid the bills that they owed, and they checked out of the hotel with the front desk agent wishing them a safe flight and imploring them to come back to the hotel when they decided to return to Jamaica.

Malakai went for the rented Toyota Camry and drove it up the lobby and put in their suitcases and drove off the resort property. Rose looked back at the hotel as they were driving through the hotel gate and said, "I do not want to go home as of yet. I love Jamaica."

"We will come back another time my queen," said Malakai.

"Kai, promise me you will take me back to Jamaica when the time is right," said Rose.

"Woman, I *promise* to take you back to Jamaica," said Malakai.

Malakai continued to drive and as they drove past the Bauxite Company in Discovery Bay, Rose asked Malakai to pull over on the right at a place called Columbus Park. Malakai and Rose got out of the car, looking at the breath taking view of the harbor and the beautiful clear blue water when Rose said, "I want to tell you I am very appreciative of you taking me to Jamaica. I want to tell you also I am deeply in love with you and if I do not get the opportunity again, I will always love you, and want to be a part of your life always."

Malakai looked at Rose directly in her face, took both hands to hold her face, and kissed her passionately and deeply and said, "I carry your essence and your spirit with me always. I am deeply in love with you and I do not want to be without you."

They continued kissing until they went back into the car and continued on their journey to the airport. They arrived at the airport around forty-five minutes later with Malakai parking the car at the departure section and quickly getting out to take the suitcase out of the car. Malakai told Rose to check in and that she would see him inside the departure gate of Caribbean Airline because he would have to take the rented car back to the car rental agency.

Malakai took the car back to the car rental agency and settled his account.

Malakai then went to the Caribbean Airline desk and checked in at the counter. He then went to their departure gate where he saw Rose. He called her and took her to the various duty free shops where they bought rum, perfume, cologne, and some beautiful, designed t-shirt. After they were finished shopping, it was time to board the plane. They boarded the plane and sat in business class.

Soon after they departed for the John F. Kennedy International Airport to New York.

Chapter 13

Wallenstein, Thornbird, Vallencourt, and a couple senior agents were in the boardroom late Saturday night, strategizing, when Wallenstein suggested that he had a hunch that hopefully may pay off in the acquisition of the amulet. He asked Vallencourt to adjourn the meeting as he left the boardroom and called an agent named Sandro. He told Sandro he wanted him to follow Wildflower the following morning to church. Clandestinely.

***

It was a warm beautiful Sunday morning the next day and Wildflower was on her way to church. She was intentionally followed by a black Ford Explorer driven by one of the Alliance Organization agents. Wallenstein requested that the agent follow her to church and to follow Reverend Watkiss home at the end of the service to see where he resided in the community.

As she arrived and parked, the black Ford Explorer parked around a hundred yards from her car. The agent's job was not to enter the church but stay put and follow the Reverend home. Wildflower had given the agent a picture of the Reverend and the car he drove to the church.

Wildflower entered the church dressed immaculately – all in designer; matching high heels and handbag. Most of the men and a few of the women in the congregation turned around to stare, admiring her beauty. She took her seat in the church as Reverend Watkiss continued to preach to his congregation about being a good Christian and ensuring that their soul is right with God.

After the service, Wildflower sat in her seat waiting on the Reverend to greet and say goodbye to his congregation. As all the people left the church, the Reverend came over to Wildflower and said, "Hello, my dear, I hope the spirit of the Lord shines his light on you this morning."

"Cut the shit, you know who I am. Do you have any information for me?" asked Wildflower.

"I have no information that will be of any use or help to you," said the Reverend.

"I have something that can help *you*. I am looking for a white male. That's all I've got for now. Will that help?" asked Wildflower.

"White male, huh… quite a lot of those around… But I will see what I can come up with to assist you in retrieving the amulet," said Reverend Watkiss.

"Don't disappoint us, Reverend. Goodbye for now," said Wildflower.

Wildflower walked out of the church, mindful of the fact that Reverend Watkiss was not going to willingly help her retrieve the amulet. She came to the realization that she would have to put her plans in place to force information out of him. She was desperate and whatever she had to do, she would – all in the name of the amulet. Even if it meant chopping off the Reverend's head.

She did not trust him. She often wondered if he was revealing everything to her honestly about who had the amulet or its whereabouts. She walked down the steps and nodded her head to agent Sandro as she entered her car and drove away from the church.

***

Around two and half hours later, Reverend Watkiss came outside, sat in his his Honda Accord, and drove away from the church. Agent Sandro allowed three cars to go ahead of him before he started his own began following the Reverend. Sandro followed him until he entered the Canarsie area of Brooklyn. The Canarsie area was a middle class area in the southeastern borough of Brooklyn. The Reverend parked his car at the entrance of a yard with a garage door. Sandro quickly parked his on the side of the road, behind several cars. He observed the Reverend as he took his attaché case out of his car and then closed the door. Walking over to his house, he took out his house, unlocked the door, and went inside. Sandro quickly became invisible and followed him inside.

Agent Sandro's mission was to observe Reverend Watkiss and report back to Wallenstein what he saw or heard in the house. Sandro, in invisible form, followed the Reverend around the three bedrooms. He observed that there was no other person living in the house. Sandro went into the living room, looking to see if he could see any pictures of a family member but was unable to ascertain anything in his quest. Reverend Watkiss went into the kitchen to prepare his dinner and Agent Sandro took the chance to rifle through some papers in the Reverend's living room. Sandro could not find anything in the papers, so he promptly left the house, satisfied that he had gotten all the basic information.

Agent Sandro went back into his car and drove to Manhattan to his home.

The next morning, he went to work at the Alliance Organization headquarters in Manhattan and went directly to Wallenstein's office. Wallenstein was already there. Sandro gave him the Reverend's address of Canarsie, Brooklyn. Sandro furthered told Wallenstein that Reverend Watkiss lived alone and did not seem to entertain guests. Sandro gave Wallenstein a few more details then left his office.

Wallenstein was glad to receive the information from Sandro about Reverend Watkiss. He knew time was running out and he had to put all his plans at the forefront to recover the amulet.

Wallenstein went into Vallencourt's office and told him of his plan to acquire the amulet by using Wildflower. He stipulated that there was a possibility that the plan may not work, but if it did, he knew it would be worth the effort. Vallencourt gave Wallenstein his blessing to go ahead and execute his plan by Friday, because time was of the essence, and presently, that was the only plan they had of acquiring the amulet. Vallencourt implored Wallenstein also to be careful and not to put himself in any unnecessary situation. Wallenstein promised Vallencourt that he would be careful. Wallenstein spent a few more minutes chatting, then bid Vallencourt goodbye.

***

Friday night at around eight thirty, Reverend Watkiss came out of the shower. As he was about to dry off his body, he heard the front doorbell ring. Hurriedly, he finished drying off, sprayed some cologne on his body, tied a white towel around his hip, and ran to the front door, wondering who was it was so late at his house. He opened the front door and was flabbergasted when he saw Wildflower. Reverend Watkiss composed himself and asked, "What are you doing at my home?"

"Are you not going to invite me inside?" asked Wildflower.

"I do not think it is a good idea" said Reverend Watkiss.

"I need to speak to you urgently, so please allow me," said Wildflower.

Reverend Watkiss moved from behind the door and Wildflower entered the house. She was dressed in a Versace design tight fitting red dress that accentuated her gorgeous body. He black high heels complemented her look. Her curvaceous bosom was left half exposed to be looked at and desired by any man with breath in his lungs. Wildflower looked around the house and asked, "Are we alone?"

"Yes, we are. Please state your business and leave," said Reverend Watkiss, quite concerned with Wildflower's unexpected visit.

Wildflower looked at Reverend Watkiss' half-naked body and smiled. "I did not know you had those lovely muscles on your body. It's because you are always covered in that stupid gown."

"What do you want?" asked Reverend Watkiss.

Wildflower looked at Reverend Watkiss and laughed, knowing that he was quite uncomfortable with her in his home. She stopped smiling, teasingly turned around intentionally for Reverend

Watkiss to see how her dress clung to her lovely bottom and asked, "Anything on the amulet?"

"No, I have not come up with anything. The information is too vague for me to garner anything about the amulet," said Reverend Watkiss.

Reverend Watkiss looked deep into Wildflower's beautiful face, trying to decipher what was going on in her head and what she wanted. As he was staring into her face, she flicked her finger, and he was hypnotized, focused only on the beautiful woman in front of him.

Wildflower knew she would not be able to get any information from him by just asking him questions. She knew she had to seduce him and said, "Listen to my voice, and only my voice. You and I are lovers and we have not seen each other for many months…"

As Wildflower stopped speaking, Reverend Watkiss grabbed her with his huge arms and kissed her hungrily and with a passion like a man who had not had a woman for years. Wildflower was surprised by the sensation he awakened in her body. She had not had sex in a while… not with a woman, nor a man. She had to tell herself to focus on the task at hand and not the man that was on top of her, kissing her with unbridled passion. She was enjoying the, Reverend… he was very adventurous. She pushed him away and led him to the bedroom.

As they entered the bedroom, Wildflower turned around and Reverend Watkiss unzipped her dress from the back. He started kissing her lips then her neck and as he was kissing her, she loosened the towel around his waist. She smiled when she saw the huge penis on the Reverend. She pushed him on the bed while she finished taking off her red dress to reveal a lacy black bra and lacy black G-string panties. Wildflower slowly took them off, putting on a show for the Reverend. She went on the bed and lay on top of him, and they started kissing each other as if they were some teenaged lovers.

Reverend Watkiss gently moved Wildflower off on top of him and switched position with her as he continued kissing her and slowly moved his lips to her neck, then slowly traced his tongue to her ample breast. Reverend Watkiss squeezed, teased, and sucked her breasts with great relish and hunger. Wildflower squirmed and wriggled as Reverend Watkiss' tongue moved between her legs and her inner thigh, she writhed under the sensation which seemed almost electric. She could not bear the intense sensation anymore and she screamed with ecstasy, climaxing as she held Reverend Watkiss' head between her thighs.

She was glad that she was the one who'd had the orgasm, because if it was Reverend Watkiss, the hypnotism would wear off, plus, she would be much more in control of the situation now that she had achieved her orgasm.

Wildflower quickly got on top of Reverend Watkiss and started kissing him slowly and deliberately, using her tongue to tease him as she performed fellatio. The feeling was so intense that Reverend Watkiss held Wildflower's head for a minute for the sensation to subside. As the sensation subsided, Reverend Watkiss allowed Wildflower to resume but she could feel his penis getting more engorged in her mouth. She stopped her tongue teasing allowing him more time to be less excited as she stared directly into his eyes.

After around a minute, Wildflower went and straddled Reverend Watkiss. She was facing him directly as she used her hand to slowly direct his huge penis inside her vagina. She grimaced slightly as she felt the extent of his penis inside of her body. She started to thrust slowly, not wanting for him to get overly excited and climax, thereby ruining her plan.

Wildflower always thought the closest you could be to a person was when you were both naked, vulnerable, and intimate. As she reached out with both hands to his face and held his head, Reverend Watkiss begun to thrust deeper and more forcefully into her vagina. She took her right hand and pressed his pelvic area to slow down his thrust, because she could not afford for him to climax and end the fun. She reached out with both hands and held his head and said, "Michael Watkiss, I am the long-lost love of your life! I need to know who has the amulet of Osiris."

Reverend Watkiss was in a deep trance, but he could understand Wildflower's question. Deep somewhere in his subconscious, he was trying to fight her by not answering. Wildflower realized that he was trying to resist, so she got off him.

Reverend Watkiss used both of his large hands and slid himself back into Wildflower. Wildflower was trying hard not to enjoy the man and his large gift. As Reverend Watkiss slid his penis inside her, she could feel the awesome power of his erection as he thrust deeper inside her body. She reached out with both hand and held his face again and asked, "Tell me who has the amulet?"

Reverend Watkiss uttered a sound, sounding like the letter "R," but Wildflower could not understand, so she asked again, "Tell me who has the amulet?"

"Rose…" said Reverend Watkiss.

Wildflower was getting quite excited when she heard the first name of the person, but she wanted a surname and asked, "Rose who?"

There was total silence as Reverend Watkiss continued to thrust deeper inside her vagina. Wildflower removed her vagina from Reverend Watkiss penis, and he slid his hand under her rear and dragged it back on his penis. Wildflower could feel Reverend Watkiss' penis getting more engorged and she knew he was about to ejaculate any moment. She put her hand on his head again and asked, "What's her full name?"

"Rose Winter!" said Reverend Watkiss.

Wildflower was totally perplexed because she knew Rose Winter and was even at her apartment. She knew Rose was not of their kind so she must have had an accomplice. She looked at Reverend Watkiss and asked, "Who of our kind is Rose's accomplice?"

"It is Rose and Mal!" said Reverend Watkiss.

Just as Reverend Watkiss was about to call the other person's name, he quickly switched position with him on top of Wildflower on the bed and he continued thrusting deep inside her vagina. He climaxed in a few seconds shooting a load of thick semen inside her vagina.

Wildflower clicked her finger and ordered Reverend Watkiss to go into a deep sleep. She looked at him, sleeping on the bed, and she thought of killing him for lying to her, but she pushed the thought out of her mind. Wildflower was glad that she followed her instinct and got maybe a priceless lead to where they may recover the amulet.

She hurriedly dressed and said to the sleeping Reverend, "You are no longer hypnotized, and you will not remember any of this." She looked around ensuring that nothing of her remained in the house. Satisfied she, left the house, leaving not a trace of her visit.

***

When Wildflower finally arrived at her Manhattan apartment, she was exhausted but excited. They finally had some concrete evidence on who had the amulet. She went into the bathroom and took a warm bath. Her mind was racing through the evening events with the Reverend.

Satisfied with her shower, she came out and called her father on the phone and told him that she wanted to have a meeting tomorrow at nine o'clock in the morning.

"It's the amulet," she told him, then hung up.

Drifting off to sleep felt too easy. After all, it had been quite the *tiring* act with the Reverend.

Wildflower dreamt of fire and experiencing unbearable pain… she was burning, and it was consuming her life force. She woke up out of her dream, sweating and greatly troubled. *What an odd dream*, she thought. How could fire consume her life force when she was a child of fire and light.

She went to the bathroom, took a towel, and dried the sweat from her forehead and went back to bed.

Wildflower woke the next morning and got her shower. She dressed in her designer outfit and went to work in her Benz. On her way, she picked her phone, dialed the Alliance Organization in Manhattan, and spoke to someone about the retrieval of the amulet.

At nine o'clock sharp, everyone was gathered in the conference – with the exception of Wildflower. Wallenstein took charge of the meeting and told the gathering that for the first time, they knew of the amulet's whereabouts. Wallenstein told the members of the Alliance Organization that with the instrumental aid of Wildflower, a woman by the name of Rose Winter of Brooklyn was involved with the disappearance of the amulet. Wallenstein told the members that they or a few of the agents needed to go by Rose's place in Brooklyn to her address, and either ask her for the amulet the easy way or "the hard way."

Roberto Sanchez, who was sitting in the conference room around the table, could not believe what he heard about Rose Winter. He was an agent now because of the demise of Rochester and he was wondered if he should contribute to the conversation.

Roberto decided, then said, "Excuse me, I have something to say… I met the woman who you are talking about, Miss Rose Winter. I went on a dinner date with her few months ago."

"What else can you tell us about her, and do you know who her friends are?" asked Vallencourt.

"I really do not know much about her, or her whereabouts. She is an extremely beautiful woman and extremely cautious. I went on one dinner date with her and could not even get her phone number or her address. I tried to take her to my place to spend a little time with her and she told me to fuck off. I left without paying for the dinner…" said Roberto.

"So you wanted to fuck the woman on the first dinner date, and because she did not go home with you, you did not pay for the dinner. You are a real piece of work. I am glad she told you to fuck off," said Wallenstein. There was laughter in the room.

"She seemed to be a very cautious and independent woman and getting the information, or the amulet, may not be as straight forward as we expect but if I have to torture her to get the information, I will," said Vallencourt.

Vallencourt soon adjourned the meeting after deciding a plan of action. He decided to take four agents along with Wallenstein, Thornbird and Roberto to Brooklyn to retrieve the amulet from Rose Winter.

They left at midday, driving two cars. Vallencourt was quite elated, knowing that for many months, this was the first lead they had about the whereabouts of the amulet. He was extremely glad that he had appointed Wallenstein to be the lead agent in the recovery of the amulet because without him, they would still be in the dark.

As the two cars continued to drive at breakneck speed, Vallencourt thought it would be a huge advancement to his position if he could just recover the amulet and deliver it to his superior within the organization.

With Wallenstein directing them, they arrived at Rose's apartment complex within an hour and a half. Wallenstein got out of the car along with Vallencourt and went to the front. They pressed the apartment buzzer, but they got no response.

Wallenstein continued to press the buzzer, but they still got no response. Vallencourt looked crestfallen and said, "She is apparently not at home, therefore let us wait until someone comes outside the building, then we can go inside."

"That seems a good idea, and we can search her apartment if the amulet is there," said Wallenstein.

They waited for around ten minutes until a Caucasian boy of around eight years old came down and opened the door. They quickly held the door and Thornbird, Vallencourt, and Wallenstein entered the apartment building. As they reached Rose's apartment door, Wallenstein looked around to see if there were any onlookers. He did not see anyone, so he took out a master key and unlocked the door and entered Rose apartment. The men entered the apartment and started looking around. They started searching the apartment thoroughly for the amulet and were warned by Vallencourt to put everything back in place when they were finished searching each room.

Vallencourt searched the apartment eagerly, but could not find anything. He went inside the bathroom and looked. He noticed that it had not been used for weeks because there was no accumulation of water on the shower curtain or in the bath. He left the bathroom and went back into the living room where he saw a picture of Rose and took out his cell phone and photographed it. He sent it to one of the agents outside in the car.

Wallenstein came into the living room with a stack of Rose's letters and asked, "Has any one of you found anything as yet?"

"We found nothing of consequence, and she does not seem to be sleeping in the apartment." said Thornbird.

"You are correct about that assessment. Her bathroom has not been used in weeks, and it therefore tells me she is gone away on some long trip," said Vallencourt.

"Where could she have gone?" asked Thornbird.

"That is the million-dollar question. Where has she gone, and does she have an accomplice…" Vallencourt wondered aloud.

"I think I may have something. I have a touching, beautifully written letter from a man expressing his feelings to Rose and how he missed her, but the writer just signed the letter "M." I think that is the person we are looking for. I honestly think if we find Rose, we have a conduit to the person who may have the amulet. I suggest we leave one agent to watch the apartment. Our inside man can get us the answers we need upon this woman's arrival," said Wallenstein.

"That sounds like a very good idea," said Vallencourt.

They all ensured that they put everything back in place in Rose's apartment, then they all drove back to Manhattan. Vallencourt told the agent that he sent Rose's photo to remain behind and watch the apartment.

Wallenstein was still hopeful, although it seemed they were always one step behind in trying to recover the amulet. He thought whoever Rose's man was, he was the one behind the theft. He wondered if Rose's man was part of some larger organization or if he was a solitary individual, taking or settling some long grudges against the Alliance. He knew whoever the individual was, he was of their kind, but why that individual would go the extra length to steal the amulet and kill everyone else trying to recover it was beyond him. He was quite baffled and intrigued not knowing the answer to the puzzle.

***

As the black Cadillac Escalade sped toward Manhattan, Vallencourt was a little deflated because he thought he would get some answers leading to the recovery of the amulet. He was still very apprehensive, as if the weight of the world was on his shoulder. He knew that failure to deliver the amulet was like a man with a foot on a landmine, with the realization that if he got off the bomb, he would die, putting an end to his existence on earth.

He was doing his damned best to ensure that the bomb did not go off, because all his hard work and dedication to the Alliance Organization would be for naught.

The Alliance Organization was like an exact task master: result-oriented. Achieving goals was the only thing that matter and nothing else. Excuses were not tolerated, if they were, only at the expense of one life force. The Alliance Organization demanded a heavy price for failure which was engrained in the psyche of any new recruit.

Those having given their entire lives to the Organization, well, they knew all too well the price of failing.

Chapter 14

As the Caribbean Airline flight landed on the tarmac at the John F. Kennedy International Airport, Rose took out her cell phone from her handbag and called her friend Angela Stanton to come and pick them up in the next forty-five minutes.

Rose and Malakai disembarked from the plane and went into the customs area to have their passport stamped. They went to baggage claim next. Malakai took possession of the suitcases, and they went outside to wait for Angela.

Rose and Malakai waited outside for around five minutes when a dark blue BMW X7 pulled up along the side of the curb near where they were standing, and a gorgeous African American woman dressed flawlessly in a white pantsuit opened the driver seat door and ran toward Rose. Both women warmly embraced as if they had not seen each other for years. Angela Stanton released Rose from their embrace, and Rose turned towards Malakai and said, "This is Angela Stanton, my best friend. Angela, meet Kai, my man."

Malakai extended his right hand, shook Angela's hand and said, "Pleased to meet you."

Angela held Malakai's hand looked intensely at him as if trying to assess him, smiled and said, "The pleasure is all mine. I am looking at Rose quite happy, tanned, and her skin and face glowing all because of you. Her face glowing seemed all orgasmic as if you were fucking in all the hotel rooms in Jamaica."

Malakai started laughing quite hysterically and Rose said, "Kai, I forgot to tell you she is quite irreverent. We were not doing any such thing in Jamaica. We swam, ate the local cuisine, visited different places and talked."

"Okay, Rose, if you expect me to believe that cockamamie story, I am Mother Theresa and also a virgin," said Angela.

"Is that not so, Kai?" asked Rose.

"The truth is, Angela; we were having sex constantly. I could not get enough of her, nor she of me," said Malakai.

"I like you even more now and thank you, Malakai for answering honestly unlike that prude of a friend. Malakai, please open the back and put the suitcases in the car, and also drive while Rose and I go in the back to gossip," said Angela.

Malakai put the two suitcases in the back of the car while Rose and Angela went around the backseat and started chatting about her Jamaican vacation. Malakai entered the car and drove away from John F Kennedy International Airport. Malakai turned on the car radio and turned up the volume slightly, not wanting to hear what Rose and Angela were saying to each other about their vacation.

As Malakai drove through the turnpike, he reflected on how he missed Jamaica, the food, the people, the warm blue sea water, reggae music, and the closeness to nature. As Malakai continued to drive, the traffic started to build up, causing bumper-to-bumper driving. Malakai hated the buildup of traffic, and it was one of the few things he hated about city life. The heavy traffic continued for miles until around twenty minutes, when Malakai came off the arterial road and switched to a less busy road.

Malakai continued to drive a little faster until he approached the neighborhood where Rose lived, and he slowed the car and turned on the service road. As he was driving, looking for a parking spot on the service road street, he saw a black Escalade. Malakai knew that the Escalade belonged to the Alliance Organization. He continued to drive away from the service road street and turned around and suggested to the ladies that they go to a Chinese restaurant to get some food because he was feeling quite hungry, and the ladies consented to his request.

Malakai turned and asked Rose to borrow her cell phone. Rose gave Malakai the phone, and he took the phone and turned it off. Malakai did not know what was going on, but he wanted to take all precaution. He put the cell phone in his pocket and continued driving, all the while looking in his rearview mirror to ensure he was not followed by any car. Realizing that he was not followed, Malakai drove up to a Chinese restaurant.

Malakai parked the car, and they all entered the Chinese restaurant. The restaurant was quite exotic, with a nice ambiance. There was jazz music softly playing throughout the restaurant with Chinese decoration and numerous paintings, painted by Chinese artists. A lady escorted them to a nicely decorated table with a red tablecloth. They sat, and Malakai immediately ordered wanton soup. A waiter brought the wanton soup, and Malakai devoured the wanton soup rather quickly, and he then reached into his pocket and took out four hundred dollars and gave Rose and told her he had to go somewhere and he would be back within a couple hours. Malakai asked Angela to use her car, and she gave him her permission.

Malakai left the restaurant quite baffled, wondering how the Alliance Organization was able to find out about Rose and even where she resides. He entered Angela's car and drove away, knowing he had to get some answers. Malakai drove to a liquor store and bought a bottle of Johnnie Walker Black Scotch whisky, the day newspaper and a black cellular tape. He drove back to where Rose lived and parked around a block away from Rose's apartment. Malakai took the Onoro sword from his waist, pressed the knob, and the elongated blade came out, and he wrapped the newspaper around the sword and used the tape to bind it. He took the amulet out of his pocket and hid the amulet under the driver's seat. He could not afford for the amulet to fall into the hands of the Alliance Organization. Malakai took the key out of the car, locked it and put it into his pocket.

Malakai took the bottle of the whisky, opened it, splashed some of it on his shirt and used some of it to splash his face. He started walking with the Onoro sword as a walking stick to support his feigning drunken state and with the bottle of Johnnie Walker Black Scotch whisky in his left hand. Malakai walked towards the black Cadillac Escalade, but instead of going to the black Cadillac Escalade, he went to the next car, a Toyota Camry parked beside the black Cadillac Escalade, started knocking and said, "Beverly, open the room door. I promise I won't beat you anymore."

Malakai, sensed that there was no one in the Toyota Camry, kept knocking on the car until he eventually staggered over to the black Cadillac Escalade and kept on knocking on the black Cadillac Escalade's second passenger door and said, "Beverly, open the room door. I promise I will not beat you anymore. I want to have sex with you."

Suddenly, the second passenger door was opened by the agent in the front seat. The agent stretched across to open the door and shouted, "You drunken fool, stop knocking on my door. There is no one named Beverly in my car."

As the agent stretched across and opened the second passenger door, Malakai instantly looked inside the car and realized that the agent was alone and was of his kind. Malakai, in an instant, jumped into the car, pushed the agent back into the front seat, closed the passenger door and took the sword and held it against the agent's neck and said, "I am going to ask you a series of questions, and if you do not tell me the truth, I am going to take this Onoro sword and chop your fucking head off." Malakai could see the terrified look on the agent's face and asked, "Do you understand what I am saying?"

The agent went into full panic mode as Malakai pushed the blade closer to his neck, and he felt the cold, unforgiving steel of the Onoro sword against his flesh said, "Yes, I do understand what you are saying."

"Are you the only agent here?" asked Malakai.

"Yes, I am the only one here," said the agent.

"What are you doing here?" asked Malakai.

The agent hesitated to answer Malakai's question, and Malakai pushed the sword closer to the agent's neck, precipitating a small amount of blood to appear on the sword. The agent, seeing the blood on the sword, said, "I am waiting for this lady named Rose Winter."

"Now we are getting somewhere. Why are you waiting on Rose Winter, and what are your orders when you see her?" asked Malakai.

"I was ordered by the Alliance Organization to call them when Rose returned home to her apartment. The Alliance Organization wants to question her about the disappearance of the amulet of Osiris. That is all I know," said the agent.

"Do you know Rose Winter?" asked Malakai.

"I have never met her, but I have a picture of her on my phone. Three senior agents went to her apartment to search for her, but they did not find her, so they sent the picture of her to my phone from her apartment," said the agent.

"Show me the picture of Rose on your phone?" asked Malakai.

The agent took his cell phone and showed Malakai the picture of Rose. Malakai took the phone, deleted Rose's picture, turned off the phone and disassembled it to ensure that it could not be tracked. Malakai ordered the agent to start the car and to drive away from the apartment complex. The agent started driving slowly until, about a mile, Malakai spotted a slightly isolated forested area consisting of trees and shrubs. Malakai told the agent to pull off the road and drive to the isolated area. Around a hundred yards, Malakai told the agent to stop the car and ordered the agent to come outside. As the agent came outside, Malakai took the sword and chopped off his. Within two minutes, everything started turning to dust, and a gentle wind came and blew it away slowly into the surrounding trees.

Malakai took the rest of the taped newspaper that was on the Onoro sword, cleaned it off and put it back in his waist. He discarded the newspaper along with the agent's phone and then drove away from the area back to Rose's apartment. Malakai parked the Cadillac Escalade, ensured it was properly closed and took the keys. He walked to where Angela's car was parked, opened it, took the amulet from under the seat and placed it in his pocket. Malakai hurriedly drove away to the restaurant hoping he did not stay away too long from the girls.

Malakai arrived at the restaurant in the next fifteen minutes, and as he entered, he saw the ladies drinking and chatting, enjoying each other company. Malakai went by Rose, kissed her gently, and asked, "Did you lovely ladies miss me?"

"We both did. Rose and I were chatting, and she was telling me what fun you and she had in Jamaica. I was thinking maybe next time you can take me with you, and we have what the French say a ménage a trois. Do you not think it is a great idea?" asked Angela.

Malakai was totally flabbergasted, not even knowing how to respond, but he regained his composure and said, "Angela, I see you do not like me much. Rose will chop off my head, and I love to keep it where it is."

Angela was not going to accept defeat and gave up that easily because she wanted to get into this man's head space. She wanted to know the type of man Rose was involved with and wanted to know if this man was worthy of her friend. Angela took up the glass she was drinking wine from, looked intently into Malakai's eyes and started twitching her tongue on the glass in a flirtatious manner and said, "It was not my idea; it was Rose's suggestion because we generally share everything."

Malakai was even more baffled because this beautiful African American woman, who was Rose's best friend, was clearly engaging in a light-hearted flirtation with him, and he did not know how to react or what to say in that brief moment. There was no doubt he was attracted to her, but he knew there was no way in hell Rose would allow her best friend to flirt with him, much less have a threesome. He knew he had been set up by Rose to test him, so he said, "Angela, you are an extremely beautiful and gorgeous woman, but I am madly in love with your friend over there. She makes me want to be a better man every day, and I am just trying to please her the best way I know how."

The woman started laughing, and Angela held Malakai's hand and said, "You have certainly aced our test. I was just wondering what type of man you are, but you have certainly restored my faith in men that you do not all think with your dick."

Malakai looked a little uneasy, breathed a sigh of relief and was glad that he did not make a fool of himself and, most of all, happy he said the right thing at the appropriate moment. He looked at the two women, smiled, and said, "I know you were not sincere, so I did not fall for your ruse."

"Kai, do you think I would allow you to sleep with my best friend?" asked Rose.

"Can we change the subject ladies? I am feeling quite uncomfortable with regards to this subject," said Malakai.

"I am glad you are feeling uncomfortable and want to change the subject. Let me tell you, it would not be your head I chop off, but your frigging dick if you ever sleep with my best friend," said Rose.

"I am feeling more uncomfortable and petrified for my dick now that it has been threatened. I promise you, my darling, I am not going to sleep with your best friend or anyone else for that matter. Can we change the subject now? I need something to eat before we go," said Malakai.

Malakai ordered a seafood platter, which was a combination of shrimp, lobster, and fish served with white rice. He hurriedly ate the food, enjoying the combination of the different textures of the food in his mouth.

After Malakai finished eating, Rose paid the bill, and they left the restaurant. As Malakai was driving over to Rose's apartment, he was petrified because he knew that the Alliance Organization was closing on him and he had a small amount of time to disappear, and he would have to take Rose with him if he wanted to preserve both their life. Malakai knew he could not tell Rose who he was, but he knew he would have to tell her something about why she could not stay at her apartment. He wondered if telling Rose some of the details of his life if she would ever trust him again and wondered if it would be the end of their relationship.

As Malakai drove on the service road where Rose's apartment is located, he parked behind the black Cadillac Escalade. Malakai came out of the car and opened the passenger door for Rose and Angela to exit the car. Rose came out of the car, and Malakai pulled her aside and said, "Rose, what I am about to say will impact our relationship, but for now, I need you to trust me and come with me. I will explain to you where we are going, but for now, I am begging you to trust me for now."

"Will I be safe with you?" asked Rose.

"You are always safe with me as long as my body breathes life. My body, my love, they belong to you, my darling," said Malakai.

Malakai took the small box with amulet, and the suitcases out of Angela's car and put them in the black Cadillac Escalade. Rose opened one of the suitcases and took out the gifts he bought in Jamaica for Angela. Angela thanked Rose, and they hugged and kissed each other. Then Angela bid goodbye to both Rose and Malakai.

Malakai opened the Cadillac Escalade door and noticed that Rose was hesitating as if contemplating the idea to get in and asked, "Are you coming with me?"

"I want to go inside my apartment for a few minutes," said Rose.

Malakai feared that Rose would make such a request. He promptly locked the car's door and followed Rose to her apartment. Rose opened her apartment door and went inside. Malakai looked around and said, "Rose, please do not turn on any of the faucets or flush the toilet."

Malakai did not want anything to be disturbed because he knew the Alliance Organization agents probably would be back at the apartment looking for clues to Rose's whereabouts and the agent that Malakai terminated his life. Rose looked around the apartment, satisfied everything was okay. She closed the apartment door, and they went into the car. Before they drove away from the apartment, Malakai turned on Rose's phone and told her to upload everything that was of importance to her to her Google account and turn the phone off when she was finished. Rose took five minutes to upload all the content on her phone that she wanted to her Google account, and then she turned her phone off. Malakai immediately started the car, and they drove away from the apartment.

Malakai drove for around fifteen minutes until he stopped at a truck stop off a highway and said to Rose, "I know you have a lot of questions, but for now, I will provide the answer to these questions later. I want to make a serious proposal to you. If I gave you one hundred thousand dollars in cash, would that be satisfactory payment for your time with me?"

"That is all my time with you is worth?" asked Rose.

"How about two hundred and fifty thousand dollars in cash, and the added bonus is you will never see me again?" asked Malakai.

Rose stared at Malakai, wondering what was going on in his mind and asked, "Kai, do you truly love me?"

"Without a doubt, I do love you with all my heart," said Malakai.

"If you do love me, please stop trying to push me away because I am not for sale. Your money is of no consequence to me. I am not in a relationship with you because of your money. I see the man you are, and I am proud to call you my man and lover. I know you enough that you do not want me to go away. I do love you and I will always want to be part of your life come what may. I am one of those ride-or-die women," said Rose.

"Thanks for the reassurance. I really wanted to hear that. No matter the circumstances, you always have my heart," said Malakai.

They both got back into the car, and Malakai continued driving until they entered the state of New Jersey, where they stopped at a gas station to buy gas.

******

Vallencourt and his entourage were driving as fast as possible to Rose's apartment in Brooklyn. He had called the agent earlier in the day and got no response, and he had no idea what had befallen the agent. Vallencourt was angry because every time he seemed to be getting somewhere leading to the recovery of the amulet, something generally happened, leaving him further in the dark. He thought that whoever had the amulet always seemed to be one step ahead of him, and he pondered if they had been assisted by the great God above heaven. He swore to himself if he found out who stole the amulet, he would ensure that they endured torture that they had never imagined possible. Vallencourt thought that the agent was one of the better trained but wondered what had befallen him and why he was not answering his cell phone.

They arrived at Rose's apartment shortly, parked on the service road and started looking for the black Cadillac Escalade. They did not see the agent or the car. Vallencourt decided to visit Rose's apartment. He took out the master key and opened the entrance door, and Wallenstein, along with Thornbird, went upstairs to Rose's apartment. When they entered Rose's apartment, it was the same as they left it the last time they were in the apartment. Wallenstein went into the bathroom and looked inside the bath and the toilet to see if it had been used recently but found no trace it had been utilized for weeks. Wallenstein came outside and went into the other two bedrooms but found nothing had changed from the last time they were in Rose's apartment.

They all assembled in the living room, and Wallenstein said, "No one has been in this apartment since we left here; therefore, we have to put out an APB to all our agents in the field to look out for the black Cadillac Escalade. If we find the black Cadillac Escalade, maybe we will find who has the amulet. Also, I have a friend at one of the phone companies. I will ask her to track her phone and who she talks with the most."

"That seems like a good idea. I am going to call headquarters in Manhattan to broadcast the APB immediately to all our agents in the field," said Vallencourt.

Vallencourt made the phone call to Manhattan, and they left Rose's apartment.

*****

Agent Chang was about five feet six inches of Chinese ethnicity, possessing thick black hair and a black moustache. His face was clean-shaven with the exception of the moustache, and he had on his dark Ray-ban glasses. He was about to drive into the gas station at Camden in New Jersey when he got an APB on his cell phone about the black Cadillac Escalade and the license plate number. He looked at the black Cadillac Escalade exiting the gas station and stared intently to make sure that the license plate was the correct one that came on the APB. Agent Chang realized it was the exact car, and he drove away from the gas station without buying any gas. As he started pursuing the car, he drove as fast as his dark blue Honda Accord could, trying to catch up to the black Cadillac Escalade.

Malakai looked into the rearview mirror and noticed a dark blue Honda Accord speeding as if trying to overtake him. Malakai was not one hundred percent certain that the driver of the dark blue Honda Accord was chasing him, so he continued to drive at a steady pace, observing the Honda Accord. Agent Chang suddenly overtook two cars trying to catch up to Malakai, and he realized instantly that the driver of the dark blue Honda Accord was in hot pursuit. Malakai was a little puzzled about how the Alliance Organization was able to catch his whereabouts that quickly, but he suddenly realized that he was driving their car and also the license plate attached to the car.

Malakai pressed on the accelerator of the Cadillac Escalade and said, "Rose, we are being followed by the dark blue Honda Accord behind us. Please buckle up securely because I will be driving extra fast."

Rose ensured that she was buckled securely with the seatbelt, and Malakai started pressing the gas accelerator. Malakai was driving quite fast, overtaking as many cars on the highway, but he was unable to lose the driver of the Honda Accord. Although Malakai was a couple of hundred yards ahead of his pursuer, he knew that the driver could see his car just as how he could see the Honda Accord. Malakai's mind was racing, trying to figure out how to elude his pursuer.

Malakai finally came to a stop at a traffic light, and he decided to use the old, trusted stop light trick to elude his pursuer. After a few minutes, the traffic light turned green, and Malakai was in the center of the road. In the lane where Malakai was, the cars behind him started blowing their horn for him to proceed, but Malakai turned off his engine and pressed the hazard button, and the car light started flashing, indicating that there was a problem onboard. Some of the cars in the lane behind Malakai started cutting into the other lane, cutting off the car in the other lane – precisely how Malakai expected they would react. Malakai had his eyes firmly on the driver of the Honda Accord as the cars from his lane were cutting off the car from the Honda Accord lane. Just as the light was about to change to red, Malakai turned on his car engine and pressed the gas accelerator and his car shot across from the oncoming traffic as the traffic light turned red.

Agent Chang was furious with rage as he realized what the driver of the black Cadillac Escalade was trying to do, by holding up the traffic that he was unable to pursue their car. As the cars in the other lane were cutting over on his lane, he was frantically blowing his horn for the other car to get out of his way, but the other cars kept cutting in his lane were just ignoring him, making him more furious, as little sweats started emerging on his forehead. Agent Chang started banging the steering wheel and continued blowing the horn when he suddenly looked at the odometer and noticed that the gas gauge was red. Agent Chang suddenly stopped blowing the car horn and resigned to the idea that he was not going to catch the black Cadillac Escalade.

Agent Chang suddenly saw the traffic light turn red as the black Cadillac Escalade shot across the road, leaving him behind as the car he was pursuing disappeared from his eyesight. Agent Chang, totally disappointed, knew that his immediate aim now was to get to a gas station to fill up his gas. He finally arrived at a truck stop off the highway and went to a gas station. After he filled up the gas, Agent Chang called the headquarters in Manhattan and spoke with Vallencourt. He told Vallencourt he saw the car with two people on board, a male and a female, and when he was chasing them, they eluded him at the stoplight.

Agent Chang further told Vallencourt that he was not sure where in New Jersey they were going or if they were going to any other States. Vallencourt told Agent Chang to keep searching in the area, and if he saw them again, he must call in immediately on his personal phone. After a few more minutes, Vallencourt hung up the phone.

Chapter 15

Malakai continued driving. Confident that the dark blue Honda Accord was no longer pursuing them, he started driving a little slower, not wanting to cause an accident on the road. He drove until they arrived in the state of Pennsylvania. Malakai drove to a motel where he checked in as Mr. and Ms. Parker. The motel was not one of those fancy ones but one that possessed just the basic amenities of a clean bed and a television set in the room. Malakai was just looking for a place that was clean and where Rose could sleep comfortably. Malakai went into the bathroom and took a shower. He came out of the bathroom with a towel wrapped around his waist and put on shorts and a white t-shirt. Rose went into the bathroom afterwards with her toiletries and lingerie.

When Rose came out of the bathroom, Malakai was in bed watching the television. Rose walked near the bed wearing a black teddy. The black lingerie accentuated every inch of her curves as if it were made for her body. The material was quite lacy and barely covered Rose's ample breasts. Rose looked at Malakai, staring at every inch of her body, and asked, "Do you approve, sir?"

"Yes, I do approve. I am just excited like a schoolboy, grateful and overjoyed to see you in your lingerie," said Malakai.

"I am pleased when my man is pleased to look upon me as the most desirable woman. It makes me so excited and amorous like I am right now," said Rose.

"Model for me, and I will sing for you," said Malakai.

"Okay, I will model for you when you start singing," said Rose.

Rose started modeling for Malakai in her black teddy, twisting and twirling, while Malakai started whistling and clapping his hands in appreciation of this beautiful woman. After Malakai finished whistling, Rose climbed into the bed and kissed Malakai intensely and passionately with wild abandonment. Rose took the lead in their lovemaking, and Malakai did not mind and even enjoyed it when Rose took the lead.

Rose stripped Malakai of his shorts and t-shirt. She stared at Malakai's body and his huge, erect penis, pleased within her mind that she could awaken his desire. She felt empowered, excited, turned on and liberated with this man, *her* man. She was at an age where she was comfortable with her body, knew what she wanted in bed, what gave her pleasure and savored different experiences with her man. Her body was relaxed, hungry and desirous of Malakai's body as she enveloped her mouth around his penis. She could feel the ebb and flow and the strength of his erection as her tongue circled and teased as she pushed it deeper into her mouth. She was enjoying the taste of this man's huge, engorged penis in her mouth, maybe a little too much, or maybe because she was so comfortable and relaxed, and the intensity of the moment was too much. Rose started to grip Malakai's body tighter as her body shook, and her orgasm came like torrential rain.

Malakai took Rose and laid her head on his chest, not talking but enjoying the serenity of the moment. Malakai was grateful for the time they had together because he loved this woman like none other and knew that this type of love comes once or twice in a lifetime, and some people search their whole life and never find it. Now that Malakai thought he had found that love, he wanted Rose by his side more than ever, secure in the knowledge that Rose was his woman.

After a few more minutes, Malakai got up and took the teddy off Rose's body. He turned her around, entered her from behind, and started thrusting and thrusting until he asked Rose to change position and go on top of his body. Rose complied as she began to thrust on Malakai's engorged penis. As Malakai's hand reached up and held Rose's soft, lovely breasts, Rose leaned her breasts towards Malakai, and he gladly, ravenously accepted them in his mouth. Malakai sucked on them like a voracious animal, savoring the feel, softness, and taste of Rose's breast. Rose was quite turned on with Malakai's mouth sucking on her sensitive breasts, it gave her a tantalizing feeling, and with his hands wandering over her body, she climaxed just as Malakai ejaculated inside her vagina.

All the energy in Rose's body was well spent, and within five minutes, she fell into a deep sleep with Malakai's arms embracing her body. Malakai went to sleep soon after making love to Rose.

Malakai got up around seven the next morning and went into the bathroom to urinate and brush his teeth. As he came out of the bathroom, Rose woke out of her slumber and rushed into the bathroom to urinate and brush her teeth. She came back into the bed, and Malakai quite turned on, seeing Rose in her lingerie, reached out and grabbed Rose and pulled her closer to his body. Rose instantly felt his erection, and she pushed him away and said, "No more sex until you tell me what is going on and where we are going."

Malakai sat up in the bed and started pondering what he was going to tell Rose. He knew he was not going to tell her everything, but he knew he had to tell her something, at least to calm her anger. He thought he owed her an explanation for why he took her away from her apartment. He got out of bed, went into his jeans pocket, took out the amulet, showed it to Rose and said, "This amulet is what everything is all about. Some immensely powerful people who control this world are searching for it, and they will kill anyone who possesses it."

"Is it extremely valuable?" asked Rose.

"Yes, it is extremely valuable, but I would say it is priceless," said Malakai.

"So why are these powerful people going after you, or are they just searching for the amulet?" asked Rose.

"That is an exceptionally good question, and I am not sure of the answer. I know these men would move heaven and earth to acquire the amulet back," said Malakai.

"You mean these powerful men had the amulet in their possession? Please tell me how you acquired the amulet?" asked Rose.

"Yes, they had it in their possession briefly. The amulet came from Egypt and when the courier was about to deliver the amulet to these powerful men, a good friend of mine in Egypt called me to retrieve it.

Rose got out of bed, put on her shorts in an angry manner, and said, "So you *stole* the amulet? I am in a relationship with a man who is a fucking thief. Good God, I am damned. I really know how to choose a man to be in a relationship with. So, these men who are searching for the amulet, would they kill us if they find us with the amulet?" asked Rose.

"I do not want to scare you, but they would kill us without the slightest thought or hesitation. Please do not panic and be terrified," said Malakai.

"How can I not be terrified and panicky when a group of men are looking for me to probably kill me?" asked Rose.

Malakai looked at Rose and noticed she was terrified and bewildered and said, "When you are in danger you have to force yourself to remain calm and try to outthink your opponent Rose."

"I am not you, and I was never in my life pursued by the law, nor in a relationship with a man who is a fucking thief," said Rose.

"Firstly, let me state categorically I am not a thief. If I were a thief, I would want to sell the amulet to the highest bidder. My sole purpose is to see this valuable, priceless artifact destroyed before it falls into the hands of these men who are looking for us. Secondly, we are not being pursued by the law but by a criminal organization who may have some element of law enforcement in their pocket," said Malakai.

Rose was still visibly upset and sarcastically said, "I feel so much more comforted knowing that I am being chased by a gang of criminals who does not have any scruple to kill me or may even rape me."

"No one will rape or kill you as long as I am alive on this earth, so please be calmed," said Malakai.

"Kai, I am scared," said Rose.

"Look at me and repeat what I am saying. I am, therefore, I can. This means because you exist in this space and time and are alive, there is always hope to get out of any situation or to do anything you set your mind to, and it comes with belief in yourself. Do you understand what I am saying?" asked Malakai.

Malakai got out of bed, reached for Rose's hand, and she extended hers, and he pulled her in his arms, and Rose said: "Yes, I do understand what you are saying and irrespective that I am angry with you, I am always comforted when I am in your arms."

Malakai, smiling and slapping Rose on her buttocks, said, "It is nice to know that I have the magic touch over you."

Rose, in pretentious annoyance, pushed Malakai away from her and said, "Get away from me, you pompous bastard."

"I need for you to understand that I am not doing this for any selfish purpose or any form of personal aggrandizement, but if those wretched men get hold of the amulet, it will alter the balance between good and evil in this world. I also need you to understand that I may not be with you always, but know that I will do everything in my power to protect you and keep you out of danger," said Malakai.

"I know you love me and will protect me. You have proven yourself to be a decent man, and I do not doubt you, but I do have a lot of unanswered questions like, what were you doing on Mount Marcy with the amulet?"

"I was looking for a place to hide the amulet. But when I ran into you on the mountain, I thought the better decision was to have you hold it and keep it safe for me. It turns out it was the best decision because I ran into those men who were searching for the amulet after I had given it to you, and they searched me," said Malakai.

"So you used me to get the amulet away from the men who searched you?" asked Rose.

"Well, I would not say used, but I would say is assisted in getting the amulet away from the men who searched me. I need to tell you those men are the same criminal organization that killed my parents when I was a baby. I was playing hide and seek with my parents in their room when I ran under the bed. The door suddenly opened, and three tall, muscular white men came into the room and killed my parents. I do not know if it was the sight of fear in my parent's eyes; I did not make a sound, and I could see everything from under the bed. They killed my parents and left the house. Around an hour later, Rodigan, who was a friend of my parent, came rushing into the house, only to find me crying. He took me out of the house, and we stayed in America for around two years until he took me to Jamaica to live with him." said Malakai.

"Oh my God, I am so sorry to hear about the murder of your parents. I apologize for calling you a thief," said Rose.

"That is okay. I am glad you are with me, and for the record, I am sorry I got you involved in this situation, but know this: if it is anyone I want to be around, it would be you," said Malakai.

"So what is the plan going forward?" asked Rose.

"I am asking you to stay with me for a few weeks until things calm down before we return to New York. I want to take you to Western Pennsylvania in Amish country to stay for a few weeks," said Malakai.

"Have you been there before?" asked Rose.

"Yes, I have been there before. A good friend of mine lives there; his name is Ephraim. We have to blend in the community, so we have to dress like them and follow their religious practices," said Malakai.

"Do I have to buy clothes?" asked Rose.

"No, there are plenty of clothes in Ephraim's house. I need to tell you that it is a different world from what you are used to, but if you ingratiate yourself in the community you will be fine. The Amish are exceptionally fine people, and are close to nature, but you cannot tell them why we are there. Is that okay with you?" asked Malakai.

"Yes, it is okay with me. I promise you I will not blabber my mouth," said Rose.

"Are we good now with each other?" asked Malakai.

"Yes, we are good with each other," said Rose.

"Then come back into the bed to have a last sex escapade because where we are going, I cannot even look at you. Seriously though, we will be staying at separate quarters, and we will have to respect and observe the Amish religious practices, morals and norms," said Malakai.

Rose went into bed with Malakai, and they made slow, passionate love in their motel room. After they were finished, they went back to sleep until they woke up in the afternoon, where they showered and started putting on their clothing. Malakai asked Rose to dress quite conservatively by wearing a long dress or skirt. They went and checked out of the motel soon after, and as they were checking out of the motel, Malakai asked the desk clerk for a call to Ephraim's neighbor to tell him what time they were coming to his home.

Malakai and Rose then left the motel and drove to a restaurant. Malakai was feeling extremely hungry, and as they entered the restaurant and were shown to their table, he ordered two Philadelphia pepper pot soups, which was basically a stew made of tripe, vegetables and plenty of peppers. After the soup, they had the world-famous Philadelphia cheesesteak. Cheesesteak is synonymous with Philadelphia, as the Eifel Tower to Paris or Big Ben to London. Philadelphia cheesesteak is an amalgamation of fried strips of steak, melted cheese, and onions. Malakai and Rose both enjoyed the meal, and as Rose was wiping her mouth with the napkin told Malakai when they were returning home, she wanted one to take back to New York.

Malakai and Rose left the restaurant with their hunger for food satiated; they started driving to western Pennsylvania. As they drove on the road, Malakai observed the beauty and length of the trees and sometimes of the verdant forest. Malakai opened the car window to allow the clean, fresh Pennsylvania air to come into the car. It felt quite therapeutic for Malakai to have the wind blowing clean, fresh air on his face; it was as if it was blowing away his troubles.

As Malakai gazed out of the car and looked at the lush green vegetation and the wide varieties of insect life, and thought that life does not exist anywhere else in the universe apart from planet Earth. He furthered the thought that life only exists because of a Great God who created life on our blue planet.

As Malakai continued driving and observing the huge acres of cornfields, he thought only a great God could ever conceive of allowing for the soil on planet Earth to be fertile so it could produce food for humans, birds, insects, and other animals to satisfy their hunger. Malakai continued thinking that this was one of the things that makes planet Earth unique because this phenomenon of rainwater falling from the sky to help with the fertility of the soil producing food does not happen on any other planet. He thought human beings are truly blessed, special, and cared for by God. Malakai scoffed at the idea that is espoused by atheists that God does not exist and that life on earth came about by accident. This idea, he thought, was just abject garbage because the complexity and diversity of life on planet Earth could only be conceived by a great God. There was no accident in the formulation of life. Life had to be conceived and actualized by a great God.

Malakai ridiculed people who claimed they were agonistic and did not know what to believe, whether God exists in a spiritual sense. This idea by agonist to Malakai is a coward way out from making or taking a decision when the simplicity of the evidence is right in front of you, staring you in the face because for something to exist, there must be a creator, and that creator is God. Nothing in this life on earth is created inadvertently; all things are created by God.

Malakai and Rose were soon in Lancaster County in Western Pennsylvania in Amish country. Lancaster County, where the past is quite steeped, but there is a mix of modernity as tourists visiting the area can see horse-drawn carriage driven by an Amish gentleman, antique shops and genuine Amish cook food at the restaurants. The Amish are mostly found in the western part of the state of Pennsylvania in Lancaster County, which is one of the oldest Amish settlements in the United States of America. The Amish religion is very steeped in tradition, and their Christian faith is extremely conservative in their biblical belief. The Amish live a remarkably simple lifestyle that is close to nature. They tend to shun modern technology because they feel that modern conveniences like electricity drive the community apart. They are very modest people, and because of their religious training, the Amish people tend to disregard individualism and self-importance.

The Amish clothing is quite standardized within the entire Amish community. Amish men and boys wear dark-colored suits, broad fall trousers with suspenders and black broad-brimmed hats. Amish men grow their beards to symbolize that they are married, but they do not have a moustache. Amish men who are unmarried keep their faces shaven until they are married. Amish married women wear quite modest cape dress with an apron to cover it. The dress consists of long sleeves and a full skirt, covered with a shawl on the bodice. Amish women do not wear jewelry, and they do not cut their hair. Amish women fix their hair in some form of braid or bun and cover it with some form of white cap if they are married and a black cap if they are unmarried. The Amish women believe that dressing plainly and modestly sets them apart from modern society and its deleterious societal impacts.

The Amish are involved in dairy farming. Dairy farmers sell their milk at the market and also utilize it for cheese production. The Amish are also involved in poultry farming of chickens, turkeys, and ducks. Some Amish are also involved in sheep and goat rearing for their milk and meat consumption. Amish are also involved in agriculture farming of corn, tobacco, tomatoes, lettuce, Brussels sprouts, peppers, and broccoli. Agriculture farming, though quite labor intensive, provides work for The Amish family and also teaches the younger generation an appreciation for hard work.

Malakai drove off the main road through some cornfields and into a large property with a two stories farmhouse with a protruding chimney painted with a white color. Ephraim's house was the first one coming into the Amish community, and Malakai was thankful that he would not be subjected to the prying eyes of the other Amish families. The barn door of the farmhouse was left open by Ephraim, and Malakai drove inside and parked. Malakai came out of the car and opened the door for Rose and held her hands as they started walking towards the house to meet Ephraim and his family. Malakai met Ephraim many years after he left Jamaica and was travelling through the state of Pennsylvania. Malakai went to Lancaster County because he wanted to immerse himself in the traditional Christian religion and he met Ephraim and his family, and he resided with them for many months.

Rose and Malakai approached the porch where Ephraim, Ruth, and his five children were to greet and welcome them to their home. Rose noticed that the porch on the house was rather quite large with lots of chairs. Rose asked Malakai why the porch on the house was so large, and Malakai explained that because there were no televisions, telephones, or computers in an Amish family home, the porch was used as a place to have leisure time, to sit and relax and to chat and even to entertain other family members.

Ephraim Bergkamp was of Dutch ancestry, middle age with a slight paunch. He was dressed in dark pants, a white shirt, and suspenders supporting his pants. He had this wide smile on his face, displaying white teeth. Ruth was of Dutch ancestry also with a slightly round face and quite overweight. She was dressed in a plain black dress covered by an apron and a white hat on her head. The five children consisted of three boys and two girls. The three boys were named Samuel, who was fourteen; Saul, who was ten; and Jonas, who was the youngest and was six. The girls were Josephina, who was twenty years old, beautiful and fiery under the concealed black hat, and Mary, who was eleven years of age.

As Malakai and Rose approached the door, Ephraim, smiling, opened his arms, hugged Malakai and said, "Welcome to my humble home, my friend; it is so good to see you."

Rose thought that Josephina was extremely beautiful and noticed that she had had this quizzical expression on her face. Rose also noticed that Ephraim spoke in a thick, Pennsylvania Dutch accent and seemed warm and friendly.

Malakai hugged Ephraim, Ruth and the children and said, "Everybody, this is Rose, my woman, and the love of my life."

Ephraim and his family all greeted Rose warmly and welcomed her to their home. Inside the house, Rose noticed that there was no electricity, but the house was spacious, modest and lit by gas lamps and a lot of ambient lighting coming from outside through windows. The furniture inside the house was all beautifully made, consisting mostly of tables and chairs. Inside the spacious kitchen area, there was a stove and a refrigerator, all powered by gas and a lot of glass jars where the Amish family preserved their fruit, vegetables, and meats.

Rose, Malakai, Ruth, and Ephraim all chatted while the children went to their beds. After an hour, Rose was shown to her room and given some clothes by Ruth. The room was quite nice, with a coffee color wooden handcrafted bed that was queen-sized. The sheet on the mattress seemed handmade of a quilted variety. Malakai went into the barn and opened the car, took one of the suitcases to Rose with her toiletries and kissed her good night while he went back to the barn with a sleeping blanket given to him by Ruth. Malakai opened the sleeping blanket and, laid it on some hays in the barn, and went to sleep.

Rose locked her door, and went to the bathroom to brush her teeth. She came out of the bathroom, undressed and went into her bed. She missed Malakai having him beside her, the feel of her soft skin rubbing against his body. She was missing his embrace and his hand on her breast when they slept. Rose stared at the ceiling of the bedroom until she finally went to sleep. She was in deep sleep when she started dreaming of being tied up and calling for Malakai. As she was tugging violently on the rope to free herself, she woke up out of her dream. The realization dawned on her that she was dreaming, and she went back to sleep clutching her pillow.

Malakai woke in the morning and took off his shirt because he was feeling rather hot. He took out his toothbrush and toothpaste from the suitcase in the car and proceeded to brush his teeth. Malakai washed out his mouth and the toothbrush in a sink in the barn. As he was putting the toothbrush and toothpaste back into the car, he heard a sound and suddenly looked around to see Josephina with some clothing in her hand, she said, "Good morning, Mr. Malakai, mommy told me to give you these clothes."

"Good morning to you, too, Josephina; it is good to see you. Please tell your mom and pop thanks for me."

Josephina stared at Malakai's half-naked body and said, "You are certainly looking good and fit."

Malakai knew she had a crush on him since she was a fourteen-year-old teenager, but he thought she had gotten over him, now she was a beautiful young woman. At fourteen, Josephina was just a freckled-face young girl infatuated by the first man that Malakai thought looked different from her family, but now she was an extremely beautiful woman, with all the freckles gone from her face.

"Be careful who you pay compliments to, Josephina; I still remember you as that fourteen-year-old freckled-faced kid that I considered my friend and nothing more," said Malakai.

Josephina bit her lips and said "I am no longer a freckled face kid that you left here ages ago. I am a vibrant woman now, who wants to see the world and see what it can offer."

Malakai knew that talking to her from when she was fourteen that she wanted so much more than what the Amish community could offer, and that dream of her was not diminished now that she had grown into a beautiful young woman. She always told Malakai when they were alone that she wanted to see the wider world, to travel and see how other people live, and to experience different facet of life.

Malakai knew that if she ventured on her dream of travelling the world, it would bring dishonor and excommunication from her church. Malakai pleadingly said, "Josephina, please put away that childish fantasy from your head because you are aware of the ramifications that it would bring to your family and your church."

"Malakai, I am tired of living a lie. I tried desperately to put those thoughts away from my head. I pray constantly, asking God for some sort of solace, but my prayers have not been answered. Do you know what it is like to live your life feeling trapped?" asked Josephina.

Malakai had thought she had outgrown her dreams of travelling the world. Malakai sympathized and even empathized with her desire because he understood the unfulfilled desire that gnawed at the core of your soul when your life is left unfulfilled. Malakai replied, "I am not in your shoes, but for what it is worth, I do understand and sympathize."

"Thank you, that is all I was asking for, a little understanding," said Josephina.

"I have a gift for you," said Malakai.

Josephina's face lit up and asked, "What is it?"

Malakai opened the car and opened the suitcase, took out a small package and gave Josephina. Josephina accepted the gift package, looked inside and said, "Thanks for the perfume."

"You are welcome, but I have something else that I want to give you." Malakai unclasped a silver amulet around his neck, pinned it around Josephina's neck, and said, "I know your religion is against wearing jewelry, but I am asking you to keep it on you always, to protect you from evil spirits and to be a shield to those who want to harm you," said Malakai.

Josephina looked at the silver amulet, concealed it under her blouse, and said, "Thank you again."

"Please promise me that you will always wear it on your body," said Malakai.

"Okay, I promise you I will always wear it," said Josephina.

"By the way, you are welcome anytime to talk. Plus, I see you are a woman now and an extremely beautiful one at that," said Malakai.

"Oh, I see you noticing me then, that I am a woman now. It was just not my imagination that you were looking at me intently," said Josephina.

"Josephina, behave yourself, because I would not dishonor my woman or your father whose property I am living on. By the way, why are you not married?" asked Malakai.

"I choose not to be married as of yet. I do want more out of life more than to be spitting out the next generation of Amish children," said Josephina.

Josephina left the barn with a cryptic smile, and Malakai hurriedly put on the pants, shirt, and hat that Josephina brought. He went outside and straight into the tobacco field, where Ephraim and the boys were working in the hot sun. It was summer, and tobacco harvesting was a busy period for the Ephraim family. Ephraim was into corn and tobacco cultivation, and also operated a small dairy farming business. Some Amish communities shunned tobacco cultivation, but the Amish order in Lancaster County did not have a problem with it. The tobacco plant is essential for cigarettes and chewing tobacco manufacture. Growing tobacco was a great cash crop for most Amish families in Lancaster County that cultivated it.

Ephraim and the boys were cutting the stalk of the tobacco plant with shears, one plant at a time in a row. Due to the fact that it was the summer holiday, the boys had a break from school, so they had to help in the tobacco field. Malakai took one of the shears and joined Ephraim and the boys to cut the broad leaves of the tobacco plants. The leaves of the tobacco plant were allowed to stay in the sun to soften them briefly, and then the leaves were then put on a lath. After the laths were stacked with enough tobacco plant leaves, they were hitched on a horse-drawn cart and taken to a tobacco shed or barn for curing. The curing process of the tobacco leaves took around two months, and by that time, the tobacco leaves turned to a smooth, dark brownish color. In late November, they were taken off the lath, stripped off the tobacco stalk, and the leaves were packaged and sold at an auction in the Town of Lancaster County.

The sun was wilting the energy of the men and boys, but the women took lemonade and water to the men to quench their thirst. Ruth and Rose served the men the liquid refreshment in the hot sun in the tobacco field. As Malakai was drinking some of the cool water, he smiled and said, "Hello, Miss Winter, you look very Amish."

Rose smiled, took her hand, and wiped some sweat that was on Malakai's face, and said, "So do you, Kai."

Rose held Malakai's hand, and they walked a couple of yards away from the group. Malakai looked at her and asked, "How are you holding up?"

"I am doing well. Living without the amenities of modern convenience is a new experience for me, but it honestly makes you appreciate the things that you take for granted. Plus, I am learning to cook the Amish way. We are preparing lunch for the men," said Rose.

After a few more minutes the women left the tobacco plant field, and as they walked away, the sun was becoming intensely hotter. Malakai wondered why the Amish were not overly worried about skin cancer, knowing that they did not use sunscreen. Malakai knew that the Amish looked at sunscreen lotion as a modern convenience and avoided it. Malakai went over and asked Ephraim about the occurrence of skin cancer in the Amish community. Ephraim explained to Malakai that because they wore protective clothing and hats, skin cancer was not very prevalent in the Amish community. Malakai also thought that that one of the contributory factors of the low incidence of skin cancer in the Amish community was their diet. With the Amish eating as much natural food as possible, it contributed to the development of their immune system to help fight off cancer cells.

Malakai, Ephraim, and the boys continued to toil in the hot sun in the tobacco field until around midday they were called for lunch. They washed their hand under a pipe outside and then went inside, where the women served them lunch. Lunch consisted of spicy oven-fried chicken, baked potatoes, homemade bread, and canned vegetables. The males hurriedly ate the food without leaving a morsel on their plates and drank lemonade. They then returned to the tobacco plant field, where they worked until late evening.

As the week went by, Malakai continued to work in the tobacco field during the day and came home in the evening. One evening Malakai came home and went into the barn and had a shower. Malakai came out of the shower and dressed in his Amish attire then went into the car. He pulled back the front seat, turned on the car radio to a rhythm and blues station and started sleeping to the sound of slow, melodious music.

Around an hour later, Malakai heard a banging on the car's window, and he opened his eyes to see Rose. He opened the door, and suddenly, the sky opened, and rain began to fall, pelting the zinc on the barn. Malakai pulled Rose into the car right on top of him and started kissing her slowly and passionately. Rose pulled her lips from his and said, "I came to tell you to come for dinner."

"You are my delicatessen," said Malakai.

Malakai continued to kiss Rose, and his hand explored the softness of her body. He missed having her beside him, and he wanted to rip the Amish dress off her, but he could not, and he laid Rose on the driver seat while he got up and lifted her dress over his head and buried his head between her soft, supple, inviting thighs. The scent of her perfume engulfed his nostrils, and he bathed in the aroma of her femininity of long-held cherished womanhood. The first thing Malakai noticed was that Rose was not wearing any panties. As he tasted her, the aroma of her body was like the freshness of rainwater on a hot and humid day to a thirsty traveler in the desert. Malakai thought that Rose tasted and smelled just as a woman should taste as he used his tongue and finger to explore and probe her inner thigh. Rose enjoyed the heightened sensation of Malakai's tongue and hand probing, exploring her body and was using all her will power to prolong the sensation. The sensation was electric, coursing throughout her body as she writhed under Malakai's probing tongue. As Malakai's tongue probed her body, the sensation was too intense, and Rose started to scream as her body seemed to quiver as she firmly clutched Malakai's head between her thighs.

Malakai got up from between Rose's legs and unbuttoned his pants, which dropped to his knee. Malakai then lay in the seat and put Rose on top of him in the car. Malakai inserted his penis inside her and pushed his hand under Rose's dress, and held Rose's hips while she thrust on his penis until he ejaculated inside of her body. When they were finished copulating, Rose lay on Malakai's chest, listening to the radio, playing beautiful soulful rhythms and blues music. The rain stopped falling, and Malakai gently eased Rose off his chest and asked, "Why are you not wearing any underwear?"

"I came here and saw you sleeping so peacefully, and I was so turned on watching you, I took them off and inserted them in my apron. I really miss you, not having you beside me in the bed," said Rose.

"I miss you, too, my darling. We will soon be gone from here soon, and by the way, I am glad you took your panties off. There is a bathroom in the barn, you can clean up in there," said Malakai.

Rose and Malakai went into the bathroom, cleaned themselves up and went to have dinner with Ephraim and his wife. Ruth and Josephina served dinner consisting of pork chops with sauerkraut and potatoes. After dinner, the family went on the porch and played board and card games.

As they were all playing scrabble, a horse-drawn carriage came into the yard, and a young, tall Amish gentleman came on the porch, and Ephraim introduced him to Malakai and Rose. His name was Edwin Davids, and he was of Dutch ancestry. Edwin was smartly dressed in customary black pants, a white shirt and a black hat. Edwin was trying his utmost best to court Josephina and to win her affection. Edwin took part in the Scrabble game, after which he and Josephina separated themselves and went to a different part on the porch to talk about their future.

Malakai glanced to where Josephina and Edwin were and could see that Edwin was smitten with Josephina. Malakai liked Edwin. He was well-mannered and had a boyish charm. Malakai wondered whether Edwin would be able to satisfy Josephina's roving mind within their relationships if it did materialize. Malakai knew that Josephina would not be subservient or to submit to any man. Because she was not willing to submit to any man, hence the reason why she was not married. Josephina was not willing to just cook, clean, and procreate for any man. She thought her life should be so much bigger and better than those mundane duties of a woman in Amish society. Josephina felt trapped in her world that she no longer desired, and she was fearful for herself and her family if she left her home that she only knew to embrace modernity in a new society.

She accepted the fact that if she left, her family would abandon her, and the church that she grew up in would also excommunicate her, and she would be a pariah. Josephina was so torn inside her mind, and the only person she spoke to about it was Malakai.

Edwin was doing his best to win her affection and to charm her, but her mind was elsewhere, and he was just a distraction to the ordinariness of her life.

The other family members started retiring to their beds, giving Edwin and Josephina greater privacy. Malakai kissed Rose goodnight and went to his sleeping area by the barn. Around one o'clock in the morning, Malakai was awoken by the sound of a horse neighing. Malakai got up and, quickly, put on his shirt, and ran to the horse-drawn carriage. Malakai asked, "Edwin, can I have a few minutes of your time to speak to you?"

"Certainly, Mr. Malakai," said Edwin.

Edwin hitched the horse on a post and came off the carriage in the early morning, and Malakai asked, "I want to speak to you about Josephina and what your intention is towards her?"

"I am very much in love with her, but honestly, the feeling has not been reciprocated. I do not know if I am coming or going with her because I sometimes think her mind is elsewhere. I tell her I am in love with her and she responds, saying that is nice to know. I honestly love her with all my heart, but the fact of the matter remains that she seems an extremely complicated girl…" said Edwin.

Malakai could hear the frustration in Edwin's voice, and he empathized with Edwin. Malakai knew Edwin's trying to get across to Josephina and her not being responsive to his feelings or affection being quite exasperating to any man or a boy in love with a girl. Malakai could not tell Edwin that Josephina was unsure if she wanted to be in Lancaster County much less to be married to a man. Malakai looked at Edwin and said, "Edwin, if you really love her as you claimed, you got to listen to her, what she says, and most importantly, you have got to be patient with her."

"I have been very attentive to her because I love her, and I hope someday to marry her, God willing," said Edwin.

Malakai could see that, without a doubt, Edwin loved Josephina, but he was unsure if Edwin would be patient, and he could also detect the level of frustration he had with Josephina. Malakai knew that, like a lot of young men who are interested in a girl, but because the girl has her standards and most young men have no patience, they missed out on a genuinely great woman who could be their ideal soul mate or ideal partner. Men sometimes forget that the woman is the prize, and she must be elusive and sometimes unattainable.

For what is life's value if it not to strive for something elusive and unattainable in a lifetime? Malakai said, "For what it is worth, I am on your side. I like you, and I will talk to Josephina on your behalf."

"I would be in your debt if you could speak to her on my behalf," said Edwin.

"Have a safe ride home," said Malakai.

As Edwin departed Ephraim's property, Malakai went back to sleep in the early morning.

Chapter 16

The next day, it was Sunday; Ephraim and his family were invited to his neighbor's home for church service, and he asked Malakai and Rose to accompany them to the church. The Amish are very deeply religious people whose beliefs centered on God, faith, humility, families and their communities. In modern society, people who want to attend church service go to a fixed address where the church is located but Amish church services are held in the homes of the individual members. The church services are held every other Sunday in the homes or a barn of one of its congregation members. Amish home services are quite small, consisting mostly of neighbors, family, and friends. Amish church services are very much regimented in terms of women being seated before the men enter and the women sitting in one area of the room. The men sit in another area facing the women.

As Ephraim's family, Rose and Malakai, entered their neighbor's home for church service, the women were seated on chairs and benches. After they were seated, the congregation selected two preachers and a bishop, all male from among the congregation. Females are never chosen to be bishops or preachers according to Amish rules but assist with the selection of hymns. The congregation began to sing hymns from a hymnbook known as Ausbund book, followed by preaching for around three and a half hours. Rose was quite impressed by the preachers utilizing reading of scriptures from the New Testament of the bible, and prayers because they were not using a written text. The church service culminated with more beautiful singing from the hymnbook.

After the church services ended, Rose and Malakai were introduced by Ephraim to the members of the congregation, and Rose noticed that they all kept calling them "English." Some of the Amish women excused themselves and went and assisted with the food in the kitchen after the church services. The meals were served to the older adults first, then to the younger ones at the same place where they held the church services. The meal generally consisted of pickled beets, cheese spread and bread, cookies, and pie, served with coffee, tea, or water.

In the afternoon Ephraim, Ruth, Malakai and Rose left their neighbor home, leaving the children behind, except for Jonas, who was just six years old. For Amish children, after church, it is generally time to socialize with each other to find a mate. Where Amish young people socialize is quite limited, so they socialize after church, and the boys visit the girl's homes with their parents' consent. Courtship in Amish communities generally begins for girls at age fifteen and for boys at age sixteen.

After Ephraim left, a young man with broad shoulders with a sheepish grin on his face approached Josephina, who was sitting alone on a bench said, "You are certainly the prettiest girl in the whole church yard, and I'd like to introduce myself to you. I am Elias van Bommel, and I am visiting from Ohio."

Josephina looked at the young man smartly dressed in black pants and a white shirt with his hat covering most of his head. Josephina was not really enamored with men who were at her height. She loves men who are tall, men who tower above her height. "I am Josephina; please to make your acquaintance. I saw you staring at me, and I was wondering why you were gazing at me like that?" asked Josephina.

"I was smitten by your beauty and was kind of unsure if I should envelope myself in the cloak of courage and put myself at your mercy, to tell you I want to begin courtship with your parents' permission and blessing," said Elias.

"I see you are a man who is very direct and uses words cleverly. I see no reason why you cannot ask my father permission to see me if you so desire," said Josephina.

"I have to be very direct when I see my future wife, the mother of my many children," said Elias.

"We just met, and that is all you see me as, a blasted breeding machine?" asked Josephina.

Elias was quite baffled by Josephina's response and did not know how to take it. He just smiled at Josephina's question, choosing to ignore the question and not respond. It was the first time he saw an

Amish female talk to him that way. It dawned on him that Josephina was a feisty woman, not likely to be subservient to his male authority. He was, however, intrigued by Josephina's beauty, and at the same time quite puzzled by her boldness. He thought and wondered if it was some sort of foreshadowing of their relationship if they eventually got married. Elias wondered if, as a man, he would be able to wield the power in their relationship. Would he be the man of the house or a coequal partner with Josephina? He knew he was not raised to be a coequal partnered with any woman. He knew he would have to be the overlord in their relationship, and he could not for his life cede authority or be a coequal partner to any woman because his father, who raised him, would be in the same yard as his wife to be and would certainly look down on him with disdain.

Josephina cleared her throat and asked, "I see you are ignoring my question, but I am insisting on an answer. My original question is that, is all you see me as to service you, breed, cook your food, wash your clothes, and raise your many children?"

"I honestly do not know how to respond to you. I have never met an Amish woman like you before. If I am to be honest, I am totally intrigued and also flabbergasted by you, and it seems that anything that I might say will be wronged," said Elias.

"That response may go down well with another young girl, but not with me. I have seen the power dynamics of Amish females, and it is not one I am enamored with because it is my life that will be affected as long as I exist on this earth," said Josephina.

"Can we change the subject? I do not think I like this conversation," said Elias.

Josephina did not care about the uncomfortableness of Elias to the subject at hand; moreover, she did not particularly like or was attracted to him that much because of what he was going to say, because of all the power dynamics in the home and the outside world going to reside with him as a male and as a man. Josephina did not like the roles bestowed on females, especially the roles of females in Amish society. She hated the restrictions placed on Amish women, from restrictions on clothing, gender roles and even on who she could date.

"It is easy for you to say that we must change the subject, but my life will not change if we do get married. I am expected to play my role as a dutiful Amish woman, and where does that leave me?" asked Josephina.

"You will be my loving wife, the mother of my many children. What else do you want?" asked Elias.

"Much more than you can give or offer me," said Josephina.

Elias thought that Josephina was not pretentious and wondered if he was a moth attracted to the flame. Elias thought Josephina was the most attractive Amish girl he had ever laid eyes on, and he wanted her even though her attitude was much to be desired for a woman. Elias thought that the yearning that Josephina has, performing household chores, and taking care of him sexually, would be extinguished with motherhood. Elias asked, "Since I cannot offer you all you need because I am not God, I still would like to come and visit you at your home if it is okay with you?"

"That is all up to you," said Josephina.

"Then it is settled then. I will ask my uncle to come and see your father if I can come by your house to see you then," said Elias.

Elias left, and Josephina went back to rejoin a group of young girls who were singing a more up-tempo religious song. After they were finished singing, Josephina went back to sit on the bench and she began to think about Malakai. She was infatuated with Malakai from the first time they met as a young teenager. She would spend countless hours questioning Malakai about the outside world, and she became fascinated with Malakai's answer. Whenever Malakai went into the town when she was a young fourteen year old, he would buy books for her, and she would carry them clandestinely to her room and read and reread them and get lost in the characters in the books. Malakai would buy books where the main protagonist would be female to help empower her as a young girl.

Josephina was extremely enthralled by the outside world because of the many books that she read and sometimes got lost in the exploitation of the many female characters. She was grateful to

Malakai for cultivating and fostering her love of reading and helping her understand the wide capabilities of her brain. Malakai always told her, that her brain is where there is no unfettered access to think big, dream big, and to make things happen on a wide scale. As a person, you can live inside your mind, yet be mindful that there is a life outside with material needs that need to be fulfilled as a person.

Josephina read and knew the capabilities of females when given the opportunities to do anything just as their male counterparts are afforded in society. She wanted a husband, but just not now, at this stage in her life. She did not want to be saddled down with a husband, or children. She told herself she was just twenty; there would be plenty of time for her husband and children after she had lived her dreams. She wanted to see the world and wanted to experience it somehow, but she was not sure how to go about it. For Josephina, not living her dreams felt like a slow, agonizing death, as if a part of her very being had been ripped apart.

Josephina thought whenever Elias came to visit her home, what would they talk about because they did not have anything in common that would cement their relationship. She liked Edwin for sure because she could see that he genuinely loved her, and he would be patient with her without any qualms on his part as a man. She could see herself definitely with Edwin because he seemed as if he would listen, be understanding, and be responsive to her feelings as a woman. She could see immediately that she did not have any connection with Elias, and it dawned on her that all he wanted was to start a family immediately. She thought, Elias was talking about having a family; he was visiting Lancaster County primarily to seek a wife to take back to Ohio.

Josephina continued thinking and was becoming quite frustrated about the hold the Amish church has on the community, even on the topic of raising a family. In the Amish church, contractive is not permitted, and it was imperative for the members of the Amish church to abide by the edict of the church. Although she was a virgin, she knew enough that a modern woman who is in charge of her sexuality is a woman who is totally free, free to make her own decisions, most of all, free to make the decisions of how many children she wants to have, or not to have, free to make her own decisions who she wants to sleep with, free to go where she wants to go, and free to work. These limitations placed on women in a patriarchal society, more so in the conservative Amish communities, tend to marginalize the female gender.

It was these limitations placed by the Amish church on their lives that drove Josephina to rebel by not marrying or having children. There were enough suitors coming by her house from when she was fifteen, wanting her to be their wife. Josephina thought that her life as a woman was so much more than replicating the role of the last generation by pouring out the next generation of Amish children.

Around ten o'clock in the night, Josephina's father came for her in the horse-drawn buggy and she entered the carriage grateful for him in not putting any pressure on her to choose a husband. She loves her father, respects how he treats her mother and takes care of her brothers and sister. Josephina thought that if she left the Amish community, it would impact him more than any member of her family because, as head of the family, the recrimination would fall on him, and Josephina felt like she was in a catch twenty-two situation; if she stays in the Amish community, she would be unhappy, and if she left it would bring unhappiness to her family.

A few more minutes and they arrived home. Josephina went straight to her room and into the bathroom, where she took a shower. She came out of the bathroom, put on her pajamas, and went straight into her bed. As she lay in the bed, somewhat comforted from the outside world, she started thinking about her situation and felt despondent, and suddenly, her tears came down like a cascading waterfall. She grabbed one of the pillows and put it over her head to muffle the sound of her crying in her bedroom. She cried, feeling like a caged trapped animal. Her solace was eventually eased, when she fell asleep, and she started dreaming that she was a huge wild bird. In her dream, she flew with wild abandon, relishing the experience of flying and soaring above the clouds.

The next morning, Josephina got up and assisted her mother with the preparation of breakfast for the family. After they finished eating, Ruth told Josephina that she must go and get ready to accompany her father into the town to buy groceries. Josephina hurriedly dressed and went outside to see her father waiting for her brother to bring the horse-drawn carriage. Josephina turned and embraced her father and said, "I love you, father for taking care of all of us, and especially me in not pressuring me to take a husband."

"You are my beloved daughter, the firstborn, who I will always love. It is your life to pick a husband who you think is suitable. It is not my place to choose for you," said Ephraim.

Josephina embraced her father and kissed him on his cheeks just as her brother took the horse-drawn carriage. She entered the carriage, and they were off into the town. Josephina liked going into the town, although sometimes they were teased and mocked by the younger boys for being Amish and ignoring technology. Irrespective of that Josephina enjoyed the town, to see the hustle and bustle of everyday people trying to make a living and going about their business. In a weird sense, watching these people gave her a sense of normalcy of what might be possible with her life.

As Josephina and her father entered the town of Lancaster, modernity challenged their Amish ethos as cars, trucks and buses zoomed by, making where they came from look like a distant memory. There were shops, restaurants, bars and the bright lights of the town confronting and inviting them in the modern world. Ephraim stopped at a hardware store and entered the establishment while

Josephina remained inside the carriage. Josephina's legs were feeling a little cramped, so she stepped outside and stood beside the horse-drawn carriage. As Josephina stood waiting, a man walked up to her and said, "I have been all over the world, to Europe, the Middle East, Asia, the Serengeti regions of Africa, and I have never beheld a woman all natural and as pretty as you."

Josephina looked up to see a tall, extremely handsome young man staring intently at her, and she blushed slightly at the man's compliment. He was smiling, revealing white teeth and a devilish smile. The man was dressed in blue jeans, sneakers, and a dark blazer. Josephina said, "Excuse me, please move along English."

"Where is my manners? I am Jerimiah, and I was so struck by your beauty; that I had to come by and say hello."

For some reason, Josephina wanted to tell him to move along, but the words refused to come from her mouth. As she looked at his handsome face, she got lost in the aura of his friendly disposition, and she said, "I am Josephina. Please to meet you, Jerimiah."

"Please tell me how I can see you because my beating irrepressible heart will not be the same again?" asked Jerimiah.

"You will not be able to see me again because you are not of our kind," said Josephina.

"Please do not tarnish our moment with the triviality of something as small as the role we play in this life. Let me take out a card and give you my number," said Jerimiah.

Jerimiah took out a card with his number and handed it to Josephina. She hesitated for a brief moment, then took the card with Jerimiah's number and said, "Please leave now, because I do not want my father to come out here seeing me conversing with you, an outsider."

"Okay, I will leave if you promise me you will try to call my phone number," said Jerimiah.

"I promise, I will call you as soon as it is possible. Now please leave," said Josephina.

Josephina playful pushed Jerimiah away; as he was going away, he said, "My beating irrepressible heart will not rest until I hear from you, you beautiful Amish girl," said Jerimiah.

As Jerimiah walked away, Josephina was surprised at herself that she was definitely attracted to this man, a stranger who was not of her world. She smiled at herself at how playful she was with this man, even by touching him as if they were some long-lasting friend. She gazed at him from a distance, watching him walking, and suddenly he turned around, smiling and waving at her. She returned his smile and turned away, blushing at her reaction to Jerimiah. Josephina knew that Jerimiah had definitely made an impression on her, and for a brief moment, her brain was in overdrive as she felt flustered by Jerimiah's charm. Josephina thought how odd for a fleeting moment, she made a connection with a man who she may never see again, but whose smiling face was firmly implanted in her mind.

Around ten minutes later, Josephina's father exited the hardware store, and they went to the supermarket to pick up groceries. Both Ephraim and Josephina went into the supermarket, and Josephina took out the list of things she needed to purchase for their household. They left the supermarket soon after Ephraim loaded the groceries in the carriage, and they made their way home.

*****

Wallenstein was in the Manhattan office waiting on some answer about the trace he had put on Rose's phone. A knock was made on his office door, and a young Caucasian man who was interning in the office came in and relayed the same information from the last couple of weeks that Rose's phone was turned off or taken apart because there were no cell towers wherever she was picking up the phone signal. He was quite irritated by the amount of time dedicated to acquiring the amulet. Wallenstein had put a trace on Rose's cell phone, and the last person she called on her cell phone an Angela Stanton. Wallenstein was hoping that Rose would call Angela's cell phone again and it would help locate her, but there was no such luck.

Vallencourt came into Wallenstein's office and said, "Good news, one of our own, who I was expecting for the last couple of months, is finally arriving on earth. He came in from the Sagittarius galaxy last night, and he will be able to locate our elusive quarry that has the amulet."

Vallencourt pressed the intercom in Wallenstein's office and asked his secretary to allow the gentleman to come into Wallenstein's office. Within two minutes, a tall Italian-looking gentleman came into the office wearing a blue blazer with dark Italian designer pants and an extremely dark glass. He was quite muscular, and his hands were as muscular as Vallencourt. Vallencourt ushered the man to take a seat.

Vallencourt introduced the man to Wallenstein as Alessandro. Vallencourt asked Wallenstein to show the photo that he had on his phone of Rose and showed Alessandro. Alessandro took the phone from Wallenstein and looked at Rose intently, memorizing every detail of Rose's features and asked, "Do you have any idea where she is at the moment?"

"To be honest, we do not have any idea where she is at the moment. The most we can tell you is that she is in the United States of America. An agent encountered her and the mastermind who has the amulet in New Jersey, about a week ago, but he lost her trying to pursue her in his car. They may be anywhere, such as New York, New Jersey, Pennsylvania, or Florida, for that matter," said Wallenstein.

Alessandro gave back the phone to Wallenstein and asked, "When I do find her should I confront her, or should I call you first?"

"You need to call us because we need to question her," said Vallencourt.

"What about my compensation?" asked Alessandro.

"I cannot bring you into the inner circle as yet, but if you accomplish this task, I will personally fast-track you to the inner circle of the Alliance Organization," said Vallencourt.

"Good, that is all I was expecting. I will commence the search later in the night. I will use the office window to ascend in the clouds," said Alessandro.

Vallencourt told Wallenstein to facilitate Alessandro in the use of his office at night. Alessandro left Wallenstein's office soon after and went on the streets of Manhattan, visiting Time Square and other areas of Manhattan. He stopped at a Chinese restaurant and had some food. He left the restaurant and continued on his sightseeing tours of Manhattan, and then in the night, he went back to Wallenstein's office.

Alessandro was alone in Wallenstein's office, and he proceeded to undress, and when he was completely naked, he opened the office window. The rain had started falling and was pouring down on the streets of Manhattan. Alessandro jumped out the window, and as he jumped, he transformed his entire body into a flaming light and ascended into the clouds. As he soared above the black nimbus stratus or rain clouds, he started fixing his gaze on New York State. He started scanning with his eyes becoming a red ball of fire, lighting up the night sky as he analyzed every individual within New York State. Alessandro's power was quite unique and there were just a few individuals of his kind that possessed that awesome power to see and identify every individual on earth.

Alessandro could not identify anyone who looked like Rose in New York State, so he turned his gaze to New Jersey. As he started scanning New Jersey State, a most stern voice descending from the black cloud said "The person who you are looking for is under my ward. Please desist from rendering assistance to an organization that is unworthy in the eyes of the Most High and the laws of mortal."

Alessandro looked up to see an individual of extremely dark complexion with dark piercing eyes, dressed in a white robe extending to his foot and sandals, walking on the dark clouds heading towards him with anger on his face. Alessandro had an idea who it was, but he was not sure because he had never met the individual before, so he asked, "Permit me to ask whom I am addressing?"

"You are addressing the angel Gabriel, the messenger, and the servant of the one true living God."

Alessandro heard of him and knew he was not matched in terms of the power that Gabriel wields, but he was certainly not going to abandon his task of searching for Rose. Alessandro thought he would be very strategic in how he addresses Gabriel, so he asked, "When you say they are under your protection. Do you mean Rose Winter and?"

"That is exactly what I meant. They are under my protection, so please go on your way and do not come back here searching for who is under my ward. If you do not heed my warning, there will be serious consequences on your part," said Gabriel.

Alessandro was hoping that Gabriel would reveal the other person's name under his protection, but his answer was bereft of any second name, and he dared not repeat the question. Alessandro knew that Gabriel had already picked up that he was searching for information, so he thought he would go back to Manhattan headquarters and return later in the night or the next night. Alessandro, still transformed into flame, descended from the clouds back to the high floors of Wallenstein's office at the Manhattan headquarters. He put on his clothes and waited until the morning for Wallenstein and Vallencourt.

At approximately eight o'clock in the morning, Wallenstein entered the office, followed by Vallencourt. Alessandro told them that he searched all of New York, but she was not in New York State. Alessandro further told them as he was searching in New Jersey, he encountered Gabriel who told him to stop the search because they were his ward. Vallencourt was indignant and asked, "You mean to tell me that the two people we are searching for are protected by our sworn enemies?"

"Yes, that is what I am telling you, and that maybe one of the reasons why you had difficulty finding Rose," said Alessandro.

"So what is the plan going forward?" asked Wallenstein.

"I am planning on going up back in the stratosphere tomorrow night, and I am hoping Gabriel will be gone by then, and hopefully, I will be able to see Rose," said Alessandro.

"That sounds like a good idea, but please be careful because, for now, you are our only hope of finding Rose. We have agents all over the country searching for them, but they seem to have disappeared from the face of the earth," said Vallencourt.

"I am touched because I never knew you cared about my well-being," said Alessandro.

Vallencourt heard the sarcasm in Alessandro's voice and said, "You are the only one on our team who has that type of power, and I would not want to lose you. That is all it is, so please do not mistake my concern for anything else" said Vallencourt.

"It is duly noted," said Alessandro.

Alessandro spent a few more minutes in Wallenstein's office, then went on the road to have breakfast and to have some leisure time while he waited for the night to ascend into the clouds. Alessandro returned to the Manhattan building in the night and went back into Wallenstein's office. He opened the office window then transformed into a fiery flame and ascended into the clouds.

It was a lovely night as Alessandro moved above the clouds quite tentatively and cautiously as he looked and gazed above the horizon. Alessandro started to attend to his task. He peered down on the State of New Jersey and started scanning the State for Rose and her companion. He completed scanning New Jersey and did not detect Rose. Alessandro knew he had to scan from State to State if he was going to detect Rose's whereabouts, and as he started scanning the State of Pennsylvania, a bolt of lightning hit him in his head. Alessandro fell into a prostrate position on the clouds. He immediately looked around to see Gabriel approaching with an angry look on his face and said, "I warned you not to come back in the clouds to search for my wards."

Alessandro was terrified, and he knew within himself that he did not have the power even to confront such an awesome foe as Gabriel. Alessandro knew the only way to get out of the situation was to flee as fast as possible to earth. Alessandro got up off the clouds and started to run, and as he started running, Gabriel stretched his hand towards him, and another bolt of lightning struck Alessandro in his head, and he fell with pain coursing throughout his body.

Alessandro got up off the cloud, petrified and at the same time feeling lucky to be alive because he knew Gabriel could destroy him in seconds. He continued to flee, and as he reached the lower clouds, he realized something was very much wrong with his eyesight. Alessandro suddenly realized that the bolt of lightning coming from Gabriel destroyed his eyesight. He gazed down to earth and realized he could not see much, and Alessandro realized his power was gone and he could not do anything about it. He transformed himself into the fiery flame and went back to earth as quickly as possible to Wallenstein's office at the Manhattan headquarters.

On reaching Wallenstein's office, Alessandro breathed a sigh of relief, glad he escaped the wrath of Gabriel. He quickly dressed, looked outside the office window, and realized that his vision was only normal like everybody else on earth. His eyesight was not able to penetrate objects like before his altercation with Gabriel. He started to ponder what utility he would have in the modern world without his superpower vision. His vision was his "calling card"; it was the reason why people called him for certain jobs, and even why people wanted to associate themselves with him because his superpower vision brings him respectability, and without it, he suddenly fears for his future. He had this sudden premonition to flee from the building, but for some unknown reason, whether the onset of melancholy or losing his power, he pushed the idea out of his head. Alessandro pushed two of the office chairs together and laid on them; he fell into a deep sleep with the last thought on his mind that in the morning, his vision would be restored to its full power.

The next morning, Alessandro was awakened by the sound of the office door, and he opened his eyes to see Wallenstein walking into the office. He got up off the chair, put on his shirt and went to the office window. Alessandro stared out the window to see if his vision could penetrate beyond the many buildings. He was unable to see beyond the buildings, and he suddenly felt isolated and dejected, fearing for his future.

Vallencourt entered the office and asked, "Did you locate Rose?"

"I searched all of New Jersey, and they were not in that State. As I was searching the state of Pennsylvania, Gabriel suddenly appeared, and I had to flee. As I was fleeing, he hit me with a bolt of lightning to my cerebral cortex, making me incapable of using my superpower vision," said Alessandro.

"Is your superpower vision permanently damaged?" asked Vallencourt.

Alessandro was quite hesitant in how to respond to Vallencourt, and he said, "I am not sure if my vision will return tomorrow or the next day or if it is damaged permanently."

"So you are useless to me then. I do not have the time to wait on you to heal, or if you will ever even recover," said Vallencourt.

Vallencourt's spirit was crushed, and the hard work of trying to recover the amulet always comes to naught. At some point, he told himself there would be a reckoning when his lord and master came calling for the amulet. Vallencourt thought he was cursed in the worst way possible, and he now knew for sure that Rose was protected by his sworn enemy. Vallencourt thought that even if they were protected by the angels of heaven, on earth, the Alliance Organization was the ultimate power. Vallencourt looked at Alessandro and said, "Since you are no longer of use to us, please leave the building."

"What about my compensation to promote me to the inner circle of the Organization?" asked Alessandro.

Vallencourt was enraged hearing Alessandro asking for compensation when the task that he asked him to accomplish was nowhere near finished, and in a fit of anger, he picked up the sword that was lying on Wallenstein's desk and swung it forcefully at Alessandro's head. The sharpness of the sword and the force that was applied decapitated Alessandro's head completely, and Vallencourt said, "Take that as your fucking compensation."

As Alessandro's head fell to the ground, blood started spraying in all directions. Wallenstein smiled briefly as he moved from around his desk. He took the sword from Vallencourt's hand and wiped the blood on the sword on Alessandro's dead body. Wallenstein took the sword and put it on his desk, and two minutes later, Alessandro's body turned to dust. Vallencourt, seething with anger, said, "Wallenstein, please ask the cleaning staff to come and clean up the office."

Vallencourt left Wallenstein's office for his office, still angry but at the same time trying to formulate another plan to recover the amulet. He was hoping by now the many agents that he had on the ground in the various States would come up with something by now, but so far, he was out of luck.

Chapter 17

As the weeks went by Elias came by Josephina's house trying to win her heart and to take her back to Ohio. But of all her suitors, she was the least interested in Elias, because she thought that there was something about him and his personality that she could not decipher about this man. She could sense that he would not listen to her, especially in a male-dominated Amish society. After chatting and playing board games for three more hours, Josephina shook his hand and bade him goodbye in the early morning hours. Elias entered the horse-drawn carriage and drove away, and Josephina watched as the horse-drawn carriage left her father's premises. She did not want to seem impolite, but she wanted so badly to tell him not to return to her home. She went to her room, took off her dress, put on her pajamas and went to her bed.

Josephina could not sleep, and she started thinking about Jerimiah. For many nights and days, all she thought about was seeing him, and she wanted desperately to hear his voice again, whispering in her ears. She missed seeing his handsome, smiling face with those set of beautifully arranged white teeth. She longed for that playfulness that she had with him, if only momentarily, and she wanted to know more about him, his travel to the various continents that she had only read about in school textbooks. She was infatuated with the image of Jerimiah, and she could not speak to anyone about him to her family.

Josephina finally nodded off to sleep and started dreaming about Jerimiah. In her dream, Jerimiah was in her bed. As Jerimiah's hand reached for her, she pushed his hand away playfully, and he grabbed her again, stared into her eyes, kissed her long and hard, and then started making love as he tore off her clothes. He traced his tongue over her supple, inviting breast, and the sensation seemed all too intense. Josephina woke from her slumber feeling a tingling dampness between her inner thighs. She got out of her bed and went to the bathroom and thought that her wet dream was a little too real and intense more than her ordinary dream. After she came back from the bathroom, she went back to bed with a firm assurance of what she was going to do in the coming days.

****

Josephina got up early in the morning and assisted her mother and Rose with the preparation of breakfast for the family. After breakfast, she assisted with washing the dishes and then told her mother she was going to see her friend Rossana. She got dressed, took the horse-drawn carriage and went to her friend's house. Rossana lived quite a distance from Josephina, and her father operated a large cornfield.

As Josephina drove passed the large cornfield, she was having second thoughts about what she was about to do, as she clutched the reins of the horse-drawn carriage with one hand, pushed her left hand in her apron pocket and took out the card with Jerimiah's number.

Josephina stared at the number trying to get some sort of solace of what she was about to do that may change her life. She continued on her way, hoping and praying that her little adventure would not embarrass her family or her church.

Josephina drove into Rossana's father's premises, got out of the carriage, and greeted the mother and three other women who were in the kitchen cooking lunch for the men who were in the cornfield. She ran up to Rossana, who was coming from upstairs to the house, embraced her tightly and kissed her on the cheeks. Rossana was five years younger than Josephina with long black hair. Rossana took Josephina to her room, and the two girls chatted. Afterward, Josephina told Rossana that she wanted to use their cell phone to make a call to a stranger. Rossana's family operated a large cornfield. They opted to make use of cell phones to help them with their business, similar to a number of Amish families in Lancaster County. Rossana gave Josephina the cell phone and excused herself from the room.

Josephina took out Jerimiah's card and dialed the number. A voice came on the phone and said, "Hello."

Josephina took a brief moment to respond. It was that unmistakably friendly male voice that she longed to hear, whispering in her ears. Josephina cleared her throat and said, "This is Josephina, the girl you met a couple of weeks ago, and I promised I would call you."

"Oh my lord, please tell me I am not dreaming," said Jerimiah.

Josephina laughed heartily and said, "No, you are not dreaming. I promised you I would call. Now I am calling. I am a woman of my word," said Josephina.

"Let me be honest with you, I was not expecting you to call, much less remember me. I am so excited to hear your voice. I have dreamt about you constantly, hoping that you would call. Now that you have called, I think I am a more hopeful and an extremely optimistic person. By the way, how are you doing?" asked Jerimiah.

Josephina was quite excited hearing this man's voice and was so intrigued by him asking about her welfare, and she said, "I am good, but you are aware I am taking a serious risk calling you from my friend's house because you are an outsider."

"Believe it or not, I do understand the social pressure you must be going through to even call me must be unbearable" said Jerimiah.

"It is an unbearable amount of pressure, especially to even be talking to you as an outsider. If anyone found out about me talking to you, I would be ostracized and shunned in the community," said Josephina.

"I will not have you ostracized or shunned in your community. I would not be able to live with myself," said Jerimiah.

Josephina thought that this man showed understanding of her predicament, and she was moved in a visceral kind of way. Josephina was getting emotional and she calmly asked, "What now between me and you?"

"What I am about to say, please do not take it in any way disrespectful, but I would love to see you again, even if it is discreetely. I would love to see you again, even if it is a few passing minutes. I am aware that I cannot come to your house to see you because, as you said, I am an outsider, and I know enough that I would not be welcomed," said Jerimiah.

Josephina bristled at the thought of seeing Jerimiah again, but she did not see any way that was even remotely possible given her situation of living in an Amish community. In her heart, she desired to see him again, but even if she dared risk it to see him, it would be so perilous for her if anyone found out about her dalliance with an outsider not of her faith. She was not so sure she was concerned about her faith because sometimes she questioned everything about her religion. Josephina was concerned about the social stigma what it would do to her family and the ostracization that she would almost certainly endure, including her family. Josephina pushed the thought out of her head, pushed caution to the winds and said, "I would love to see you too, but for the life of me, I do not see how it would be possible."

"A human life that is worth living is a life that is about taking chances," said Jerimiah.

Josephina smiled and said, "Some chances are not worth taking, especially when the consequences can be so devastating for one of the parties. Josephina asked, "Do you think you are worth the risk?"

"I can say I am worth it for you to take the chance, but in all honesty, in the end, the onus is going to be all on you. I do desperately want to see you, but if it is not possible, it is just not possible," said Jerimiah.

"By the way, do you have a car?" asked Josephina.

"Yes, I have one," said Jerimiah.

Josephina thought long and hard about what she was going to say next, and for a brief moment, she was going to throw caution to the wind and said "I would love to see you also. You can pick me up tomorrow at exactly eight o'clock."

Josephina and Jerimiah chatted for a few more minutes and she gave him the direction where she lived in the community. She hung up the phone call soon after and thanked her friend for the phone. She left her friend Rossana and went home excited and nervous at the decision that she had made about seeing Jerimiah as an outsider. As she was on her way home, she stopped the horse-drawn carriage at Edwin's home and told him to be at her house at seven o'clock tomorrow evening. She was not too proud of the plan she was putting in place, but if she planned to succeed, she had to use Edwin as a cover for her devilish scheme. She left Edwin's home and went home.

As Josephina reached home, she was just in time for dinner. She had dinner with the family and then retired to her room to think about the day's events and her impending plans. She went into the bathroom and had a quick shower then retired to her bed. She did not want to sleep, but because there was no one to talk to, she had to keep everything 'bottled up." She was so excited and nervous, but so looking forward to seeing Jerimiah. She could not stop thinking about Jerimiah, what he likes, and most importantly, what were his expectations of an Amish girl. She eventually fell asleep, dreaming about being in Jerimiah's arms.

Josephina woke up the next morning and went downstairs to assist with making breakfast for the family. After they finished eating, she washed the dishes. She was a nervous wreck, but she tried to maintain her composure, and did a few chores around the house during the day and watching the clock. As the afternoon approached, she went into the kitchen and assisted with dinner preparation for the family. She wanted to do everything as before so no one would become suspicious about her plans for the evening. After eating her dinner, she told her mother that Edwin was coming by the house.

Josephina went to her room and had a bath. She came downstairs at exactly seven o'clock dressed in a regular Amish dress, but she had on a blue sweater that her mother had knitted and used a small amount of the perfume that was given to her by Malakai. Edwin's horse carriage was just arriving at the yard. She went to the front porch to greet and welcome him to her home. They sat on the side porch and chatted, and Edwin held her hand, gazed into Josephina's eyes, replete with desires for her, and expressed his love and devotion as any man intending to marry a beautiful woman. Edwin told Josephina of his desire to marry her when she was ready, but instead of celebrating the good news, she brushed him off, and told him she was not ready as yet and wanted more time.

Around a quarter to eight o'clock, Josephina told Edwin she wanted to go for a ride in his horse-drawn carriage. Edwin complied, and Josephina went into the horse-drawn carriage. They left the premises and were riding and chatting in the horse-drawn carriage when Josephina told Edwin that she felt like walking back to her house to enjoy the cool evening breeze fully. She further told him to come by her house another evening. Josephina got out of the horse-drawn carriage and started walking back to her house. As Edwin horse drawn carriage was out of sight, she turned around and started walking in the other direction. She did not want Edwin to suspect anything or become jealous seeing her meeting, much less entering another man's car. She felt terrible how she had to use Edwin to get out of her own yard to see Jerimiah, but if it were how she had to see Jerimiah she would bear the guilt of it.

Josephina walked for another two minutes when she saw a black-tinted car parked at the side of the road. She walked cautiously near the car and noticed it was a black Toyota Camry. The window of the car opened suddenly, and a hand pushed out started waving at her frantically. She then pushed her hand into her apron pocket, took out a pen and paper wrote down the model, license plate of the car and Jerimiah's name with her name. She then pushed the paper into an extremely small empty water bottle that she took out of her apron pocket.

Jerimiah opened the car door, Josephina entered, and he stared at her for around ten seconds from her face to her feet. Jerimiah smiled at her, almost grinning and said, "Welcome to my humble little car. I am so pleased to see you because, for a moment or two, I thought you would not show up."

Josephina noticed that he was dressed in blue jeans, a white shirt with a long sleeve that he rolled up, and white sneakers. Josephina thought that Jerimiah looked even more handsome than the first time they met. "Good to see you too. I told you I am a woman of my word, and I would be able to see you. Now, here I am. So what's the plan?" asked Josephina.

Jerimiah continued smiling. "I thought we could go for a drive out and chat. I take you back to your house in the next hour or two. How does that appeal to you?" asked Jerimiah.

"That sounds okay, but make it an hour. I do not want to provoke suspicion at home," said Josephina.

"Great then, I will have you home in the next hour. By the way, you certainly look extremely attractive, and I love the look with the blue sweater. It does blend well with your dress," said Jerimiah.

"Thank you very much for the compliment and for even noticing my dress. In our Amish culture, we do not cherish individuality because the elders in our church say it can be a form of pride that will drive the people and community apart. On this auspicious date, I thought I would wear it because the sweater is certainly beautiful," said Josephina.

"You know, you certainly sound very radical to be in a very conservative Amish community," said Jerimiah.

"Well, if my outlook on life were not very radical, I would certainly not be out here with you, cognizant of the consequences if anybody found out," said Josephina.

Jerimiah started the car, and turned on the car radio to a rhythm and blue station, which started playing a soulful, soothing song named "Half the world away" by Paul Johnson. It was the first time Josephina was hearing the song and she listened keenly and suddenly started humming along to the song. They drove and chatted with each other. Whenever there was a pause in their conversation, there was the soulful soothing music on the radio that Josephina was singing and enjoying herself. The music, the conversation they were having, and most of all, she was enjoying being in the company of Jerimiah. She did not regret being in the company of an outsider, apart from Malakai, for the first time in her life. She was even conscious that she was very much attracted to Jerimiah.

As they entered a small town, Jerimiah parked the car at an establishment and told Josephina that he would soon be back as he entered a dimly lit shop. Jerimiah came back around ten minutes with a brown paper bag. In the bag were four non-alcoholic drinks. Jerimiah opened two of the bottles and gave one to Josephina, which she accepted. "Are you trying to get me drunk so that you can have your way with me?" asked Josephina.

"That would be impossible to achieve, considering the drink is non-alcoholic," said Jerimiah.

Josephina was laughing heartily. "I am only messing with you because I knew they were non-alcoholic."

Jerimiah turned around the car in the direction where they were coming from and told Josephina that he was taking her home because he did not want to keep her out too late, and her parents to become overly concerned about her whereabouts and call the police. Seeing the car heading in the direction where they came from, Josephina let down her guard a little, feeling much more relaxed in the company of Jerimiah. Josephina glanced at Jerimiah and smiled and thought he was certainly respectful of her, and most of all, he did not cross any boundary with her in the short amount of time they were spending together in the car. All in all, she thought it was well worth the risk of seeing this man, a stranger, and an outsider.

As they were driving home, Jerimiah said, "I have enjoyed spending time with you, and I would like to see you again. I would like to take you to dinner in the next two days, if it is not a problem?"

Josephina was thrilled that Jerimiah wanted to see her again because the feeling was mutual. As she pondered on her response, her mind was racing, "I would love to go to dinner with you, but you would have to pick me up at the same location at exactly seven o'clock."

"Okay, we have a dinner date then," said Jerimiah.

As they approached the area where Jerimiah had parked earlier, he stopped the car, stretched his hand towards Josephina, held her hands and asked, "Can you please tell me your dress and shoe size?"

Josephina was quite curious as Jerimiah still held her hand. She could feel and sense the attraction that she had for this man, a stranger to her and also an outsider. Josephina started to blush and said, "I am a size six, and my shoe size is seven."

"Great then, I guess I will see you in the next two days," said Jerimiah.

Jerimiah released Josephina's hand, bade her goodbye, and drove off in his car. Josephina walked around a hundred and fifty yards towards her gate; she was feeling quite excited and a little nervous. As the cool night air blew on her face, she started wondering if she was tempting fate by planning on going on an actual dinner date with Jerimiah. Josephina arrived at her gate, which she opened and entered. She quickly walked towards the house and saw her mother and father on the porch. She greeted them and told them that she was going to her room and retired for the night. She was not in the mood to converse with her family tonight. She wanted to be by herself with her inner thoughts to process the night's events.

Josephina entered her room, went straight into her bathroom, and took a quick shower. She came out of the bathroom, put on her pajamas, and went straight into her bed. She liked being in her bed whenever she had a lot of stuff on her mind. She started thinking about Jerimiah. She was glad that he was charming, courteous, thoughtful, and respectful about her situation. She was well aware that she was attracted to him, and especially when he held her hand, she was shuddering and blushing slightly at his touch. She was hoping that he did not notice her reaction to his touch when he held her hand.

Josephina continued thinking, even if she did get into a relationship with him, where would the relationship go, since she could not foresee a future with Jerimiah? In addition, the shame and ostracization that it would bring to her family being involved with an outsider. Josephina was in a quandary, and she could not see a solution to her problem. She was most definitely attracted to Jerimiah like no man before and she definitely wanted to be involved in a relationship with Jerimiah, but such a relationship would be fraught with the utmost of difficulties for her and her family. Josephina eventually drifted off to sleep with her heart eagerly set on seeing Jerimiah.

Josephina woke up early the next morning and went downstairs to assist in the preparation of the family breakfast. After breakfast, she cleared the table and washed the dishes. She could hardly concentrate on her task of washing the dishes as her mind was solely focused on seeing Jerimiah the next day. She was quite excited and scared at the same time, hoping that no one in her community would find out that she was planning on seeing an outsider. She was steadfast in her determination to take the risk of seeing Jerimiah, because, for some reason, the excitement was totally consuming and overpowering, and it was taking her to uncontrollable heights. She was aware that she had been rebellious against the conservative Amish rules and regulations that dictate her life that she totally abhors like a yoke around her neck.

As the hours and minutes of the day passed by, Josephina was giddy with excitement, and she did not feel stressed in seeing Jerimiah, but in a weird way, she felt liberated like a modern woman.

Josephina felt liberated because, in seeing Jerimiah, she was doing it of her own volition.

The stress and pressure to choose an Amish husband was something she constantly rebelled against, and she relished the opportunity to rebel against the Amish church and the dictatorial hold the church has over their life, especially females. While males in Amish society have the opportunity to party and even sow their wild oats before they are married, females have no such opportunity, even if they do so desire for their own life. Accordingly, the Amish church dictates that after the males in Amish society are married, they are to be dedicated to their families and the church. The centrality of the Amish church within their life that teaches them to eschew individuality causes more resentment within Josephina. The church dictates how to behave, how to dress, dictates the avoidance of modern conveniences, and even choosing an Amish husband, which retard the gene pool in the eyes of Josephina. Josephina believes that individuals should be free to decide who they want to marry from whatever race or creed, thereby strengthening the gene pool.

In the evening of the next day Josephina told her parents that she was going by her friend Rossana's house and would be back later in the night. As she closed the gate and started walking, she felt bad that she had to lie to her parents in order to see Jerimiah. Josephina started walking in the opposite direction to her friend's house. She was glad that her house was the first one entering into the community. She started walking a little more briskly because it was nearly seven o'clock.

Josephina walked nearly a hundred yards when she saw Jerimiah's car parked at the side of the road near some cornfield which was on either side of the road. She hurriedly walked up to the car, and Jerimiah came and opened the car door for her to enter. Jerimiah was wearing tight black jeans and a blue blazer and said, "Good evening, Josephina; I have been counting the hours and minutes all day yesterday, hoping time will speed up until I see you again."

Josephina looked at Jerimiah's smiling face displaying white teeth, and retorted, "I have been looking forward to seeing you also; therefore, the feeling is reciprocal."

Jerimiah laughingly said, "I, therefore, can just take you away and never return."

"I do not know about that, because I left your name, cell phone number, model and licensed plate number of your car just in case anything happened in my room," said Josephina.

Jerimiah drove off and turned on the car radio to his favorite rhythm and blue station, which was playing soft melodic music. Josephina, for some reason, felt happy and excited as the soothing rhythm and blue music surrounded them in the car. Josephina thought that irrespective that she did not know Jerimiah much, she somehow felt at ease around him and was feeling quite carefree, as she pushed back the car seat.

As they continued driving, Jerimiah said, "I have something to say to you, but please do not take it the wrong way. We are going to have dinner at a restaurant and hopefully enjoy ourselves and I do not want anyone to stare at you to make you feel uncomfortable. I appreciate you for whatever you wear. Those superficial things do not concern me, but to make other people feel comfortable, they do not look at you as out of place. I recommend that we stop at my place, and you can change into something more appropriate."

"Are you taking me to a store to buy a dress?" asked Josephina.

"No, I have bought them already. The last time I saw you, I asked you what dress size you wore, and I bought three extremely short dresses. These dresses are so short they only cover your waist," said Jerimiah.

Josephina looked at Jerimiah, laughing and said, "I see you have jokes, but I tend to dress modest and respectable as a lady."

They drove for around another two minutes when Jerimiah drove into a premises with a modest four-bedroom house. Jerimiah got out of the car, opened the passenger door, and said, "Please go inside the house and in one of the rooms, you will see three dresses with shoes to match the dresses with other stuff. The dresses and the other stuff are all yours, so select the dress you want to wear on the date with me. I will be right here in the car waiting with bated anticipation on you."

Josephina got out of the car, and Jerimiah gave her the keys to open the front door. Josephina took the keys, walked up a few marbled color steps and opened the front door. She cautiously entered the house. In the living room was a large brownish leather sofa, a rather large sixty five inch flat screen television, and the floor was fully carpeted. Josephina left the living room and entered the dining room with a beautifully designed Italian-looking mahogany table that seated six. She left the dining room, saw the kitchen and washroom, turned around in the other direction and peeped into the first bedroom, which was the master bedroom. Inside was a king-sized bed.

Josephina went from room to room and noticed one of the room doors was locked, but she saw the dresses and black Fendi handbag lying on the bed in another room. Josephina looked at the three dresses and thought they were extremely gorgeous and something that she had dreamt about when she was at home in her bed. The dresses' colors were red, black, and dark blue, all different styles. Josephina started undressing in the room, and for some unknown reason, she decided to close the door and locked it just in case Jerimiah decided to come inside the bedroom.

Josephina stripped naked and tried on the black, and red dress first; then, she changed into the blue dress. She decided she was going to wear the blue dress because it was a close-fitting dress with a revealing breast line. It reaches to her ankle but had a high slit come up to her thighs. Josephina felt provocative and sexy in the dress. She put on the black high heels shoes, let out her hair and looked into the mirror. She was totally pleased with her immediate transformation from her plain Amish dress. She took up a bottle of perfume and sprayed it on her skin.

She looked at herself in the mirror again and felt absolutely beautiful in the dress, like she was transformed into a princess. Ever since she was a child, she had wanted desperately to dress in a modern dress but never got the opportunity because of her Amish upbringing. She continued to look into the mirror, and tears welled up inside her eyes. It was that feeling of getting an opportunity for the first time in her life to try something so trivial that she had always wanted to do but never got the opportunity. As she stared into the mirror and the beautiful image of her reflected back to her, it was as if it was some sort of long-held validation that she was a beautiful woman finally dawned and registered to her finally as tears started emerging from her eyes. She waited a few minutes and then wiped her tears away with her hands.

Josephina then took up the Fendi handbag, opened the door, walked out of the house and locked the front door with the key. Josephina walked towards the car and could see Jerimiah sitting in the car, waiting on her patiently. She walked towards the car and asked, "Are you pleased with the transformation, sir?"

Jerimiah came out of the car and said, "I think you have me confused with someone else. I am here waiting on a lady in the house; her name is Josephina."

Josephina took her handbag and playfully hit Jerimiah and retorted, "You bastard, I know you were messing with me."

Jerimiah started laughing and said, "You look so beautiful and desirable that for a moment, I did not recognize nor believe it was you."

Josephina looked at Jerimiah appreciatively and said, "I am thankful to you for making me feel so beautiful and special."

Jerimiah, slightly curtsy towards Josephina, opened his right hand and said, "My only aim is to please you, and I am glad that you like the dress."

Jerimiah opened the passenger door of the car and Josephina entered, and they drove away from the house. They were soon at their destination at the Cameron Estate Inn which is located in Mount Joy in the rural area of Lancaster. The Cameron Estate is a bed and breakfast inn located on fifteen acres of land. The Cameron Estate offers fine dining to its guests and the wider public just wanting to have a fine dining experience. The inn offers a very historic nineteen-century feel to it with modern amenities.

Jerimiah parked the car and went and opened the passenger door for Josephina to exit the car. As they were walking towards the entrance of the Cameron Estate, with Jerimiah's arm embracing Josephina's arm, he asked "Do you think it was even remotely possible that you and I would be on a romantic date?"

Josephina pursed her lips before responding and said, "Even if an angel descended from the heavens and told me that you and I would be going on a romantic date, I would not believe that angel."

They laughed, and Jerimiah said, "I can imagine the risk you are taking and the social pressure of dating someone who is not of your world. However, having you under my arms and being close to you seems to be worth the risk."

"I am glad that I took the risk to see you irrespective of everything," said Josephina.

They entered the front entrance of the Cameron Estate, where they were greeted by a friendly hostess who took them to the restaurant where Jerimiah had made a reservation. The restaurant was beautifully decorated, and the table was covered with a white tablecloth. When they arrived at their table, Jerimiah pulled out Josephina's chair. Jerimiah ordered a bottle of white wine and encouraged Josephina to taste it. Josephina looked at Jerimiah and asked, "Do you know that the consumption of alcohol is not tolerated within my religion? In addition, I do not know what your intention is with me tonight," said Josephina laughingly.

Jerimiah ignored Josephina's question, poured a small amount of the wine into a glass, and told Josephina to taste it. Josephina tasted it, relished the taste in her mouth and said, "I am breaking all the rules that I have lived by all my life, firstly not to associate with, much less date an outsider, and secondly, not to drink alcohol."

Jerimiah, with a wry smile on his face, said, "You have done all those things, and you are still here. I promise to take you home safe and sound, so please do not concentrate on trivialities and frivolities."

The waiter came and took their order. Josephina ordered baked salmon fish, while Jerimiah ordered Ahi tuna steaks. The meals tasted quite sumptuous with local herbs and spices quite pronounced and flavoring the meals. When the main course was finished, they had chocolate cake for dessert. They continued drinking the white wine when Josephina asked Jerimiah, "Where was the most interesting place you have visited?"

Jerimiah took a moment to think about the question and responded, "Africa would stand out as the most interesting place I have been. I am speaking mostly about the Serengeti region of Africa, which comprises the region of north Tanzania to southwestern Kenya. In the Serengeti region, you see the largest migration of animals in the world. It is truly fascinating to see so many mammals in one place migrating. It is truly a sight to see over a million wildebeests and also zebras, gazelles, and buffalos."

" It does sound truly fascinating to witness such an occurrence of so many animals migrating. I have always been fascinated with travelling to see what the world is like," said Josephina.

" Hopefully, one of these days, you will be able to travel to see the world as it is, and just the different types of people that occupy the different countries," said Jerimiah.

" I do hope so," said Josephina.

Jerimiah paid the bill for the dinner, and they went outside on the lawn of the estate with Jerimiah holding Josephina's hand. They continued to chat and flirt with each other until it was time for them to depart the premises. They drove back to Jerimiah's house, where he gave Josephina the key to open the front door. Josephina exited the car and went inside the room to change into her Amish dress. She went into the room, but this time, she did not lock the door. She undressed in the room, keeping on her bra and panty, hoping that Jerimiah would come inside the room.

Josephina stared at her nakedness in the mirror with the amulet that Malakai gave her prominently displayed around her neck. She stared in appreciation at her body with the high heels on her feet. She waited a few more minutes to see if Jerimiah would come into the room. He did not enter into the room, and she took up the Amish dress off the bed and put it on and she walked out the house a little peeved to see Jerimiah waiting by the car. Josephina walked up to where the car was parked, and Jerimiah held her right hand; she fell into his arms, and he kissed her softly and gently on her lips. Josephina was trying to catch her breath when Jerimiah embraced her more tightly and kissed her more aggressively, this time around her neck.

After Jerimiah released Josephina from the tight embrace, he said, "I want to come inside the room, but I had to restrain myself. I want to see you more often than you can imagine, but I am weak when it comes to you."

Josephina, acting stoic, smiled and said, "Can we go now because I do not want my parents to be overly concerned about my whereabouts."

Jerimiah opened the passenger door of the car and Josephina entered, and he drove her home. Jerimiah stopped the car at the exact area where he picked up Josephina. As Jerimiah turned off the car ignition, he said, "This is the worst part of the night to see you leave."

"It was a lovely date. I enjoy every moment with you immensely," said Josephina.

Josephina took her right hand, held Jerimiah's face, and kissed him deeply and intensely. After they stopped kissing each other, Jerimiah asked, "I'd love to see you in the next four days at the same time if it is possible?"

"I do not see any reason why it would not be possible," said Josephina.

"I'd love to take you to a dinner theatre club in the town," said Jerimiah.

They kissed one final time and bid goodbye to each other, and Jerimiah drove off as Josephina walked towards her gate. As she pushed the gate to enter the premises Josephina felt elated as a broad smile was plastered over her face. She greeted her parents, who were inside the house and went straight to her room.

Josephina went to the bathroom to take a quick shower to cool down her overheated body. She stayed in the shower longer than she intended as the water poured down on her body, her soapy hand gently exploring, tantalizing her body, as she touched herself over and over until she climaxed in the shower. Josephina finished her shower, came out, put on her pajamas and climbed into her bed.

Josephina tried her absolute best to sleep but it was a failing effort as she was thinking about Jerimiah. The sky seemed to suddenly open, and rain started to pour down on the housetop. She suddenly felt lonely and missing Jerimiah's touch and his kisses, especially on her neck. She wished there was a telephone in her house so that she could call Jerimiah to hear his voice and, more or less, talk endlessly like a normal couple in the modern world. Suddenly, the soothing rhythm and blue music that Jerimiah was playing in his car, "Half the World Away" by Paul Johnson, started echoing in her brain, and she started humming to the songs. Josephina thought the song lyrics were so apt because she and Jerimiah seemed like they were "Half The World Away," and she wanted desperately to be with him in her bed.

Chapter 18

Malakai and Rose were in the barn in the car, chatting and listening to rhythm and blues music on the radio. The car's front seats were pushed back, and Rose lay slightly on Malakai's chest. Malakai's hand was caressing Rose's back, and as his hand wandered, Rose said, "I truly miss having you beside me in the bed at night."

"We will soon be back together in your warm, lovely bed in New York City. I promise you," said Malakai.

Rose laughingly said "Please do not worry, because I am definitely holding you to that promise. If not, we will have to go our separate ways, and it will be the last you will have me in your arms."

Malakai took his right hand, slapped Rose on her rear, and said, "You are mine, and I am yours no matter the season or time of the year."

Malakai kissed Rose softly and tenderly and whispered in her ears that he loved her no matter where they were, as long as they were together on this adventure that they called life. They stayed in the car until it was getting late, and Malakai followed Rose to the front porch of the house, where he kissed her goodnight and went back to the barn. As Malakai arrived back at the barn, he saw Josephina standing, waiting on him beside the car. Malakai opened the car and said, "Hello, Josephina. What can I do for you?"

Malakai pushed up back both front seats to their original position, and Josephina came into the car and said, "You told me that whenever I want to talk, I can always come to you. Therefore, I am here now, and I want to talk to you, but whatever I say to you, it is between both of us."

"I told you that whenever you want to talk, you can always come to me, and whatever you say to me, it will be treated confidentially," said Malakai.

Josephina took a moment hesitating, biting and licking her lips, not sure how to broach the topic of what she wanted to say to Malakai until finally; she said, "Malakai, you know that I am dissatisfied with my life and especially the hold the Amish Church has on our community. In expressing anguish and rebelling against the doctrine of the church, I think I may have committed a sinful, reproachful act."

Malakai, quite concerned about what Josephina may have done, asked, "Please tell me what is of concerned to your pretty little head?"

"A few weeks ago, I went into the town of Lancaster with my father to do some shopping. While he was in the hardware and I was waiting outside, beside the horse-drawn carriage, I met someone, and he gave me his number. I went by my girlfriend's house and used her father's cell phone to call him. I have been seeing him discreetly and even went on two dates with him."

"What is the matter with that?" asked Malakai.

Josephina hesitated in answering Malakai's question, not sure how her response to the question would sound or perhaps not wanting Malakai to condemn her. She continued, "The problem is that he is not of our faith. He is an outsider, but I like him so much. He is the only man other than you that I have been interested in so for."

Malakai allowed Josephina's answer to his question to sink into his brain before responding to her statement. He was well aware that if Josephina continued to see this man, what would it mean to her, and her family if anyone found out about her transgression? Malakai sighed and asked, "Are you going to continue to see this man?"

Josephina thought long and hard at the question and, with a firm determination, answered, "Yes, I want to continue to see him again discreetly. I think I am falling in love with him. I think of him constantly, and you are the only person in the world I could talk to and share my feelings about him without you castigating my behavior."

Malakai thought Josephina seeing this man, an outsider from her community, would not end well, and it would only cause heartache to Josephina and her family if they found out about her affair. He was not sure any advice given to Josephina she would be even willing to accept if it was negative.

He pleadingly asked, "Can I ask you, for the sake of your family and even your well-being, not to see him again?"

Josephina responded angrily to Malakai and said, "I am not a child. I am well aware of the ramifications of my actions if I continue to see him. I tried several times to push the thoughts of not seeing him out of my head, but it was of no use. I go to bed thinking of him, and I wake up thinking of him all day. By the way, his name is Jerimiah."

Josephina started becoming emotional and started crying, and Malakai leaned over and held her head against his chest. Malakai allowed Josephina to cry on his chest, hoping that somehow it would be therapeutic, after a few more minutes, Josephina stopped crying, and Malakai asked, "When next are you going to see him?"

"I will be seeing him in the next couple of days," said Josephina.

"I would love to tell you not to see Jerimiah anymore, but I know you would ignore that advice. Please be careful and do not let him pressure you to do anything so that you cannot look at yourself in the mirror the next morning. Please do not take any unnecessary risks and come to me whenever you want to talk," advised Malakai.

Malakai opened the car door and Josephina got out, and she kissed Malakai on his cheeks and bid him goodnight as she walked back to the house. Malakai was not comfortable with the news that Josephina shared with him, but he was comforted by the fact that

Josephina was an extremely smart woman. Malakai wondered if he was doing the right thing in not telling Josephina's parents. If he told Josephina's parents, he would immediately lose the trust of Josephina, and it would cause a big family crisis. There was no easy solution out of this crisis and Malakai was hoping that everything would work out in the end, even if he did not believe or immediately see a way forward.

******

The next evening, all the family members were on the porch when Elias came by and greeted everyone, and he and Josephina went to the back porch. Elias had this somber look on his face. He sat down on the chair and said, "Seeing you looking so beautiful lifts my despondent spirit, and my troubles seem inconsequential."

"Thanks for the compliments. What kind of trouble are you in?" asked Josephina.

"I will have to return to Ohio shortly because my father died, and I will have to assume my position as head of my household," said Elias.

Elias was deceitful but he thought that he had no choice in the matter of affair of the heart. He had this wild, abandoned desire for Josephina, and he reckoned he had to use whatever means to win her heart. Elias thought that playing the sympathy card might work if it got him the desired goal of winning Josephina's heart.

"I am so sorry to hear about the death of your father. How are you holding up?" asked Josephina.

Elias was thrilled to hear the level of concern in Josephina's voice. He thought the right amount of sympathy might just work for what he wanted to ask Josephina. Elias lowered the pitch of his voice to try to get the maximum amount of sympathy from Josephina and said, "I am trying to cope and be strong for my family, but the news of his death is quite hard to take and make sense of it all."

Josephina drew closer to Elias and laid his head on her bosom to comfort him about the unfortunate death of his father. As Elias's head was on Josephina's bosom, he took his hand and embraced Josephina's waist, and he could feel the warmth of Josephina's body. Elias held Josephina's body against his, reveling in the momentary pleasure and hoping somehow that it would be permanent having this woman in his life. Josephina withdrew from the embrace and asked, "Is there anything I can do to help to soothe the pain of losing your father?"

Elias took a few seconds before responding and thought everything went well so far as he had planned, but now was the moment to ask Josephina what he came by the house for and now was the pivotal moment to play on Josephina's emotions. Elias did not care whether sympathy or empathy or anything else that got him the desired goal of what he wanted from Josephina.

Elias cleared his throat and said, "Josephina, I am in awe of your mind and how you see the world. I think you are the most beautiful Amish woman I have ever seen. I am in love with you and would like to ask you, for your hand in marriage and take you to Ohio."

Josephina, totally flummoxed, not expecting a marriage proposal, stared into space as if she was peeping into an alternate universe. Josephina, not knowing how to respond, held Elias's hand in her own hands. Josephina did not want to tell him anything negative because of the death of his father, and compounded his misery. She thought long and hard about how to respond and decided just to tell Elias the truth. She held his hand firmly and said, "Elias, I am sorry to disappoint you, but I cannot marry you. I am not in love with you, and I certainly cannot move to Ohio with you."

Elias released his hand from Josephina, angered by Josephina's refusal to accept his marriage proposal and asked, "Josephina, please answer me honestly. Is there someone else?"

Josephina could see the anger and hurt in Elias's eyes, and she wished that there had been a way to erase the pain, apart from accepting his marriage proposal. Josephina averted her eyes from Elias and looked downward on the floor, trying to formulate a way to answer his question to lessen the hurt and pain to Elias. She could not formulate anything more than to answer honestly and said, "Yes, there is someone else that I am in love with, and I am sorry to tell you this;

it was not my intention to hurt you, especially on such an occasion as on the death of your father."

Elias was more furious than ever with the awareness that Josephina chose someone else, and he was bitter and asked, "Are you a loose woman? You must be because you are seeing me and someone else. Where I am from, they called that type of woman a two-faced whore."

Josephina was stunned and apoplectic at the same time, having been disrespected in her own home. She was going to raise her voice when she thought that her parents were on the side of the porch, and did not want them to hear what she was talking or arguing about with Elias. Josephina calmly said, "Please leave now, and never venture on my father's premises again. You are a disrespectful piece of crap, and I am so glad in my wildest thought never to make a decision to be with a piece of crap like you."

Elias got up, stormed off the porch, went in his horse-drawn carriage and left the premises. Josephina blew a sigh of relief, glad to see the back of Elias and to have someone of that ilk out of her life. She thought that if she had made the fatal mistake of being with someone of that disposition, she would be so unhappy in her life. She somehow felt good inside, not having to dwell on what might have been if she had decided to go and live in Ohio with Elias.

From she was a teenager, she always remembered what Malakai taught her about relationships; "It was not the big things, while they can be important, it is always the small things that tell who a person is and what that person is capable of in life. If you meet a man and he is always inconsiderate of you, and by chance, you entered a relationship with him, he will be inconsiderate throughout the relationship; that is just life and not rocket science. People's nature does not change. People's personality is just what it is, and it especially comes to the forefront, especially in adverse circumstances."

As Josephina's mind was lost in her thoughts, her mind drifted to Jerimiah and how he was thoughtful about her welfare and been respectful of her, not even coming inside the house when she was undressing to buy those gorgeous dresses, not wanting anyone to stare or for her to feel uncomfortable when they were on the dinner date.

Josephina did not know where dating Jerimiah would end up, but she was so attracted to him, that she enjoyed being in his company and staring at his handsome face into those devilish blue eyes. Josephina accepted the fact that she was falling in love with Jerimiah irrespective that he was an outsider. She questioned herself why she was so attracted to Jerimiah and wondered if it was because it was forbidden love. Since the time she was a child, she was taught how to behave, how to dress and her role within Amish society. She wondered if it was her way of rebelling against those strict Amish rules why she was so attracted to Jerimiah and wanted to be in his company.

Josephina soon after, went upstairs to her room. As she lay in the bed, she was counting the hours eagerly anticipating the next day when she would see Jerimiah. As she started sleeping, she started to dream. She was dreaming that she was in a huge cornfield, and there was a huge circle of colors encircling her. They kept changing from one color to the next until the colors just enveloped her, until she was fully naked, running barefoot on the grass. Suddenly, the colors disappeared, and a loud, piercing shrieking sound seemed to be coming from all around, disorienting her senses; she looked up to see a huge black bird with wings extended, and she started to run through the cornfield. Josephina, as she was running, turned around to see a fox running at her at a maddening speed. Josephina kept on running as she turned her head around to see how close the fox was, but there was no fox but a barking, menacing Doberman dog. Josephina started running faster to create some distance between her and the Doberman dog. Josephina turned her head to see how close the dog was, but suddenly, she saw a huge, ferocious white wolf with piercing blue eyes running twice as fast as the other two animals. The wolf caught up to her and suddenly sprang at her. Josephina woke out of her dream, instantly breathing heavily in the bed.

Josephina was sweating profusely in her bed, wondering what her dream indicated and what it meant. As she took a towel and wiped her forehead, Josephina could not fathom what the dream indicated, so she went back to sleep.

Josephina was walking towards Jerimiah's car the next evening with the cool breeze blowing across her face. She was almost giddy with excitement to see Jerimiah. When she reached up to the car Jerimiah was waiting outside the car. He opened the passenger door, and Josephina entered into the car. Jerimiah closed the door, went around, opened the driver's side door, entered the car, and drove away from the area to his residence. As they drove into the yard, Jerimiah parked the car, reached over to Josephina, and kissed her passionately. He gave her the front door key and told her to go and get dressed for their date while he waited outside.

Josephina went inside the house and entered the room where the dresses were located. She quickly undressed and tried on the red dress. The red dress had a split front. The split went up halfway up to her thighs, and the dress clung to her body as if it was sewn on it. Josephina put on the black high heels shoes and looked at herself in the mirror. Josephina realized that the silver amulet that Malakai gave her was on the front of her dress and took it and placed it inside her bosom.

Josephina sprayed on her perfume, picked up a small handbag on the bed and walked out of the house. As she locked the door, Jerimiah was smiling and said, "My, my, you certainly take my breath away. You look so beautiful, and I am so honored to have you in my arms."

Josephina blushed slightly at the compliments and said, "Thank you for the nice compliments and thanks for making me feel so special. It is duly noted and appreciated."

"It is my job to make you feel special if I am to be worthy of your company. Always remember you are the prize, and I am just hoping by all means to be a worthy recipient," said Jerimiah.

Jerimiah kissed Josephina on the cheeks and opened the car door. Josephina entered, and they drove away from Jerimiah's house. As they were driving, Jerimiah had his left hand on the steering wheel and with his right hand held Josephina's hand. Josephina felt at eased and relaxed in Jerimiah's presence, and she was never sure she could feel so at ease in a man's presence, more so an outsider not of her world.

They drove into the town of Lancaster, where they entered the Dutch Apple Dinner Theatre. Jerimiah parked the car, opened the passenger door and escorted Josephina inside the Dutch Apple Dinner Theatre. Josephina felt excited and confident, although she was visiting a theatre for the first time in her life. She thought that these simple things that most people take for granted were so novel to her, but she was going to relish the moment because she did not know when she would have this kind of experience again in her life.

As Josephina held onto Jerimiah's arms as they walked inside the theatre, she could see lots of people staring at her approvingly, especially the men. There was a large gathering of people inside the theatre. The stage was beautifully decorated, and the dinner tables were covered with elegant red tablecloths. Jerimiah and Josephina were escorted to their table by a friendly female host. The meals were served buffet styled by friendly staffs. They had honey-baked chicken served with rice, and for dessert, they had strawberry swirl cheesecake.

After they had consumed their meals, they watched the showing of The Wizard of Oz. The show was cleverly produced, and the actors and actresses were quite professional in their performances as they went through their various acts. They left the Dutch Apple Dinner Theatre soon after the show ended and drove back to Jerimiah's house.

As they were driving back on an isolated road, Jerimiah kept looking in his rearview mirror and said, "We are being followed by four men on motorcycles."

Josephina spun her head around to see four Caucasian-looking men on motorbikes riding their bikes at an even pace. Jerimiah sped up the car to create some distance between the car and the motorbikes. The men sped up their bikes, and one of the riders caught up to the car and overtook it. The rider of the bike that overtook the car sped away from the car, rode around a hundred and fifty yards ahead, and stopped in the middle of the isolated road.

Josephina was feeling quite panicky at the situation, and she looked across at Jerimiah, and she could see a wry smile on his face.

As she was about to ask Jerimiah a question, the other three bikes overtook the car and stopped in the middle of the road where the first biker was parked. Jerimiah reduced the speed of the car and stopped at the side of the road around twenty yards from the bikes.

The first rider that overtook the car took off his helmet and walked towards the car. He was a tall blonde gentleman wearing a brown leather jacket, black jeans and brown cowboy boots. His blonde hair was tied in ponytail fashion with a red bandanna. He walked up to the car casually, bent his tall body frame, lowered his head and said, "Good evening, Jerimiah, and your lady friend."

"Hello, Lonnie," said Jerimiah.

Jerimiah attempted to open the car door, and Lonnie pushed back the car door slamming it shut, preventing him from exiting the car. Josephina realized what was happening and started to become quite scared, being trapped in the car. Lonnie gazed steadfastly at Jerimiah and said, "We need for you to pay us for all the work we are presently doing for you, and the previous assignment which you did not pay us. The current assignment of searching for the two individuals is not easy, and gas is not free in this economy."

"Okay, let me out of the car and let us talk," said Jerimiah.

Lonnie moved away from the door, and Jerimiah came outside the car. The other three bikers came by closer to where Lonnie and Jerimiah were chatting, and they were all dressed in blue jeans and black jackets, and all were sporting long, disheveled looking beards. Jerimiah moved a little distance behind, and away from the car, deliberately outside of Josephina's earshot.

One of the bikers named Jerry said, "We need our pay now, or else you got to bear the consequences of our fist."

Jerry started grinding his hand knuckles together to form a fist and asked, "Are you going to pay us now, or do we have to take our own action to force you to pay us?"

Jerimiah knew he did not have the money to pay them, so he thought the only way to extricate Josephina and himself from the situation was to be partially honest with them on the one hand and be deceptive on the other hand. Jerimiah, in a stern voice, said, "Listen to me, gentleman. I do not have the money with me at the moment, but by next week, I will have the money to pay you."

All the men started laughing loudly, and Lonnie said, "Since you do not have the money to pay us. We will take your woman in the car and return her to you when you have the money, but do not expect her to be in one piece when we return her to you."

Jerimiah knew that the men were not joking, and they had every intention of taking away Josephina; where they would certainly rape her continuously, and this would almost certainly destroy the plan that he had for Josephina. Jerimiah started laughing hysterically and using his right hand to slap his right knee while he bellowed out pretentious laughter, "You guys are making me laugh too much. That is the best joke I heard all day. You four guys need to be working in a comedy club."

Seeing Jerimiah laughing hysterically, the men's disposition changed, and they became quite angry at Jerimiah. Jerry angrily said, "Hey shithead, if you do not pay us what you owe us, we are going to take your woman and rape the shit out of her, until you bring us the money you owe us."

Lonnie started walking back towards the car, and Josephina, who was looking at what was happening, saw the man approaching the car, and she locked both car doors. Josephina was terrified inside the car and knew whatever the men were arguing over with Jerimiah was not going well. She knew she was in danger and was looking frantically inside the car for anything that could be used as a weapon. She opened the glove compartment and saw a small knife. She took it out and concealed it in her right hand beside the lower side of the driver seat.

Jerimiah started staring intently at the three men in front of him, and suddenly his eyes were bloodshot, and his eyes were the color of crimson. The three men saw the transformation of what was happening with Jerimiah, and they stood back, quite terrified and frightened of Jerimiah. Jerimiah kicked the first man in his stomach, and he fell on the ground, grimacing with pain, while the other two men started circling Jerimiah. The second man, Jerry, lunged at

Jerimiah with his right fist, and Jerimiah sidestepped the man's attack and punched the man in his ribs. Jerry screamed with intense pain as it coursed throughout his body, and he fell to the ground.

The third man saw his two companions on the ground in intense pain but did not know what to do, and the fearful expression showed on his face, similar to a deer caught in a car headlight. He wanted to run away but was afraid, fearing the wrath of his companion and being branded a coward by his travelling comrade. The man leaped at Jerimiah with his outstretched hands, trying to force him to the ground, but Jerimiah evaded the man's grasp and spun around quickly and kicked the man under his rib cage, as he fell to the ground in pain, similar to his companion.

Jerimiah diverted his attention to the last man standing beside the car, shouting at Josephina to open the car door. The man was shouting and said, "Bitch, for the last time, opened the car door."

The man, in total anger, smashed the passenger window of the car with his fist and opened the car door. He pushed his hand inside the car and placed his hand on Josephina's left hand, trying to drag her out of the car. Josephina took the small knife that she had in her right hand and plunged the knife into the man's right hand. The man released Josephina's hand immediately as blood started pouring off his hand. The man did not see Jerimiah running at full speed as he was concentrating on the cut on his hand. Jerimiah leaped off the ground as he was in proximity to the man and landed a karate kick to the man's chest. The man fell over on the ground, grimacing with pain, and Jerimiah went over the man and snidely said, "Never dare to disrespect me or my companion again, else next time I will take your life."

The man was moaning in pain as the blood was pouring off his hand, and Jerimiah said, "I also expect you to keep on looking for the two people."

Jerimiah went back into the car and drove away, feeling confident that he had sent a clear message to the men that he would not tolerate their threats. Josephina was quite excited, and her beating heart was just slowing down from the excitement of the man trying to drag her out of the car. She reached out and held Jerimiah's arms because she wanted to feel close to him, and to have some reassurance that the danger was truly over. She somehow felt confident and relaxed with Jerimiah, especially how he dealt with those men with their despicable behavior.

As they were driving to Jerimiah's home, Josephina asked, "Jerimiah, why did those men want to get into a confrontation with you?"

"I asked them to carry out a task, and they did not fulfill their end of the bargains; therefore, I refused to compensate them until they fulfill their end of the contractual agreement."

Josephina, not sure what to make of Jerimiah's response, said, "All this confrontation over failing to live up to a contractual agreement?" Josephina mused and asked, "Do you not think it is a little gratuitous for somebody to be having a confrontation over unfulfilled work?"

Jerimiah smiled and said, "I think it is a little juvenile and unseemly, but people can act and behave irrationally sometimes."

They arrived at Jerimiah's home, and as Josephina was opening the car door, Jerimiah held her hand and said, "I am coming inside. I cannot hold out any longer, and I am hoping you are ready to go the ultimate distance with me tonight."

Josephina knew that at some point, the moment would come for her to make the decision whether she should engage into a sexual relationship with this man. She thought long and hard many a night in her bed, but somehow, being with Jerimiah brought a certain clarity that she was ready to go the distance with him and be his woman. Also, the fact that she was in love with him made the decision a rather easy one to make, although she was a little hesitant because she was a virgin and was not sure of all the intricacies of making love to a man.

She smiled shyly, held Jerimiah's hand, and said, "Let's go inside the house."

They went inside the house, and as Josephina was walking ahead of Jerimiah into the backroom where her clothes were, he gently held Josephina's hand and told her he was taking her into the master bedroom. Jerimiah turned on the light in the bedroom to an almost dim lighting, giving an almost reddish display of colors. It was the first time Josephina was going inside the master bedroom. As she walked in, she saw the huge king-sized bed neatly made up with lavender-colored sheets. Jerimiah held Josephina's hand, and he kissed her long and hard, relishing the taste of her lips as his hands wandered over Josephina's body.

When Jerimiah ceased kissing Josephina, she said, "Please be gentle because I am a virgin."

Jerimiah grinned and laughingly said, "If you were not a virgin, you would not be here for me to feast."

Jerimiah then continued kissing Josephina, tracing his tongue over her lips down to her neck to the carotid artery. He licked and tasted her neck, where Josephina's carotid artery was similar to a lion licking an animal they had just killed before tearing its flesh apart and eating it. As Jerimiah was licking Josephina's neck, he inserted his hand through the slit of her dress and allowed his hand to wander all over her body. He could feel her young, supple, vibrant breasts, but he was not satisfied. His hand continued to wander to her pert, luscious posterior, where he relished the touch and the sensation.

As Jerimiah's hands wandered over Josephina's body, he started taking off her dress. Jerimiah was hurryingly taking off Josephina's dress and her bra. He flung the bra on the bed and turned Josephina around, smiling appreciatively at her body. Josephina's dress came off to her waist and she pushed Jerimiah away slightly to step out of the dress and took off her underwear. Josephina was now completely naked, only having the amulet and her high heels. Jerimiah took off his shirt and pants, reached for Josephina and took her into the bed.

As they were in bed, Jerimiah said, "I have dreamt for many a weeks and days having you in my bed, and now you are finally here. I think I am the luckiest man alive."

"I have also sat in my room many a night, wondering what it would be like to be with you in your bed. I have no regrets, though, because I want to be here, to be in your arms and make love to you and share my virginity with you," said Josephina.

"I am so honored that you decided to share your virginity with me," said Jerimiah.

Jerimiah reached over and gently grabbed Josephina, pulled her closer to him and started kissing her passionately. He moved his mouth off Josephina's lips and started slowly tracing his tongue to her neck and to her young, supple breast, where he enveloped them in his mouth. Jerimiah removed his mouth from Josephina's breast and started kissing her neck. As he continued kissing her neck on the bed, the sensation became too intense for him, and his eyes started to become blood red. Jerimiah's lips started to become drained of all the blood in them and became extremely white, and suddenly, two large teeth appeared in the lower and upper portion of his mouth, looking more like the fang of a wild animal like a wolf.

As Jerimiah was about to sink his fang into Josephina's carotid artery, she shifted her body, and the silver amulet she was wearing around her neck started shining a bright, piercing white light at Jerimiah's face. Josephina was totally unaware of the light coming off the amulet and the effect it was having on Jerimiah. The light hit Jerimiah's face, and it was the most intense pain he had ever felt in his entire life. Jerimiah screamed at the intense pain, ran into the bathroom, and locked the door.

Josephina was totally bewildered at the sight of Jerimiah's naked body running into the bathroom and slamming the door. She wondered what was happening to Jerimiah and why he had to run into the bathroom. Josephina wondered if she had done something to him but for the life of her, she could not fathom what had happened to Jerimiah. She knew she was a virgin and did not know much about making love to a man, but she was not aware of anything she did wrong. She started to panic wondering if he did not find her appealing and desirous as a woman. She got out of bed, quickly put on her bra and panty, and ran into the back room to put on her Amish frock.

Jerimiah was in the bathroom, wondering why he was experiencing so much intense pain. He looked into the mirror at his face, and it was extremely swollen. There were some huge red blotches, and his face seemed as if he was run over by a truck. Jerimiah looked down at his body, and suddenly realized his whole body was covered in red blotches, and there was intense pain permeating his entire body. He could not make sense of what was happening, but it suddenly dawned on him that his life force was nearly terminated if he had stayed in bed with Josephina. Jerimiah suddenly came to the realization that whatever was happening to him had something to do with Josephina.

As Jerimiah was in the bathroom, he wondered what type of being Josephina was. He was quite puzzled because he had thought she was a normal Amish girl for him to feed on her virginity. The red blotches that covered his body told him that maybe Josephina was not what she seemed like, a normal Amish girl. Jerimiah was racking his brain, wondering if he should even open the bathroom door. He was suddenly afraid for his well-being, and as sweat started covering his face, he heard a knocking on the bathroomdoor. "Could you please take me home now?" said Josephina.

Jerimiah was frightened and did not even know how to react to Josephina's request. He was relieved that she wanted to go home, indicating that she would not hurt him anymore, and Jerimiah said, "Please give me a few seconds before I take you home."

Jerimiah then looked into the mirror and started concentrating as his eyes became fiery red, and miraculously, his entire body, which was covered with red blotches, started to heal instantly. He quickly put on his pants, shirt and a sneaker and timidly opened the bathroom door. Josephina was standing by the bathroom door with a tense look on her face, and Jerimiah said, "Come now, let me take you home."

They went into the car and Jerimiah drove away from his house. There was total silence in the car. Neither Jerimiah nor Josephina spoke to each other because Jerimiah was terrified of Josephina, and Josephina, unsure of what transpired within the house, blamed everything on herself and her own insecurities.

When they arrived near Josephina's home, Jerimiah did not stop at the usual place; instead, he stopped just out of sight of her home and said, "Goodbye, Josephina."

Josephina opened the passenger door and exited the car. Jerimiah drove away without even looking back at Josephina walking towards her home. As Jerimiah drove away, the tears came streaming down Josephina's face. She knew it was the last time she would see Jerimiah again, and to make matters worse, she could not pinpoint what caused the breakup of their relationship. The cool summer night air offered her no form of solace, as her tears came down in torrents and seemed cemented on her beautiful face.

Chapter 19

As the days and weeks went by, Josephina robotically did all her house chores. There was no joy in her daily house chores or appreciation of life. She went to bed every night crying over Jerimiah until her pillows were soaked with her tears. She missed hearing Jerimiah's voice and seeing his handsome face. It finally dawned on Josephina that she was intensely in love with Jerimiah but accepting that she had lost him forever, and it was the hardest thing to overcome in her mind. To make matters worse for Josephina, she was unable to relate her ordeal to Malakai because it was too painful for her to bear.

One night, when everyone went to their bed, Josephina crept out of the house and went to see Malakai in the barn. Malakai was in the car listening to rhythms and blues music when Josephina knocked on the car. Malakai opened the car door and Josephina got in the car. Malakai smiled at her and said, "Hello, my friend."

Josephina said, "Hug me as if I am your girl for only tonight. I need to feel you embracing me tonight."

Malakai pulled back both front seats to lay flat and laid on it and embraced Josephina with her head on his chest and his arms on her shoulders. Malakai knew and could sense something was wrong with Josephina. As the rhythms and blues music played in the car, Malakai was hoping Josephina's problem was not too catastrophic, and they might hopefully resolve it in the barn. He knew that

Josephina would tell him the problem that was affecting her when she was comfortable and ready to talk, but for now, he did not want to pressure her as if he was her interrogator.

Josephina laid her head on Malakai's chest for around twenty-five minutes when she started to cry. Malakai gently rubbed her back and said, "Let your tears flow, because I am here for you no matter what the circumstances."

Josephina cried until there were no more tears left, and she wiped away the tears and said, "He ended our relationship without even telling me why. I am so devastated because I love him. The pain in my heart is unbearable, and everything I tried to mitigate the hurt does not work. I cry every night in my bed, hoping the pain will go away."

"What happened? Why did he end the relationship?" asked Malakai.

Josephina took a few minutes and took a deep breath and said "I am honestly not sure what happened. We were coming from a dinner theatre when four bikers stopped him. He got out of the car, and they engaged in a fight. He defeated them, and then we went to his house. I wanted to offer my virginity to him because I love him dearly, and when I took all my clothing off apart from the amulet, which I promise to keep on at all times, he ran naked into the bathroom shrieking like a little girl in intense pain."

Malakai mused for a moment and said, "I am terribly sorry to hear about your ordeal, but you have to put it behind you and move on with your life. Sometimes in life, you have to put the bad experiences in life behind you and move on because that is what life requires in some instances. I know you want closure in your relationship with Jerimiah, but in life, sometimes there is no closure, and you have to move on to continue living your life no matter what the circumstances."

"I want some form of closure, but more than that, I want to see him, talk to him, and I want to know the reasons why he ended our relationship. I want you to take me to see him now," said Josephina.

Malakai pondered for a moment and said, "I think it is a bad idea to just show up at his house at this time of night without an invitation from Jerimiah. Can't you put it behind you?" asked Malakai.

"I honestly do not think I can put it behind me. I need some form of clarity and closure of our relationship. The constant pain and anguish of thinking about him left a narrow hole in my heart. At night, when I am in my bed, I cry nonstop, wondering what happened or what I did wrong," said Josephina.

Malakai could see the pain on Josephina's face and knew for sure she was in love with Jerimiah. He hugged her and said, "Hush, my friend, if you do not reconcile the pain and heartache will go away in time. Anyway, I will take you to see him. Let me get dressed."

Malakai pushed back the car seats in their upright position and drove out of the premises with Josephina. Along their journey in the night Josephina gave Malakai directions to Jerimiah's house. They soon arrived at their destination, and Malakai drove into the premises and parked his car beside Jerimiah's car. Josephina used her hand, wiped her face, opened the passenger door and told Malakai that she would be back shortly as she exited the car. Malakai sat around the steering wheel, watching Josephina walking toward the front door wondering if he did the right thing in taking Josephina to see Jerimiah.

As Josephina arrived at the front door, she was nervous, not knowing if Jerimiah would be glad and excited to see her or if he would even welcome her inside the house. As she was about to knock on the front door, Josephina pushed the door and walked inside the house. There was dead silence inside the house. She walked quietly, ensuring that her shoes did not make any noise inside the house. She could see a bright light inside the master bedroom. She walked inside expecting to see Jerimiah in bed, but he was nowhere in sight. She went inside the bathroom to see if he was inside there, but there was no Jerimiah.

Josephina walked quietly to the other rooms to see if Jerimiah was inside, but she did not see him. She walked to the last room in the house, where there was a faint red light. She thought how odd she had never been in that room before, but she recalled that the room door was always locked, as if Jerimiah did not want anyone in that particular room. Josephina heard a sound and realized that Jerimiah was in the room. The door was slightly ajar, and Josephina pushed it slightly for her to see inside the room. Josephina peeped inside, and she noticed that there was no bed or any other furniture inside the room but a rack with an Amish dress hung on it. Suddenly, she was horror-struck and gripped with fear with what she saw, and she wanted to run, but for some reason, the fear and horror gripped her body, and her limbs seemed unable to move because of what she was looking at in the room.

Josephina stared in horror at the round-spinning metal-wheel contraption in the center of the room that was elevated off the floor by an iron base around three feet thick. Tied to the contraption was a young Amish girl who was totally naked and much younger than Josephina. Josephina noticed that the contraption could rotate at any angle, and Jerimiah was feeding or sucking the blood from the girl's neck. Jerimiah could not see her as his back was turned toward the spinning contraption with the young girl tied to it, and her mouth was stuffed with a rag to prevent her from making any sound. Josephina noticed that Jerimiah would take a break and sink his teeth or fang into the girl's neck, sucking more blood in his mouth. When Josephina saw the fang coming from Jerimiah's mouth, Josephina was more petrified as she covered her mouth, ensuring that no sound escaped her mouth.

As Josephina stared transfixed at what was happening in front of her, the Amish girl on the contraption saw her, but she was unable to shout for help because her mouth was stuffed and covered with a piece of cloth. The Amish girl was powerless to put up a defense as her hands and feet were tethered to the contraption. Jerimiah continued to suck all the blood out of the young Amish girl's body as her life ebbed away, and Josephina could see the fear, terror in the eyes and face of the young Amish girl who seemed resigned to her fate of an agonizing death.

Josephina woke from the trance-like state of terror and fear that gripped her as she tried to pull back the door, but the door suddenly made a creaking sound, and Jerimiah looked around and saw Josephina. Josephina no longer tried to close the door gently. She slammed the door shut and ran out of the house towards Malakai's car. As Josephina reached outside, she shouted loudly and frantically at Malakai to start the car. Malakai heard the frantic scream and opened the passenger door for Josephina to get inside the car. Josephina, in total panic, said, "Start the ignition and drive away quickly."

Malakai turned on the ignition, and as he was driving out of the premises, he saw the front door burst open, and a tall Caucasian man came running out the door. Josephina frantically said, "Drive as fast as possible away from this house."

Malakai, driving extremely fast looked at Josephina and could see that she was frightened and extremely terrified and asked, "What is the matter?"

Josephina tried to catch her breath and said, "I went inside the house discreetly because the front door was unlocked, and I went into all the rooms searching for him, but he was nowhere in sight. I eventually went into a room that he kept locked, and I saw him sucking the blood of a young Amish girl tied to a round metal contraption with her mouth stuffed with a rag to prevent her from making any noise. I think she is dead by now. When he saw me, I ran out of the house."

Malakai could not believe what he had heard from Josephina. Everything sounded so surreal and incredulous, but he was happy that she had the good sense to run out of the house. Malakai, trying to calm down Josephina, said "You did the right thing by running out the house to where I am. You will be safe with me. Everything will be okay now."

"Malakai, did you think he was grooming me for the same fate that befell that young girl?" asked Josephina.

Malakai pondered the question and said, "I honestly think that the same fate would have befallen you. The question is, why the same fate did not happen to you?"

"Well, I am extremely thankful and grateful to the God in heaven that such a fate did not befall me. I somehow do not believe Jerimiah was human because I have never seen in my lifetime any human being with those fangs coming out of their mouth and feeding or sucking on the blood of another person," said Josephina.

Malakai looked in the rearview mirror and saw that a car was chasing them and realized it was Jerimiah. Malakai started pressing the gas pedal of the car and said, "Jerimiah is chasing us; please put on your seat belt because I am going to be driving fast."

Josephina did as Malakai instructed her by putting on her seat belt. Josephina was getting scared as she turned around and could see Jerimiah's car gaining on them. Josephina bit her lips and said, "Malakai, he is gaining on us. Please drive faster."

Malakai knew that Josephina was extremely nervous. He extended his right hand and held her hand to calm her down because he could see the fear in her eyes. As Jerimiah's car came closer, Malakai slowed down the car because he came to the realization that he had to confront Jerimiah. Malakai was hoping Josephina was not in the car, but he knew that her life would be in greater danger if he did not confront Jerimiah. Malakai squeezed Josephina's hand and said, "Josephina, I am going to stop and confront him because if I do not, your life will be in great danger. I am not going to allow you to live like that, to be looking over your shoulder every time you go outside your house."

"I do not think it is a good idea for you to confront Jerimiah. I see what he is and what he is capable of because he is a beast, and I do not think you can argue with a bloodthirsty beast," said Josephina.

"I do not see a way out but to confront Jerimiah. If I do not confront him now, I would be putting you, and your family in great danger because he will kill all of your family to get to you. I could not do that, so we will have to end the problem here, and now," said Malakai.

Malakai drove until he saw a clearing in a cornfield brilliantly lit by electric light from a light post. The clearing in the cornfield was around a quarter acre, and Malakai drove off the road into the clearing near the cornfield and parked the car. Jerimiah drove behind Malakai and parked around a hundred yards from Malakai's car. As Malakai was about to open the car door, Josephina said, "Please be careful and do not take any unnecessary chances with him because he is a killer."

"I will be careful. If he is beating the crap out of me and basically killing me, please drive away immediately before he can get to you," said Malakai.

"Please remember I cannot drive; therefore, if he kills you, he will also kill me," said Josephina.

"Guess I will have to be extra careful then," said Malakai.

Malakai opened the car door, and as he was about to walk towards Jerimiah's car, Josephina opened the passenger door and ran towards Malakai. As Malakai looked towards Josephina, she ran into his arms, embraced him, grabbed his head, pushed her tongue into Malakai's mouth and started kissing him passionately as if it was their last day on earth. Malakai was quite shocked but responded by kissing Josephina.

As Josephina and Malakai were kissing, Jerimiah came out of his car angrily, started clapping his hand and said, "I have been searching for the occupants of this car for weeks. I am going to enjoy killing the man that I have been searching for weeks, and then I am going to drink the blood of that virgin bitch."

Josephina and Malakai continued to kiss until Malakai pulled away and said, "By continuing to kiss me, you are aware you are just irritating him more than is necessary. I can imagine he wants to kill me more than ever, seeing you kissing me."

A wry smile came over Josephina's face, and she said, "Let him get angry and jealous; who the hell cares? He may let down his guard so you will more easily dispose of him."

Malakai stopped kissing Josephina as she went back into the car, seething with rage, being called a bitch and blaming herself for getting involved with this two-faced beast of a man. She felt nothing but disdain and hatred for Jerimiah and thought someone that she was so madly in love with only hours earlier, but now she only felt contempt and revulsion. Josephina went into the car and sat around the driver's seat. Josephina quickly locked the car door and turned down the window.

Jerimiah went back to his car and opened the car trunk and took out a sword. He walked back towards where Malakai was waiting patiently in the open area of the cornfield. As Jerimiah was approaching, Malakai put his hands hand into the air and asked, "Before we start fighting can you tell me what you are?"

Jerimiah, smiling quite confidently in his ability to dispose of Malakai, because he did not see Malakai with a weapon, said, "I do think it is appropriate for me to tell you what I am before I dispose of you. I am a shapeshifter, and I drink the blood of young virgin girls to stay young and alive. I can take the shape of anyone I want, be it an animal or a human being. What is so funny is that the Alliance Organization has been searching all over the country for you, only to find you right in my backyard. I am only sorry that I ran out of the house without my cell phone trying to catch that bitch, Josephina, or else I would be able to call them and tell them that you are in my backyard."

Malakai took off his jacket and gave it to Josephina. Malakai then pushed his hand into his right jeans pocket and took out his sword. Malakai then pressed the button on the metal object, and the long, elongated steel blade emerged as he took his fighting stance. Seeing the flaming steel blade emerge from the metal sheath, Malakai could see the surprise look on Jerimiah's face.

Jerimiah, seeing the sword emerge from the metal object, was quite flabbergasted. His eyes became a fiery red, and he transformed into a Japanese sword fighter. Jerimiah used his sword and immediately lunged at Malakai. Malakai, in turn, used his sword to block Jerimiah's attacks and as they continued attacking each other, neither of them was making any headway with their constant sword attack because both were skillful swordsmen.

Malakai was well-trained in sword fighting by Rodigan, but he had nothing but admiration for his opponent. Every attack and lunge Malakai made at Jerimiah, he anticipated and blocked with artful ease like a skillful matador. Malakai knew that he had to defeat Jerimiah somehow, but his opponent was so skillful, and he was just hoping that his stamina would outlast Jerimiah. He knew he could not allow Jerimiah to defeat him because his life and Josephina were in great danger.

Jerimiah used the sword and lunged at Malakai, and he blocked it. Jerimiah, in an instant, kicked Malakai's foot, and Malakai started falling, but as he was falling, Malakai used the sword as an anchor and somersaulted in the air. Jerimiah rushed over to where Malakai somersaulted trying to chop at Malakai's head. Malakai, in a crouching position, immediately used his sword to block Jerimiah's sword directed at his head. As Malakai was in the crouching position, Jerimiah's stomach was exposed, and Malakai used his right hand and muster all the power in his hand and punched Jerimiah in his stomach.

The force of the punch knocked Jerimiah over, and he fell to the ground. As he fell, Jerimiah was transformed back into his original form and gasping for air.

They continued fighting, neither one making headway against the other, and Malakai started noticing that the blow from Jerimiah's sword was not as forceful as before, and he realized that Jerimiah was losing stamina. Malakai made contact with Jerimiah's stomach and slashed it. Jerimiah yelled out in agonizing pain as blood started oozing out of his stomach. Malakai saw the blood oozing from Jerimiah's stomach and knew he had to be more cautious than before because Jerimiah was more dangerous now than before because he was like a trapped animal.

Malakai and Jerimiah continued fighting until Malakai asked, "Please tell me why you did not kill Josephina?"

"Please keep that bitch away from me," said Jerimiah.

For the first time, Malakai realized that Jerimiah was scared of Josephina. As he continued to fight Jerimiah, Malakai remembered Josephina telling him that she was totally naked in his bed with only the silver amulet around her neck, and he ran scared into the bathroom. Malakai instantly started shouting at Josephina and said, "Josephina, come out of the car."

Josephina heard Malakai calling her to come out of the car, but she was scared for her life. She eventually opened the car door tentatively and walked towards the men. As Josephina was walking towards the men, she heard Malakai shouting, "Josephina, open the front of your blouse and expose the amulet."

Josephina hurriedly ripped open the blouse and exposed the silver amulet. Suddenly, a flash of bright rays of light emanated from the amulet, hitting directly on Jerimiah's whole body. Jerimiah screamed so loud that it echoed throughout the cornfield. Jerimiah's face started turning red and swollen, and Jerimiah dropped the sword as his face and his whole body started to peel away into blotches. Jerimiah dropped to the ground in a fetal position and started screaming like a trapped animal, drawing and gasping on his last breath of life.

Josephina walked closer to Jerimiah, laying on the ground and asked, "Who is the bitch now?"

Jerimiah, too weak to respond to Josephina's question, mustered all the energy in his body, got up off the ground and tried to walk to his car. As he was walking away, Josephina ran behind him with the amulet held in her hand directed at Jerimiah's back. Jerimiah's entire body started to peel away, and he was covered with blood. As he was about ten feet from the car, he fell to the ground. Josephina, feeling more emboldened, walked right behind Jerimiah with the powerful rays from the amulet draining and destroying Jerimiah's body. Jerimiah got up off the ground and made one last effort to reach the car so he could escape from Malakai and Josephina.

As he reached the car door and was about to open the door, he fell to the ground, and his entire body turned into a red bloody mush.

Josephina put back the amulet around her neck, and Malakai came behind her and said, "Remind me not to piss you off, because you certainly took your revenge and frustration on Jerimiah."

"I was certainly angry thinking about the amount of young, innocent Amish girls this piece of trash killed, and that was certainly his intention towards me, if you were not around. I am even angry at myself for allowing this filth to sweep me off my feet with his devious intention," said Josephina.

Malakai held Josephina's hand and said, "It is over now, and you are safe. Think of him as a bad memory and put him out of your mind. By the way, go into the car and look in the glove compartment; you will see a box of matches and some newspaper; take them to me. We are going to burn his car and the mush that is Jerimiah."

Josephina went for the box of matches and newspaper and gave them to Malakai. Malakai told her that what she witnessed there tonight was just between the two of them and not to relate the incident to her friends or family. Malakai lit the match with the newspapers and threw them in the car and some on the bloody mush that was Jerimiah. The car and the red mush started burning in the cool night air. Malakai and Josephina then drove away from the area. As they were driving there was suddenly a huge explosion as Jerimiah's car exploded in the cool night air.

Chapter 20

Malakai and Josephina arrived back at her father's premises, and Malakai parked the car in the barn. Josephina looked at Malakai and asked, "The silver amulet that you gave me to wear, what is it?"

"It is the only thing that I have of my parents. They said it is to protect me from evil spirits and people on this journey on earth. I think it is the only reason why you are alive. When we were fighting, I realized he was afraid of you, and I remembered you telling me that you took all of your clothes off except the amulet, and he ran into the bathroom. I, therefore, deduced that it was the amulet because of which he was fearful of you," said Malakai.

Josephina looked quite pensive and then said, "I am more puzzled and bewildered by what I have just witnessed in the transformation of Jerimiah. I cannot imagine that something like Jeremiah exists or that I understand the universe in some small ways, but I realized I do not. I am even more puzzled and even excited to discover what more is out there in the wider world."

Malakai then mused and responded, "This world that we all live in is not what it seems. Your human brain comprehends everything in a material or physical sense because that is what you experience, but this world is so much more complicated and intriguing. I will explain to you more in-depth one of these days if we see each other again."

"You know what is so funny? I was blaming myself that I repulsed him when I saw him run into the bathroom. In retrospect, seeing Jerimiah run naked into the bathroom was certainly a funny sight," said Josephina.

"You cannot repulse any man that has a pulse in his body. You are a beautiful, intelligent woman that any man would be glad and proud to have as his woman. Let me ask you a question; why did you kiss me?" asked Malakai.

"I have been in love with you my whole teenage years. You never reciprocated nor took advantage of me, and for that, as a woman now, I am grateful and have the utmost respect for you. I chose to kiss you because I never wanted to die and never tasted the feel of your lips on mine. Plus, I wanted to piss off Jerimiah," said Josephina.

Malakai laughingly said, "You are the devil, but it is time to go to your bed."

Josephina looked into Malakai's eyes and said, "I want to stay with you tonight. I will leave early in the morning before my parents wake up. I want to lay on your chest and feel your embrace. I want to be close to you just for tonight."

Malakai consented, and he pressed back the two front seats laid on them with Josephina lying on his chest. Josephina said, "Of all the men I have known apart from my father, you are the only man I have ever truly felt comfortable with and to even kiss on the lips. By the way, Malakai, I need to speak to you seriously about something that is going to affect my future, and I do not know how you are going to react to it."

"What is it?" asked Malakai.

"I do not think I can stay here any longer in the community. I want to see the world, and I cannot shut away my passion and hide my desire any longer. Therefore, I would love to come with you when you are departing Lancaster County," said Josephina.

Malakai was stunned because he was not expecting such a request from Josephina. Malakai knew he had to disappoint her because such a request would surely cause friction within her family. Malakai cleared his throat and said, "Josephina, please think clearly about what you are saying because embarking on such a course of action would cause excommunication from your church and friction within your own family. You know I love you, but I cannot be a part of that decision you are making to leave your community."

Malakai could feel Josephina's body stiffen up because she did not want to hear anything negative to dissuade her from leaving her Amish community. Josephina's voice tone changed, and she said, "I have made my decision already, and neither you nor anyone else is going to dissuade me from leaving the community. I am tired of living a lie; I want to live for myself for once and not be forced to marry and immediately breed like I do not have a choice in the matter. It is my life; I choose to do what I want, or when I want, and I want to go to school and become a doctor, and it damn sure is not going to happen here, in my community. Being with Jerimiah was not all bad. Yes, he was a pretentious bastard, but it taught me that life is fleeting, and it must be enjoyed while you can, and you cannot live your life for anyone but yourself and God. I will talk to my family, and if they cannot understand, they will lose me forever, but I will continue to live my life."

Malakai did not respond to Josephina immediately because he was processing everything she had just said in his mind. Malakai said, "I will help you, but not in the way you expect because I cannot take you with me on the road. I need to do some preparation as to where you are going to live in New York. Also, I am leaving here in the next two days, but you cannot speak to your parents about your desire to leave, until I am gone. I will be responsible for your living and school expenses. I do not want to give your parents any impression or idea that I am responsible for you leaving your Amish community because I would rather you stay and get married. Therefore, I beg of you not to mention my name when you are explaining your desire to leave your community because you are doing it of your own volition."

Josephina reached over, grabbed Malakai and kissed him passionately. After a few minutes, they stopped kissing each other, and Malakai said, "I see you are well practice in receiving and giving pleasure."

"I am glad that you realize that I am a vibrant woman and not the starry eye teenager who was so in love with you," said Josephina.

"I know you are not a teenager anymore, and I see with my eyes fully open that you are a vivacious woman. Are you okay with what I have suggested about moving to New York?" asked Malakai.

"It is perfectly fine with me. I would not have kissed you if it was not okay. I promise you I will speak to my parents about leaving the community when you are long gone," said Josephina.

Malakai stretched his hand over to where the suitcase was, opened a zipper at the side, took out some money and gave it to Josephina. Josephina started counting the money, and Malakai said, "You are going to need the money if you are going to travel to New York. I was hoping I would give it to you as a wedding present."

Josephina finished counting the money and, with wonderment in her eyes, said, "It is over five thousand dollars."

"You are going to need the money to travel and to buy a new wardrobe. However, I would suggest not buying any clothes until you are in the city. Not much sense in aggravating your parents because they will not take kindly you leaving your community," said Malakai.

Josephina, for the first time, looked a little sad and said, "Thanks for the money. My parents will not take kindly to me leaving the community, but they will understand after a while when I am gone. At least I hope they will understand that I want more out of life than what the Amish community can offer."

Malakai tried to empathize by hugging Josephina because he knew that the conversation with her parents would be extremely difficult because her parents were stuck in their old ways of thinking, pledging allegiance to the church and their community.

Malakai thought he tried one more way of dissuading her and said, "Living in the city can be difficult at times; the constant noise, the large number of people, traffic and smog can be a tad exasperating on your mind and body. You will miss the quietness and peacefulness of your community, and most of all, you will miss your parents and your siblings."

"I have thought of all those things already. I know without a doubt I am going to miss everything you just mentioned, but that does not mean I am going to be limited by the community and even the genuine affection of my family and not take the opportunities that the wider world has to offer and to see," said Josephina.

Malakai looked at Josephina and smiled because he knew he was looking at himself in her eyes. He saw the wandering spirit that wanted to see the beauty and peculiarness of this beautiful planet. He could never imagine himself being restricted to one area and not wanting to see other areas on the planet. Malakai knew that she was determined to leave and that there was no way he was going to persuade her to stay in the community. He knew if it was him, he would be gone already from the community. Malakai then said, "See you in New York City. I will pick you up at Grand Central Station in New York, whenever you choose to come to the city."

The broad smile returned on Josephina's face, and she said, "Thanks for finally understanding my plight."

"I understand your situation since a long time ago, but I just wanted to dissuade you from coming because of the dilemma it is going to cause the family. By the way, also look about your identification. You cannot function without identification in a big city," said Malakai.

Malakai took out a pen and paper and wrote his and Rose's phone numbers and address and his email address and gave them to Josephina. He told her to call or email before she came to New York. Josephina's face radiated happiness as she said, "Now that I have said what I wanted and you have given me your support, I can depart the community. Once again, thanks for your support, and for understanding my situation. I was going to leave the community with or without your support, but now that I have your support, I guess things will be a little less uncomfortable for my family."

Josephina opened the car door and exited the car and said, "I guess this is where I bid you goodbye."

Josephina, with a cryptic smile on her face, said, "This is goodbye." She grabbed Malakai and kissed him passionately one last time then she left the barn.

As Malakai watched Josephina walk away and the faint taste of her lips on his mouth, he wondered if he was doing the right thing in assisting her, leaving the one community that she had known all her life. He knew that Josephina was deeply unhappy, and it was because of her family that she stayed in the community. But now she was ready to move on to the next phase of her life and move away from the Amish community, irrespective of whatever upheaval it will cause her family, and the church. Malakai wished, at times, things were monochromatic and not shades of grey because he thought things would be a hell of a lot simpler.

******

The next day, Ephraim's family, Rose and Malakai, were at the dinner table having a large amount of food that Ephraim's wife had prepared for Malakai and Rose's departure from their community. The food consisted of baked pineapple chicken, baked potatoes and baked bread. They all ate heartily then they went to the back porch to chat and play board games. As the hours passed by and the board games became tiresome, they all felt sleepy, and the family retired to their beds.

In the morning, Malakai and Rose were ready to depart the farm. One of the boys assisted Rose with her suitcase from her room and carried it to the barn. When it was time to depart, they all hugged each other, and the family bid Malakai and Rose a safe journey back to New York City. Malakai and Rose drove away from Ephraim's premises around six o'clock in the morning.

As they were on their way on the open road, Malakai opened the car window for a moment to allow the fresh morning air in the car. Malakai was not quite ready to depart Ephraim's premises, but he thought he had no choice as he did not want to endanger Ephraim's family. To come into contact with Jerimiah, who was searching for him and working for the Alliance Organization, meant that it was only a matter of time before they found him and maybe put Ephraim and his family in danger. He would not be able to forgive himself if anything happened to Ephraim's family.

Rose was looking forward to embracing modernity again and said, "It was a nice learning experience living in an Amish community. The simple amenities like electricity, listening to a radio, watching television, and using a cell phone in a modern world and not having any concerns about it, is a reminder that we can do away with those things for a while and not stress out our body and mind."

Malakai laughingly said, "Most Americans would go insane if they are deprived of these modern amenities for a day, much less a week. Truth be told, it would be good for most people just to de-stress themselves from the modern world."

Malakai and Rose continued chatting and listening to rhythm and blues music as they made their way to Pittsburgh City, Pennsylvania. It was a long journey from Lancaster to Pittsburgh, which took around four and a half hours. Malakai realized that Rose was tired and hungry from the long Journey as they entered the city. He was planning and sorting out their accommodation first, but Rose was famished so he thought to get her some food.

Malakai drove on Oakland Avenue in Pittsburgh and stopped at Uncle Sam's Sandwich Bar to order Philly Cheese Steak. Uncle Sam's Sandwich Bar is a small venue with friendly staff. The cheese steak was prepared quickly and served with lots of French Fries. Malakai and Rose devoured the meal in no time and left the establishment after their hunger was satiated.

As they drove past a haberdashery, Rose told Malakai to stop the car, and she took some money from him and went inside, while Malakai waited inside the car. Rose soon returned, and they drove to a motel in the Pittsburgh area. They checked in for two nights and paid cash at the front desk. The room that they checked in was quite clean, with the bed beautifully made up and a house phone on the bed side table. The bathroom was quite clean, with fresh towels in it. As Malakai put down the bag with their clothes and closed the door, Rose jumped on the bed and said, "I am so exhausted from the long journey. I am just going to get a shower and get some sleep."

"After not spending time together for such a long time, that is all you want to do?" asked Malakai.

Rose smiled, then burst out laughing and said, "Yes, Mr. Malakai, that is all I want to do. To get a shower and get some sleep."

Rose got up off the bed and started unpacking the bag. She then started undressing in front of Malakai in her black lacy matching bra and panty. She then went to the bathroom to take her shower. Rose came out of the bathroom soon after with a towel firmly wrapped around her body. Malakai then went into the bathroom and took his shower.

Malakai came out of the shower totally naked and into the room. Rose was in the bed, covered with the sheet. As Malakai approached the bed, he dragged away the sheet to reveal Rose's naked body. Malakai looked at her nakedness appreciatively and said, "That is a sight I have not seen for many weeks, and I so miss seeing you like this, naked in a bed."

Rose pulled the sheet away from Malakai, and it fell on her, covering up her body; she said, "I have missed you more than I could ever imagine, and I have missed you, especially in the nights."

Malakai removed the sheet and entered the bed. Rose instantly lay on Malakai's body, and Malakai kissed her hungrily and passionately as they started to make love in a fierce, and frenzy way in the motel room. The rhythm of their lovemaking was a constant ebb and flow like a cascading waterfall. Rose orgasms soon after, her body shaking uncontrollably as Malakai ejaculated deep inside Rose's body. They were both exhausted after their lovemaking session ended, and they went to sleep with Rose curled up under Malakai's arm.

They woke up later in the night, and both took turns and went to the bathroom. After they came back into the bed, they made love just as fierce as before until they were well spent; they went back to sleep. As Malakai was just about to nod off to sleep, he thought Rose's body was like a drug to him where there were no medications. His lust and desire for this woman was like no other that he had ever encountered in his life.

They woke up late the next morning, and Rose suggested that they order from Uncle Sam's Sandwich Bar for some more Philly cheese steak. Malakai agreed, and they used the phone in the room and called Uncle Sam's Sandwich Bar to order the food. The order arrived shortly, and Malakai paid the man who delivered the food. Rose turned on the television in the room and started watching CNN, as they ate the food. After they finished eating, Malakai told Rose that he would have to take the car to a garage to service it because he did not think the car would be capable of making the long five-hour journey to New York if he did not change the oil filters and maybe the plugs.

As they continued watching the television, suddenly, there was breaking news about Anthony Bourdain's death by suicide. Both Rose and Malakai were stunned by the news of Anthony Bourdain's death because both were avid watchers of his television show "Parts Unknown." The news affected Malakai more because by watching the show, he would live vicariously through Anthony Bourdain's experiences of going to these different countries and highlighting their varied cultures and their foods. It was a program that showed local people talking about their experiences on various subject matters in their respective countries and also their hopes and aspirations.

"Anthony Bourdain will certainly be missed because he was truly unique in every sense of the word," said Rose.

"Sometimes people do not understand what they mean to other people. I do not think Anthony Bourdain understands the love and appreciation people had for him and his television show. May his soul rest in peace," said Malakai.

As they continued watching television in bed, Rose suggested that they spend the day in bed with each other and take the car to the garage the following morning. Malakai agreed, and they watched television, chatted, slept, played, and made love to each other. As Rose lay snuggled under Malakai's arms, she said, "I am truly happy when I am with you, and most importantly, I am so in love with you."

Malakai smiled mischievously and shouted, "She is in love with me, people, but what not to love about me."

Rose, not hearing Malakai reciprocate the word, took her foot and kicked Malakai off the bed, and he fell on the carpet. They laughed uncontrollably, and Rose said, "You pompous bastard, I love you with all my heart."

Malakai climbed back on the bed and said, "You know I am just playing with you. I am in love with you, woman, now and always. Your body is like a drug to me, and I always want to stay high on it."

Rose grabbed Malakai and kissed him passionately, and It was the way Malakai made her feel wanted, secure and confident like no relationship before with any man. She did not doubt Malakai's love for her because she could see it in his eyes. As Rose stopped kissing Malakai, she asked, "What is your favorite part of my body?"

Malakai pondered the question and said, "It is really hard to answer the question. I love every part of your body, but if I were to choose, I would say your brain. You are extremely intelligent and smart, and I am in awe of your resourcefulness most of the time."

"I honestly thought you were going to say my ass because your hands are always on my bottom," said Rose.

Malakai laughingly said, "That is part of the magical attraction I have for you, but there is no denying that I love your ass for sure."

Malakai jumped off the bed and said, "I feel like going on the road. Get dressed; we are going on The Three Rivers Sightseeing Cruise of Pittsburgh."

Rose got off the bed and went into the bathroom to take a quick shower. They left the motel soon after in the late afternoon to go on The Three Rivers Sightseeing Cruise of Pittsburgh. Malakai and Rose arrived at the dock and drove around until they found a parking area. They went and paid the fee to go on the boat, which was under fifty dollars.

The cruise was a one-hour tour of the city of Pittsburgh to see the old and new buildings on the waterfront. On board was a narrator who gave details about the historic buildings, bridges, and about Pittsburgh. As they sailed on the three rivers, the Monongahela, Allegheny, and Ohio Rivers, Rose thought from where she was sitting beside Malakai in the open air on the third deck that it was a highly informative and educational tour of the city of Pittsburgh.

After they came off the boat, Rose was hungry, and Malakai drove to McCormick and Schick's Seafood and Steaks Restaurant to have dinner. The restaurant was beautifully decorated with a white tablecloth, and the cutleries were nicely assembled on the table. The restaurant was packed with people having their meals. Malakai and Rose were ushered to their seat in a private area away from the crowd. They had lobster and a bottle of white wine for their meal. They dined and chatted enjoying each other company until it was time to leave the restaurant.

On their way home to the motel, the car dashboard service light started flashing, and suddenly, the engine of the car started to sputter, but Malakai continued to drive until they arrived back at their motel at around ten thirty in the night. They both went into the bathroom, where they took a quick shower and went into bed, where they made love, and then went to sleep.

Malakai woke the next morning at eight o'clock. He got dressed and told Rose that he would be back as quickly as possible, but she must order breakfast. He kissed her and slapped her on her bottom as he left the room for the garage.

As Malakai closed the door, Rose went back to sleep in the bed. She woke up for around an hour and went to the bathroom to take a shower. She came out of the bathroom, dressed in her shorts and turned on the television to watch the news. She picked up the phone that was on the bedside table and called Uncle Sam's Sandwich Bar for some more Philly cheese steak. The cheese steak arrived in the next twenty minutes, and she ate, enjoying every morsel of the meal. After she finished devouring the cheese steak, she had some drinks and continued to watch television.

As Rose was watching the television, she suddenly started thinking about her friend Angela Stanton. She thought she would give her a call on the house phone. She remembered Malakai telling her that she was not to make any calls on her cell phone. She thought that her cell phone was taken apart; therefore, there was no harm in using the phone in the room. Also, the fact that she thought that there was no way that by using the phone in the motel, they would be able to track them or their whereabouts in Pennsylvania.

Rose picked up the phone on the bedside table and started dialing Angela's number. Angela answered, and they chatted like two long-lost school girlfriends. Rose had missed her friend and longed to chat, and gossip like girls all over the world. They continued to chat for another hour until Rose hung up the phone and continued watching television while she waited for Malakai to return from the garage. As she continued to watch the television, she fell asleep on the bed.

****

Meanwhile, in the Manhattan office in New York, Wallenstein received an urgent call on the office phone about Angela Stanton's cell phone that they were monitoring to find some clue of the whereabout of Rose. The caller told him that they had put a tracker on the last phone number that Rose had called, Angela Stanton and that it was almost a certainty that Rose Winter was on the line chatting to her presently, and they traced the number to a motel in Pittsburgh, Pennsylvania. Wallenstein jumped out of his soft, cushy office chair, took out his cell phone and called a number in Pittsburgh to go immediately to the motel to apprehend Rose Winter. Wallenstein gave the man all the essential details about Rose, including sending him a picture of her on his cell phone. Wallenstein warned the man about the possibility of Rose not being alone in the motel room, and that he should be extremely cautious because of Rose's companion.

The man who received the call from Wallenstein is a thirty-five-year-old, tall, lanky Caucasian policeman named John Warren. He jumped in his police cruiser and called his partner, a bald middle-aged Caucasian policeman with a slight paunch named Steve Roberts. They drove to the motel as quickly as possible without the siren because this was not an official police matter. They arrived at the hotel within five minutes and ran to the front desk, showed the agent who was working on Rose's picture and explained to him that they needed to speak with her immediately, and the front desk agent gave the policemen Rose's room number. They hurriedly went to Rose's room.

Rose was sleeping when she heard a knocking on the door. She got up off the bed and went to the door, thinking it was Malakai returning from the garage. As she opened the door, two policemen barged into the room, almost pushing her aside, and the tall policeman went and looked into the bathroom, and as he returned, he asked, "Are you Rose Winter?"

Rose, visibly upset seeing the two policemen barge into the room, said, "Yes, I am Rose Winter. What can I do for you, officer?"

"We have some questions we need for you to answer; therefore, we need for you to come with us so we can take you down to the precinct. Please go and put on something more suitable than the shorts," said John.

Rose took up her bag with her clothes and went into the bathroom. She was in full panic mode. She was hoping somehow Malakai would walk in the room and "smack the crap" out of the policeman who wanted to take her away to the police station. Rose stared at her face in the bathroom mirror, trying to prolong her stay in the bathroom and trying to figure out a way to extricate herself from the situation. She could not think of a way out of the situation, so she put on her jeans, a white blouse and her sneakers. She opened the bag and took out the things that belonged to Malakai, such as his pants, shirts and underwear and threw them in the bath.

John took out his private cell phone, called Wallenstein and said, "My partner and I are in the motel room. We have apprehended Rose Winter, and she is alone in the room. What do you want me to do with her?"

Wallenstein was on the other line and hearing the news that the policemen had Rose Winter in custody. Wallenstein was ecstatic, and it was the best news he heard in these many months of searching for Rose Winter. Wallenstein cleared his throat and said, "She is to be returned to New York immediately. Take her to Camden in New Jersey, and from there, I will make arrangements with someone else to pick her up and take her to New York."

John hung up the phone with Wallenstein and turned to his partner and said, "We will have to take her to New Jersey, and from there, someone else will take her to New York."

As John was about to call Rose, his private cell phone rang, and he looked at the phone screen and realized it was Wallenstein. John answered the phone, and Wallenstein instructed him to write on a piece of paper that the Alliance Organization had Rose in their custody and a phone number, and to call a number if they wanted to see her alive again by the next couple of days. Wallenstein hung up the phone, and John did as he was instructed and left the note on the bed.

Rose left the bathroom door ajar so she could hear what the two policemen were saying to each other about taking her to New York. Rose quickly took a pen and paper out of her bag and quickly wrote on it that she was to be taken to New York by two policemen. Rose threw the paper on the floor and opened the bathroom door with her bag in her hand.

Rose and the two policemen left the motel room with her bag. She was escorted in the Toyota cruiser where she was seated in the back. The two men sat in the front of the car feeling incredibly happy hoping for a big remuneration for delivering Rose to the Alliance Organization.

Rose was sitting in the back of the speeding car, feeling very terrified and not knowing what would happen to her, but she tried not to display it on her face. She bit her lips and forced herself to remain calm, and she whispered a quiet prayer in her mind, asking God for his guidance and protection. She was hoping that Malakai would find her somehow and rescue her from the two policemen. She hoped that when Malakai returned from the garage, he would find the note that she hurriedly wrote and come and rescue her from her abductors.

Chapter 21

Malakai drove back to the motel around midday. He parked the car and hurriedly walked to the room. As he entered the room, he called out Rose's name, but there was no answer. Malakai glanced into the bathroom but did not see Rose. He went directly into the bathroom to see if she was taking a shower, but as he pulled away the shower curtain, he saw some of his clothing in the bath. Malakai immediately knew something was wrong, and he took all his belongings out of the bath and carried them towards the bed. As he was about to put his belongings on the bed, he saw a note.

He put down his belongings on the bed, picked up the note and read it. As he read the note, his worst fear came to be, and his heart sank as he sat on the side of the bed. The Alliance Organization had Rose, and he did not know where they had taken her, and how they would treat her, having her in their custody. Malakai was nervous, fearing for Rose's safety, and he knew they would want to trade her for the Amulet of Osiris, but he could not allow that dark power to be unleashed on this world. He knew that her life would be in grave jeopardy if he did not accede to their request.

Malakai was thinking about all the possibilities of what could happen to Rose when he had a sudden urge to urinate, and he got up off the bed and went into the bathroom. He urinated, and as he was washing his hands in the sink, he saw a piece of paper on the floor.

Malakai dried his hand on the bathroom towel and then took up the piece of paper. Malakai saw immediately it was Rose's handwriting, and he was glad to see that she had the resourcefulness to write a note to him irrespective of the situation, and not allowing him to waste time searching for her in Pittsburgh.

Malakai gathered up all his belongings and put them in a large plastic bag that was in the room. He looked around the room to ensure that he did not miss anything, and then walked out and closed the door. Malakai then went by the front desk to pay his bills. The agent printed out his bill and showed him that he made a long-distance call to New York. Malakai paid the bill, realizing that Rose had made the call to New York. As Malakai was about to leave the desk, he asked the front desk agent, "Has anyone been to his room when he was away this morning?"

"Two Caucasian policemen came here around ten thirty inquiring about your woman. They left with her carrying a bag to their car," said the front desk agent.

Malakai thanked the front desk agent for the information and then took his plastic bag to his car. He put the bag in the car and then drove away from the motel to New York City. Malakai was glad for the small number of details by the front desk agent. Malakai was wondering how the Alliance Organization was able to track them, but he realized that whoever number Rose called the Alliance Organization was tracking that person's phone. Malakai suspected that the number Rose called was more or less her friend, that beautiful African American woman named Angela Stanton.

As Malakai continued to drive to New York City, he knew that he had little time to play with because the Alliance Organization would want to interrogate Rose about his whereabouts and how or what she knew about her companion. He prayed that they would not torture her for the information. Malakai did not want Rose to aggravate them, because they would use torture to inflict unbearable pain on her body. He could not bear to live with himself if they tortured her, knowing that he would be the cause of her pain and suffering.

Malakai was quite worried for Rose and wondered if she could bear the strain of the ordeal she was about to undergo in her life. He knew he had to call the number they left but he wanted to be in New York. He was driving at breakneck speed to seek some answers about Rose's potential whereabouts in New York. As he considered the situation, he knew he could not turn over the amulet to the Alliance Organization, and he could not abandon Rose to them because they would surely kill her without the slightest hesitation.

Malakai knew he was in a catch twenty-two situation, and he knew he could not abandon Rose and give the amulet to the Alliance Organization because it would be hell on earth. As he contemplated his situation, he wondered if the love of a woman would be worth unleashing all the dark power of hell on earth just to see her safe and secure and back in his arms.

****

Meanwhile, Rose was in the back of the Toyota police cruiser, speeding as if they were on a car chase trying to apprehend criminals. Rose could see the tall policeman staring at her through the rearview mirror, but she was unsure why he was staring at her in that manner and sometimes smiling and licking his lips. As she looked at the two men, she noticed they were smiling and exchanging glances at each other, and she suddenly felt uncomfortable and asked, "Officer, can you tell me which state we are in?"

The shorter policeman turned around and started flicking his tongue at Rose, and suddenly, it dawned on her they were leering at her and had this lascivious smile on their face. As the shorter policeman stopped flicking his tongue, he said, "We are in the state of New Jersey, sweet cheeks, but we are going to stop soon and have some fun with you before we deliver you to those big city boys in New York."

The two policemen let out a raucous laughter and started slapping each other knees. It suddenly dawned on Rose that the two policemen wanted to rape her, and she was not about to be a willing accomplice to their immoral demands. The policemen drove off the road and entered a wooded area. Rose took out a plastic water bottle out of her bag. As she was about to open the plastic water bottle, the

402

car soon came to a stop at a shadowy, dark, wooded area. She put back the plastic water bottle in the bag and slung it over her shoulder.

The shorter policeman came running out of the car and opened the car passenger door. As the shorter policeman opened the door of the car, he unbuckled his pants, and it fell to his knee. He climbed into the car and tried to push Rose to lay flat on the seat. She avoided his hands, and he fell on Rose. Rose pushed him away with all the strength she could muster, stretched out her foot, and kicked him under his ribs. The power of Rose's kick was so powerful that the policeman fell out of the car on the ground with his pants at his knees. The shorter policeman was screaming with the pain so excruciating near his lower ribs. Rose quickly jumped over him with the bag over her shoulder and started running as fast as she could into the woods.

The taller policeman who was in the front of the car saw what was happening, and he came out of the car in a mad dash and started running after Rose. In his desperation to catch up to Rose, who was escaping from him, he did not see a thick piece of rotting wood in his path; he slipped and fell over the rotting wood.

As Rose jumped out of the car, she noticed that the car was parked at the side of some isolated rural road. Rose did not have a clue as to where she was running to, but she noticed that the area was quite rural with a lot of trees. She started running toward the trees, trying to get away from her abductors.

Rose kept on running until she was quite a distance away from the policemen. She looked back to see the policemen struggling to catch up to her, and she was thankful to God that she was dressed in sneakers and jeans pants.

Rose was now fully in the woods and could see no sign of the two policemen. She kept on running but at a slower pace than before, and she thought that all those times climbing mountains and hiking had just paid off big time because it had allowed her to escape her abductors. She kept on running at a slower pace until she started walking, secured in the knowledge that she had eluded the two policemen. Rose stopped for a moment, took out the plastic water bottle, and had a drink. After she finished drinking, she looked in the forest for a thick piece of tree branch. She found a piece of tree branch lying on the ground around four and a half feet. She wanted the tree branch to use as a weapon just in case she encountered any ferocious wild animals.

As Rose walked through the forest with her stick in her hand and her bag slung over her shoulder, she was not fearful as she got accustomed to the different sounds of the forest. Rose thought more or less she was somewhere in New Jersey, maybe some miles away from the Camden area. As Rose walked through the forest, she could see tall trees of different varieties and lots of squirrels busy climbing trees. Rose walked until she came upon a small creek with some deer quenching their thirst for water.

Rose looked right and left and did not know which direction to take as she stared at the flowing creek water. She closed her eyes and muttered a prayer to God for guidance and protection and to show her which direction to take. As she was there deliberating, she heard a rustling sound behind her, and she turned around swiftly, expecting to see a wild animal. Still, unexpectedly, she saw a tall, dark man with the smoothest olive complexion and extremely white teeth. The hair on the man's hair was as dark as his complexion. The man was dressed in a white robe, carrying a white rod in his hand, and his feet were just a simple sandal. He approached Rose and said, "Sorry to frighten you, my child. I am Gabe, and I see you are wondering which direction to take on your journey."

"I am Rose, and you are right. I am wondering which direction to take to the nearest town," said Rose.

"Go right and follow the creek until you come upon two trees that fell in the water. When you arrive there, turn left and walk until you see a cabin. Please do not stop at the first cabin. Continue walking until you see a cabin marked Moosehead. Look carefully for the second cabin because it is well hidden, and you can stay there for two days and then you proceed on your way by following the creek downhill. The cabin belongs to a friend of mine, so you will be safe there, my child. There is plenty of canned food in the pantry and nice bed linen in the room. You will be safe there as if you were in your own home," said Gabe.

Rose extended her hand and almost grabbed Gabe's hand as he extended his hand to shake hers. The first thing Rose noticed was that his hand was so warm, and she said, "Thank you from the bottom of my heart. I really do appreciate your kindness, and again thanks."

"All praise and thanks belong to the Great God of heaven and earth, my child. Safe travel," said Gabe.

Gabe proceeded to walk away before Rose could even respond, and she proceeded to walk away and follow the creek downhill. As she was walking away, she suddenly heard Gabe say something, but the wind seemed to carry away the sound. Rose turned around to see if she could see Gabe, but he was nowhere in sight. She continued to follow the creek she thought meeting Gabe was almost surreal and spiritual at the same time. Rose thought even Gabe's mode of clothing seemed unreal in the forest.

Rose walked around a mile before she came upon the two trees that fell in the creek. She immediately turned left and walked more than a mile before she saw the first cabin. She did not stop as was instructed by Gabe but continued on her way in the forest. It was getting dark, so she walked a little more briskly through the woods. She was searching for the cabin, but she could not see any cabin. As she stopped at a huge tree with a large canopy, some birds that were in it had flown away, and Rose looked and realized that the huge tree concealed the cabin. She walked to the front of the cabin, and the name "Moosehead Sanctuary" was carved on the door.

Rose hurriedly climbed on the steps of the cabin and pushed the door. It was opened, and Rose entered and locked the door. It was a small cabin, extremely clean and very rustic looking, with a small kitchen, two bedrooms and one bathroom and a small fireplace. The furniture inside the cabin was all made of wood, but the chairs had cushions. Rose went inside the rooms and saw two queen-sized mattresses. She then went into the kitchen, and there was a small gas stove attached to a twenty-five-pound gas cylinder. She searched the kitchen for a box of matches on the counter, but she did not see any. She opened the pantry and found lots of canned food and matches. Rose took one box of the match and lit the gas lantern that was in the cabin. The cabin lit up, and Rose felt a little more relaxed and thankful to God.

Rose was feeling quite hungry, so she went back into the kitchen, took out one of the tin Campbell soup and heated it up in a small pot. She consumed the Campbell soup, but her hunger was not sated so she opened one tin salmon and poured it in a frying pan to heat it up. As the salmon was frying, she poured some ketchup on it. After it was finished, she ate it with some unopened crackers she found in the pantry. She drank a lot of water after the meal was finished, and afterward, she washed the few dishes she used in the kitchen sink.

Rose then went into the bathroom and took a shower. The water was quite cold, but Rose was quite unconcerned, as she was quite tired from the running and the long walk through the forest. After she completed her shower, she then retired to one of the bedrooms and slept peacefully throughout the night.

****

After Rose escaped from the two policemen who were chasing her in the woods, they came back quite angry and frustrated out of the woods and walked back towards the road to the police car. They knew that there would be severe consequences for them in allowing Rose to escape into the forest. They sat in the car, trying to come up with something to tell Wallenstein why Rose escaped from their custody. They knew they had to conceal the fact that they were trying to rape Rose when she escaped into the woods. They finally settled on a story, and the tall policeman picked up the cell phone and called Agent Chang first and told him where they were and told him that Rose had escaped into the woods. The policeman hung up the phone after being instructed by Agent Chang to remain where they were to ensure that Rose did not come out of the woods.

As the two policemen waited in their car, Agent Chang drove up to their car and parked his car. Agent Chang did not exit his car but remained inside his car. Around five minutes, the two policemen exited their car when they heard the sound of a helicopter. Agent Chang came out of his car and started waving his hand to signal to the helicopter. The helicopter landed shortly in a clearing beside the road, and Vallencourt, Wallenstein, and Thornbird, emerged from it.

Agent Chang walked towards the men and shook their hands. All the men that emerged from the helicopter were wearing their black suits, with the exception of Vallencourt, who was wearing blue jeans, a dark jacket, and a black Ray-Ban glass that covered his face. Vallencourt walked up to the two policemen and asked, "Please tell me why you allowed Rose to escape from your custody?"

The taller policeman saw the stern look of all the men around him and became extremely nervous; he started to perspire slightly and said, "We stopped the car and parked on the side of the road because Rose told us that she was not feeling well and needed some fresh air. When we stopped and opened the car, she ran into the woods. We pursued her, but somehow, she managed to elude us in the woods."

"What was the instruction given to you?" asked Vallencourt.

"To deliver Rose to Agent Chang for him to transport her to New York," said the tall policeman.

"Since both of you have not delivered Rose to me per my instruction, let's go up in the helicopter to see if we can see her on the ground," said Vallencourt.

The two policemen, the pilot, Wallenstein and Vallencourt, who was seething with rage, went into the helicopter. The pilot then flew the helicopter in the direction where the policemen told him they last saw Rose in the woods. The pilot circled the helicopter, but there was no sighting of Rose. The pilot went back and forth with the helicopter circling the area, peering intensely into the woods, but they could not locate Rose. After twenty minutes, Vallencourt told the pilot to take the helicopter to a higher altitude.

When the helicopter was around twenty-three thousand feet in the air hovering over the woods, Vallencourt got up and opened the helicopter door and said to the two policemen, "I need to know now, what happened with regards to Rose. Why do you allow her to escape from your custody?"

The tall policeman, looking more nervous and sweating more profusely than before, said, "I told you before we stopped because Rose was feeling sick."

In one swift motion, Vallencourt unbuckled the tall policeman's seatbelt and pushed him out of the helicopter. Within less than a minute, they all looked downward to see the policeman's body all splattered on some rocks in the forest. As the helicopter moved away from the area they then turned to the shorter policeman. He was looking extremely nervous and terrified and started to sweat profusely. Vallencourt turned to him and asked, "I need for you to tell me what happened with the lady that was in your custody?"

The shorter policeman, seeing what happened to his partner, thought that he better told them the truth with regard to Rose's escape and hoped that the same fate may not befall him by being thrown out of the helicopter. He thought he would put all the blame on his dead partner because a dead man tells no tales. The short policeman cleared his throat and said, "My partner wanted to rape Rose, so he stopped at this area near the wood because of the isolation. I tried my utmost best to dissuade him from taking such a course of action, but he would not listen. He told me he was the senior officer, and I must respect his wishes. He stopped the car and went around the back where Rose was and tried to rape her, and as he was taking off his pants, he grabbed Rose with his hand, and she avoided him somehow and kicked him in his ribs, and he fell over, and she ran out the car into the woods. I tried to run after her, but I fell to the ground. She ran extremely fast in the woods and disappeared, and we were unable to locate her in the woods."

Vallencourt looking quite pensive, said, "That was not too difficult, to tell the truth, but telling me the truth will not save your sorry ass. I instructed you to deliver Rose to Agent Chang in Camden, and you ignored my instruction. If you had followed my instruction, you would be rewarded, but now your reward is death. Please unbuckle your seatbelt and jump out of the helicopter, now."

The policeman unbuckled the seat belt and got out of his seat; as he was nearing the helicopter door, he opened it, turned around, drew his service revolver, pointed it straight at Vallencourt's stomach and said, "I am not jumping out of this helicopter to my death. I will kill you all with my gun before I jump out of the helicopter. I want you to instruct the pilot to land the helicopter now, or I will shoot you right here in the gut."

Everyone in the helicopter started laughing, and Vallencourt asked, "Do you know who you are threatening with a gun?"

The policeman raised the gun towards Vallencourt's chest and said, "Tell the pilot to land the helicopter, now."

Vallencourt turned to the pilot and said, "Elevate the helicopter to another five hundred feet."

The policeman suddenly felt the helicopter going upward instead of downward, and he stared at Vallencourt with pure venom and hatred in his eyes and started shooting the gun at Vallencourt's chest. The policeman, in total incredulity, saw Vallencourt absorbed all the bullets that were aimed at him in his chest and still standing in front of him with a wry smile on his face. The policeman, in total disbelief, could not understand what was going on as he was emptying the magazine clips into Vallencourt's chest. He stopped the shooting and asked, "What are you?"

The smile disappeared off Vallencourt's face, and he said, "Not fucking human, you piece of shit."

Vallencourt, in one quick motion, kicked the policeman out of the helicopter. As the policeman was falling, he suddenly started shooting the gun in all directions until he fell and died on a huge boulder.

The pilot continued to search the area for Rose, but they were unable to see any sign of her, until Vallencourt asked the pilot to land the helicopter because it was getting dark. The pilot landed the helicopter, and Vallencourt instructed Thornbird to drive the police cruiser and lit it on fire before pushing it over a precipice. Vallencourt turned to Agent Chang to follow the police cruiser and to return with the Thornbird.

******

As Wallenstein sat in the helicopter pondering what he was going to do if Rose's accomplice called him about Rose's whereabout and he did not have her in their custody. He had instructed the police to leave his number on the piece of paper, but what if Rose's accomplice called him and there was no Rose? How will they retrieve the amulet? The idea was to exchange Rose for the amulet but now Rose had escaped, and they do not have the amulet. Wallenstein thought they must do everything in their power to find Rose in the woods. They waited around twenty minutes until Agent Chang returned with Thornbird. Vallencourt then took Agent Chang aside and spoke to him; then, they all boarded the helicopter and flew away, with the exception of Agent Chang, who drove away from the area.

Rose woke the next morning at the sound of rain pelting on top of the cabin. She looked at her watch and saw it was ten o'clock. She was surprised that she slept so late, but she was aware that the long walk and escaping from those crooked police officers made her extremely exhausted from running and walking into the woods. She got up off the bed feeling reinvigorated from a well-earned rest and went into the bathroom to empty her bladder and brush her teeth.

Rose then went into the kitchen and started searching in the pantry for something to eat for breakfast. She found some powdered milk and some Kellogg's frosted flakes. Rose looked about some tea and then had the frosted flakes. After consuming her breakfast, Rose started exploring the cabin until she found a small radio. She turned it on but was not satisfied with the station that was playing, and she turned the dial on the radio until she came upon a rhythm and blues station. She carried the radio back to her room and went back into the bed. As the soothing, soulful music kept on playing, she missed Malakai. She eventually dozed off to sleep as the music kept on playing in the background.

Rose kept on sleeping until she started dreaming about the place where she met Gabe. In her dream, she could see his smiling face displaying those extremely full white teeth. She somehow started to remember what he was saying to her when they last met when he was making his departure in the woods. In her dream, Gabe extended his hand and said, "My sweet, dear Rose, I am always there to be a guide for you in this life. Tell Malakai that he is not there as yet, but he is on the right path."

As soon as Rose remembered what Gabe had said, she suddenly woke out of her dream. Rose started staring intently at the ceiling of the cabin, pondering who or what Gabe was and what he meant about Malakai. She thought he was a ghost, but his warm smiling face and his warm hands told her that it was unlikely an apparition. Rose was wondering how he also knew Malakai's name as she sat in the bed pondering her encounter with Gabe and wondering if she had conjured up everything in her mind. She soon dispels that notion out of her mind because it was Gabe who directed her to the Moosehead cabin.

Rose got out of bed and started looking outside the window. The rain had stopped falling, but she could not see much because of the tree canopy that basically covered and concealed the cabin. Suddenly, she saw two men in camouflage clothing being dragged by two search dogs on a leash running past the cabin, going furthered in the woods. It suddenly dawned on Rose that they were searching for her, and she felt a sense of security inside the cabin and somehow felt more relief that she followed the instruction given by Gabe not to stop at the first cabin. She was certainly thankful for the showers of rain that certainly erased her tracks, and any trace of her whereabouts in the woods. Rose suspected that the dogs were there to scare her out of her hiding, if any at all possibilities, that she was in the woods.

Rose was now even more puzzled by Gabe because, without his help, they would have her in their custody. It dawned on Rose the humongous resources of the Alliance Organization that they could muster men to pursue her so quickly in the woods.

Rose went and turned the volume of the radio down and checked to ensure that the back and front doors were closed securely because she knew at some point the men would reemerge from the woods. She was not planning on going anywhere other than to stay in the cabin where she felt safe from the outside world. She went into the kitchen and cooked white rice and tinned salmon and added ketchup to add taste to the meal. After she ate, she washed up the dishes and went back and sat in a chair and started reading some old magazines.

Around some minutes to seven o'clock in the evening, Rose heard barking dogs. She got up from the chair where she was reading the old magazines and opened the window slightly. As she looked outside, she caught a glimpse of four men and their search dogs coming back from the woods. Rose felt quite apprehensive, but the men and their dogs ran passed the cabin, and Rose whispered a prayer of thanks to God. After the men and dogs were out of her sight, Rose went back to reading the magazines. After a few more hours of reading, Rose went to the bathroom and took a quick shower then went to bed. As she lay in the bed sleeping, she began to dream about Malakai and being in his arms.

Chapter 22

As Malakai drove into New York, he decided to stop by an old acquaintance of his to get some information about the possibilities of where the Alliance Organization might be holding Rose in New York. Malakai's acquaintance's house was located on the outskirts of the city. The house was in an isolated area from his neighbors and had a huge yard. Malakai parked the car by the gate, came out of the car and walked toward the gate. The gate was unlocked, and Malakai pushed it aside and walked towards the house which was around three hundred yards. Malakai entered the premises and noticed that the lawn was extremely well-manicured, looking like a green carpet.

Malakai walked toward the house, and started admiring it. It was a beautiful two-story house painted orange in color. As he kept on walking, suddenly, four large ferocious Doberman dogs came running towards him at a fast pace. Malakai knew immediately that the dogs were guard dogs, and they would rip the flesh of an intruder. Malakai immediately took a dominant stance by clenching his hand muscle towards his chest, screaming at the dogs to sit and looking the dogs directly in the eyes. The dogs looked Malakai cautiously in his eyes and somehow maybe saw a kindred spirit. They say that the eyes are a window into the soul of a person, but most animals can see human beings for who they truly are, whether they are a good or a bad person. Suddenly the dogs started licking the bottom of Malakai's jeans pants foot, and he immediately started stroking them with his hand.

Malakai and the dogs walked towards the house, where someone was watching them from behind a window drape. Malakai arrived at the door and was about to knock on the door; it suddenly opened by a tall, muscular, broad shoulder Caucasian man with black hair and a thick moustache. The man's name was Wainwright, and he and Malakai were somewhat similar; both were loners, but Wainwright was from the Sagittarius Galaxy. He hugged Malakai, slapped him on the shoulder and said, "Kai, welcome to my humble little house. It is good to see you after such a long while. Come inside the house."

Malakai went inside the house which was quite spacious and beautifully decorated with various artwork. They entered the living room, and Malakai said, "It is good to see you also after such a long while, my friend."

Wainwright motioned Malakai to have a seat on the brown leather sofa and asked, "What can I do for you, my friend?"

Malakai took in a deep breath and said, "The Alliance Organization took, or I should say kidnapped, a friend of mine, and I would love to get her back somehow. I was wondering somehow if you would know where in New York they would be keeping her in their custody."

Wainwright looked at Malakai and saw that he was deeply troubled and said, "Sorry to hear that about your friend. I know for a fact that they will not take her to their Manhattan headquarters, but they will most likely keep her at some isolated house, a warehouse or some isolated farmhouse out of the city. I am sorry to tell you this, but it is quite unlikely that you will get her back, much less see her again."

"That is what I am honestly afraid of, that I will not be able to see her again," said Malakai.

"For what it is worth, I have a friend who works at the Manhattan headquarters in the security area. I could ask a few questions of him discreetly, and you could call me back within a week; if I hear anything, I will convey to you any information," said Wainwright.

"That would be great. I would be so appreciative if you get any information," said Malakai.

"So are you going to tell me what you have for the Alliance Organization why they kidnap your woman?" asked Wainwright.

Malakai grimaced and said, "It is not that I do not want to tell you, my friend, but the less you know better it is for your safety and well-being. These people are after my head, and I cannot add yours or put you in a compromise situation."

Wainwright got up off the sofa and said, "Walk with me to the gym."

Malakai got up off the sofa and started to walk with Wainwright through a passage in the house to the fitness center when Malakai asked, "Can I please borrow your cell phone to make a call?"

"Certainly," said Wainwright. He turned back into one of the rooms, picked up the cell phone that was charging, and gave it to Malakai.

As they arrived at the fitness center in the house, Malakai noticed that it was a large room with a few weightlifting machines. Malakai pressed the power button on the phone, and the phone light came on and requested the phone user code. Malakai turned around and asked for the access code for the phone, and Wainwright gave it to him without the slightest hesitation. Malakai turned around and took the paper out of his pocket and started dialing the number that was left in the motel room in Pittsburgh when he heard Wainwright say, "There is a bounty for your woman, Rose Winter head and yours, but apparently no one knew who you are."

As Malakai was about to dial the last digit of the phone number, he turned around to face Wainwright when he heard him utter Rose's name, but as he was about to turn, he got hit in the face by Wainwright, and he fell on the ground on the carpeted floor. Malakai looked up from the ground to see Wainwright approaching him with a beautifully sleek sword. Malakai quickly rolled away from where he was, got up off the floor, and went to the other end of the gym.

"I am about to chop off your fucking head if you do not give me the amulet so I can return it to the Alliance Organization. They made anyone who brought the amulet to them an offer that they simply could not refuse. It is an offer to have a seat on their council and unlimited power," said Wainwright.

"So you are going to sell me out for power and prestige. I thought you eschewed those things when you left them to be by yourself and to serve a higher cause more than yourself," said Malakai.

Wainwright smiled and said, "I was trying, waiting on a liberator, but I realize that I do not have the patience, grace and diligence; therefore, I would rather go with the team that seems to be winning at the moment. I do not hate mankind like they do, but I prefer to have my sway over them and be worshipped than not be."

"I am terribly sorry for you, my friend. As the old saying goes in *Matthew 16:26, for what it profits a man to gain the whole world and lose his soul?* Having all the powers and material possessions will not bring you happiness or for you to be a good person. It is those things that you eschew that bring you happiness, patience, grace, diligence, humility, and to reach out to God that is greater than all of us combined."

Wainwright, full of confidence, especially not seeing Malakai with a weapon, held the sword near his ribs with his elbow and started clapping Malakai's speech and said, "Bravo on your speech, but there is an old motto that you never looked a gift horse in the mouth meaning do not question the value of a present or a gift. You arrived at my house as a well-wrapped gift to present to my benefactor, the Alliance Organization. I never told you that I rejoined them shortly since the last time we saw each other. My only aim now is to take back the amulet to my brothers in the Alliance Organization so they can bring hell to this earth. Nothing you can say or do will stop my quest to bring that about especially now I do not see you with a sword to fight. I am asking you one last time to hand over the amulet, or I will chop off your head."

Malakai did not want to fight Wainwright because he was an old acquaintance and knew that he struggled constantly to stay on the path of what is right and good in this world and his inability to reach beyond himself to a higher power that comprise a force of good in this world. Malakai knew he could not allow him to retrieve the amulet and give it back to the Alliance Organization, so he resigned to the fact that he would have to fight Wainwright. Malakai looked intently at Wainwright and said, "We have known each other a long while. I beg of you, let us not do this and fight because one of us will have to die."

"As the great William Shakespeare said in. *Hamlet, to be or not to be meant,* one of us will surely die, and it is certainly not going to be me. The old adage goes that our types who are born farther away from the Milky Way Galaxy are stronger and therefore unbeatable by one such as you," said Wainwright.

"I am sorry it has to come to this wherein I will have to fight you. By the way, I never told you I do have a sword, and my sword is the great equalizer. Therefore, whichever galaxy any of my enemies is from, I have my trusty Onoro sword to even my fighting chance," said Malakai.

Malakai took off his jacket and took out his Onoro sword. Malakai pressed the button, and the elegant, sleek, flaming blade emerged like a well-trusted friend. The sight of the flaming blade drained the confidence that Wainwright had, and Malakai smiled, aware that the sword effect on most of his enemies. Wainwright lunged at Malakai with his sword, and he evaded the attack. Wainwright made a quick chop at Malakai's head, and he blocked the sword. They continued pressing the attack on each other back and forth until Wainwright made one quick, desperate chop at Malakai's head. As Malakai blocked Wainwright's sword, it broke in pieces, and Wainwright, totally terrified at seeing the sword break in his hand, froze for a second within an instant, Malakai chopped off his head, and his blood sprayed all over the carpet.

Malakai wiped off the blood that was on his sword and pressed the button, and the blade retreated into the sheath. He picked up his jacket and put it on and inserted the sword in it. Malakai then went upstairs to ensure that there was no camera system in the house to record him decapitating Wainwright. Totally satisfied that there was no camera system in the house, Malakai came downstairs and picked up the charger for Wainwright's cell phone and inserted it in his pocket.

Malakai then went into the living room and sat on the sofa. He reached for the house phone and dialed the number that was left in the Pittsburgh motel. A man answered the phone and said, "Hello."

Malakai, rather unsure and nervous, said, "I am Peter Mack. To whom am I speaking with?"

"You are speaking to Wallenstein; what can I do for you?"

"I am calling about the woman, Rose Winter; you are holding or kidnapped, I should say. I need her back unharmed."

Wallenstein, who was slouched over in his office chair, stood upright instantly in his office chair when he heard the caller on the other end of the phone line mention Rose Winter's name. Wallenstein cleared his throat and said "We have been searching for you more than a year now. Do you have the Amulet of Osiris?"

Malakai hesitated for a moment and said, "Yes, I do have the amulet, but you cannot have it until I have Rose safe and sound by my side. If, by any chance, you hurt a hair on her head, I will kill you all one by one, and you will never see the amulet. In addition, I know for a fact your master will kill you if you do not deliver the amulet to him; therefore, it is in your interest to keep Rose unharmed."

"That is a given that we will not harm Rose, but if we do not receive the amulet, we will certainly kill her and burn her body. I need for you to bring the amulet to our Manhattan headquarters, where we can exchange Rose for the amulet," said Wallenstein.

Malakai hesitated to respond, thinking about the offer presented to him by Wallenstein. If he did not accept their offer, they would certainly kill Rose. Malakai knew he was in a bind; if he gave them the amulet, they would destroy the world, and if he did not, they would certainly kill Rose. Malakai said, "The offer to exchange the amulet for Rose must take place at a neutral territory and not at your headquarters where you may set a trap to kill me when I hand over the amulet."

Wallenstein thought about what Peter Mack said and knew that the Alliance Organization did not have Rose in their custody. Any suggestion by Peter Mack would be okay by him as long as they can retrieve the amulet. Wallenstein, trying to be amenable, then said, "A neutral territory sounds fine by me. Where would you suggest we do the exchange?"

Malakai thought for a moment, then said, "We do the exchange in public view; therefore, I would prefer we do it at Kings

Plaza Mall in Brooklyn on the second floor near the entrance of the Old Navy Department Store tomorrow evening at six o'clock."

"Sound great then; we will see each other at six o'clock tomorrow evening," said Wallenstein.

"Before we end the conversation, I need to speak to Rose to ensure that she is okay, and you did not torture her for any information about me," said Malakai.

Wallenstein, hearing the request from Peter Mack, started cursing his luck, and his disposition changed instantly, similar to a cornered animal. There was no Rose in their custody, much less even knowing her whereabouts, and Wallenstein did not even know if Rose was alive or dead. Wallenstein tone of voice changed to a much sterner, sinister tone and said, "We cannot allow you to speak to her at this moment."

"Then we do not have a deal, and I will certainly not be in Brooklyn tomorrow evening," said Malakai.

All the blood seemed to drain from Wallenstein's face as he listened to Peter Mack's pronouncement that he would not meet with him the following day to recover the amulet. Wallenstein knew he had to come up with a plan quickly, so he said, "Please hold on while I take the phone to Rose for you to speak to her for one minute."

Wallenstein knew that the only way he could continue to deceive Peter Mack was to change his voice and pretend to be Rose.

As Malakai waited for around two minutes, a soft female voice came on the line and said, "This is Rose."

"This is Peter speaking to you. Are you okay?" asked Malakai.

"Yes, they are taking care of me properly, but I miss you, honey," said Wallenstein.

A light bulb suddenly went off in Malakai's head when the person at the end of the line said, Honey. Rose has never used that type of expression to refer to him, and he sternly asked, "Rose, what is my favorite part of your body?"

The question totally flummoxed Wallenstein. He thought that he was doing a good job pretending to be Rose, and suddenly, he got this question from Peter Mack out of the blue. Wallenstein hesitated for a moment before answering the question, wondering if Peter was like most men who love a woman's ass or a woman's breast. Wallenstein, unsure of how to respond, said, "Honey, my breast is what you love the most on my body."

Malakai intuitively knew it was not Rose but an imposter pretending to be her, and he was filled with dread and fear. Malakai was filled with rage because the other person on the other end of the line was trying to deceive him, and he said, "Please get the fuck off the line and put on Wallenstein for me to talk to."

Wallenstein knew he had said something wrong, but he did not know what, and as he held the phone in his hand, trying to figure out what went wrong, he said, "Hello."

"You are trying to deceive me by putting that woman on the line, who was not Rose. I want to speak to Rose now, or there is no deal, and you can forget seeing the amulet again if I cannot speak to Rose," said Malakai.

"Hush now, you are one of us, and you would utilize the same chicanery to deceive me to get back Rose. Let me state honestly, that I am sorry for trying to deceive you. You wanted to speak to Rose, but she is not with me at the moment. She is locked up in a warehouse far from here. I will be at the warehouse in the next four days; therefore, I will allow you to speak to her in the next four days if you call back my number, and then we can make the exchange for the amulet.

"I accept your contrition, but if anything like this happens again, I promise you, you will not see the amulet. I will call you back in the next four days," said Malakai.

Malakai then slammed down the phone in anger and wondered if he could believe anything that Wallenstein had said about Rose. He sat on the sofa, wondering why Wallenstein would want him to call back in the next four days. He knew that the Alliance Organization was desperate for the return of the amulet, but why in heaven's name would they want to prolong the retrieval of it? Malakai started to wonder if they had killed Rose, but he pushed the thought out of his mind. Malakai thought Rose was too valuable to them alive, if they wanted to trade her for the amulet.

Malakai, with his brain in overdrive, had an epiphany and started wondering if the Alliance Organization did not have Rose in their custody. He thought that was the only way they would want him to call back in the next four days. He leaped out of the sofa and gathered all his stuff and left the door ajar for the dogs to come and go in the house. Malakai left the Wainwright's house feeling much better than before as he walked towards his car parked at the gate. He entered the car and drove away from the premises in a higher than when he came to Wainwright's house.

****

Wallenstein sat at his desk processing the conversation he had just had with Peter Mack after he hung up the phone. Wallenstein thought he finally had the mastermind in his grasp, but he did not have Rose to trade for the amulet. He took the office phone off the base and started banging it on his office desk and said, "Shit, shit, shit. I am cursing my damn luck."

After a few more minutes, Wallenstein calmed down, picked up the phone and called the secretary to tell her to announce that there would be a meeting in the conference room in the next ten minutes. Wallenstein then got up from around his desk and went to the bathroom to urinate and wash his hands. As he was drying his hands, he caught a reflection of himself in the bathroom mirror. He stared at his face to ensure that everything was okay, then left for the conference room.

As Wallenstein entered the conference room, Vallencourt, Thornbird, Sanchez, and a number of senior agents were seated around the conference table. Wallenstein took his seat and said, "Ladies and gentlemen, I think we are close to retrieving the amulet. I just spoke to Peter Mack, who has the amulet. Our problem is that he wants to exchange the amulet for Rose, whom he thinks we have in our custody. We, therefore, have to exert all our resources to find her immediately, and I mean in the next three days. I told him that we were holding Rose in a warehouse in upstate New York, so he will be able to talk to her in the next four days."

"Could we not get a female to pretend that she is Rose?" asked Vallencourt.

"I have tried that, and he caught on that it was not Rose he was talking to; therefore, we will have to get Rose in our custody by whatever means, or else we can forget about retrieving the amulet. I mean expending multiple resources, our kinds and humans, to the last area where she was last seen. I was thinking we offered a monetary reward of around fifty thousand dollars in cash to the human if they came across and apprehended her," said Wallenstein.

Thornbird, looking puzzled and envious at the same time that Wallenstein was put in charge of the investigation instead of him, asked, "Peter Mack, is he one of us? Did you ask him which galaxy he is from?"

"I can tell you categorically that he is one of us. I did not ask him which galaxy he was from, because I was trying to deceive him with the female voice, and I did not wish to anger him more. I think he is from an extremely far galaxy because no one from any near galaxy would dare challenge us," said Wallenstein.

"If he is one of us why the separation and been our arch enemy?"

Vallencourt let out a deep laugh and said, "When our ancestors were cast out of heaven, there were a few who became disillusioned with our god, the morning star and separated themselves from us. They wanted to re-enter heaven again, but that was lost cause or a fool's errand. These renegades saw us as the enemies, and we see them likewise. They live on earth by their own rules and no one else. I have even encountered some who do exceptionally good deeds for human beings, trying to please our master enemy somehow so that he will somehow look upon them as redeemable and hopefully find their way to heaven again."

Sanchez looked pensive and, as if a light went off in his head, asked, "Is it possible for our kind to be redeemed?"

"No, it is not possible. When our ancestors were cast out of heaven, our accursed lots were cursed by the maker of the universe, never to return to heaven. Therefore, I choose to serve the morning star as my god and rule here on earth. My motto is simply, if you are not with us, you are against us; therefore, if you are not with us, you are the enemy, and you must die," said Vallencourt.

"I see," said Sanchez.

"Back to our business of how to retrieve the amulet," said Wallenstein.

"Okay, I will call Agent Chang to send out the word about the fifty thousand dollars in cash, and I will send all my agents to New Jersey to look for Rose," said Vallencourt.

"Great then, if there is nothing else to discuss, the meeting is adjourned," said Wallenstein.

They all filed out of the conference room back to their respective office. Wallenstein, as he sat back in his soft chair around his desk, somehow decided to call back the number that Peter Mack had called him on, but as he dialed the number, it kept on ringing without anyone answering it. He hung up the phone and called the information technology department to check on the number and location.

Chapter 23

Rose got up early the following morning and prepared her breakfast. She ate her breakfast quickly and cleaned up the cabin. After Rose finished the cleaning, she started hunting for anything within the cabin that she could take on her journey. She found a rather large sharp knife and a bear pepper spray, which she packed in her bag. Rose then went into the bathroom and took out a blond wig that she had bought in the store in Pittsburgh. She had bought the wig to change her looks for Malakai, and now she thought if anyone was still looking for her, they would have a more difficult time seeing that now she was now a blond woman. She then covered her head with a black New York Yankee baseball hat. Rose then went into the kitchen cupboard, took out three small water bottles, and put them in her bag. She took the bag, slung it over her shoulder, and left the cabin.

As she started walking, a cool morning breeze began blowing gently over her face. Rose looked ahead but could see no other human apart from some deer grazing around two hundred yards away on some fresh green plants. She continued walking, enjoying the birds chirping and flying away, when she came upon them suddenly, frightened at the sight of her presence in the woods. Rose was glad she was in her blue jeans and sneakers as she walked through the woods. She walked the path that she came and soon passed the first cabin. She continued on her journey and soon reached where the two trees fell in the creek. She continued on her way, following the path where the creek ran downstream. On the bank of the creek were some small stones that were baked in the soil caused by the splashing of the water, allowing them to shine brightly in the early morning sun.

Rose was feeling hot as she was sweating more profusely, and as she came around a bend, some deer that were drinking the cool creek water ran away, frightened at the sight of her presence in the area. She continued to walk along the banks of the creek when suddenly, around five hundred yards ahead of her, she saw a huge black bear drinking water in the middle of the creek. Rose froze for a couple of seconds, hoping that the bear did not see her as she backtracked stealthily like a ninja warrior. She started to backtrack without making the slightest sound. The bear was still drinking from the creek, and Rose was walking backward gingerly, not making the slightest sound. Rose suddenly stepped on a piece of dry twig, and it broke, and the bear looked up instantly in Rose's direction and stood upward on his two hind legs. The bear seemed as if it was around ten feet in length, ferocious-looking and with muscle strewn all over its body.

Rose continued to walk backward but at a faster pace now that the bear was aware of her presence in the woods. The bear did not move out of the creek but let out a huge bellowing sound that seemed to echo throughout the woods. Rose was now around nine hundred yards away from the bear, still walking backward, and she did not want to run because she knew no human could outrun a bear, but at the same time, she did not want to confront it. She knew that bears sometimes killed human beings when they felt threatened, but she was glad that she had the bear pepper spray in her bag and the huge knife.

Rose was around nine hundred and fifty yards when suddenly the bear made a mad dash out of the water and started running in her direction. Rose thought that she had enough distance between her and the bear, so she started running away from the bank of the creek, but instead of running back to where she was coming from, she made a side way dash into the woods. The vegetation was thicker, but she was still going downhill and running at breakneck speed. The bear, seeing that Rose had run in a sideway direction, followed also, thereby cutting off the distance that it would take to catch up to Rose.

Rose slowed down a bit, opened her bag, and reached for the knife and the bear pepper spray. She closed the bag and held the knife in her left hand and the bear spray in her right hand as she kept on running in the forest. She realized that the bear was gaining on her as she could hear it rushing through the undergrowth as the vegetation seemed to give way as it trampled it. The vegetation was now becoming less thick as she entered an area with some large trees. She continued to run among the trees in a zigzag fashion, hoping that the bear would lose interest in the chase. Rose suddenly turned around to see if she could see the bear, but she was unable to, and she kept on running but at a slower pace in the woods. She stopped and listened to see if she could hear the sound of the bear, but she could not hear anything. She opened her bag and put away the knife but still kept the bear pepper spray in her right hand as she walked among the tall trees.

Approaching some rather large pine trees, Rose saw some squirrels busy gathering pine nuts. She stopped and admired the length of the trees which seemed to be around seventy feet extending in the sky. Rose stopped for a moment, took out one of the small bottles of water and took a drink. She then resumed her trek throughout the woods with her bear spray in her right hand. Although she was away from the banks of the creek, she kept walking in the direction where she could hear the flow of the water.

Along her journey out of the woods, Rose saw animals of various kinds, such as the elegant whitetail deer, coyotes, raccoons, and chipmunks. As she continued her trek, she suddenly saw some birds fly away as she approached. Rose looked ahead but could not see what would cause the birds to be disturbed and wondered if it was her presence in the woods. She then looked behind her and was quite startled by what she was seeing in the bush. It was the same huge black bear running through the bushes and fast approaching where she was standing near an oak tree. Rose did not want to confront the bear on the ground because she thought that the speed and force that the bear was approaching her might knock her over, and she would be at the mercy of the bear. Rose knew she had a few minutes, so she ran towards an oak tree, quickly put away the bear pepper spray in her jeans pocket and started climbing the tree.

Within a few minutes, she was in the oak tree, sitting on a branch. She knew bears were very adept at climbing, but she wanted to face the bear where she had the upper hand and not in a vulnerable position. She knew that if the bear climbed the oak tree, the bear's eyes would be exposed, and she would be able to aim the spray more accurately at its face. Rose was at the second branch when the bear approached the oak tree. The bear was even bigger and even more ferocious looking now that it was closer, and the bear claws were the largest Rose had ever seen. She was aware that they were meant to tear flesh, and it gave her an uneasy feeling.

Rose could sense the confusion within the bear as it looked up at Rose in the tree. The bear lifted itself on its two hind legs and let out a huge growling sound that seemed to shake the surrounding trees. The bear started to climb the tree and suddenly stopped, seemingly more confused when it saw that Rose was climbing downward toward a tall tree branch. It occurred to Rose that she did not want to kill the bear, and if it climbed too high when it dropped out of the tree, the fall might kill it. Also she did not want the bear to climb to the first branch and thereby have a greater support of the branch and would more likely put up a more fierce resistance.

As Rose climbed downward to the first branch and waited on the bear, it started to growl and somehow seemed to become irritated at seeing Rose patiently waiting on it. At around four feet away from the first branch, Rose took out the bear pepper spray from her pocket, removed the lid, aimed it directly at the ferocious-looking bear eyes and sprayed it. The spray hit the bear's eyes with deadly accuracy, and it started to growl more loudly. Rose aimed the spray directly into its mouth and some more in the bear's eyes. The bear became angrier and started to climb, and as it climbed closer to Rose, it felt the full effect of the bear pepper spray in its eyes and mouth. With one final growl, the bear lashed at Rose with its claw, fell to the ground and ran off in the direction where it came from growling and running as fast as possible as it could towards the creek. Rose laughed at seeing the large bear run away, and she thought more or less the bear was running towards the creek to wash the pepper spray from its eyes and mouth.

Rose quickly climbed down the tree, hoping that the bear had learned its lesson not to attack human beings. Although she was alone in the forest Rose was quite pleased for staring danger in its eyes and had the will and tenacity to overcome it. Rose walked briskly through the woods because she did not want the night fall to catch her in a strange place. She walked until it was around four in the afternoon, and she saw a strange sight in the distance. She ran towards the strange sight quite excitedly and was glad to see some semblance of civilization.

Rose was not sure what she was seeing as she ran towards the strange sight. As she got closer, she could clearly see a huge burning cross in a clearing, and some people gathered around it in a semicircle. The people who were gathered around the huge burning cross were not able to see her because numerous trees were blocking the view. Rose drew closer to the gathering and started observing the people. She could see numerous shaven head Caucasians men, but she could not see any women. As the cross burnt, the men started marching in a circle around it, clapping and chanting, "We hate Jews, we hate Blacks, we hate Mexican, and most of all, we hate Faggots. The only good Jew is a dead Jew. The only good Black is a dead Black. All Mexicans must die, and Faggots we shot on the spot. It is our constitutional duty to protect our country from these parasites. The future of our white children depends on us, as we fight to protect our rights of white privileges."

Rose's heart sank as she saw the mostly young men in their twenties displaying such rampant ignorance and seeing the men. Rose thought she was near civilization somehow but thought the men's behaviors were very questionable and almost uncivilized in the twenty-first century. As the young men kept on chanting in the woods, Rose suddenly realized that it was an initiation ceremony to induct these men into a skinhead hate group.

Rose, who was crouched near a tree, got up and walked stealthily past the group of men no longer desirous of their help in the woods. She was angry, thinking that young men could waste their lives engaging in a useless emotion like hate. She thought if those young men knew of the benefits of intermingling the different races, they would not be in the woods chanting nonsensical catchphrases. She thought that basic things like food would not be as enjoyable if people of different cultures did not intermingle and share their unique cuisine. Sports, science, technology, business, international diplomacy, arts, languages, and even jurisprudence are all borrowed from different races.

As Rose walked along, she was irked thinking that people could hate other people for no reason more than the mere fact of the color of their skin, or they look, or dress differently than what they are used to in their small towns or villages. She questioned why another human being would inculcate a child with hatred and disdain for another human being if they were not mentally unstable. A child is not born with hate but is taught to hate by their elders, or peers.

The concept of treating some people as sub-human makes it possible for enslavement, and taking away their rights goes far back to ancient civilizations. But in the modern twenty-first-century society, where most human knows that they will have to interact with one another, go to school, work, bear children, form a business, participate in the economy, and treat people differently, it is wrong. Rose thought that living in a cosmopolitan society is an exhibition that we are all one race that is the human race, and a reminder that we are all God's children, the most important of his mortal creation.

Rose walked around another mile before she started to see a smidgen of civilization in the form of people camping in the woods. Rose continued to walk by the many campers she saw in the woods. It dawned on Rose that it was a holiday camping ground somewhere in New Jersey. She continued walking until she saw an elderly Caucasian couple in their sixties sitting beside a Recreational Vehicle. The recreational vehicle was quite elegant, modern looking and painted in a bone white and brownish color. The vehicle had a large windscreen and large side windows at the front. Rose noticed the name of the recreational vehicle was "The Freedom Traveler."

The elderly man was very tall and had on a cowboy hat. His face was overly broad, and he had this friendly disposition. He had a thick white moustache, and his face was covered with freckles. He was dressed in khaki cargo shorts and a green t-shirt. The elderly woman seemed as if she was a couple of years younger than the man. She had long gray hair and an extremely pretty face. She had on blue jeans, and t-shirt and sandals.

Rose approached the elderly couple, who did not notice her, and said, "Hello, I am Savannah Parks."

The elderly man and woman spun their head around and scrutinized Rose. The elderly man, with a big wide smile on his face, extended his right hand and said, "I am Big Bob, and this lovely lady is my wife, Mary Joe Cox. We are pleased to meet you, Savannah."

"I am travelling from early this morning, and I was just wondering if, by any chance, you are going to New York?" asked Rose.

Mary Joe, with concern on her face, said, "No, my dear, we are not going to New York. You seem very tired. Have you eaten?"

"No, I have not eaten since morning," said Rose.

"Can we invite you to have dinner with us in our mobile home?" asked Big Bob.

Rose, who was extremely hungry from the long trek through the woods, said, "You are too kind, but I would be very appreciative of the meal."

"I was preparing baked chicken in the oven. It should be finished by now. Let us go inside to eat," said Mary Joe.

Rose and the elderly couple went inside, and the spaciousness of the recreational vehicle blew away Rose. Inside the recreational vehicle were areas for a bedroom, bathroom, fridge, sofa, television, dream dinette, and closet. Mary Joe set the table, and they had baked chicken with baked potatoes, and for dessert, they had freshly baked chocolate cake. Rose enjoyed the meal immensely and thanked her hosts for the meal. As they ate the chocolate cake, Rose asked, "Which part of the country are you folks from?"

"We are both from the great State of Texas. I married this lovely lady over twenty-five years ago, and I would do it all over again," said Big Bob.

Rose looked at the elderly couple and could see the love they had for each other in their eyes. Rose was in awe of their relationship and could not help saying, "Congratulations on having such a beautiful, long-lasting relationship." Rose, quite pensive, said, "I have to ask, what makes your relationship last so long?"

The couple laughed heartily, and Mary Joe said, "Thanks for the nice sentiments about our relationship lasting these many years, but I must tell you, a relationship is not beautiful; a flower is beautiful. A relationship is hard work that must be caressed and cushioned. I remember about ten years into our marriage, he went away for a weekend with that big-breasted prostitute Ruth Ann. It took me many months to forgive him, but I did because I love him. The question that you asked about why our relationship lasted so long is, I think you have to have love and commitment to each other, even though that love, and commitment will be tested as you go along in your life."

Rose gently and playful slapped Big Bob's hand and said, "Shame on you for being disloyal to your wife."

"I did regret it, causing her pain and, most of all, to lose faith in me for a brief period. Sometimes I think it is some primal urges in most men that we have to act out to remind us we are men with shortcomings, and we are capable of dastardly behaviors irrespective of which one of our loved ones we hurt," said Big Bob.

"We are all flawed creatures with our individual shortcomings, but it is how each one of us deals with it and move on with our life," said Rose.

Mary Joe looked down at the table and said, "Some individuals do not have the opportunity to move on. Savannah, I hope I do not shock you too much, but I am dying. I have cancer of the blood, an aggressive form of leukemia. I decided I did not want to endure pain and suffering while undergoing chemotherapy. I decided I wanted to see the country, to see the beauty of nature, and people as they go about their business before I die and not sit in a hospital bed. I want to die with dignity, on my own terms and not anyone else."

Rose reached over and held Mary Joe's hand and said, "I am terribly sorry to hear of your diagnosis, but I can truly tell you on my journey on this earth I have never met any human more dignified than you. My boyfriend would surely love you because I do not know of anyone who loves nature and this planet like he does. I think you and he are kindred spirits; if he was battling cancer, I know he would want to follow in your footsteps."

"I would love to meet him since he is my kindred spirit," said Mary Joe.

Rose looked at Big Bob and asked, "How are you dealing with Mary Joe's cancer diagnosis?"

Big Bob clasped his hands together, and tears came to his eyes; as he wiped away the tears, he said, "Not too good. I have asked God many a nights why take her from me so soon, but I got no response. A voice came into my head, and I cannot tell you if it was the voice of God, but the voice said I have not taken her as yet; therefore, enjoy the moment you have with each other. I bought the recreational vehicle and started travelling the country, enjoying nature and meeting people, and, most of all, spending a great deal of time together. It is so therapeutic for me that I honestly did not know I would enjoy it this much, that I sometimes forgot about the cancer diagnosis."

"My diagnosis is a stark reminder of the preciousness of life, especially when you are about to lose a loved one. It does highlight the fleeting nature of life that things that generally offend you, you suddenly realize the inconsequential nature of stuff you worry and fight about," said Mary Joe.

"You are right about the brevity of life and the stupidity we as humans engaged in. On my journey here, I saw some young men engaging in an initiation ceremony, pledging to some racist skinhead group. I was so angry I could not bear to look at them wasting their life just hating people for no good reason," said Rose.

"We as men do some pretty crazy stuff, and sometimes, we just follow the crowd and their peers. Most of them are just clueless young men, trying to fit in as they make their way through this complicated world, sometimes not even aware of the hurt they cause other people not looking like them. Sometimes, because of their unawareness, we have to pray for them, hoping they will turn their life around and away from hate," said Big Bob.

"That is so profound, and I guess you are right about them. Mary Joe, I see why you love him so much. I will pray to God for you that he will give you as much time with Big Bob as possible," said Rose.

"That is so sweet of you, my dear. My sweet child, do you ever lose faith in God when you see the endless suffering wrought upon people's lives, and also wars?" asked Mary Joe.

"I used to lose faith on a regular basis. I used to struggle with the concept of a Great God who created everything in this world but created untold suffering for people and animals. The funny thing is that when I met my boyfriend, he reaffirmed my faith in God. Sometimes I think he is like an angel to me," said Rose.

"I would love to meet your boyfriend. He seems like a real gentleman and a real man," said Big Bob.

"Savannah, if you are in no hurry to reach New York, we would be happy if you could stay with us for the next two days. There is enough space for us to accommodate you. We will be leaving here in the next two days to the great state of Pennsylvania," said Mary Joe.

"I would be honored to stay with you for the next two days. Thanks for your hospitality," said Rose.

Mary Joe got up and turned on the television, and they all watched until around nine o'clock. Rose got up, went into the bathroom, and took a nice warm shower. After she finished her shower, she put on her shorts and t-shirts. At around ten o'clock, they all retired to bed. Rose was extremely tired because of the long trek through the woods. She slept peacefully throughout the night and woke up the next morning feeling refreshed and revitalized as she stretched her body.

At approximately seven o'clock Mary Joe and Rose went into the kitchen to look about breakfast. They prepared corned beef hash and eggs for breakfast. After they finished eating their breakfast, which was quite delicious, Rose washed the dishes. Both ladies left Big Bob in the recreational vehicle, watching television. The ladies went for a walk, indulged in some bird watching and also took the view of the local wildlife. The ladies chatted like long-lost mother and daughter while also inhaling the clean, fresh air at the campsite.

As they were under a rather large oak tree looking up at some birds, Mary Joe was feeling a bit tired, and they decided to return to the recreational vehicle. Rose could not help but feel sorry for Mary

Joe for the terrible cancer diagnosis. She really liked Mary Joe and admired her serenity in spite of the deadly prognosis. She took out a pen and paper and asked Mary Joe for her cellular number and she gave Rose.

They arrived back at the recreational vehicle to see Big Bob still watching television. They both joined Big Bob, watched the news on the television and argued about it, from politics to international affairs. Both ladies were quite liberal in their views of the world, while Big Bob from the great state of Texas was quite conservative in his outlook. They all watched the television until they all fell asleep on the sofa.

Rose got up and went into the kitchen to prepare dinner while Mary Joe and Big Bob slept. Rose took two bags of shrimp out of the refrigerator and started to prepare them for cooking. Rose took out a large skillet and inserted some cooking butter into it. As the butter melted, she added the shrimp, and pepper. Rose stirred the shrimps for around six minutes until the colors changed slightly, and she then added some garlic to the shrimps and continued to stir it. Rose then added some chicken stock and lemon juice to the skillet and allowed it to boil for a few more minutes. She turned down the stove to allow the shrimp to cook slowly. She then boiled some long-grain white rice to serve with the shrimp. As Rose was preparing the broccoli Big Bob woke and asked, "What smells so good?"

"I am preparing garlic butter shrimp for dinner. It will be ready in the next five minutes after I finish preparing the vegetables," said Rose.

Mary Joe woke up feeling famished and excited to taste Rose's cooking and glad in some way that she did not have to cook dinner. Rose set up the small table and shared the food. After she finished sharing the food, she called Mary Joe and Big Bob to the table. They all took their seat and held each other hands while Mary Joe prayed and said, "Lord, we ask you to bless this food that we are about to consume. We ask you to bless all of us around the table and for your eternal love and guidance in our lives. We ask for your continued love and forgiveness for our sins as we strive to forgive those who wronged us. These and other mercies we ask in your son's name of Jesus our savior."

They commenced eating the meal with all of them relishing the taste of the food. Big Bob paused for a minute from eating and said, "Savannah, you certainly can cook. You are like a daughter to me and Mary Joe that we never had. I can speak for both of us that we love you and wish you the best on your journey."

"I concur and feel the same way. We will definitely miss you and always remember you," said Mary Joe.

Rose was touched by the outpouring of love from Big Bob and Mary Joe, and she said, "I love you too. You reminded me of my parents before they both passed away. I will always have you in my thoughts."

Mary Joe poured the white wine that was on the table in each glass. She then said, "I want to make a toast. To Savannah, may our friendship continue, no matter the seasons of the year, no matter where we are, may we always have a listening ear for each other."

They all drank the wine to Mary Joe's toast and laughed and chatted over the meal. At one point Rose even felt a little guilty not telling them her real name. She pushed the thought aside, telling herself that not telling them was for their own safety and protection if she encountered any unsavory character. They eventually got up from around the table, and Rose helped clean up the table, while Big Bob washed the dishes.

Rose and Mary Joe went outside the vehicle to take in some fresh air, hugging each other as they walked around the area, aware it was their last night together at the campsite. Rose knew she was going to miss them because Mary Joe and Big Bob reminded her somewhat of her parents. She somehow wishes that she could do something to help heal Mary Joe's cancer or to lessen her pain. They stayed outside for around two hours; then they went back into the vehicle, where they played card games and watched television before retiring to their bed.

The next morning, they were outside having pancakes for breakfast. Big Bob had set up a small table under a tree, and as they were eating, a police car pulled up near where they were having breakfast. A tall female police emerged from the police car along with her male police companion. Both police officers were smartly dressed and carrying their service revolver in their holsters. The male police officer was around in his late twenties and the female police officer seemed as if she was the senior officer.

Rose's body tensed up, seeing the police officer as they walked up towards them where they were having breakfast. The female police officer said, "Good morning to you folks. I am Officer Woodley, and my partner's name is Patterson."

Big Bob put away the pancake and said, "Good morning to you, officers. I am Big Bob, and my wife Mary Joe, and my daughter Savannah. What can we do for you this lovely morning?"

"We are looking for a female that was in our custody but escaped. We heard that she was in this area, but we were unable to locate her. Have any of you folks seen a black hair female around five feet seven inches tall?" asked Officer Woodley.

"We have not encountered any such individual. We have been here for the past week, and we have not encountered any black hair female wandering through the woods," said Big Bob.

Rose could feel the intense stare of the two police officers. She did not want to seem too apprehensive, so she continued to consume the pancake and drink the orange juice. The younger male officer was stationary, while the female officer kept on moving, and looking intensely at Rose from every angle. Rose realized all of a sudden that there was an intense manhunt for her capture by the police. She was so glad that she had bought the blonde wig in Pittsburgh that now concealed her appearance. Rose kept eating the pancakes not wanting to talk or answer any question from the police officer, so they may not be able to detect or pick up anything from her speech pattern.

"Which area of the country are you folks from?" asked Officer Woodley.

"We are from Texas, officer. Why these many questions? Are we persons of interest?" asked Mary Joe.

Officer Woodley smiled and said, "No madam, we are just trying to eliminate certain individuals we come across. We will have to walk further down the line to make some more enquiries about the female we are pursuing. That is all, folks. Have a good day."

The two police officers walked away, and Rose breathed a sigh of relief. She stopped eating as the police officers departed and started drinking a good portion of orange juices to help digest the large portion of pancakes. Having finished her drinks, Rose reached over and squeezed Big Bob's hands. Big Bob and Rose got up off the folding chair and embraced each other, not one saying a word. After they finished embracing each other, Big Bob said, "In some other life or in some other worlds, you are my daughter. I can feel your spirit and know that you are a good earthly person, and I am honored to know you."

Big Bob then kissed Rose on her cheeks, and they embraced again, with him rubbing Rose's shoulder. Mary Joe, seeing Rose and Big Bob embracing, said, "I am feeling left out over here."

Rose motioned to Mary Joe, and she got up off her folding chair and came over and all three of them embraced, not saying a word. They all sat and chatted under the tree with a keen awareness that it was their last day together, and they may not see each other again in their lifetime. After a few more minutes, Rose got up and carried the dishes inside the small kitchen. She started washing the dishes, and a tear came rolling off her face. She was concerned about Mary Joe's health and knew she was not long for this world of the living. Rose was washing the skillet and lost in her thoughts when she heard Officer Woodley say, "I came back to ask you one question, Savannah, if that is your real name. Were you always a blonde, or is it a wig you have on your head?"

Rose froze when she heard the question. She quickly regained her composure and said, "It is my natural hair." Rose then asked, "Officer Woodley, where is your partner?"

"My partner is making an inquiry with the other campers further down the road. I told him to go ahead while I picked up something. I left in the car, but I had a sudden hunch that you are wearing a wig, and I wanted to check it out for myself."

Rose then said, "Goodbye, Officer Woodley. I told you it is my natural hair, so our business is concluded."

Officer Woodley smiled and asked, "Not so fast. If it is your natural hair, let me feel it, to satisfy my curiosity?"

"That is not going to happen. You will just have to take my word that it is my natural hair. I will not allow a stranger to touch me as if we are some long-lost friends," said Rose.

Officer Woodley folded her hand, held it at chest level and asked, "If you are not the fugitive we are searching for, let me check your head that you are not wearing a wig?"

"I see we are at a stalemate because I will not allow you to search my hair to clarify some twisted curiosity on your part," said Rose.

As Rose was finishing her sentence, Officer Woodley walked up to her in the kitchen and slapped her on her ass with her hand. Officer Woodley then proceeded to grab Rose's breasts and cupped them with both hands. Her right hand then moved upward to Rose's head to feel her hair. Officer Woodley felt Rose's hair, and the realization dawned on her that Rose was indeed wearing a blonde wig. She immediately released the hold that she had on Rose and was moving backward to take out her service revolver when Rose picked up the skillet pan that she was washing, swung it around, and hit Officer Woodley on the head. Officer Woodley fell on the kitchen floor in the recreational vehicle like a sack of potatoes. Rose was angry and took great offense that Officer Woodley's hand was all over her body.

Rose quickly dried her hands on a kitchen towel and checked Officer Woodley's pulse to ensure that she was not dead. Officer Woodley was unconscious but was still breathing, and Rose was glad that she did not kill the police officer. Rose quickly stepped over Officer Woodley's body and went outside. She walked straight to where the police car was parked and opened the front car door. She looked inside and saw that the car key was in the ignition. Rose went inside and drove the car to the side door of the recreational vehicle. She got out of the police car and called Mary Joe and Big Bob, who were watching her from under the tree. Rose explained to them that Officer Woodley was unconscious in the kitchen, and she wanted help to lift her in the back of the police car. Rose told Mary Joe to pack up the folding chairs and small table because they would have to leave the camping area immediately.

Big Bob and Rose carried Officer Woodley's body out of the recreational vehicle and put her in the back of the police car. Mary Joe was putting the last of the folding chairs in their vehicle when she walked towards Rose and said, "I guess this is goodbye. Please take care of yourself and be careful."

"No matter where I am, I will always remember both of you. I will call when I am in New York. Take care, and I love both of you," said Rose.

Rose hugged them and ushered them into their vehicle. She grabbed her small bag and put it in the front of the police car. The recreational vehicle drove off with Mary Joe waving goodbye to Rose, standing by the police car. As the recreational vehicle was out of sight, Rose opened the front of the police car, and as she was about to enter the car, she saw some handcuffs. She took one, opened the back of the car, and put it on the unconscious Officer Woodley. Rose suddenly had an idea that if she was going to drive the police car, she should look like a police officer. Rose quickly took Officer Woodley's hat and inserted it into her head. Rose then went and drove away with the unconscious Officer Woodley in the back of the police car.

Chapter 24

Rose felt relieved and safe that at least she had a mode of transportation to move from the area. Rose drove around two miles when she stopped at the side of an isolated road. Rose came out of the police car and went around the back, where she opened the door and pulled the unconscious police officer out of the vehicle onto the side of the road. As Rose was about to close the back door of the police car, she noticed that Officer Woodley started regaining consciousness. Rose hurriedly closed the door, rushed around and jumped into the police car. She started the car, and as she was about to drive off, Officer Woodley was fully conscious and started shouting, "You bitch, come and take off the handcuff now, or you will be sorry."

Rose sped off, and around three hundred yards, Officer Woodley somehow managed to get hold of her handgun from her holster, and with her hand still in the handcuff, she started firing at the car. Due to her hand being handcuffed, Officer Woodley's aim was off-targeted, and she was firing wildly at the car. Rose looked in the rearview mirror when she heard the shots and smiled when she saw Officer Woodley firing quite indiscriminately with the gun. She accelerated the car and was out of sight of Officer Woodley.

Rose drove until she was on the highway, where she settled into driving the stolen police car. She felt more at ease as she was on her way home to New York to her beloved apartment. As she drove the car, she started planning her next move because she did not want the police to take her back into their custody. Rose decided at some point she had to abandon the police car because the members of the Alliance Organization would be looking for her, and the police may be putting up roadblocks searching for her to bring her into their custody. Rose then decided that she would abandon the police car at the second or third truck stop and look for a drive to New York.

Rose drove past the first truck stop and continued driving until she drove past the second truck stop. She continued driving, all the while looking to see if she saw any police roadblocks ahead of her, but she was unable to see any on her journey to New York. Around an hour and a half, she drove into the third truck stop and parked between two Sports Utility Vehicles. She hurriedly took off the police cap, then she took off the blonde wig and put it in her bag. She then took a hairbrush out of her bag, and brushed her hair, and also applied some lipstick. As Rose exited the police vehicle with her bag, she thought that if the police were searching for her, they would most likely be searching for a blonde woman.

Rose walked towards a fast-food restaurant and went into the bathroom. She came out of the bathroom and went inside the restaurant where there were quite a few people having their meals. She joined the line at the cashier and ordered some fries, fried chicken, and some fruit juice. Rose waited for five minutes before receiving the food. After she received the food, she went by a table that was unoccupied and she sat down and ate the food.

Rose ate the food and started observing the patrons coming into the restaurant and wondered which one of them seemed harmless that she could ask for a ride to New York. As she was there observing the patrons in the restaurant, two Caucasian men in priest garments came to her table and asked, "Excuse me, Miss, can we sit with you to have our meals?"

"By all means, sit and have your meals," said Rose.

"Thank you, my child," said the older-looking priest.

Rose glanced at the two men and noticed that the older one appeared to be in his late fifties. The older man seemed quite friendly, with a round face and smooth golden hair that was thinning out, and the other man had dark hair and a straight face with piercing brown eyes. He was much younger and appeared to be in his early forties. Rose somehow got an uneasy feeling about the younger man as she glanced at him consuming his meal. The younger man stopped for a brief minute and said, "Where is my manner? I am Jonathan, and the fellow next to me is Andre. How are you doing today?"

Rose decided she did not know who to trust at this particular moment. Therefore, she would not reveal any pertinent information, especially to two strangers, irrespective that they were priests. She looked at the men directly in their eyes and said, "I am Scarlett, and I am doing fine."

"What a fine, beautiful lady doing at a truck stop?" asked Andre.

"I am just visiting family in New Jersey, more specifically my sister," said Rose.

"It is good to have family, especially when it is a close-knit family. All my family is in New York," said Andre.

"So you are going to New York?" asked Rose.

"Yes, that is where we are going. Hopefully, we will be there in the next three hours" said Andre.

Rose looked at the two men, deliberating within her mind if she could ask to accompany them to New York. She was not sure she could trust the younger priest, Jonathan, but the older priest, Andre, had a friendly disposition. She had a funny feeling about them, but somehow, she decided to take the gamble and asked, "I am having mechanical trouble with my vehicle. Would it be possible if I could accompany you to New York?"

"Certainly, we would be glad to assist you with a ride to New York," said Jonathan.

Rose was hoping she was doing the right thing even though in the back of her mind was a voice telling her not to go with these men.

Rose finished eating and said, "When you gentlemen are finished eating, we can all go."

Rose excused herself from the table and went to the lady bathroom to clean herself up for the long journey to New York. In the bathroom she muttered a silent prayer to God for his guidance and protection. Rose came out of the bathroom and went back to the table where the two men were waiting, as they had finished eating their meals. They departed from the restaurant and walked to the parking area. They walked towards a seventy two metallic blue Dodge Polara Sedan. Jonathan opened the front door and Rose entered the car. Jonathan then entered the car and took his seat in the front, while Andre went in the back seat.

They drove away from the truck stop with Rose quite vigilant because she was in the company of the two strangers. Rose started admiring the thick vegetation and the different varieties of trees. Rose could also see the sea ahead as the roadway move ever closer and closer to the edge of a precipice. The edge of the precipice was only separated at times by small rock wall and at times no barrier.

Around four miles into their journey Jonathan stopped the car on the roadside and Andre opened the back door and exited the car. Andre, then opened the front passenger door where Rose was and pointed a Glock nine-millimeter gun at Rose's stomach and said, "Move over bitch. I am going to sit beside you and ask you some questions and I need some answers."

Rose sat closer to Jonathan as Andre came into the vehicle and sat beside her sandwiched in the front seat. Andre was no longer the smiling oval face priest. His whole disposition had changed and now he looked like a menacing thug. Jonathan started the car and they drove off again with Andre pointed the gun straight at Rose ribcage. Rose could feel the coldness of the metal of the gun as it pressed against her blouse nearly touching her skin. Jonathan then asked, "Are your named Rose Winter?"

Rose hesitated in answering Jonathan's question because, apart from her being fearful, it was the first time in her life that someone had pulled a gun at her and threatened her life. She tried to remain composed and calmly said, "No, I am not Rose Winter. My name is Scarlett Jones."

Andre looked at Rose and, in an ominous tone of voice, said, "If you do not tell us the truth, I will kill you, and throw your body out of this moving vehicle like a dog." Andre then exasperatedly said, "Let me ask the question again. Are you Rose Winter?"

"I told you already that I am not Rose Winter. My name is Scarlett Jones; however, if you want me to play your sick, twisted, sadistic game, I could be Rose Winter, whoever that may be," said Rose.

Both men looked at each other and started laughing, and Jonathan said, "I see you want to fuck with our minds, bitch, but it will not work. I have a picture of you that was sent to my phone offering a rather large reward for anyone associated with the Alliance Organization that can capture you and bring you in alive.”

“Would it not be a surprise, for you to take me to your organization and find out that the person you brought in is the wrong girl? What would your colleagues in your organization think of you? I imagine they would think you are nothing more than a damn halfwit. I suggest that you let me out of this car, and we can all go our own merry way,” said Rose.

“Irrespective that you denied you are Rose Winter we will take the chance and take you to the Alliance Organization. If we handed you over to them and you are not Rose Winter, then we will discard you however we see fit after we have some fun with you,” said Jonathan.

Rose’s mind was racing, trying to figure out how to extricate herself from this situation she practically placed herself in, and she realized that they were not going to hurt her because they wanted to exchange her for the amulet. Rose thought she would just talk and try to be friendly to the two men and asked, “Where in New York are you taking me?”

“We are taking you to a warehouse in Upstate New York,” said Jonathan.

“Please do not tell her anything because you never know what is going on in her head,” said Andre.

Jonathan suddenly slowed the car, took out his phone, and said, "Scarlett, please turn around." As Rose turned around, Jonathan took a picture with his phone and said, "Now I will be able to send a picture to Wallenstein to confirm who you are. Therefore, there will be no ambiguity of who you are."

Within an instant, Rose saw that Andre had moved the gun from her ribcage. She took her elbow and slammed it in Andre's face, and the gun fell from his hand onto the car floor. As Rose slammed her elbow into Andre's face, it allowed her space to use her foot to kick Jonathan's head. The kick to Jonathan's head forced him to lose his grip on the car steering, and the car plunged over the precipice. As the car went over the precipice and fell over, the three occupants of the vehicle were gripped with sheer terror.

The car hit the water with a loud splash and suddenly started sinking with all three occupants. As the car started to sink Jonathan and Andre tried to open the left and right door of the car. They were unable to opened the car door. The car was fully submerged, and water was pouring into the car as it continued to sink to the bottom of the ocean floor. Both men were still desperately exerting pressure on the car door frantically trying to open it, but the water pressure formed a barrier.

Rose was sandwiched between the two men as she stood up and pushed her head up to the roof of the car which was not filled with water. She inhaled the few remaining oxygen in the roof of the vehicle as it continued to sink furthered to the ocean floor.

As the car hit the ocean floor with a slight thud the car door finally gave way. Rose realized that the car door was opened, plunged herself near the roof of the car where she was breathing the last amount of oxygen, and as the men were about to swim to the surface, she stretched out both hands and held both their foot. The men started to panic and kick frantically at her using up valuable oxygen in their lungs. Rose after a few more seconds released the hold she had on the men feet. Just as Rose released the men feet, they started to swim towards the surface but suddenly, out of nowhere two large white sharks grabbed them by the shoulders and swam off with them along with a trail of blood darkening the ocean water.

Rose saw the sharks attacking the men and carrying their body away in the sea. She swam to the front of the car with her bag tied firmly around her waist. She swam on top of the car and used the hard material surface of the car top to push off and swam to the surface. As she reached the surface she started gasping for oxygen and blowing sea water out of her mouth and nostril. She looked towards where the shore was and saw that it was quite a distance away. She summoned all her energy and started swimming to the shore. The sun was intensely hot thereby warming the water, but it seemed to drain all the energy out of her body.

As she continued to swim to the seashore in the distance, a white yacht came in front of her and blocked her path. From where Rose was in the water, she could see three Caucasian people on board the luxury yacht beckoning her to come on board. Rose hesitated because she did not know who these people were, and she did not know if she would be in more danger. She decided to go on board the yacht because she did not imagine the three people on board the luxury yacht would want to hurt her and also, they would not know her situation.

Rose swam towards the luxury yacht and noticed it was around sixty feet. As she swam towards the yacht, she saw the name of the vessel, "Helen," painted in bold black letters. She climbed aboard and was greeted by three people, a woman and two men. The woman was a beautiful long long-legged blonde looking quite elegant, dressed in a white blouse and blue shorts. One of the men was a tall, muscular man clean, shaven with a quite handsome face. The other man had black thinning hair with a broad oval face that was quite greasy. He was short and fat with a huge paunch dressed in a t-shirt and white shorts and sneakers.

Rose walked towards them but could not figure out their nationalities. The woman stretched out her hand and spoke with a thick English accent, "Welcome aboard, my dear. We saw you swimming in the sea and thought you may require some assistance.

My name is Maria Petrova, and the tall gentleman is Igor, and that fat man is my husband, Alexander Petrova."

Rose did not know what to make of the three people but went and shook their hands and said, "Thank you for rescuing me from the sea water. I am Dawn Wood. I am pleased to meet you all."

Three strangers exchanged a sly look, and Alexander said, "Go downstairs and have a shower and get out of those wet clothes. My wife will assist you with some dry clothing."

Rose went downstairs with Maria and took a shower washing the saltwater from her body. Rose finished having her shower and as she was about to step out of the bath Maria handed her a towel and Rose wrapped it around her body. Maria then said, "You look so beautiful let me take a picture."

Maria took up her cellular phone and took one picture of Rose then assisted Rose with clothing as she was similar in size. As Rose was brushing her hair she asked "Maria, what nationalities are you, and your companions?"

"We are all Russian nationalities. You are safe with us. My fat darling of a husband, Alexander will not bother you. He is only concerned with drinking vodka and stuffing his mouth with bacon or for that matter any kind of food. Igor will not even look at you unless what you American say, only if you have a long, big dick" The woman started laughing heartily until Maria asked, "You do not have a big dick, Dawn?"

Rose laughing said "No, no, I am all female. I do not have any male part."

Maria grinning said "Too bad because I certainly could use some male parts. I am just a pretty little fixture on Alexander arms, nothing more. You American called it a trophy wife but I certainly do not feel like a trophy. I guess that the life I chose, I suppose. I dreamt to be with a rich Russian man, but I did not know I should have dreamt of one that not only rich but have something in the hips as well and not only in the tongue."

The women continued laughing enjoying each other company until Maria asked "Dawn, can you stay with me for a few days?"

Rose hesitated in answering Maria question. She certainly liked Maria, but she did not know enough about them to want to spend a few days. As Rose was about to respond, Maria said, "Please say yes because it would be really nice to have an extra female companion onboard. I beg of you to say yes. It would lift my spirit to have a female companion to talk with on this beautiful yacht."

Rose smiling and hoping at the same time that she will not come to regret her decision nodded her head to Maria. Maria then invited Rose to the kitchen to get something to eat and drink. Maria told her that Igor had prepared some chicken soup. Rose gladly accepted the chicken soup meal because she was hungry and thirsty from the ordeal in the sea with the two men. After Rose finished eating, she had some orange pineapple juice. The two women then went on the upper deck and continued with their chatting as they sat in two lounge chairs.

As the two women were on the deck chatting, Alexander was at the other end of the yacht, dialing a number with a disposable cellular phone. The cellular phone rang that Alexander was dialing, and a man who was of Russian nationality answered with a gruff voice and said, "Hello."

"Yuri, it is me Alexander. I called to tell you we have the girl. You can make the call to Wallenstein and tell him that your business associate have the girl. Tell him we need fifty million dollars in cash and not the fifty thousand that is offered, or else he will not see the girl alive. Tell him that you need the money by midday tomorrow."

"Is there any negotiation with regard to the amount of money for the girl?" asked Yuri.

"There is no negotiation with regards to the amount of money for the girl. They want her desperately so they will have to pay for her. Yuri do not stay on the line with Wallenstein more than necessary. Tell him your demand and destroy your phone instantly the minute the conversation ends. I have the numbers for all the other disposable phones so keep them nearby. We cannot be careless if we are to pull off this caper and be successful. The Alliance Organization is a thousand times more dangerous than the regular Russian Mafia so be extra careful" said Alexander.

"If they do agree to our terms, where do they drop off the money?" asked Yuri.

"I will text you the information where I want the money drop off after you call the second time, and also a picture of the girl that you are going to send to them because they are going to want some sort of evidence that you have got the girl," said Alexander.

The men ended their phone conversation soon after, and Alexander started pondering his next move. He knew he was taking a huge risk, but he had no choice. He was running out of money, and he was desperate to embark on such a caper to take on the notorious Alliance Organization. He had his lifestyle to maintain and keep up appearances among his criminal colleagues and society. He knew he would lose his yacht, and his mansion in Milan, Italy, and without a doubt, he would lose his lovely trophy wife, Maria.

The fifty million dollars to Alexander represented in some way a sort of challenge to his manhood that he is still capable of pulling off the big caper. He knew he would be right back on top of his game, and he would be full of pride if he could make this a successful heist from the Alliance Organization. The Alliance Organization would represent the zenith of his criminal career if he were able to pull off such a daring feat. Alexander accepted that such great risks come with unparalleled danger, but if successful, it would come with great rewards. He knew he would be celebrated by his peers in the criminal underworld worldwide, and his stature would only advance to legendary proportions.

After Yuri hung up the phone with Alexander, he started thinking and wondering about the consequences of such a venture he was about to engage in, and he knew what he was about to do had never been done to the Alliance Organization; the idea of someone blackmailing them is so unheard of and quite foreign. There has never been a challenge to their authority on planet Earth, and if anyone dares to question their authority, they generally do not have long on this earth.

Yuri was in the restaurant at the truck stop when Rose came inside to have her meal. He was waiting on her to finish her meal so he could follow her to her car and kidnap her, but he had to adjust his plans when the two priests came in the restaurant. Yuri had no choice but to follow the motor vehicle which the priests were driving and watched in horror when the motor vehicle went over the cliff and into the sea. Yuri composed himself and called Alexander to come and rescue Rose from the ocean.

Yuri picked up the disposable cellular phone and dialed Wallenstein and the person at the other end of the call answered and said "Hello, this is Wallenstein speaking. How can I help you?"

A man in a cold calculating gruff rasping voice came on the line speaking in an accent that Wallenstein was not familiar with said

"We have her in our custody and if you want to see Rose Winter alive you will have to pay us fifty millions dollars in cash. We will call and tell you where to drop off the money tomorrow."

"Whom am I speaking to?" asked Wallenstein.

"Bitch, my name is not yours to concern with. Anyway, you can call me Professor X. Please acquire the money in cash, and tomorrow, I will call you with the instructions on where to drop off the cash," said Yuri.

"Wait a god damned minute. I will need some sort of evidence that you have Rose in your custody and you not playing some kind of trick" said Wallenstein.

"That will not be a problem. Since you are a good little boy, I will indeed send you a picture of Rose to prove we have her in our custody. I will send the picture of her immediately to prove to you without a shadow of doubt that we have her in our custody" said Yuri.

Yuri took the phone and sent the picture of Rose that Alexander had sent earlier to Wallenstein's phone. Yuri was a little uncomfortable being on the phone longer than he expected with Wallenstein.

Wallenstein received the picture of Rose with her body wrapped in a white towel standing in a bathroom. Wallenstein looked at it and knew the picture was, indeed, Rose without her makeup. Wallenstein then said, "Yes, the picture is indeed Rose. I need to ask you about the money that we are to deliver to you in cash. Fifty million dollars is quite a vast sum of money. Could you take Ten million dollars for your troubles?"

Yuri was quite mad been on the phone this long and when he heard Wallenstein making a counteroffer to his proposal and he said "Listen to me you bitch, there is no negotiation on the offer. If we do not get the money by tomorrow, we will kill her, and you will never be able to exchange her for the amulet. Also do not try to trace the phone, because I am going to dismantle it as I am finish talking to you. Now that we have established that there is no negotiation on the money, please go and get the cash and wait on my call where to deliver the money. Goodbye."

Yuri immediately dismantled the phone and breathed a sigh of relief. He knew that was only round one and the Alliance Organization was going to intensified their efforts to find Rose and whoever has the temerity to blackmail them for money.

Chapter 25

Meanwhile back at the Manhattan headquarter of the Alliance Organization Wallenstein was fuming and wondering who dare to blackmail their organization and called into question their authority that they were the master and overlord of this planet. He could not imagine that someone had the temerity to dare blackmail their organization. Wallenstein then had an epiphany that whoever was behind the blackmail seemed to be someone that was affiliated to their organization.

Wallenstein anger subsided and he called Vallencourt into his office and relayed the information to him that someone had Rose Winter into their custody and wanted fifty million dollars in cash. Wallenstein took up his phone and showed the picture of Rose in the white bath towel wrapped around her body. Vallencourt looked at the picture intently and asked, "Do you have any idea who has her in their custody?"

Wallenstein looked pensive for a minute and said "I have no idea who they are but the man that called me spoke in a foreign accent. I am trying to remember where I heard that accent before, but it escapes my memory for now. Also, something in the back of my mind tell me it is someone that is familiar with us and our ways of doing business."

Vallencourt looked through the office window seething with rage inside his mind and unsure of what was going on or what was happening to the organization that he love and oversee for so many years. Vallencourt anger subsided and he turned to Wallenstein and asked, "Anything in the background of the picture seem familiar?"

Wallenstein looked at the picture more intently then said "The background seems like an elegant bathroom in a house or an apartment. That is all I can detect in the background."

"Let us play their game for now, until we see what they are up to, and let us facilitate all their demands until we have Rose in our custody then we bring down the wrath of hell on them. I will personally look about the money and put it in a briefcase" said Vallencourt.

Vallencourt exited Wallenstein's office to sort out the money. As Vallencourt walked out of the office, he immediately devised a plan to teach those people who thought they could dare to blackmail him and the Alliance Organization. Vallencourt realized that the people who were behind the scheme to blackmail him had some knowledge of the Alliance Organization and knew the vulnerable state he was personally in to retain leadership of the organization. Vallencourt knew the blackmailers had intimate knowledge of the structure of the organization and knew that failure to recover the amulet more or likely will result in his replacement as the head of the Alliance Organization and most likely termination of his life. As

Vallencourt tried to rationalize what was going on, he decided he would go through the organization from top to bottom to find out who in the organization was betraying him and somehow devising a plan to replace him as the head of the organization. Vallencourt thought all those issues will have to wait because the most immediate problem now was to get Rose Winter in their custody so they can exchange her for the amulet.

*****

Rose and Maria were on the upper deck of the yacht laying in two white lounge chairs drinking Mai Tai and staring at the sea. As Rose was savoring the taste of the Mai Tai drink with the combination of the pineapple juice and Caribbean rum, she asked "Maria what the best place you have visited?"

Maria started thinking and finally said "Of all the place I have visited and love, I would say Paris without a doubt. The beauty of the place, the history, the people, the language, the food, the beautiful museums and the stunning architecture of the buildings, and most of all, my handsome French lover Henri Michel."

The women started laughing, and Rose asked, "Does Alexander know of your French lover, Henri Michel?"

"Are you crazy? Alexander would kill both of us. When he is away on business and meeting with his French whores in Paris, I generally tell him I am going to the museums and meet up with Henri Michel" said Maria.

"Have you ever been to France, Dawn?" asked Maria.

"No, I have never gone to Europe, but hopefully, one of these days, my boyfriend will take me there," said Rose.

"I think if you can afford to visit the country of France you should go and indulge in the food, visit the Eifel Tower, museum, and learn the history of the place. I certainly think you will leave feeling more learned. I do not think you will leave with any regret" said Maria.

As the evening wore on Maria told Rose that she must accompany her to the kitchen to prepare dinner. Maria decided that she was going to look about shrimp Alfredo for dinner. She boiled the pasta in a large stainless steel pot. Maria then took a large skillet and cooks the shrimps. She added butter and garlic and stirred. Afterward she added Parmesan cheese and chopped broccoli. Maria continued stirring the shrimps until it was fully cooked When the meal was fully cooked Maria asked Rose to set the table. She then shouted to Igor and Alexander to come and have their dinner.

The shrimp Alfredo was served quite hot and tasted delicious, and they all ate and as they were eating Rose caught Igor staring at her intensely as if she did not belong at their dinner table. It suddenly gave Rose an uneasy feeling, but she could not fathom why he was staring at her in that manner. After they completed eating the shrimp Alfredo, they had chocolate cake for dessert and drank white wine.

Alexander excused himself from the table and went on the upper deck took out a Cuban cigar, and started smoking it while he stared over the horizon. As he puffed the cigar, he started coughing and spat the saliva into the seawater. Alexander stared into the horizon, not looking at anything in particular, but was nervous about tomorrow as he smoked the cigar, hoping that it would calm him somehow and bring about some sort of solace to his nervous disposition.

******

The next day around nine o'clock in the morning Wallenstein's cellular phone rang and he answered saying "Hello, this is Wallenstein."

"This is Professor X; do you have my fifty millions dollars in cash?" asked Yuri.

"Yes, I do have your fifty millions dollars" said Wallenstein.

When Yuri heard Wallenstein said that he had the money he felt excited and thought that they might really pull off the blackmail caper. Yuri composed himself and said "Wallenstein, this is not going to be a straight swap, meaning you give us the money and we give you the girl. It is not going to work like that. I want you personally to take the money to a grimly apartment in Brooklyn. I do not want anyone from the Alliance Organization to follow you. If by any chance I see anyone following you the deal is off. Is my instructions clear?"

"Your instructions are clear; however I need to know when I will get the girl and also which apartment in Brooklyn should I take the cash?" asked Wallenstein.

Yuri let out a rather sinister laughter and said "Because I know your power and what you are capable of, I do not want to be anywhere near you that you can chop off my fucking head and hold it out as a memento. When you are on your way to Brooklyn, I will call you and tell you which area in Brooklyn and apartment to drop off the money. When you are in the apartment, I will call you and tell you where the girl is. Do you comprehend all I am saying to you?" asked Yuri.

"I do comprehend what you are telling me, and I will follow your instructions" said Wallenstein.

"Good, then you need to leave your office and start driving to Brooklyn now. I will be watching you" said Yuri.

With the last statement made Yuri hung up the phone feeling quite excited thinking of the big payday he was going to make when he receives his portion of the fifty millions dollars.

As Wallenstein hung up the phone Vallencourt walked into the office with the briefcase and Wallenstein relayed all the information to him from the caller. Wallenstein then asked, "Should we go along with their game?"

"We do not have any choice. We will have to play their games until we get what we want from them" said Vallencourt.

"I need to tell you something which I do not think you are going to like. As I have said it is a suspicion on my part, but I have a feeling that I am right. This blackmail caper I think it is one of our kind, trying to extort money from you. More to the point, I think it is one of us that work presently in the Alliance Organization trying to dethrone you from been top of the organization and may want to replace you" said Wallenstein.

Vallencourt thought for a moment and said "It occurs to me too, but I cannot for the life of me figured out who could be so bold and calculating within our organization. I just need to have Rose Winter within our custody so we can retrieve the amulet and afterward I will leave no stone unturned trying to figure out who is behind the blackmail."

"I am to depart now to deliver the briefcase with the money in Brooklyn," said Wallenstein.

Wallenstein reached for the briefcase, and as he touched the handled of the briefcase, Vallencourt said, "let me take the briefcase to the Cadillac Escalade for you."

Vallencourt and Wallenstein left the office and took the elevator to the street level where the black Cadillac Escalade was parked beside a Mercedes Benz. Vallencourt opened the vehicle door and put the briefcase in the front passenger seat. Wallenstein entered the vehicle and as he was about to turned on the ignition Vallencourt pushed his right hand into his pants pocket and took out a small device and gave it to Wallenstein and said, "When you are leaving the apartment please pressed the button on this device to ensure that it is turned on."

"What type of device is this, and more importantly, what does it do?" asked Wallenstein.

"Please do not concern yourself with the device at the moment. Please remember to turn it on before you leave the apartment" said Wallenstein.

They bid each other goodbye and Wallenstein drove off to Brooklyn.

Wallenstein was entering Brooklyn when his cellular phone rang and he said, "This is Wallenstein."

It was the same gentleman voice that called him earlier blackmailing him, only this time he was using a different cellular phone. The man voice came on the line and said "You are to drive to East New York and enter a public housing building. I will text you the exact address in East New York for you to take the money. Please take the elevator and go on the ninth floor to room nine D. The door is unlocked so please leave the briefcase on the bed and I will call you once you are in the room to tell you where to pick up the girl. Please do not leave the room until I call you on the phone."

The other caller hung up the phone and Wallenstein sped up the vehicle to East New York. Wallenstein soon got the text of the address in East New York, and within two hours he was entering the public housing complex. The housing complex was totally surrounded by some huge iron rails cemented in concrete. Wallenstein parked the vehicle in the complex and turned off the vehicle ignition. He sat in the vehicle and looked around and noticed the people were mostly African American and Hispanic.

Wallenstein opened the vehicle door and noticed some children playing on the asphalted playground. He took the briefcase and exited the vehicle. As he walked towards the front of the building, he thought the briefcase was heavy as lead. Wallenstein arrived at the front of the building and pushed a door to enter the building where the elevator was located. As he was about to push the elevator button the elevator came down and four young African American came off it.

Wallenstein was about to enter the elevator when two young men one African American and a Hispanic around in their twenties entered the elevator. Both young men were wearing blue jeans, sneakers, and t-shirts. As he waited for the elevator the different smell of people cooking filled his nostril and he remembered one of the reasons why he did not like apartment setting.

The elevator came down and opened, but this time, no one came off it, and Wallenstein entered on it. As Wallenstein entered the elevator, he saw the two young men who entered the elevator earlier in the corner. The African American man closed the elevator door and asked, "Which floor are you going to?"

"I am going to the sixth floor," said Wallenstein.

As the elevator door closed and started moving upward, the Hispanic man pulled a gun out of his waist, pointed it straight at Wallenstein's chest and said, "I am going to need the content in that briefcase, now."

"That will not be possible. I cannot give you the content of what is in the briefcase because it is not mine" said Wallenstein.

The Hispanic man used his left hand and reached for the briefcase and Wallenstein pushed him to the elevator wall. The Hispanic man was clearly furious been pushed by Wallenstein and said, "If you do not give me the briefcase, I will fucking shoot you in this elevator, right here, and now."

Wallenstein and the Hispanic man stared at each other and the Hispanic man lower the gun to Wallenstein's stomach. The African American man who was beside the elevator door shouted, "Shoot the motherfucker, take the briefcase, and let's get off this elevator."

Wallenstein looked into the Hispanic man eyes, and he seemed wild and dangerous, like a wild animal. Wallenstein put down the briefcase to deescalate the situation and said "Okay, take the briefcase."

The Hispanic man reached for the briefcase and put it between his legs. The Hispanic man advanced towards Wallenstein, staring menacingly and sanguinely at him because he had the gun in his hand said, "We are going to teach you a lesson, boy, that when we request that you give us the briefcase, there should be no hesitation."

The Hispanic man swiftly lifted his right hand with the gun in the air and tried to hit Wallenstein in his face. Wallenstein, in one swift motion, avoided the blow to his face and reached out and took the gun from the Hispanic man's hand. Wallenstein pointed the gun at the two men and said, "Please let me have my briefcase."

The Hispanic man pushed the briefcase toward Wallenstein. The elevator arrived at the sixth floor, and Wallenstein shouted, "Keep the elevator door closed. I need to teach you both a lesson. Whenever you see a stranger come into your apartment building, you welcome him and not try to steal from him." Wallenstein waved the gun in the air, pointing it at the two men and asked, "Is what I am saying clear to both of you?"

Both men shook their heads in unison, indicating that they understood, although they were frozen with fear. Wallenstein looked at the two men, and he could see fear in their eyes. Wallenstein then said, "I hope you have learnt your lesson. Please open the elevator door."

The elevator door opened, and Wallenstein looked outside but did not see anyone, and he waved the gun at the two men to leave and as the Hispanic man was about to walk outside the elevator Wallenstein lifted his foot and kicked him on his backside. The Hispanic man fell on the ground and as Wallenstein was about to turn to the African American man, he made one dash out of the elevator. Wallenstein smiled, pushed the gun in his pant pocket. He closed the elevator door and pressed the button for the ninth floor.

Wallenstein arrived on the ninth floor and came off the elevator. Wallenstein walked along the corridor until he saw room nine D. He pushed the door and it opened, and Wallenstein walked inside the apartment. The apartment was dingy and smelled as if there was no one was living there for weeks. Wallenstein turned on the light in the apartment and noticed it was a two bedroom and a kitchen and a small living room. The rooms were dusty with no sheets on the bed. Wallenstein left the briefcase with the money on the bed and went into the kitchen which was also dirty with a few unwashed dishes in the sink.

Wallenstein went outside the living room and sat in a chair. As he was waiting, he turned on a flat screen Samsung television. The television station was set to MSNBC and Andrea Mitchell was on presenting the news of the day. Wallenstein watched the television while he waited for the phone to ring in the apartment.

******

Meanwhile, Yuri was in a one engine boat speeding towards where Alexander and Igor were awaiting his arrival on the yacht. The boat was on full throttle as it cuts the choppy seawater. Yuri was cognizant that time was extremely limited because Wallenstein was waiting on the phone call in the apartment. Yuri wanted to get as far away from Wallenstein and the Alliance Organization when they deliver Rose Winter into their custody.

As the boat sped towards the yacht in the warm water on the New Jersey seacoast Yuri took up one of the many disposable cellular phone and was about to call Wallenstein then thought better of it and put back down the phone. He thought calling him now would not allow them to get as far away as possible from the New Jersey coast. He thought he would allow Wallenstein to wait in the room until he reached the yacht.

Yuri steered the boat through the sea water and soon saw the yacht in the distance. Yuri suddenly realized that they were around ten to fifteen miles from the New Jersey coast. He hoped that Rose did not realize that the yacht had drifted that amount of distance. Yuri sailed the boat alongside the yacht and tethered it to it. He promptly took out the disposable phones and his other belongings and took them on the yacht. Yuri went back on the boat and removed the engine and took it on the yacht.

Yuri then climbed aboard the yacht to the upper deck where Alexander, Igor, Maria and Rose were looking and waiting on him to come onboard. They hugged and greeted each other like long lost friends. Maria turned to Rose and said, "Yuri this is our friend Dawn and our golden ticket."

Rose on hearing what Maria had just said about her been a golden ticket suddenly felt panicky, and her heart began to race as if she was running a marathon. It dawned on Rose that she was suddenly in real danger. Yuri smilingly extending his hands said "We can all stop the pretense. All of us knew who you are. You are Rose Winter, and as Maria so eloquently put it, you are our golden ticket worth fifty millions dollars."

Rose angrily turned to Maria and asked, "So all of this was an elaborate guise to allow me to stay on board?"

"Not all of it. I really like you. Alexander wanted in the initial stage when you came aboard the yacht to imprison you in the cabin. I convinced him that you are no threat, and to allow you to walk freely and not be tied and bounded in a cabin. My plan worked because while Yuri was negotiating with the Alliance Organization you were here safe, and on the yacht."

Rose forced her anger to subside and started to wonder how she can extricate herself from this situation. She knew these Russian mobsters would want to exchange her for the fifty millions dollars so they would not want to harm her, because she was their golden ticket. As Rose was thinking Alexander said "Rose, now that you know what we are about, we will definitely have to keep you in one of the cabin. Yuri, please escort Rose to the cabin and ensure that she stay there."

Yuri escorted Rose to the cabin, followed behind by Maria. Rose and Maria went inside the cabin while Yuri stayed outside guarding the door. Inside the cabin Rose looked at Maria with pure disdain and said "I knew we did not know each other long enough, but I thought somehow we made a friendship connection. I did not know that all you see me as was a fucking meal ticket?"

Maria looked a little sad and said "Rose, I am sorry to deceive you, but Alexander made all the decisions within our relationship. It was his decisions to blackmail the Alliance Organization. Yuri, Igor, and I are just following any scheme he comes up with, hopefully to better all our life."

"So you are just going to hand me over to the Alliance Organization then go on your merry way with your fifty millions dollars. Do you not care what they might do to me?"

"I do think about it but there is nothing I can do. We are not going to hand you over to the Alliance Organization the way you are thinking. We cannot be anywhere near those people. They would destroy us in a second. We will be hundreds of miles away when they come and pick you up" said Maria.

Rose turned and looked Maria directly in her eyes and asked, "Are you going to assist me to escape?"

Maria looked away from Rose and said "I am terribly sorry, but I cannot assist you escaping from Alexander. Alexander will kill me if I assist you."

Listening to Maria words and her refusal to help her all hope drained from Rose face and she angrily said "Since you are not going to assist me escaping, please get the fuck out of the cabin. I do not want to be in your presence any longer."

Maria left the room and Rose sat on the bed wondering how long her travail would last, and if it would be all possible to escape from these Russian mobsters. Rose got off the bed and took off her shorts that she was wearing and put on her jeans and sneaker. Ruse thought that whatever lay ahead of her, she would be better suited to be in her jeans and sneakers.

******

On the deck of the yacht Yuri took up one of the disposable phone and as he was about to dial the yacht started going farther and farther from the New Jersey coast. Yuri dialed Wallenstein's phone and said, "I see you are sitting and watching my television set" Yuri then cleared his throat and asked, "Do you have the fifty millions dollars?"

Wallenstein froze when he heard the man telling him that he was sitting and watching television. He immediately looked around and saw various small cameras all around the living room. He was angry with himself for not seeing the cameras and suddenly realized that he was up against an enemy that was cautious and deserving of his respect. Wallenstein then said, "Yes I have your fifty millions dollars in a briefcase on the bed."

"Go inside the bedroom and open the briefcase so I can see the money," said Yuri.

Wallenstein walked inside the bedroom and opened the briefcase and said, "The fifty million dollars is all there in the briefcase."

Yuri felt quite exhilarated seeing the money in the briefcase and asked, "Please take out a batch of the money and remove the seal so I can see properly the denominations of the money?"

Wallenstein pushed his hand into the briefcase and took out a fresh batch of money. He removed the seal from the single batch of money to reveal freshly printed hundred dollars bills. He then inserted the money back into the briefcase closed it, and asked, "Now that you have seen the money where I can pick up Rose?"

"Not so fast, our arrangement remains the same. I call the shots and not you. Here is what going to happen. You are going to leave the apartment without the briefcase with the money, and on your way back to Manhattan I will call you to tell you where Rose is, therefore, please leave the apartment and I will call you shortly with the information."

Wallenstein hung up the phone walked out the bedroom and into the living room. He opened the entrance door and as he was about to close the door, he pushed his hand in his pants pocket and pressed the switch on the device. As he pressed the switch on the device, he heard a click, and he closed the door.

Wallenstein walked towards the elevator and saw two attractive African American women waiting on it. The elevator stopped at their floor and Wallenstein said hello and all three of them went on it. Wallenstein came off the elevator and walked towards his vehicle and proceeded to drive towards Manhattan.

****

Rose got up off the bed when she heard a knocking on the cabin door. She opened the door to see Yuri standing at the doorway. Yuri looked trouble in his face, and he said "Time to go Princess. Your time on the yacht has expired. I am sorry to hand you over to them, but we extorted a lot of money from them and when they pick you up, we want to be hundred of miles away. Please follow me."

Rose did as she was instructed and followed Yuri down to the lower deck of the yacht. Yuri pointed to the small boat attached to the yacht and said "That is your boat for the time been until they pick you up, or if you somehow make it to the shore and escape before they arrive. Good luck and I really mean it."

Rose entered the small boat and sat down, just as Yuri was unfastened the rope that attached the small boat to the yacht Maria came running down the stairs with a small package containing bottle waters and four energy bar snacks and a Nike cap and gave it to Rose. Rose took the packages and threw it in the corner of the boat. Maria then waved goodbye to Rose, and she turned her back. The yacht sped away cutting through the seawater until Rose could barely see them in the distance.

Rose took up the packages that Maria gave her and took out the Nike cap and put it on her head to protect her face from the biting sun. She looked around in all direction at the open sea to see if there was any passing boat whereby, she would be able to ask for help but she could see none in the distance. Rose could no longer see the New Jersey coastline and realized that she was quite a distance in the open sea.

A gentle wave came and pushed the boat, and Rose wished that she had two oars to row the boat in the direction of the shoreline. She took one of the energy bars, ate it, and drank one of the water. She turned around, and she could no longer see the yacht. As the boat continued to drift slowly to the shoreline, Rose started to wonder how Malakai was doing in his effort to locate and save her from the Alliance Organization.

Chapter 26

Wallenstein was entering Manhattan when his cellular phone rang, and he answered and said, "Wallenstein here."

"Since you paid the fifty million dollars and I promise to tell you were Rose Winter is, and I am a man of my word. She is in a boat around a couple of hundred miles off the coast of New Jersey. She does not have an oar to row the boat so the boat will drift to the shore by night fall if she does not get any assistance from a passing boat. I will send the picture of her in the boat, so you will have to hurry if you want to retrieve her and have her in your custody. I will send the exact longitude and latitude location where we left her when I send the picture. I guess this is goodbye then, it was a pleasure doing business with you and the Alliance Organization" said Yuri.

After the caller hanged up Wallenstein call Vallencourt and told him to get the helicopter ready because they were going to New Jersey to pick up Rose. Wallenstein soon arrived at their Manhattan headquarters and was in the process of parking the vehicle when the picture of Rose in the small boat came in on the phone and her location. Wallenstein ran quickly to the underground elevator which took him to his office. Vallencourt and Thornbird were there waiting on him to arrive, and all three of them hurriedly climbed the stairs to the helipad on the roof, where a helicopter with a pilot was waiting on them to climbed aboard.

They all boarded the helicopter and it elevated and flew over the high buildings of Manhattan to the New Jersey shoreline. Wallenstein gave the pilot the exact location where they were supposed to pick up Rose. Wallenstein was tensed with excitement because these many months of trying to get Rose, and every time they all failed to get her into their custody. Wallenstein was hoping that this time would be different because they just gave away fifty millions dollars and if they do not have Rose in their custody shortly, all the blame would be on him, and no excuses would be tolerated by the company.

The pilot was flying the helicopter quite fast and pretty soon they were flying over the New Jersey coastline. The pilot kept flying over a wide area far from the coastline until Vallencourt said, "I see something in the distance, looking like a small boat."

"Which direction have you seen the small boat?" asked the pilot.

"To the west," said Vallencourt.

"Okay, I see the boat now," said the pilot.

Wallenstein looked through the glass of the helicopter and could see the boat in the seawater below, but because of the distance, he could not see if there was anyone aboard the small boat.

Wallenstein could see that it was the same boat in the picture that was texted to him, and as he peered in the distance, he asked, "Can anyone see if there is anyone aboard the boat?"

The pilot then answered and said, "No, we cannot tell if there is anyone onboard. We will have to get closer to the boat."

As the pilot flew closer and closer to the small boat Vallencourt was nervous and his knee seemed as if they could not sit still for the momentous occasion. He knew this moment would be pivotal in the recovery of the amulet. He also knew that if Rose was not in that boat they would, more or less lose any chance of the recovery of the amulet.

The helicopter pilot flew closer to the boat and said, "I think I see movement in the boat. Yes, there is definitely someone in the boat, but it looks like a man in a baseball hat."

Vallencourt heart sank when the pilot said it was a man in the boat. He thought how many times we can come so close and yet end in disappointment. Vallencourt then said, "Let's go further up the coastline."

"No, do not fly away as yet. I think it is her. Take us further below so we can verify it is her," said Wallenstein.

Rose saw the helicopter hovering around the boat and knew instantly that it was the Alliance Organization people. When she first saw the helicopter, she tried to lay on the side of the boat, hoping that it would provide some sort of concealment. The boat was drifting slowly to shore, and she had hoped by nightfall, she would reach the New Jersey coastline.

The pilot flew around twenty feet near the seawater, and the helicopter rotor blade whipped the water and caused the wind to blow off the Nike baseball hat that Rose was wearing. Wallenstein, with uncontrollable excitement, said, "It is her. That is Rose Winter."

The pilot circled the helicopter around the boat, and Thornbird opened the helicopter door and pushed out the rope ladder. Thornbird then climbed down into the boat where Rose was and said, "Miss Winter, please climb aboard."

Rose knew that she could not resist the tall, muscular man who climbed into the boat, so she started climbing onto the rope ladder of the helicopter. Wallenstein could not contain his excitement and as Rose stepped into the helicopter, he looked at her similar to a lion catching prey. Wallenstein smiled, then said, "We have been searching for you all these months, and now we finally have you in our custody. Please have a seat."

Rose took a second, looking directly into the eyes of the man speaking to her, and thought that the man's eyes looked quite familiar, but she could not recognize the person. Rose took her seat in the helicopter and sat in silence, wondering what would happen to her or what they would likely do to her now that they had her in their custody. She thought they would not want to harm her because they would want to exchange her for the amulet that Malakai had in his possession. Rose felt a little more comforted by that idea but was prepared for the worst.

Thornbird climbed into the helicopter, pulled up the rope ladder, closed the door, and flew back to Manhattan. The flight back to Manhattan seemed like it took a shorter time to Vallencourt, but maybe because he was so elated that something was finally going his way. They landed on the helipad of their Manhattan headquarters, and Thornbird opened the door, and they all exited the helicopter. Thornbird walked closely to Rose as they all walked the stairs to Vallencourt's office. Rose was escorted into Vallencourt's office and told to sit down on the chair facing the office desk by Wallenstein.

******

Malakai was going all over New York seeking information about a girl that the Alliance Organization possibly had in their custody. He would go from bar to bar, to various restaurants, and clubs in Manhattan, seeking information, but each time, he would come up with nothing. On the fourth day, he took out his cellular phone and dialed Wallenstein's cellular phone number.

Wallenstein was walking to his office when a few of the senior agents were congratulating him for capturing Rose when his cellular phone rang. He did not recognize the caller number who was calling, and he hesitated in answering the phone but finally said, "Wallenstein here."

"This is Peter Mack. You told me to call back about Rose Winter. I want to speak to her before we discuss exchanging the amulet for Rose."

Wallenstein could not believe his luck just as they recaptured Rose Peter Mack called, and thought it was such an uncanny coincidence that everything was falling in place. Wallenstein then said, "Please hold on while I take the phone to her." Wallenstein walked to Vallencourt's office, gave Rose the cellular phone and said, "I have your boyfriend Peter Mack on the phone. He wants to hear your voice to ensure that you are alive."

Rose hesitated to hear the name of Peter Mack and decided not to say anything because she thought that Malakai might not want them to know his real name. Rose took the phone rather nervously from Wallenstein and said, "Hello."

Malakai, hearing the unmistakable voice of Rose, breathed a sigh of relief that she was still alive and said, "I am going to try my best to get you back safe and sound. Just hang on a little bit longer."

"Please hurry," said Rose.

Before Malakai could respond to Rose, Wallenstein dragged the phone from her hand and said, "Enough talking to Rose. Now that you hear her speaking, there can be no doubt, we have your girlfriend in our custody. Her fate is now in your hands."

Wallenstein words about Rose's fate lay in his hand and cut through Malakai's heart like a sharp knife. Malakai knew and accepted that in order to get back Rose he would have to give them the amulet. If he did not accept their demands, they would surely kill Rose. There was a moment of silence on the phone, and Malakai asked, "When are we going to make the exchange of the amulet for Rose?"

Wallenstein cleared his throat and said, "I cannot make that decision as yet. I will have to consult my boss. Please call back in the next two days at the same time, and I can tell you where and when we can make the exchange of your woman for the amulet."

Wallenstein hung up the phone and felt extremely good that within the next two days, the amulet would be in their custody after these many months. Wallenstein felt the urge to urinate and went to the bathroom. As he was coming from the bathroom, he heard an announcement on the intercom system for all senior staff to be in the conference room in the next five minutes. Wallenstein walked towards the conference room, and as he entered, he was greeted with a loud applause by the senior staff. Standing and clapping in the conference room were Vallencourt, Thornbird, Roberto Sanchez, Agent Chang, and other senior agents.

Vallencourt urged everyone to be seated and said, "Now that we are on our way to recovering the amulet so that we may bestow it on our god, the Morning Star. I would like to thank my beautiful daughter, who makes it all possible."

All the senior staff gasped in astonishment as they looked at Wallenstein. Vallencourt then said, "You can take off the mask now that we have Rose in our custody."

Wildflower started slowly taking off the mask that seemed as if it was cemented to her face. Vallencourt turned to her and said, "Thank you for all the hard work you have put into the capture of Rose. Now that problem has been taken care of; we now need to interrogate Rose to ascertain who the people are who think they can blackmail us and think they can get away with that type of action."

Wildflower finished taking off the mask and wiping her face with her hand, said, "I will do the interrogation of Rose because I have some history with her."

"Great then, the meeting is adjourned," said Vallencourt.

They all left the conference room, and Wildflower went to her office and straight into her office bathroom, where she changed out of the black pants. She washed her face and released her long blonde hair. She then put on a red Blazer women's business suit that was above her knees. She also put on her high heels and walked straight into Vallencourt's office, where Rose was sitting on a chair. Wildflower asked the two security personnel who were guarding Rose to excuse themselves out of the office.

Rose stared at Wildflower, totally flummoxed by her presence in the office, as she took her seat around Vallencourt's office chair. Rose recognized her instantly as she sat in the chair. Wildflower then asked, "I am sure you are surprised to see me here?"

"I am totally bewildered seeing you here. You are the last person I was expecting to see here," said Rose.

"I worked for this company, and I am here to ask you some questions if you do not mind. Firstly, tell me about the people that kidnapped you?" asked Wildflower.

Rose did not want to tell Wildflower anything, but when she thought about the way Maria abandoned her on the open sea, she decided to reveal everything she knew about Maria and the other men who were onboard the yacht. Rose said, "They are Russian nationals; I believe they are part of the Russian mafia. I was held on a beautiful yacht and locked in one of the cabins."

"Dammed it. I knew that the accent sounded European, but for the life of me, I could not remember that it was a Russian accent," Wildflower started writing on a notepad that was on Vallencourt's desk. After she finished writing, she asked, "How many people were on the yacht?"

"There were three people on the yacht and one man that took the boat that I was in, which made it four people on board. There is a lady onboard named Maria who is married to Alexander. There is also another man onboard named Igor. The last man that arrived today that boarded the yacht his named is Yuri," said Rose.

Wildflower was writing the information as fast as possible. She stopped writing and asked, "Do you know the name of the yacht?"

"The name of the yacht is Helen," said Rose.

Wildflower looked up at Rose and said, "You know what? You have been extremely helpful with the information. I really appreciate you giving me the information about these fucking Russian bastards."

"Can I leave now for my home in Brooklyn?" asked Rose.

Wildflower started laughing and said, "You are very funny." Wildflower continued writing on the notepad and paused for a minute, looked directly at Rose, and asked, "When we release you, can you tell me how we are going to get back the amulet?"

Rose looked at Wildflower and, without flinching, said, "Simply, you allow me to walk out of this office building, and he will allow you to continue living your life. If you do not allow me to leave, my boyfriend will kill you, one by one. I suggest you take my offer and allow me to leave."

All smiles disappear off Wildflower's face, and she said, "You have no idea what I am capable of; therefore, I will not allow you to leave. We need you to exchange for the amulet. When we have the amulet in our hand, then you can go home to Brooklyn."

"I had the amulet in my home on my kitchen table these many months, and I did not see anything so special about it. I know it is made of pure gold; therefore, it should be unbelievably valuable."

Wildflower could not believe what she was hearing and asked, "You mean to tell me when I came by your apartment, the amulet was on the kitchen table?"

"Yes, it was on the kitchen table in the fruit bowl when you came by the apartment," said Rose.

Wildflower could scarcely believe she was within proximity to the amulet and did not know because she was focusing on seducing Rose. Wildflower then asked, "How did you come to acquire the amulet?"

"When I met my boyfriend, he gave it to me to hold it securely for him," said Rose. Rose did not want to give Wildflower too much information. Rose then asked, "What importance does the amulet have apart from it being very valuable?"

Wildflower laughed and said, "I see and recognize that you do not know shit. You are just an innocent bystander caught up in the struggle between good and evil. I need to go to my office to call some people to track down that yacht. I need to get some food, clothing and toiletries for you. You will stay in my father's office."

Wildflower excused herself from the presence of Rose and walked to her office. As soon as Wildflower exited the office, Roberto Sanchez stealthily opened Vallencourt's office door, leaving it ajar, and entered with a sly grin on his face. As the door opened, Rose turned around, recognized him instantly, jumped out of the office chair, and stood on her feet. Roberto smiling, said, "You bitch, you are in my world now, in my territory, and you do not have to get up out of your soft comfy chair on my behalf."

Rose thought how uncanny that this little man standing in front of her, whom she went on that unfortunate dinner date with, was a member of the Alliance Organization. Rose curtly said, "I see they allow all sorts of garbage into this organization. This organization will not survive for the foreseeable future when they allow all sorts of putrid carcass to be a member."

Roberto was angry that this woman was insulting him at his workplace, and as he looked at her face, he could see the disdain that she had for him, and Roberto then said, "Bitch, I do not know what you just said, but I know you think that I am beneath you, like I am some sort of crap caught on your designer shoes. Well, let me tell you what I am going to do later when everyone is gone, apart from the security guards. I am going to rape the shit out of you. I am going to have my way with you every which way I want, and there will not be anyone to stop it."

As Roberto finished speaking, Vallencourt pushed the office door, which was left ajar, wide open. Vallencourt eyes were as if they were burning with anger looked at Roberto and said, "If you dare touch her, I will personally rip off your cock and shove it up your ass, then I will ram my size thirteen feet up your ass just to ensure that you will never be able to even fart and not feel pain. She is my guest until I retrieve the amulet. If she opens her legs from east to west, please look the other way."

Roberto looked totally crestfallen and then said, "I never meant any of the things I just said. I only wanted to scare her. I apologize to you and to her for the words that came out of my mouth."

"Good, now get out of my office and wait in the conference room for my daughter on what her plans are in locating that yacht," said Vallencourt.

Rose, with a devilish smile on her face, as Roberto was leaving the office, said, "Goodbye, my short friend. You are a piece of excrement."

Roberto closed the office door and Rose was glad to see him depart the office. She sat back in the office chair, staring at Vallencourt. Vallencourt then said, "You should be getting some food and clothing shortly. There is a bathroom and a small bedroom where I stay when I choose to stay in the office overnight. You will be safe there. No one disobeys my orders. Hopefully, by tomorrow, we will make the exchange of the amulet for you."

Rose sat in the chair in silence, hoping everything would work out for her and she would be safely back in her apartment the next day.

****

Wildflower, Roberto, and Thornbird were in the helicopter, flying back to New Jersey. From New Jersey, they were going to take a seaplane and fly to some location off the coast of Maine, where they would meet up with a speedboat to take them to the yacht, "The Helen." The helicopter had just landed off the seacoast of New Jersey at a seaplane base named the Hummel. From there, they boarded a seaplane, which was a fixed-wing airplane with two pontoons known as floats.

The pilot was a short, round, freckled-faced Caucasian man around in his forties. He was dressed in khaki Bermudan shorts, a red Polio shirt and black sneakers. The pilot welcomed them onboard the seaplane and told them that they would soon be at their destination in the shortest amount of time. The seaplane took off effortlessly to the sky, and from there, they sat admiring the views and the beautiful rolling ocean waves.

After what seemed forever to Wildflower, the pilot landed the seaplane in the calmed seawater, skillfully at the exact coordinates given to him by Wildflower. Wildflower, Roberto and Thornbird disembarked from the seaplane to a waiting speedboat. The speedboat was a Jeanneau Leader 805 that was quite elegant with a sleek appearance. On board, the speedboat was a tall, dark Hispanic man with a distinct black moustache and wearing a captain white hat. The Hispanic man had a huge Cuban cigar in his mouth and introduced himself as Juan Saldado as they all climbed aboard.

Wildflower was admiring the beauty of the speedboat and asked Juan, "How many miles is the yacht from here?"

"The yacht is around five miles from where we are presently. I took the liberty of speeding past them twice so they were not suspicious of my boat. I wanted them to think I was on a joy ride excursion," said Juan.

"That is a great idea. They will not see us coming. We can, therefore, surprise them and allow them to talk before we dispose of them," said Wildflower.

"Let's go and get them before they decide to leave the area," said Juan.

Juan turned on the ignition key, and the engine started, and the elegant, sleek speedboat started racing through the seawater. The speedboat was racing at maximum capacity at around thirty-two knots. The speedboat cut through the seawater with consummate ease, displaying a beautiful miniature waterfall. They soon saw the yacht lying idle in the open water from a distance. Juan raced the speedboat and stopped just two feet alongside the yacht.

Thornbird jumped onboard the yacht first, followed by Roberto. Thornbird and Roberto raced ahead to the upper deck, where they saw some people lying on lounge chairs. One of the men who was lying on the lounge chairs sprang up when he saw that the yacht had been boarded by unknown people. He raced towards a long black bag that was underneath the lounge chair and took out a Kalashnikov twelve gauge semi-automatic shotgun. Roberto saw when the man took out the gun and ran downstairs to the lower deck. Thornbird continued to walk towards the upper deck, and the man started shooting the semi-automatic gun directly at him in his chest.

Roberto ran downstairs, and as he was trying to catch his breath; he saw a slight movement of someone entering one of the cabins. Roberto ran towards the cabin only to find the door locked. Roberto stood back, braced himself and kicked off the door. Roberto looked inside the cabin and did not see anyone, and he then entered the bathroom. Roberto looked and did not see anyone, and as he turned around and was about to exit the cabin, he turned around to look inside the bath. Roberto pulled away the shower curtain to see Alexander sweating profusely on his face and had a look of unmitigated terror on it. Roberto gestured to Alexander with his hand to come out of the bath.

As Alexander came out of the bath and walked into the room, he asked, "What are you doing here?"

Within an instant, Roberto took a Glock 9mm gun from his waist, spun around from around five feet and shot Alexander in the forehead. The bullet hit Alexander, and he fell on the floor of the cabin, and he died with a total surprise look on his face. Roberto then went over Alexander's body and felt his neck to see if there was any pulse. Satisfied that Alexander was dead, Roberto took out a gun from his pants pocket and placed it into the hands of Alexander on the floor.

Roberto then exited the cabin and walked back upstairs to see Thornbird lifting Yuri by the neck around two feet off the ground. Maria and Igor were seated on the lounge chair, watching with total disbelief what was happening to Yuri. Wildflower walked around both men and asked, "I need to know who is the boss behind this operation?"

Yuri seemed totally resigned to his faith as Thornbird put him back on the ground but with his right hand firmly clasped around his neck. Yuri then said, "I do not know who the boss is. We were just given instructions by phone and told how much money to ask for the girl. Three of us would be receiving ten million dollars each if we carried out the operation smoothly."

"I need more information that you are not the mastermind behind this whole operation. The way you were talking and bullying me on the phone. I suspect you are the mastermind behind this whole blackmailing scheme. If you do not give me the name of the mastermind, I am going to ask Thornbird to break your fucking neck and throw your dead body into the sea to be eaten by sharks," said Wildflower.

"No, no, please do not kill me. I do not know anything, but Alexander would know a great deal more than me. Alexander told me that he met him once when they were about to undertake the blackmailing scheme," said Yuri.

"Where is Alexander?" asked Wildflower.

Yuri started stuttering and said," I believe he is by the lower deck."

Wildflower, quite exasperated, said, "Roberto, go and fetch him and make sure he is not harmed because I need to question him thoroughly."

Roberto cleared his throat and said, "If that fat man below the deck is Alexander, I am sorry to tell you that he is dead. I saw a shadowy figure downstairs and went to investigate. When I went downstairs, he attacked me with a gun, and I shot him, and he died."

Maria had never done an introspection for her love for Alexander because he was always there in her life, but now he was gone, her means of survival in this world. She was suddenly filled with rage and hatred towards the man who was calmly relaying the news of him killing Alexander.

As Roberto finished speaking, Maria leaped from the lounge chair straight on Roberto and started attacking him like a crazed animal. She was scratching him in his face with her hands, and as Roberto put up his hand to push her off, Maria grabbed his left hand and bit it. Roberto screamed out at the searing pain coursing throughout his body. He was infuriated at being bitten and took his right hand and pushed Maria to the ground. Maria got up off the ground and was about to leap on Roberto when Wildflower said, "Stop this altercation immediately."

Maria went and sat on the lounge chair. She was crying uncontrollably about the death of Alexander. Wildflower was irritated because she wanted to question Alexander, but now, he was dead. Wildflower went to the lower deck to look at Alexander to ensure that he was dead. She went into the cabin and looked at the body with Alexander holding a gun in his hand, and the single gunshot to his forehead.

Wildflower left the cabin and went back to the upper deck and said, "Since you three are of no help to me and cannot provide any information I may as well kill you all." Wildflower then went over to Roberto and whispered, "Go over to the other man and put a choke hold on him and break his fucking neck and throw him in the sea."

Wildflower went over to Maria and held her hand while Roberto went over to Igor, took the gun from his waist and pointed it at Igor's head. Roberto shot Igor in the head while Thornbird broke Yuri's neck and threw his body overboard. Maria started to scream more loudly, and Wildflower slapped her hard on her face and said,

"Shut the fuck up, I am not going to kill you. I am going to allow you to go free."

"What am I going to do now that Alexander is dead?" asked Maria.

Wildflower hated consoling anyone, because she was about showing strength and power and thought she would just change her mind and kill Maria, but something within her made her show empathy for this Russian female. The mere fact that she was a woman made Wildflower think she would give her a chance at life and said, "Maria, you are a woman, you are a survivor. Go to New Jersey, New York, or the state of Florida and start your life over. Make your life a new beginning. However, please do not tell anyone about what happened onboard the yacht; if you do, I will hunt you, cut out your tongue and kill you." Maria was still looking dazed and confused, and Wildflower asked, "Is that crystal clear to you?"

Maria wiped away her tears with her hands and said, "Yes, I do understand."

"Good that we understand each other. You can even change your name if you so wish for your new life. I will ask the men to remove the body from the boat, and you can clean up any blood stains before you sail away from here," said Wildflower. Wildflower gestured to Thornbird that he should assist Roberto in throwing Igor's body overboard into the seawater.

Wildflower, Thornbird, and Roberto left the yacht, boarded the speedboat, and returned to their seaplane that took them back to New Jersey. From New Jersey they were flown back to Manhattan by their waiting helicopter. The helicopter landed on the helipad of their Manhattan headquarters. It was around midnight and they all disembarked and walked down the stairs to their offices.

Wildflower was walking to her office when she turned around and went to Vallencourt's office to check on Rose. She greeted the two security guards that were placed outside Vallencourt's office. She opened the office door, went in, walked to the area where the small bedroom was and opened the door. Wildflower looked inside to see Rose soundly asleep. She closed the door and went to her office, called her dad, and told him what had transpired on the yacht. Vallencourt told her that in the morning, before she came to work, she must pick up a white dress in the store for Rose to wear when they do the exchange for the amulet.

As Wildflower came off the phone there was a knocking on her office door. She told the person who was knocking on the door to come inside the office. It was Roberto, and he said, "I am not feeling too sleepy. I would love to invite you for a drink at the club."

Wildflower was surprised at the invitation, but she did not have anything doing and she was not particularly tired, so she said "Yes, I would love to go to the club."

Roberto could not believe that she responded in the affirmative to his invitation and he was beaming with pride and he said, "Great then, lets us go to the club."

They both left the office and went to the underground parking garage where Wildflower's Mercedes Benz car was parked beside a fire hydrant. Wildflower opened the car, and they went in and drove to the club. The club was one of those high-end and because she was a frequent guest, she was escorted upstairs to a private balcony. The club was quite packed with people dancing below in almost hypnotic fashion.

Wildflower ordered a bottle of Hennessey, and they both drank, and then went dancing on the dance floor. Roberto was most impressed by her very sensual dancing skills. With Wildflower dancing closed to him in this very sensual way Roberto was turned on and decided to take a break from the dancing and went back upstairs to their table.

As they sat around their table, Roberto said, "I will have to confess to you. I am very much attracted to you and I am wondering if it is all possible that I will be able to come home with you."

Wildflower started laughing uncontrollable and said "No, no you do not understand. I accepted your invitation to come to the club because I did not feel sleepy. I am not attracted to you and most definitely I am not sleeping with you, not now or ever."

Roberto was a little peeved and said, "I see I am wasting my time. I had hopes that we would be going home to your place together."

The smile disappeared off Wildflower's face, and she said, "Let me be brutally honest with you because I do not want you to leave with the wrong impression. I swing both ways, but I am not into short men. If a man does not tower over me, I do not feel like a sexy bitch, and I like to feel I am the sexiest bitch when I am in that man's arms. Sorry, my friend, you are just not my type; you are just too short."

Roberto looked dejected and said, "I guess that is my cue to make my departure. I will see you at work. Goodnight."

Wildflower watched Roberto walk out of the club, not caring if his feeling was hurt. There was something about Roberto that she did not trust. She left the club soon after Roberto's departure. She drove straight home to her Manhattan apartment, took a bath, and went to her bed.

Chapter 27

It was around ten o'clock in the morning and Wildflower was driving to work when she remembered Vallencourt telling her to pick up a dress for Rose to wear when they make the exchange for the amulet. Wildflower was a little puzzled why Rose would need a white dress to wear for the exchange and her father seemed like he wanted it to be a secret. She stopped by the Macys store and bought a chiffon cocktail dress for Rose. She paid for the dress, left the store and drove straight to work.

As Wildflower opened her office door Vallencourt was in her office waiting on her to arrive. They greeted each other and Vallencourt told her where he wanted the exchange to take place. Vallencourt left her office soon after and Wildflower then went and checked on Rose to see how she was doing. Satisfied that Rose was okay she came back to her office to sort out some paperwork's.

It was late in the evening when Wildflower phone rang, and she answered and said "Hello."

It was Malakai on the other end of the call, and he said, "I am calling on where possible to make the exchange for Rose to get her from your custody."

Wildflower was eager to hear Peter Mack's voice. She was waiting on his call all day and hoping their business with Peter Mack would conclude tomorrow. Wildflower not wanting her voice to seem too eager said "Mister Peter Mack I am waiting on your call all day. Anyway, we will make the exchange at the Bunyan's Apple farm in Upstate New York at exactly six o'clock tomorrow. Do you know the location of the Bunyan's Apple farm in Upstate New York?" asked Wildflower.

Malakai hesitated in answering the other person on the other end of the phone call, as he was pondering the location of the apple farm. He knew the location quite well, but that place would be on their turf, quite isolated and in the open where his escape would be quite limited if anything unforeseen happened. Malakai then said "Yes, I know the location of the Bunyan's Apple farm."

"Good, we will see you there tomorrow and please be on time to make the exchange" said Wildflower.

They ended the phone call and Wildflower thought that everything will come to an end in some form by tomorrow. She was so looking forward to the recovery of the amulet to end, and she would be able to move on with her life and focus on other things.

Wildflower called her father and told him that tomorrow they would make the exchange at approximately six o'clock. She hung up the phone and continued concentrating on the paperwork in front of her when suddenly an announcement was made by Vallencourt that all senior staff must be at the Bunyan's Apple farm in Upstate New York tomorrow at approximately six o'clock.

Wildflower sat at her desk wondering what her father was up to, but she could not come up with anything that makes sense. She knew him enough that without a doubt that he was planning something ginormous maybe to cement his status as the unquestionable ultimate ruler of the Alliance Organization in this sector.

****

The next morning Malakai was around his small dining table in his Manhattan apartment finishing eating his breakfast. He got up from around the table and put the few dishes in the kitchen dishwasher. As he was closing the dishwasher his apartment door buzzer started ringing. Malakai pressed the knob to listen and a voice said "I am Reverend Watkiss, I am Rose pastor. I am asking you kindly, could you please come down to the lobby. We need to talk urgently."

Malakai was totally puzzled why in heaven name Rose pastor was at his apartment building wanting to talk to him, and for what reasons. He was having second thought wondering if at all he should go downstairs to talk to this man who he has never heard of or spoken to in his life. Malakai thought better of it and opened his apartment door and went downstairs to meet this Reverend Watkiss. When he arrived downstairs Malakai saw this tall handsome muscular looking African American man pacing back and forth in the lobby. The man was dressed in blue jeans and had on a black jacket.

Malakai approached the man and he spun around and grabbed Malakai's hand shook it and said "I am Reverend Watkiss and I know you are Malakai. I know who you are and also what you are, and what is occupying your mind. We need to talk urgently and somewhere private."

Malakai totally perplexed about the man in front of him and what he wanted from him, and he looked at the man keenly and somehow got the sense that he could trust this stranger. Malakai then said, "If you want to speak privately, please follow me to my apartment."

Reverend Watkiss followed Malakai to the elevator and to Malakai's apartment. Malakai invited Reverend Watkiss to a seat around the small dining table. Malakai then asked, "Can I offer you something to drink?"

Reverend Watkiss suddenly looked trouble as if something dire was on his mind. Reverend Watkiss looked at Malakai and said, "Water will do fine."

Malakai went to the refrigerator and took out a bottle of water and gave it Reverend Watkiss. He opened the water bottle and poured it down his throat. His thirst sated Reverend Watkiss then said "As I said before I am Rose pastor, but I am more than that. I am going to reveal to you something that only a handful of people on this planet knows. I have certain capabilities or gifts that allow me to see into the future. I know that you have the amulet of Osiris that the Alliance

Organization has been searching for these many months. I know they have Rose in their custody and wanting to exchange the amulet for her life. I came here to tell you; you cannot give them the amulet. Our world as we all know it will be destroyed if you gave them the amulet."

Malakai felt the pressured and strained of the Alliance Organization having Rose in their custody as tears started draining from his eyes, and he said "I cannot sacrifice her life for the amulet. I refuse to do it. I got her into this mess, and I will have to give them the amulet to get her back."

Reverend Watkiss then echoed a sigh of frustration and said, "We are all doomed then because if you gave them the amulet, all the dead souls of this world will be under their command to use as they see fit and not as the Creator of the universe intended."

Malakai used his hands and wiped away the tears that was streaming down his face and asked, "What must I do?"

Reverend Watkiss with solemnity in his voice then said "I know for a fact that you love Rose, but you will not defeat them by yourself. You need to call on a greater power for help. You need to call on God for his help and guidance in this time of trouble. Let him guide your path and show you the way forward because without his help you will not be able to defeat them."

Malakai then looked as if he was totally spaced out and said "Reverend Watkiss you are aware of who I am. I am not the religious type. I am aware and recognize his greatness and love. I submit to him always for he is the creator of the universe and all things within it."

Reverend Watkiss suddenly started grinning showing his pearly white teeth and said "I did not understand because I know who you are, but the spirit of the Lord move me to come and talk to you. I was even resistant, but the spirit of God move me to come and I forgot the old saying you never judge a book by its cover, or it is the substance of the man. My friend God knows your heart and he find that you are a good person. Make no bones about it, you have your failings like every one of us but on God scale he weighs us in a holistic way."

Malakai looked a little confused and asked Reverend Watkiss "Could you explain a little more for my sake?"

Reverend Watkiss then said "The battle you will be embarking on is not only one of good over evil, but it is also a battle with yourself. It is a battle to see if you are capable and willing to surrender to a greater power within the universe. If you are not capable of surrendering and submitting to God, you will be destroyed like all before you, but if you are willing to surrender then the force within the universe will come to your aid. I beg of you for the fate of the world to choose the right course."

Malakai got up from the chair that he was sitting on and Reverend Watkiss got up also and they embraced warmly. Malakai then said "Thank you for coming; it was a pleasure having you in my home. I promise you if everything works out, I will come and visit you soon."

"I am truly glad that I came to visit and meet you. I will pray for you but remember to call on God because we cannot win the war against them if God is not in our midst. God is our shield in the battle against the enemy of that magnitude. Take care my son and give them hell on the battlefield."

Malakai watched Reverend Watkiss exited the apartment and was very appreciative that he came to visit, because his presence lifted his spirit. Malakai then went into the refrigerator took out a bottle of water, drank it then went into the room and put on a light black jacket over his white t-shirt. He was wearing his blue jeans and sneaker because he thought that whatever contingencies that was ahead of him, he wanted to be ready, comfortable, and flexible in his clothing. He then went into the bathroom picked up the amulet that was on the counter surface and inserted it in his jeans pocket. Malakai also picked up the Onoro sword and put it in his waist and put on a New York Yankee blue baseball hat. He walked out the apartment and closed the door.

Malakai exited the apartment building and walked around a hundred yards away to the Cadillac Escalade vehicle that was parked on the roadway. He opened the vehicle jumped in and drove away to Upstate New York. As Malakai drove the vehicle, he was struggling, and conflicted, what he was going to do, whether to give the Alliance Organization the amulet or to sacrifice Rose life. His mind was in overdrive thinking of all the possible way to avoid giving his enemy the amulet and saving Rose life. Malakai could not figure a way to extricate Rose from the Alliance Organization without both of them been killed if he did not give them the amulet. He knew he could not sacrifice Rose life because he would be filled with guilt for as long as his life last on mother earth.

Malakai continued driving until he stopped at the side of the road trying to clear his head. Malakai did not even have a plan of how the exchange of Rose for the amulet would occur, and he knew that he could not walk into the Bunyan's Apple Farm and give them the amulet and they would in turn release Rose from their custody and they would all walk away to freedom. He became petrified and thought if he did walk into their camp and gave them the amulet, they would surely kill him for been such nuisance, and they would more than likely do unspeakable horrors to Rose if he was dead. Malakai then decided he was going to hide the amulet in some nearby bush near the farm.

Malakai restarted the vehicle and resumed driving on the road. He was still not comfortable with his plan and started to question himself if at all he would be able to free Rose from the Alliance

Organization. Malakai started to think profoundly for the first time of the possible ramifications if the Alliance Organization gain holds of the amulet. He knew that whoever was in charge of this sector for the Alliance Organization would want to hand over the amulet to their God immediately so he would be in command of the souls of the dead and unleash hell on earth. Malakai suddenly started to panic, and his chest seemed as if it was going to explode in pieces. He quickly opened the vehicle window and started inhaling deeply to get the fresh air to calm his beating heart that seemed as if it would pulverize his chest.

Malakai knew he was caught between the love of an innocent woman and humanity in general, and it dawned on Malakai that he needed help from a greater power in this world. He knew he was weak and unsure if he would be able to sacrifice the woman he loves for the sake of humanity.

As the cool evening air beat on Malakai's face he suddenly remembered what Reverend Watkiss told him that he would not be able to defeat them until he calls on a higher power. Malakai drove until he saw a huge white building looking like a church with a huge cross on top of the building. He did not even notice the name of the church as he drove off the road and into the churchyard. Malakai came out of the vehicle and ran up the steps of the church. Malakai then noticed that the church door was closed, and he looked around and noticed a Caucasian round face white hair man around five feet eight inches tall. The man was dressed in a dark pants and a white long sleeved shirts and he said "Sorry stranger but we are closed. You can come another time to worship."

"I need help desperately and I need to call on a greater power than myself. I am a wandering stranger asking you kindly if you can open the door for me to pray and worship and call on God in my time of need" said Malakai.

The man hesitated looked into Malakai face and saw the consternation on it and pushed his hand into his pants pocket and took out a key and said, "I will open the door for you to pray."

Malakai thank the man and as he opened the door and was about to turn on the electric light in the church. Malakai told him that it was not necessary, because there was enough ambient light coming from the outside, pouring through the windows of the church. Malakai could see rows of benches on beautiful ceramic tiled floor. He walked up to the front of the church, sat in the first bench and took off his cap. He sat in the bench mediating and started crying uncontrollable, cognizant that he had just couple more hours to face his enemies.

The tears poured down Malakai's face like a gently running stream. He took his hand and wiped away some of it. He then went on his knees clasped his hand together and said "The almighty God, the creator of all living things, I have come to you in my time of need and desperation. I have come to you in your one and only true son name. He states that none can be saved only in your son name Yeshua.

I am asking for your guidance, protection, and assistance in your son name, Yeshua. I am powerless and seek your mercy and guidance. Those who have taken Rose are your enemies and mine. I seek no greater help more than the return of Rose safely to me and aid me in their destruction to reveal to them you are the one true God of all mankind. Amen."

Malakai finished praying and a cold gust of wind came into the church creating an eerie echoing sound. Malakai got up off his knees and sat back on the bench. His tears were all dried up on his face and he was somehow more calmer, and after a few more minutes Malakai thank the man and exited the church. Malakai did not get an answer but his whole demeanor had changed, and he was experiencing some amount of solace and tranquility.

Malakai continued driving until he was in Upstate New York. As he drove, he started seeing large acres of huge apple farms in the area. It was after five o'clock in the evening and Malakai still had not decided which course of action, he was going to embark on to free Rose. Malakai turned off the main road to an isolated road, drove around four miles before he stopped and parked the vehicle on the side of the road.

As Malakai sat in the vehicle it seemed as if the whole weight of the world was on his broad shoulders. He thought that he had prayed solemnly and sincerely to the Almighty God, but he got no response or any sign of help to come in his moment of great trial and tribulation. Malakai opened the vehicle door and stepped on the road surfaces. He looked up and down the road and saw that it was totally isolated without one vehicle in sight.

Malakai then took off the cap he had on his head and put it inside the vehicle. He pushed his hand inside his pocket and took out the amulet out of the black box. He looked at the amulet started rubbing it with his right hand and thought why are you so special? Malakai then decided to put the amulet around his neck. As the amulet swung back and forth on Malakai's chest his heart suddenly started racing and he was about to pull the amulet off when he looked up at the sky and the clouds started turning black. Suddenly there was lightning and thunder all around and Malakai did not know what to make of what was happening in the moment.

Malakai was suddenly lifted around six feet off the ground and his whole body was transformed into a new being. He had this muscular looking body, and his skin was of the color green. His chest was covered with a tight fitting green garment that was beautiful decorated with beads made from gold, silver, and other precious metals. He had this pharaoh looking beard that was waxed in black and on his head was a double red and white crown and in his hand was a scepter made of pure gold. Around his waist was a piece of green cloth attached to a belt that covered his waist extending to his knees. His muscular legs were painted in a bronze color.

Malakai was now fully transformed into the ancient Egyptian god Osiris, the god of the dead. Malakai was aware that he was in total control of the soul of the dead and he smiled at the sudden amount of power he wielded in his hand. Malakai conscious that he was around ten feet in the air stretched forth the scepter and suddenly like magic zombie apparition started to appear on the ground. Malakai descended to the ground and as he looked at the ghostly figures numbering more than a thousand of all ethnicities. Malakai then stretched forth the scepter and said "Listen to me you creatures of dead souls. I am the god Osiris, ruler of the dead. You are all under my command and my command alone. My command to you is to go over the Bunyan's Apple Farm and kill everyone over there with the exception of one human being name Rose Winter. She is been held against her will by my enemy. Now go and do your master bidding."

As Malakai finished speaking, there was huge thunder and lightning, and the black clouds disappeared to replace by blue sky. All the apparitions suddenly disappeared, and Malakai looked up into the sky, and a blinding light pierced his eyes as he suddenly fell to the ground. Malakai was suddenly transformed back from the ancient Egyptian god, Osiris. Malakai looked away from the sky and started looking downward at the ground. Suddenly, a figure emerged from the sky to the ground.

Malakai was on the ground bowing his head to a being he had never seen or came across in his whole life. The sheer power of the being was so immense that Malakai was unable to lift his head but to stare on the ground. Malakai could not even look up at the individual face. Malakai tried everything in his power to look up at the individual, but he was unable to, and Malakai's body was trembling, and he could not understand why.

As the individual approached and asked in a rasping voice "Who dare challenge the servant of the Almighty God for the soul of the dead?"

Malakai with his stare steadfast on the ground and with his voice trembling said "I am Malakai. The God that you served, I am a believer in the Almighty God the creator of all living things. I am not here to challenge you because I am aware the awesome power you wield over the living and the dead."

"By what means did you summon the soul of the dead?" asked the being.

"I summoned them with an ancient Egyptian amulet that once belonged to Osiris. I stole it from two agents who were on their way to deliver it to the Alliance Organization in Manhattan. I think they were going to deliver it to the Morning Star for him to control the soul of the dead and to unleash them on this world to do their bidding," said Malakai.

"Let me have the amulet" said the powerful being.

Malakai hesitated then took the amulet off his neck and gave it to the powerful being. Malakai started wondering if all hope of ever rescuing Rose from the murderous Alliance Organization was going to be extinguished by giving this powerful being the amulet.

"What were you going to do with the soul of the dead if I were not here?"

"The Alliance Organization has my girlfriend in their custody, and they want to trade her life for the amulet. I was going to use the soul of the dead to help me fight them, that I might be victorious. They are waiting on me to come and trade the amulet for her over the Bunyan's Apple Farm in the next few minutes" said Malakai. Malakai then said "The Almighty God, the creator of all living things enemy is also my enemy. I beg and beseech you for your assistance to help me free Rose from the Alliance Organization custody and to return her safely in my arms."

There was total silence for around a minute. The powerful being then said "Without my help you will surely die today but because you told the truth and did not resist in giving me the amulet, I will surely help you. I question you not because I did not know the answers, but I wanted to see if you were going to tell me the truth. I was aware of your dilemma and the earnest and sincere prayer in the church. I will not give you back the amulet. This amulet will stay with me and not fall in the hands of those who would choose to usurp the dictate of the power of the Almighty God."

Malakai, quite concerned that the powerful being was not going to give him back the amulet, asked, "What am I going to use to exchange Rose's life for now?"

"That small stone beside your knees, please give it to me. I will transform the small stone into an exact replica of the amulet, and you can take it to them. They will not know the difference, only the fact that the replica amulet will have no discernable power" said the powerful being.

Malakai, still on his knees, bowed down with his face facing the ground, stretched forth his hand above his head and gave the powerful being the small stones. Within seconds, the powerful being said, "Stretch forth your hand and take the copy of the amulet."

Malakai did as he was instructed and took the amulet from the powerful being. As he took the amulet, he stared at it and realized it was an exact copy of the amulet. Suddenly the powerful being reflection shone on the stone in a fuzzy way displaying the being face full of fire and black skin. Malakai heart raced as he looked at the fuzzy image reflection on the amulet. Malakai continued to look and suddenly realized the being was a woman because he could see her ample breast in the white robe. The powerful being then asked, "Is the replica of the amulet I made satisfactory to you?"

Malakai without hesitation said, "It is an exact copy of the amulet of Osiris" Malakai then asked are you going to allow the soul of the dead to go with me to fight the battle against the Alliance Organization?”

“I will allow no such course of action. Only the Almighty God the creator of all living things within the universe controls the soul of the dead. I am the Angel of Death, and my mission and directive is to take the dead souls and lead them to a place where they will spend the rest of their life. You wanted to control the soul of the dead for your own reason and be God and for that transgression you will have to go over there alone and face your enemies alone” said the powerful being.

“Then I am doomed, and they shall surely kill me when I enter into their domain,” said Malakai.

“Yes, they will certainly kill you if I did not commit to help you. You believe in the Almighty God, a greater power than yourself and for that reason alone, I will help you. In the book of Psalm 120: 1 it states that in my trouble I cried to the Lord and he answered me. The force within the universe has seen your tears and your prayer and he has directed me to assist you to wipe away his enemies. Now stretch forth your hand and I will imprint my blood on it that when I come, I will not destroy you. I will also put some blood on your jacket that you may cover Rose face with it. Please ensure that her face is properly cover because when I come and if she looks up at me, she will be destroyed with everyone, including you” said the Angel of Death.

Malakai stretched forth his hand and the Angel of Death pierced it. Malakai could feel his warm blood running on his skin and then suddenly as the Angel of Death blood mingled with his and coldness came over Malakai entire body and he dropped face down on the green grasses. Malakai could hear when the blood of the Angel of Death hit his jacket and he felt even colder.

The Angel of Death then said "Take long deep breath and you will be fine in the next five minutes. I will see you shortly."

Malakai prostrate on the ground saw the Angel of Death back, as she walked away from him and just disappeared into thin air. She was dressed in a bone white robe to her feet, but her neck was covered by a seventeenth century Elizabethan neck ruffs that sat upright and holstered to the robe by the most precious stones that Malakai had ever seen in his entire life. Some of the stones were slight greenish coffee colors and were about the size of strawberries.

Malakai was breathing heavily, got up off the ground and shook off the few fine stones that were on his jean pant. Malakai gathered himself and walked towards the vehicle. He took off the black light jacket he was wearing and looked at it. On the jacket was the blood splattering of the Angel of Death. Malakai put on the jacket and opened the vehicle door, sat in the driver seat reliving the experience with the Angel of Death. Malakai thought how any human beings could be in that presence of so much awesome power and not be disintegrated by it. He tried his utmost best utilizing all his strength just to look at her face and he was unable to, and the experience left him drained of his energy. All he could do was to bow down in the presence of one of the Almighty God servant.

It was around five minutes to six when Malakai regained his strength, and he started the vehicle and drove away to the Bunyan's Apple Farm. As Malakai was driving and approaching the farm gate, he thought his destiny awaits, and he wondered whether his fate would lead to his destruction, or to unleash unmitigated annihilation on his enemies.

Final Chapter

Malakai drove the vehicle to the Bunyan's Apple farm gate where he was stopped by two security guards, who were dressed impeccable in black jackets and white shirts. Malakai was then directed to the parking area. He got out of the vehicle put on the baseball New York Yankee hat and started to walk to the farmhouse. The apple farm was a sprawling estate with more than a hundred acres of apple trees. Furthered in the back was a large brownish farmhouse.

Malakai continued to walk to an open spaces area where there were around fifty to sixty people gathered and dressed in their black jackets and white shirts. Malakai thought it was quite strange that everyone including the women were all dressed in the same colors as the men. Malakai was around a hundred yards away when he saw a scene that shocked him to his core. It was the sight of Rose dressed in white and tied to a long wooden ten foot pole. Rose hands were tied behind her back and attached to the ten foot pole. Malakai eyes drifted away from Rose to a large pile of woods around hundred and fifty yards from where Rose was tied to the wooden pole. It seemed to Malakai as if someone was about to make a huge bonfire but for what purpose he could not fathom.

Malakai walked up to the first individual and asked, "Who is Wallenstein?"

A female emerged from the front and said "I am he or I was he. I am no longer. I am Wildflower and you must be the infamous Peter Mack in the flesh. I dare say you certainly have big balls to just walk in on our compound without any back up. I am impressed" Wildflower eyes wandered from Malakai lower body to his upper body and smiled at the man in front of her and asked, "Did you bring the amulet with you?"

Malakai then sternly said "I need to speak to Rose first, and then we can discuss business."

Wildflower looked at Malakai like an uncontrollable student that had been brought to the principal office and the principal do not know what to make of the student. Wildflower thought that this man in front of her was giving out ultimatum and does not seem to realize that he was not in charge of the situation. Wildflower then mused and said "Okay, you can speak to her for a few seconds, afterwards we discuss business."

Malakai walked up to where Rose was tied to the wooden pole and as he walked away, he could sense the tension among the crowd. There was grim sense of foreboding in the air that heightened the tension. He arrived at where Rose was tied to the pole, looked at her, examining her while she stared back at him without saying a word. Malakai then break the silence and asked, "How are you holding on?"

Rose heart lit up when she saw the sight of Malakai walking towards the crowd. She prayed earnestly that he would come to rescue her but seeing him in the flesh she suddenly started to panic. Most of all seeing him just walking alone in their stronghold seem quite foolhardy, as if he was a madman. Rose cleared her throat and said, "I am not doing too well, but seeing you I suddenly have a semblance of hope."

"Did they hurt you?" asked Malakai.

"Not as yet but I heard one of the guards whispering to his companion that the pile of woods they set up is to be used as a burnt offering sacrifice to their god of our bodies" said Rose.

As Malakai was pondering the information that Rose relayed to him Rose asked, "Please tell me you have something up your sleeve, and you did not just walk into their compound without a plan?"

Malakai not wanting to frighten Rose said "Yes I do have a plan. I promise I will not let anyone harm you. I would walk through hell and back for you."

Vallencourt was sitting on a chair watching Malakai every move as he interacted with his daughter. He got up off the chair and started clapping his hand and said "Enough chatting mister. We have business to discuss, now."

Malakai hurriedly kissed Rose lips and walked to meet Vallencourt. They met each other in the center of the large open space and Malakai said, "I guess you are the man I should speak to."

"Yes, I am the man you should speak to. I am the leader of this sector and in full control of it" said Vallencourt. Vallencourt quite eager to get some information about the amulet asked, "Do you have the amulet with you?"

Malakai looked at the tall muscular man in front of him and said "I do not want to answer your question as yet" Malakai could see the well-oiled face of the man became redder and the anger boiling up. Malakai then asked, "If I gave you the amulet now, will you allow us both to leave the premise without any hindrance from anyone?"

A broad smile came over Vallencourt's face and he started laughing and said "Certainly, I will allow you to leave without anyone bothering you. You have my word on that."

"If you do not honor your word, you will all die right here" said Malakai. Malakai pushed his right hand into his pants pocket and took out the amulet and threw it at Vallencourt and asked, "You have the amulet now in your possession, can we depart from the compound?"

Vallencourt examined the amulet intensely, looking at every marked. The scrutiny of the amulet completed Vallencourt gave the amulet to Wildflower. Vallencourt turned towards Malakai and said "hold on Mister, I lied, you are not going anywhere. You and Rose are not leaving this compound especially now that we have the amulet in our possession. For all the stress and trouble you caused me, there will have to be some recompense of both your life. I am going to offer

Rose as a sacrifice on that bonfire to our god, the Morning Star. With regards to you, I am going to take my sword and chop off your head right here, to teach you a lesson, so no one dare steal from us again."

"I beg of you, let us depart from your compound, and do not take any action. You have what you wanted, so let us not fight and we all live to see another day" said Malakai.

Vallencourt smirked at Malakai proposal and responded "If I allow you to just walk away without any consequence, I am finish as a leader of this sector. What you did stealing the amulet allow my authority to be question and I cannot have that in my organization. Therefore the ultimate price for that is death for you, and your woman who assisted you."

Since you will not reconsider my proposal, can I ask you one favor?"

Vallencourt barked "Yes, I will grant you one favor before I kill you."

Malakai was at least glad that Rose was out of earshot and could not hear what he was telling the man he was about to fight for both their life. Malakai cleared his throat and said "Rose is not like us, she does not understand anything that we are not like her, and I want to keep it that way. I want to cover her face with my jacket so that she will not be able to see you kill me. I want to spare her that agony."

Vallencourt suddenly had this self-assurance that he was going to defeat the man that caused him so many headaches so many months. Vallencourt feeling quite confident said "Go ahead and have one last talk with your woman and put whatever you want over her head. It is the last wish I could ever grant to a man who is going to die shortly."

Malakai thanked him for the kind gesture of allowing him to speak to Rose before the man chopped off his head and end his life. Malakai walked towards where Rose was tied to the pole and as he approached her, he whispered in her ear rather sternly "I need for you to listen keenly and if you love me please do what I am going to instruct you to do. Please do not deviate from my instructions. I beg of you because I cannot survive this if you die. I am going to place my jacket over your face. I need for you to close your eyes and whatever noise you hear around you; you block them out. You will not survive if the jacket is removed." Malakai somehow felt quite worried for Rose and not even thinking about his wellbeing. As he stared at her he could see the panic in her face and he asked, "Do you understand my instruction, Rose?"

Rose face was almost ashen white, and Malakai could see the obvious fear on it as she said "Yes, you said I must keep my eyes close and ensure that the jacket is covering my face at all time."

Malakai kissed Rose lips and as he removed his lips from her, he said "I cannot survive this if you are not in my life. Everything will be over soon, one way or the other. Now close your eyes and pray to God Almighty the creator of all life until I am here to remove the jacket."

Malakai took off the light black jacket and inserted it over Rose face ensuring that it did not cover her nostril. He made one last looked at Rose again ensuring that the jacket was firmly covering her head. He was satisfied as he looked at the jacket with the red blood splattering. He walked away from Rose towards the tall Italian man for the final confrontation with destiny.

As Malakai approached the tall Italian man, he had taken off his jacket and was now wearing a white shirt and had a huge sword in his hand. Vallencourt then barked out an order to one of his men and said "Light the bonfire now. As soon as I am done disposing of this foe in front of me, we make a huge sacrifice to our god the Morning Star for giving us the victory over our common enemy."

Vallencourt finished speaking and he lunged the sword at Malakai's body which he easily dodged the blow. Malakai started moving around in circles around Vallencourt without taking the Onoro sword from his waist. Vallencourt was a little puzzle by the man in front of him as the man seemed as if he was toying with him and what was worse, he was not even holding a weapon in his hand. Vallencourt felt irritated by the man actions and took the sword and make one quick swipe at Malakai's head. Malakai was about to advance closer when he saw the blade of the sword advancing towards his head. Malakai in a flash drifted backward and smiled at how close he came to losing his head.

Malakai then pushed his hand into his waist and took out the Onoro sword. He pressed the button and the elegant sleek flaming blade emerged from the sheath. There was a loud gasp from the crowd seeing a once in a lifetime sight of the elusive, famous flaming Onoro sword. The people in the crowd started to push to come to the front to have a better view of the flaming sword.

Vallencourt could not believe what he was witnessing in front of him, and he was at a loss, briefly for words. He was watching the flaming Onoro sword been used to attack him after he had spent countless years and man-hours searching for them without success. Finally the words that escape Vallencourt's lips came back to him and he said "I am really going to enjoy killing you for the level of stress you caused me. I have been looking for the flaming Onoro swords for these many years, only to see you with it now. When I kill you, I shall take it and bestow it to the rightful owner."

Malakai and Vallencourt started fighting each other fiercely neither one given an inch as they lunged and blocked each other attack with their swords. Malakai was pleasantly surprised at the quickness of his attacker because person that tall and muscular tended to be a little slower in their agility, flexibility, and movement. Malakai was impressed by his opponent swordsmanship and realized that he was well trained and was in the fight of his life for his survival and Rose.

As the partisan crowd was cheering for Vallencourt, their leader, to squash the interloper one individual was discreetly going to the back of the crowd. That individual was Roberto Sanchez, who had an uneasy feeling about the fighting that was taking place. Roberto's gut feeling or intuition was telling him that something was amiss, and he needed to get away from the area. He had learned over the many years to trust his intuition because, from experience, it has saved him enabling him to be alive and to get out of many delicate situations. Roberto finally arrived at the back of the crowd, and he scurried to the apple trees without anyone noticing. He started running among the many apple trees until he was quite a distance away from the crowd. Roberto was now less fearful now, thinking that he was quite a distance away, and he walked through the apple trees until he arrived at the fencing that secured the property. Roberto climbed over the fence to the main road, where he started looking for a ride back to New York City.

Malakai and Vallencourt were still fighting utilizing all their energies trying to decapitate each other without success. Malakai saw an opening and leapt in the air and came down with a fierce blow with his sword to Vallencourt's head, but Vallencourt quickly blocked his sword. The fighting went on with each one trading blow and the other blocking the other with their respective swords. Although they were combatants, equally matched in a fight for survival Malakai could only admire the tenacity of his opponent. Malakai thought the fight was like a chess match and knew he had to be patient if he was at all going to defeat this stubborn opponent.

As the fight ensued around one hundred and fifty yards away from the fighting area seven high priests dressed in red robes were on their knees praying and holding up the amulet to their god the Morning Star. The seven high priests indulged in praying and incantation in order to summon the Morning Star to receive the amulet of Osiris. All seven priests put on the amulet to see its awesome power, but they were at a loss to explain why the amulet could not summon the spirit of dead souls. Finally one of the priests had an epiphany and told the others that the amulet was a fake. The priest with the idea of about the authenticity of the amulet called Wildflower and told her that the man who took the amulet to them wanted to deceive them intentionally by giving them a replica.

Wildflower was angry on hearing the news that the amulet was a fake ran to where her father was in a deadly combat with this stranger shouted "Dad, the amulet is not authentic."

Vallencourt face suddenly became red, and he was now furious than ever by his opponent. Vallencourt stood back from attacking Malakai and said "So you came here to deliberately deceive me with a fake amulet. For that you will have to pay with your life." Vallencourt then held up the sword and pointed it straight at Malakai and asked, "Did you think you could just waltz in our compound with a fake amulet and get away with it?"

"Yes, I was hoping I would get away with it. Giving you the real amulet would put your master in command of the soul of the dead to do as he see fit. That type of power belong to the Almighty God the creator of all life as it was intended."

Vallencourt swung the huge sword at Malakai's torso in a wild fashion and as Malakai was advancing it cut him and he screamed at the pain. Malakai retreated and Vallencourt started swinging the sword more wildly. Gone was the discipline approached and the patience to Vallencourt attacks but now he seemed more furious and wanted to end the combat any way possible. Malakai was bleeding not profusely from the cut to his chest. It was a welcomed sight for Vallencourt to finally lay a blow on Malakai. He was walking and at time circling Malakai trying to figure how to land the final death blow.

Malakai started to make his attacks looked laborious and at time when there was enough distance between him, and Vallencourt started using his sword for support his weight. Seeing that his opponent was getting weaker Vallencourt would throw caution to the wind and rushed into attack Malakai. At one point when there was enough space between both of them Malakai leaned on his sword and dropped to the ground. The small crowd started chanting "End it now, end his life."

With the urging of the crowd and seeing Malakai on the ground Vallencourt threw caution to the wind and advanced towards

Malakai with sword in the air to decapitate Malakai. Malakai was struggling to get up off the ground and as he shakily stood on his feet with the assistance of the Onoro sword. Seeing that Malakai was struggling to even stay on his feet Vallencourt rushed in and was in the process of bringing down his sword to Malakai's head when in a flash Malakai who was using his sword for support moved his body and swung his sword at Vallencourt exposed head and decapitated him, and his headless body started spewing blood in all direction. Unknown to Vallencourt and his cheering crowd, Malakai was pretending to be lacking stamina for the fight.

Malakai, seeing Vallencourt's headless body, breathed a sigh of relief and thanked God for defeating his enemy. Revenge, they said, belongs to God, but seeing your enemy vanquished and you are still standing is a feeling that can only compare to the ultimate ecstasy. The unmitigated joy of terminating Vallencourt's life was somehow felt quite cathartic to Malakai. Suddenly, the famous seventeenth-century French playwright Pierre Corneille quote came to mind: "To win without risk is to triumph without glory." The risk he took by giving up the amulet and totally surrendering his life and Rose to God, somehow strengthened his belief in the mighty God. At some point, Malakai knew he would have to ask for forgiveness, but for now, he just wanted to bask in the accomplishment of getting revenge for his parent's death by one of the men who orchestrated it.

As Vallencourt's body fell on the ground there was the audible gasp of silence and disbelief coming from the crowd. Wildflower seeing her father decapitated body on the ground started screaming and running towards where Rose was tied to the wooden pole with a sword in her right hand. Malakai suddenly realized that Wildflower was about to kill Rose to avenge her father death. Malakai started running after her, but it was useless she was too far ahead to make up the distance. Malakai started to panic because he knew he was unable to catch her and prevent her from killing Rose.

Wildflower was about twenty yards from Rose when suddenly a piercing shrieking noise was unleashed on the compound and a bolt of lightning and fire struck Wildflower. The bolt of lightning and fire struck Wildflower flung her in the air, and she died before hitting the ground. . Suddenly a rasping voice from the sky said, "So you all will know and acknowledge the power of the one true living God and the ferocity he will unleash on his enemies."

Suddenly bolt of lightning, thunder and fire unleashed from the sky enveloped the people who were on the compound. Malakai stopped running the instant he heard the piercing shrieking noise and bent his knees and looked down on the ground. Malakai was on the ground for a minute when he got up and ran towards the wooden pole where Rose was, keeping his eyes firmly on the ground.

When Malakai arrived at the wooden pole the jacket was still covering Rose face and her eyes were still closed liked a frightened child. Malakai whispered a silent prayer of thanks seeing that Rose was safe, and the piercing shrieking noise was still echoing as the stench of death was unleashed all over the compound. Malakai lifted part of the jacket and covered his head and said, "Rose pray with me and say the prayer of David in Psalm 23."

Malakai and Rose started uttering in unison, *"The Lord is my Shepherd; I shall not want. He maketh me to lie down in green pastures; he leadeth me beside the still waters. He restoreth my soul; he leadeth me in the path of righteousness for his namesake. Yeah, though I walk through the valley of the shadow of death, I will fear no evil, for thou art with me. Thy rod and thy staff, they comfort me. Thou preparest a table before me in the presence of mine enemies. Thou anointest my head with oil; my cup runneth over. Surely goodness and mercy shall follow me all the days of my life, and I will dwell in the house of the Lord forever. Amen"*

After Malakai and Rose finished praying there was the constant wave after wave of nonstop bolt of lightning and fire emanating from the sky. The constant piercing noise went on for around another ten minutes, and then there was total silence. Malakai waited another five minutes to listen for the slightest detectable sound, but there was nothing apart from the unmitigated silence and the palpable sound of their beating hearts. Malakai removed the jacket over his head and told Rose to keep her eyes closed and stay under the jacket.

Malakai walked around five feet and started noticing the burning bodies of the people everywhere on the compound. Malakai thought the compound looked as if a bomb had been detonated, with everything blown up to smithereens. He looked around the compound to see if there was any sign of life but could not detect any, and Malakai returned to where Rose was, took out his sword and cut the ropes that she was tied to the wooden pole. Malakai told Rose to keep her eyes closed because he did not want her to see the burning bodies and to have constant nightmares at night. He held Rose's hand and walked her to the vehicle. He assisted Rose into the vehicle then he went and opened the compound security gate. Malakai then went into the vehicle and drove away. As he exited the gate, they heard a huge explosion that seemed to echo throughout the area.

Malakai told Rose to open her eyes and take off the jacket. Rose looked at Malakai with great appreciation in her eyes with the recognition that she was finally safe with her man. Around a mile as they were driving back to New York Rose said, "Malakai please stop the vehicle, I want to talk."

Malakai drove the vehicle off the road and parked by the sidewalk, and before he could say anything, Rose unbuckled her seatbelt, jumped into his lap, and started kissing him, and he reciprocated, enjoying the softness of her lips. Rose stopped kissing Malakai and, playfully, slapped his face and asked, "What took you so long to come and rescue me?"

"I looked and questioned anyone I knew who would possibly know your whereabouts, but I came up with nothing. I finally had to call them and make some arrangements to bring the amulet to them in exchange for your safe return to me."

"Did you really give them the amulet?" asked Rose.

Malakai smiled and said, "Of course not. Someone made an exact copy of the amulet, and I gave them the fake copy."

"What was that piercing shrieking noise?" asked Rose.

Malakai did not want to lie to her, but he knew he could not reveal too much information to her because it would call into question his own existence. Malakai then said, "I gave the amulet to some good people where it would be very safe. The sound you heard was the sound of the good people arresting them and taking them away for life."

Rose kissed Malakai and then asked, "So all this adventure is truly over then?"

"Yes, my darling, it is truly over. You will be sleeping in your very own comfortable bed tonight where we will be making sweet love. I promise you no one will be looking for you because they are all apprehended."

"That is very good because I cannot take any more adventure for now" said Rose.

Malakai playfully slapped Rose on her ass and said, "Been with me is an adventure and a thrilling ride. Now let us go; I need to get you home."

Malakai drove off looking forward to spending time with Rose in her apartment. He was driving fast and was soon in Brooklyn. Around a mile from where Rose apartment was, they stopped at a supermarket to pick up some groceries. As they were finishing picking up the groceries Malakai took out a pen and paper and wrote two numbers and told Rose to go and buy the two Mega Millions Lottery numbers plus three quick prints. Malakai took ten dollars from his pocket and gave Rose while he went and paid for the groceries. Rose returned with the tickets and gave Malakai. They left the supermarket, went to buy some take out Chinese food and then drove straight to Rose apartment.

Malakai carried the groceries bags to the apartment while Rose carried the takeout Chinese food. Rose opened the apartment door and said, "It is truly good to be home."

Malakai went and assisted Rose with the unpacking of the groceries and afterward they sat around the television and had their Chinese takeout food. They spend another hours watching television then Rose went into the bathroom to take her bath. Malakai went into the bathroom soon as Rose came out and had a quick shower. When he went into the room Rose was naked in the bed. Malakai went in the bed and they made love with an unquenchable lust and desire for each other as if there was no tomorrow. Maybe it was somewhat the realization that they were both lucky to be alive, and to have each other in their life.

Early Saturday morning they got up and they made love again and slept through out the whole morning. They got out of bed around one o'clock in the afternoon. Malakai went and called the local Chinese restaurant to place an order for food to deliver to their apartment. While they waited for the food Rose told Malakai of her own adventure from when she was taken in custody by the two policemen, to meeting Big Bob and Mary Joe and her adventure on the yacht. Rose told Malakai about Mary Joe sickness and how she really made an imprint on her heart.

The food arrived shortly, and they consumed it rather slowly relishing the food and enjoying been in each other company. After they finished eating Rose cleared the table then went into the bedroom to call her friend Angela Stanton to chat and gossips.

Malakai sat in the sofa watching television and after a while started to sleep. He woke up in the next half hours to hear Rose still chatting with her friend. He suddenly remembered the Mega Millions Lottery tickets and he went and turned on Rose laptop to check the winning numbers. Malakai calmly called Rose and said, "I have something to show you."

Rose came out of the bedroom and asked, "What do you have to show me?"

Malakai pointed to the laptop and the Mega Millions Lottery tickets. Rose picked up the lottery ticket and then looked on the Mega Millions website not believing what she was looking at, and she refreshed the page website just to ensure that what she was looking at was real. The actual numbers came back, and she started to scream. Rose then leapt into Malakai's arms and said "We are rich. We won eighty nine million dollars."

Malakai smiling said "No, we did not win eighty nine millions dollars. I did win the eighty nine million dollars."

Rose pushed away Malakai hands, pouted out her lips and asked, "You won eighty nine millions dollars and you are not going to share it with me?"

Malakai's face was quite stern, and he said "No, I am not going to share it because it is not mine. It is all yours. It is for all the trouble I have caused and put you through and you never deviated or questioned your love for me. Also I wanted to give it to you to create some financial independence, so you will have to figure what you want to do with the money."

Rose leapt back in Malakai's arms and kissed him passionately, and after Rose paused kissing him and said "I have never loved anyone like how I love you. I appreciate how you care for me; you are like an angel to me."

Malakai slapped Rose on her ass and said, "When those beautiful thighs of yours wrapped around me, I am truly a fallen angel."

Malakai released Rose from his arms and asked, "how are you going to take the winnings?"

Rose thought for a moment and said, "I really do not want all that money to mess with my head, so I will take it in annuity over a thirty year period."

"Very good; I will take you to the place to collect it on Tuesday or Wednesday."

Afterward, they lay on the sofa with Rose's head buried in Malakai's chest, feeling happy as a lark and truly contented with her man.

******

Roberto Sanchez was finally making his way home. He had gotten a ride from an open pickup truck with some Mexican day workers who were returning to New York City. As he looked over the compound one last time, he could see lightning and thunder descended on the compound. Roberto smiled with himself, knowing he had done the right thing by following his intuition and departing the compound. Roberto knew and accepted that he was a coward, but he always thought that a man who ran away lived to see and fight another day.

After another two hours, the pickup truck was entering New York City. Roberto stopped the driver of the pickup and came off at a train station. Roberto entered the train station and bought a Metro Card from the Subway Station Booth. He entered the train, and he was on his way to Brooklyn. Roberto knew he was finished with the Alliance Organization, and they were almost certainly finished with him for dereliction of duty. He thought the Alliance Organization did not matter because he certainly did not believe what they believed, especially now that he was going to be rich than he could ever imagine in his wildest dream.

Around fifteen minutes time, the train stopped, and Roberto came off it and waited around five minutes for a number two train. Roberto entered the number two train which would take him to Brooklyn. He came off the train at Church Street soon after, and from there, he took a bus to where he resided in Brooklyn. He came off the bus and started to walk to his crummy, dilapidated apartment building.

As Roberto walked to the elevator, he was in high spirit thinking what he was going to do with all of his money. The elevator came down to the first floor and he went on it. Roberto came off the elevator at the ninth floor totally giddy with excitement of the caper he pulled off against the Alliance Organization. No one in history has ever blackmailed the organization much less done what he did and get away with it. Roberto suddenly felt invincible and proud of his accomplishment. Roberto walked to his door, opened it and closed it quickly, and he looked around just to ensure that there was nothing amiss in his apartment. Satisfied that there was nothing amiss he quickly went into the room to see the briefcase on the bed.

The briefcase was fully opened, and the money could be easily seen, as Roberto approached rather nervously, and anxiously knowing it was the most momentous occasion of his life. He pushed his hand into the stack of money and took up the first batch that Wallenstein had shown him, and he smiled at the sight of the stacks of hundred dollars bills.

Roberto pushed his hand again into the briefcase and took up another batch of money but this time to his horror it was a pack of paper neatly packed on top of a dollar bill. Roberto was apoplectic and as he slammed the neatly stacked batched into the briefcase and picked up another and it was the same neatly stacked of paper with a dollar bill on top. Roberto flung the stack of money back in the briefcase and suddenly out of nowhere several oval shaped sharp metal serrated edge around six inches wide flew out of the briefcase straight to his neck. Blood started to spew everywhere into the room as Roberto head was suddenly decapitated. Suddenly there was a loud explosion, and the room was engulfed in flames.

******

Sunday morning, Rose and Malakai were in Reverend Watkiss' church, giving praise and thanks to God for protecting and saving their life. It was the end of the church service, and Reverend Watkiss came off the pulpit and gave a huge hug to Rose and Malakai and said, "It is so great to see both of you on this Sunday morning." Reverend Watkiss turned to Malakai and said, "See what happened when you asked for help from God. God knows that we human beings are flawed, inadequate creatures, but if we reach out to him, he is there to provide guidance and protection to his people always."

Rose was a little confused and turned towards Malakai and asked, "How do you know Reverend Watkiss?"

Malakai smiled and said, "When I was searching for you, he provided invaluable advice, and I dare say without him, I do not think you would be here this Sunday morning."

Rose turned towards Reverend Watkiss and gave him another hug and said, "Thank you."

Reverend Watkiss patted Rose back and said, "No need to; you are like a daughter to me, and I love you." Rose released Reverend Watkiss from her warm embrace, and Reverend Watkiss turned towards Malakai and said, "I expect to see you more often now that you and Rose are an item."

"You will see me more often," said Malakai.

"Okay, I will see you another time. I will have to go and greet some of my other church members."

Rose and Malakai bid goodbye to Reverend Watkiss and walked out of the church, and as they were walking out Malakai said, "I really like reverend Watkiss, he is a good man."

They exited the church premises and went to a restaurant to have some food. They left the restaurant after consuming their food and went back to Rose's apartment. As they arrived at the apartment, Rose went into the room and changed her church attire. She picked up the phone and dialed Mary Joe's number to find out how she was coping with regard to her sickness. Rose and Mary Joe chatted for a few minutes on the phone, and at the end of their conversation, Mary Joe gave Big Bob the phone.

Malakai was lying in the sofa watching television when Rose came out of the room crying, and she came and lay beside Malakai opened his shirt burying her face in his chest as tears flowed down her beautiful face. Malakai took his hand and lifted her head off his chest and asked, "What is the matter?"

Rose started to still cry until finally she said "You remembered that elderly couple that I told you I stayed with, Mary Joe and Big Bob. Well, Mary Joe has cancer, and her husband said she is extremely sick and about to die."

Malakai tried to soothe Rose's pain by massaging her back as she continued to cry with her face in his chest. Malakai was not sure what he could do to alleviate the pain Rose was genuinely feeling for the elderly couple. He hated seeing her that way, but he knew there was nothing he could do more than be there for her, providing emotional support. Malakai then asked, "What type of cancer is Mary Joe suffering from?"

Rose used her right hand, wiped away her tears, and said, "Mary Joe has leukemia." Rose was a little pensive then asked, "Malakai, can we go and visit them in Florida?"

Malakai allowed Rose's question to percolate in his mind and then said, "I do not see why we cannot go to Florida to visit your friend."

Rose's tears dried up, and she asked, "Can we go on Wednesday?"

"Yes, my woman, we can go to Florida on Wednesday. However, I will have to take you to the Mega Millions office tomorrow with the winning ticket for your account to be credited with the money," said Malakai.

"That will be no problem. I will gladly go to the Mega Millions office tomorrow, so we do not have to worry about the winning ticket being lost. Let me go and call Mary Joe that we are coming to look for them on Wednesday."

Rose leapt out of the sofa and went into the room to phone Mary Joe to say that they were coming to Florida. After she finished talking to Mary Joe, Rose called her friend Angela Stanton and invited her to come to Florida with her and Malakai on Wednesday. Angela agreed to come with them, and Rose went and booked the airline tickets on American Airlines, a hotel, and a rental car.

Rose went into the living room and told Malakai that she had invited her friend Angela Stanton to come with them for the whole week in Florida. Malakai then asked her, "It seems like it is a girl trip. Are you sure you want me to be there?"

Rose then said adamantly, "I want you there, and if I have to tether you with a rope on me, I am dragging you there to meet my friends."

Malakai, smiling, said, "Okay, boss of me, I am coming to Florida with you and your girlfriend."

They sat and chatted, and Malakai told Rose about Josephina's situation of wanting to leave her Amish community to study medicine to become a doctor. Malakai further told her if she does leave the Amish community, they will have to accommodate her and send her to school. Rose was quite receptive towards the idea especially how Josephina's family treated them so well when they were in Lancaster County, Pennsylvania. They continued to chat and watch television until they were ready to retire to their bed.

The next day, Rose was dressed in blue jeans, a white t-shirt and a black leather jacket. Rose was also wearing a blonde wig, and on her face was dark sunglasses. Rose was practically unrecognizable as Malakai drove her up to the Mega Millions office compound to collect her cheque for the winning lottery ticket. Malakai walked her to the office and told Rose that he would wait for her in the vehicle. Malakai could not be bothered with the frivolities and picture-taking at such an event and thought it was best to get some extra rest in the car while he waited for Rose.

Malakai was in the vehicle sleeping for around an hour when Rose came back and knocked on the vehicle door. He opened the door, and Rose came inside the vehicle. She grabbed Malakai's head with her hands, kissed him tenderly, and said, "Thank you for everything, and thanks for being you. They told me that the money would not be credited to my account around the next two weeks when they collected all the money from their merchants. I told them that it is quite okay as long as the money is credited to my account. Now let us go to my bank."

Malakai drove away from the Mega Millions office compound and went straight to Rose Bank. He waited in the vehicle while she went into the bank. She came back from inside the bank around thirty minutes, and as Malakai was about to turn on the vehicle ignition, Rose said, "Take this bank card. That money belongs to both of us, and if you do not take the bank card, I do not want any of it."

Malakai took the bank card and said, "Thank you, you have aced the test. I wanted to be sure you are not one of those selfish women, but you have proven yourself to be one of those great, unselfish women, and I certainly adore you for that."

Rose was quite flabbergasted with her mouth wide open, and she started playfully hitting Malakai on his arm. Both started laughing uncontrollably until Rose asked Malakai to take her to the mall. Malakai drove to the mall for Rose to do her shopping. Malakai accompanied her as they walked from store to store. Rose finally had what she wanted, and they left the mall and drove to a takeout Chinese restaurant where they bought their dinner. They drove back to Rose's apartment, both feeling exhausted from the long day. They ate the Chinese takeout food, watched television, and later showered and went to their bed.

The next day, Rose, Malakai and Angela Stanton were on the American Airlines flight to Florida. The girls were seated together, and Malakai sat behind them, reading a magazine in first class. The American Airlines flight soon landed at the Miami International Airport, and they disembarked from the plane and went to claim their luggage. They went outside the airport and were met by a representative of the car rental company. The vehicle Rose rented was a red Kia Sorento all-wheel drive. They put their luggage in the vehicle and drove away from the airport to their hotel.

They arrived at their hotel and were checked in by a Hispanic-looking gentleman. The hotel was near the seafront, offering a spectacular view of the ocean. Their two rooms were adjoined and located on the thirtieth floor. Malakai and Rose's room had all the convenience of a kingside bed, satellite television, and a small refrigerator. They all stayed in the hotel room for fifteen minutes, then left to see Mary Joe and Big Bob.

As they were driving, Rose took out her cell phone, called Big Bob and informed him that she was on her way to visit them. Big Bob gave her directions to where they were located in a park for recreational vehicles. Big Bob then told Rose that Mary Joe was extremely weak and could not get out of bed. Rose hung up the phone and relayed the information to Malakai. Rose was now more eager to see Mary Joe and told Malakai to drive faster to their intended destination.

As they were driving, Malakai told Rose that he once saw a man assist a sick cancer patient by cooking for some food and by changing her diet over time, the patient was able to recover in a few days. They soon saw a mall and drove over there looking for a supermarket. They found a very spacious, stocked supermarket. Malakai went over to the meats section and bought ten pounds of free-range chicken livers, lemon juice, ginger, a bottle of Grace Jamaican ketchup, Jamaican Island spice chicken seasoning, wheat bread, and fresh fruit juices. Malakai paid for the groceries, and they left the establishment, resuming their driving on the road.

After thirty minutes more driving, they finally found the park in the Miami area. They drove until Rose saw Big Bob's Recreational Vehicle. Malakai parked beside the recreational vehicle. Rose hurriedly walked towards the Recreational Vehicle door and knocked.

Big Bob opened the door, and all three entered the vehicle. Rose hugged Big Bob and introduced Angela and Malakai.

Rose then ran into the room where Mary Joe was lying on the bed, extremely sick. Mary Joe's face was quite pale, and her eyes were as if she was resigned to her fate, walking along the path to death doorway. She looked up and saw Rose and held up her right hand, waving it feebly, as all the energy seemed to drain from her body. Rose rushed out of the room, crying uncontrollably and into Big Bob's arms. Malakai and Angela went into the room and introduced themselves as Rose's friend but got only a hand wave from Mary Joe.

Malakai and Angela came out of the room and sat beside Rose and Big Bob. Malakai explained to Big Bob he wanted to try something that may help Mary Joe by cooking something for her that may get her well and restore her body. Big Bob then said, "At times like this, I am willing to try anything as long as it helps Mary Joe."

Malakai went into the vehicle and took out the groceries and carried them into the kitchen. He called Big Bob into the kitchen and told him to watch what he was cooking for Mary Joe, so he would be able to cook it for her if she did recover.

Malakai washed his hands, took three of the packs of chicken liver, and put them in a container. He poured water over it and washed the chicken liver. Malakai then drained the water into the kitchen sink and poured the lemon juice on the chicken liver. After a minute he turned on the kitchen faucet and washed off the lemon juice off the chicken liver. Malakai ensured that all the water was properly drained off the chicken liver, and he poured it out into another dry container. Malakai then took out the Island Spice chicken seasoning and poured a small amount on it. He then inserted chopped onions, ginger, pepper, thyme and chopped garlic into the chicken liver. Malakai took a fork and stirred inside the bowl to ensure that the seasoning was well marinated in the chicken liver.

Malakai then turned on the stove and put a skillet over the hot flames. He poured a small amount of coconut oil into the skillet, and when it was hot, he poured the chicken liver into the skillet. He stirred the chicken liver with a fork to ensure it was not burnt. After around three minutes of stirring, Malakai poured a small amount of water into the skillet with a small amount of the Grace Jamaican ketchup. He then put a cover over the skillet and let it simmer for around five minutes. Soon, the sweet cooking scent was permeating the recreational vehicle, and Big Bob said, "I have been standing here watching you for the longest while, and I have not smelled a sweeter cooking than what you have prepared for May Joe." Big Bob then paused and asked, "My taste bud is desirous for some of the meal, are we going to get some?"

Malakai laughed heartily and said, "We all will taste a small amount of the meal after Mary Joe has eaten if at all possible."

Big Bob then turned to Malakai and said, "Even if this does not work, I want to tell you from the bottom of my heart, thank you for making the effort."

The two men hugged, and Malakai then said to Big Bob, "I want you to take the girls outside the vehicle because I want to pray to Almighty God for Mary Joe's healing. I will call you when I am ready."

"Certainly, that will be no problem," said Big Bob.

Big Bob went into the area where the girls were and invited them outside the vehicle. Malakai went into Mary Joe's room and said, "I am going to pray with you and try to assist you." Malakai looked at her and saw the agonizing pain she was going through and asked, "Whatever occurs in this room is between us and no one else. Do you understand me?"

Mary Joe shook her head, indicating that she understood Malakai's request.

Malakai then placed his right hand on Mary Joe's head and said, "Almighty God, the creator of all living things, you have seen the pain and suffering that this woman has been experiencing. We asked in your loving and merciful nature to heal her."

Malakai took his hand, pulled Mary Joe upright in the bed, and said, "Open your mouth wide open."

Mary Joe complied with Malakai's request, and Malakai opened his mouth and pressed it almost two inches against Mary Joe. Suddenly, some red liquid started to emanate from Mary Joe's mouth into Malakai's mouth. The process went on for thirty seconds until Malakai pulled away from Mary Joe, and the top half of her body fell on the bed like a sack of potatoes. Malakai rushed into the bathroom and expelled all the liquid content from Mary Joe's mouth into the bathroom sink. He washed his mouth with some water and came back into the bedroom. Mary Joe was looking a bit groggy but looking and feeling much better than before, and Malakai could see the immediate improvement in her facial appearance and asked, "How are you feeling?"

"I feel quite lightheaded as if I just unburdened myself of the weight of the world," said Mary Joe.

Malakai smiled and said, "The good news is that you are fully healed of your cancer, but as I asked you before, you cannot tell anyone, not even your husband. Over a period of time, you can reveal that because of your change of diet, you no longer have the cancer."

"Thank you for helping me heal," said Mary Joe.

"All thanks and praise belong to Almighty God, the creator of all living things," replied Malakai.

Mary Joe looked directly at Malakai and asked, "Does Rose know who you are?"

"No, she does not, and I want to keep it that way. At some time in the future, I will tell her, but not now," said Malakai.

"The truth has a strange way of revealing itself over time of who we really are. Anyway, your secret is certainly safe with me," said Mary Joe.

"You need to come and eat something now because you will faint away. I have cooked some free-range chicken liver for you. It is packed with protein, so you will be able to build up your strength rather quickly eating it for the next two weeks," said Malakai.

Malakai assisted Mary Joe out of bed, and she walked to the small dining table and sat down. Malakai then gave her a glass of fruit juice. She drank it and demanded one more glass. Malakai gave her and went into the kitchen to share the chicken liver. Malakai took the plate of chicken liver and whole wheat bread and gave Mary Joe and she started eating it.

The recreational vehicle door suddenly burst open, and Rose, Angela, and Big Bob rushed inside to see Mary Joe eating the chicken liver. Big Bob, with mouth wide open, stared at his wife in total amazement and finally said, "Mary Joe, I thought you were on your way to the other side, at death's doorstep. Now, I see you have returned to me." Big Bob put his hand around Mary Joe's neck and hugged her and suddenly started crying. Big Bob looked at Malakai and said, "I do not know how to repay you for giving back my life and love."

"Showing a stranger love and kindness, putting up Rose securely under your roof is payment enough for me. I am more in your debt because if anything had happened to her, I would not be able to live with myself. Plus, the only reason why we are here on this earth is to help each other, and when we help each other from the goodness of our hearts, God's grace and love manifest in our lives," said Malakai.

The girls went and hugged Mary Joe. Angela walked up to Malakai, embraced him, kissed him on his cheeks and said, "I finally see what Rose sees in you, and for that, I am grateful."

Malakai looked intently at Angela and thought this African American woman was stunningly beautiful. He kissed her back on her cheeks and said, "Thanks for your approval of our relationship, finally."

Angela pushed Malakai away and said, "I know sarcasm when it is spoken."

They all sat around the table while Malakai shared a small amount of chicken liver and wheat bread. As they consumed it, they drank the fruit juice and chatted. It was around two o'clock in the afternoon when they finally departed from Mary Joe and Big Bob. They all embraced each other warmly, and Malakai promised to come and take them to the hotel for dinner before they departed Florida.

They drove back to the hotel with the girls wanting to make use of the cool afternoon to swim in the blue seawater. They soon arrived back at the hotel and raced to their room to change into their swimsuits. Rose went into Angela's room, where they lathered sunscreen on each other and changed into their swimsuits. Angela wore a white hand crochet triangle bikini while Rose wore a sexy black mini microstring bikini. Both girls wore dark glasses over their faces as they walked down to the beach, followed by Malakai in his blue swim trunks holding one bag and their beach towels.

Malakai saw three beach chairs, and he spread the towels on them, ensuring that they were spread out neatly. There were only a few people on the beach, and Malakai lay on the beach chair, watching the girls playing on the sand. Malakai knew that there would be troubles ahead of him because that is life, in general, filled with stress and pressure. However, now he just wanted to bask in the pure, unmitigated joy of watching, appreciating the two beautiful, gorgeous women playing on the sands and splashing in the beautiful blue seawater with their beautiful bodies. All Malakai could mumble to himself was, *'I love this beautiful blue planet, earth.'*

The End

References

APA:

1. https://en.m.wikipedia.org/wiki/Prospect_Park_Zoo.

2. https://www.hedonism.com/what-is-hedonism/destination-negril-jamaica/

3. https://en.m.wikipedia.org/wiki/Amish

4. https://myamishindiana.blogspot.com/2015/09/growing-tobacco.html?m=1

5. https://en.wikipedia.org/wiki/Amish_religious_practices.

6. https://www.cameronestateinn.com

7. https://en.m.wikipedia.org/wiki/Mount_Marcy.